Something Borrowed

LOUISA
GEORGE

Something old. Something new...?

When Chloe Cassidy is jilted at the altar it's all her nightmares rolled into one. Her mother is convinced she's the victim of the family curse. Her sister believes she just hasn't found The One yet. But Chloe's not listening; she's too busy taking her humiliation out on the infuriating best man, Vaughn Brooks.

Three months later, *Something Borrowed*—her wedding planning business—is failing. In a last ditch attempt to save it, Chloe is forced to swallow her pride, and work with the enemy: too-hot for his own good, award-winning chef Vaughn. She soon realises the sparks flying between them are nothing to do with their dubious past, but from something else altogether...

This fun read features one sizzling chef, one spicy heroine and a whole lot of tasty trouble.

PROLOGUE

Wedding day blues for Portobello Wedding Planner

It was meant to be the best day of her life, but for local business owner, Chloe Cassidy of Something Borrowed *wedding planners on Colville Terrace, her special day ended up being something very blue instead. For, after waiting fruitlessly at the church for her dashing groom to arrive, Miss Cassidy was given the news that the 'something' her fiancé had borrowed was her best friend and bridesmaid, Amy Fisher.*

Neither Miss Fisher nor the groom, Jason Hawthorn, attended the church to face the music, but as all reliable wedding fables go, it was best man, Vaughn Brooks, who arrived to break the news to the now very blushing and very jilted bride.

Reports of a bridezilla-style meltdown and a fight between the wedding guests are as yet unsubstantiated, but three police cars and one ambulance were in attendance.

As we go to press the bride, the groom and the bridesmaid were all unavailable for comment, but mother of the bride, Bridget Cassidy, described the philandering fiancé and the arrests for disturbing the peace as having 'ruined her daughter's lifetime dreams'.

Pressing a bandage to his forehead as he left Paddington Green police station, a bruised and bloodied Mr Brooks was heard to have said that the outcome was all for the best, and that the intended couple had been a 'bad match from the start'. The question now is, after her very public jilting at the altar, will Miss Cassidy's reputation as Portobello's foremost wedding planner remain intact?

Were you there? Did you witness the fighting, the arrests? Have photos? If so, contact the news desk on info@portobello-local.co.uk

CHAPTER 1

We absolutely adore frogs. We're 100 per cent sure that a frog theme would be perfect for us. Maybe a cute froggy cake with two frogs holding hands on top? Everything in different shades of green, the bouquet, bridesmaid's dresses...' The caller exhaled an excited sigh and Chloe Cassidy tried, very hard indeed, to remain calm and positive. Difficult at times, especially when the urge to throttle a potential client almost overrode the need to fill the almost empty bank account. 'We're thinking early June next year to coincide with the frog lifecycle... D'you think we could get some real ones for the big day?'

'I don't know. It sounds...' *Hideous. No,* Chloe corrected herself, *the customer is always right. The customer is always bloody right. Even when it feels so terribly wrong.* 'Er, delightful. I'll check some details, do a bit of research on… frogs and get back to you as soon as possible. Fine? Thanks. Bye.'

Chloe threw her phone onto her desk and gave two very direct fingers to the newspaper cutting of her own failed wedding fluttering on the noticeboard as the April breeze breathed into her stuffy Portobello office—also known as her cramped, but cosy, living room.

'I hate you, Jason bloody Hawthorn. I used to turn work down. And now… look what I'm reduced to: Amphibian nuptials.'

She glowered at the fading print and the close-up image of her hand as she'd tried to cover the intrusive camera lens. Her flawless, handmade, lace-over-organza gown, which had taken three years to design and make, was just a blur.

Bridezilla, indeed. That journalist had a nerve. He wasn't the one who had to face the guests, send the presents back and pay everyone for the wedding that never happened. Plus, live with the humiliation while working on damage-control as clients fled in droves. Who the hell wanted a wedding planner who couldn't successfully organise her own wedding?

She refused to give any thought to the pain in her chest, but it was still there, a big solid blob of hurt. It was hard to work out what was worse: losing Jason, losing her best friend, losing the clients or reading about it all in the papers.

'Bad time?' Chloe's sister, Jenna, popped her head around the stripped wooden door, her usual smiles-solve-everything grin adding a shimmer to the day and immediately making Chloe feel better. If only she could be like that, even just a little, but she'd been shimmerless for months.

'Hey. No, come on in. You'll never believe this—I've just had a client asking us to do a frog wedding. A frog wedding?' She laughed, trying to shimmer and pretty much failing. 'Really?

What happened to weddings at the Ritz? Jimmy Choo shoes? Rubbing shoulders with celebrities? What's next? A shark theme? Dinosaurs?'

'At least it's a client. I hope you didn't put them off. We should be grateful... Hang on...' Jenna smiled, then ducked out of the room.

'You want a hand?'

'No, you can't fit two people plus a buggy in your tiny corridor. And, anyway, I need the exercise.'

Outside, floating softly over the hum of city traffic and happy chatter from the Saturday market just off Chloe's doorstep, bells were ringing. Another wedding. Someone else's bride and groom. Someone else's fat cheque. A whole lifecycle of happiness that most definitely wasn't hers.

But not anymore. Things were going to change around here. Onwards and upwards.

'Actually, I was very polite.' Chloe nodded, determined to count her blessings. 'And what's the bet that the frog groom will actually turn up to the wedding?'

'He might be a frog Prince Charming,' Jenna called from the hallway as she grunted with the effort of hauling the buggy up the stone steps.

Chloe called back, 'There's no such thing as Prince Charming. They're all cheating, scheming, evil—'

'Whoa.' Jenna came back in and threw Chloe a wide-eyed admonishment and a sharp shake of her head as she zigzagged behind her gorgeous three-year-old daughter, who stopped and zapped everything with a sparkly pink wand. Jenna smiled adoringly at her mini-me. 'Evie, don't listen to grumpy old Auntie Chloe. She just needs to smile; then everything will seem fine again. Boy, the market's busy today. Must be spring fever. Oh, and I've picked up Pad Thai for dinner.'

Chloe's tummy rumbled at the sight of the plastic carrier bulging with containers. 'Hmm, it smells divine.'

'Yes, well, I got you the full monty version with everything.' Jenna sighed. 'I told them they needed to do a slimmer's version for me.'

'Oh, don't be silly; you're perfect as you are.' Chloe looked at her sister's tired eyes and wished she could do more to help her. A few curves were the least of her problems. 'You've had a really rough few years and have a beautiful baby to care for. Don't be so hard on yourself.'

'Oh, I know you love me heaps and would say anything to make me feel better, but I also know I need to lose some pounds. I'm not daft. And you need to put some on, Chlo. I can see your bones. You want some of my tyres? I have spares.' Jenna grabbed some flesh from her waist and gave it a loopy stare. 'Look at this mummy tummy. Evie could use it as a trampoline.'

'Please, you look great to me.' And even though her sister still wore her ditzy smile, Chloe knew she was covering up her real feelings. Again. Somehow, Jenna had it in her head that she had to cope and never complain, that she could not allow herself to crumble. After all the harrowing upset of her sister's last few years—losing her husband to a freak accident and then facing solo parenting while heartbroken—at some point, Chloe feared, there would be fallout.

'Hi there, cheeky-face. Come here.' Chloe pushed her chair back and took hold of her niece's hand, smothering her with kisses and a tickle in the ribs. She let the resulting giggle wash over her. There was something so fresh and new about her still, a wonder that had risen phoenix-like out of the mire of sadness.

Today, Evie was dressed in a Superman outfit. Yesterday it had been a pirate. The girl was learning badassery skills from her mother. Go figure. 'Maybe you could use some of those superpowers to make me less of an old grump, Evie? Cast a happy spell with your wand? Tell me, Jenna, how do you do it?'

'Do what?' Her sister wandered over, having put the cartons on the coffee table in the centre of the room, which had filled with delicious aromas of garlic, tamarind and coriander.

'That shiny, happy people thing? How do you keep so upbeat after everything that happened?'

'One day I just woke up, looked at Evie all precious and innocent, and knew it was time to let all the sadness go. For her sake. Now I try not to think about anything negative. In fact, I've banished sadness from ever entering my life again.'

'Just like that?'

'Oh geez, come on. I'm a work in progress. It's one step at a time. Fix one part of your life, then move on to the next. Leave the past behind.' Jenna shook her head, the shimmer and glitter replaced momentarily by a sheen of pain. She may well have tried to banish it, but it was still there. 'I have this one to keep me going. I don't want to go back to that dark place. Ever. But loving Ollie, having Evie, those were my blessings. In lots of ways, I'm better off than Mum. She had two kids under five to deal with when Dad died. Look how she managed. Or rather, how she didn't.' She waved her hand as if none of what she'd been through was important. It was. So very much. 'Now... about the frogs? Swamp-themed flowers? We could have succulents, earthy tones, little frog knickknacks and motifs on the invitations. It could be fun. You remember that, right?'

Chloe looked up and met her sister's concerned gaze. 'Remember what?'

'When this job was fun. When you had fun.'

'I have fun.'

'When? When was the last time you had a good laugh, Chloe Cassidy?'

'Er... well...' Who was she trying to kid? The shocking truth of it was that Chloe hadn't had any fun since... well, since before The Jilting. In fact, when Jason had finally found balls big enough to contact her, the message she'd received via text was that he'd left her because she was just no fun anymore. Er... a wedding doesn't plan itself! Since then, too humiliated to meet up with mutual friends for drinks and parties, she'd barely left the house. 'I've had a lot on my plate.'

Jenna wrapped her in a warm hug. 'I know. It's been a tough few months, but you're allowing that to colour everything you do, sis.'

'I was let down by the two people I trusted more than anything.' Smiling certainly hadn't helped any, but then, neither had accosting the bearer of bad news... or screaming. *Bridezilla*. It was mortifying even now. 'And humiliated.'

'I know. But we're the new generation of Cassidys. We can ride the hard times and come out smiling. And you can't let it affect your work. We need the money.'

Chloe sat at her desk in the huge bay window that looked out towards Portobello market and the rush-rush of wrapped-up shoppers and grabbed some blank sheets of paper for Evie to draw on. 'Can frogs be fun, though? Suitable for a wedding? Really? What do you think about frogs, Evie?'

'Ribbit,' Evie croaked, then giggled, very pleased with herself.

'Clever girl. It gets her vote.' Jenna beamed again at her daughter then turned to Chloe. 'I think you'd better make sure that frogs are the funnest wedding theme ever, or that'll be even less we make this year.' Her sister paused, opening and closing her mouth. Opening it again, she brushed her palms over her grey woolly-tights. 'Look, I've been thinking, Chlo, maybe I could get a job on one of the flower stalls in the market? Just to tide us over... during this... financial blip. I mean, three weddings booked for the whole season… three? It's… well… maybe I could even open a shop? There's an empty one coming up for lease, just next to the pub.'

And show the world just how badly Jason's betrayal had affected Chloe? To the point where she couldn't even look after her own sister, her family? Like hell. Shame shimmied through her. There was no room for maudlin and whingeing anymore. It was time for action. She could live on the smell of an oily rag, but she wasn't going to let that happen to her sister and her gorgeous niece.

'No. No… for goodness' sake, it's only a glitch,' she answered brightly. 'There'll be more work coming in soon. I promise. I'll make it happen. There's the wedding fair coming up in a few weeks; that'll drum up some business, you'll see. And if it doesn't, then I'll jack the whole thing in and get a job back at the tax office. Pete Farrell said he'd have me back anytime.'

'Because he fancies you. But you hated that job. You said it was mind-numbing and soul-sapping.' Jenna grabbed Chloe's hand. 'Let me take the reins for a while. Until you get back on your feet.'

'No. I don't want you to take more on, not with a little one to look after. I am on my feet.' Chloe prayed for some shimmer to convince her sister that she wasn't washed up and failing. 'I just need to do some damage control and find some more clients.'

'It wasn't your fault that coward didn't turn up at the altar. Or that all those clients fled the minute they heard.' With her free hand, Jenna tucked her auburn hair behind her ears. Jenna had got the trademark Cassidy red locks and fierce blue eyes from their father. Chloe, meanwhile, had been gifted, which was the only polite way of saying *stuck with*, their mother's mousy wishy-washy midbrown. Nothing that a packet of dark mahogany dye couldn't fix.

Her own eyes, though, they were something she was proud of, dark chocolate and, she liked to think, mysterious. Jenna's startling blue ones fixed on her, gently but assertively. 'Don't take this the wrong way, lovely sister of mine, I know you're hurting, but maybe if you tried to be nicer to people when they called, they might decide that you are the planner for them.'

'I do try to be nice. I am nice.'

'Are you sure you're as nice as you can be?'

Okay, not recently. Not at all. 'Of course. I gush over everyone.'

It had taken gargantuan effort to even pick up the phone, never mind do it with a smile. Chloe's throat burned as she dragged her hand away from her sister's and started to busy herself by tidying up her immaculate desk with one hand, and stopping Evie from defacing her planner with biro swirls with the other. After shuffling paper for a minute or so, she asked the question that had been on her lips for three months. 'Okay, well, be honest, Jen, was I really bridezilla?'

There was that sunny smile again, not solving anything, but at least it made Chloe's heart thaw a little. 'Yep. Totally. Truly. Nervous breakdown kind of stuff, especially when you tried to shove your bouquet up the best man's...' Jenna's eyes flicked to her daughter, then back to Chloe as she mouthed out the letters b.u.m.

'Oh, God.' Heat flooded Chloe's cheeks. Chasing him down the aisle. Screaming. Rugby tackling him to the floor... It ran through her head like a sordid tape. The only redeeming thing was that no one had uploaded the video to the Internet—although she had a feeling the videographer would have tried if she hadn't ripped the camera from his hands and erased the whole catastrophe. Shame she couldn't do that with her own brain rewind button.

Jenna beamed and didn't even try to hide her laughter. 'Look, your attention to detail is what makes you such a fabulous wedding planner. You had that wedding nailed, my girl. It would have been the most perfect wedding ever. It would. Your clients love you—once you get them and keep hold of them.'

But Chloe couldn't get passed bridezilla. It was the ultimate nightmare for everyone in her profession. 'I was that woman.'

'Yes. You were, but you know what? I preferred seeing you like that instead of like this. At least there was emotion there, anger and passion. Now you're a shell. Empty. There's nothing there, Chloe. You've gone… somewhere. And I think that might show itself to your clients.'

Jenna was right. And it was scary to think that she'd lost her buzz. But she had—she didn't know what to do or how to get it back. Once upon a time, she'd adored this job and had jumped out of bed in the mornings. Now it was a slow crawl fuelled by extra strong coffee and a lot of dredged up desperation.

'Thing is, Jen, I don't think I…' Chloe couldn't bring herself to say the words: *I don't believe in love anymore, so how can I be a wedding planner?* Because their whole family business had been built around her and the concept of absolute love. The One. Forever. 'Til death and all that. Mum did the dresses, Jenna did the flowers and Chloe did everything else. It was a perfect business for them all. It kept Mum busy and paid for her cruises and her newest hobby of ghost hunting, which meant she went away a lot which kept them all sane, and Jenna fitted it around little Evie. They needed her. They needed this to work.

'What?' her sister urged her to continue. 'What don't you…?'

Chloe lost her nerve. Admitting anything would only send Jenna into a panic, and she didn't deserve that. 'Hey, Mum's going to be here any minute for Jane Davidson's planning meeting. We need to get down to work.'

Jenna nodded, switched on *Nickelodeon* for Evie and grabbed her notepad and pen. 'Basically, your heart's not in it anymore, is it?'

'It is. Really, it is. I love my job.' It was a valiant effort at reassurance, but there wasn't a lot she could get past Jenna.

'*Loved* your job. Past tense. That's the point.' Jenna fixed her with a sisterly stare. Over the years, they'd developed a kind of secret language. A look, a roll of the eyes—sentiments shared and understood that didn't need verbalising. 'He broke your heart and now you're off your game.'

'I'm fine. I won't let him interfere with my work. And I wouldn't take him back if he begged on hands and knees. Or hopped like a damned frog.'

It wasn't him. It was... well, it was her. It was hard to look at other people, all happy and excitable and... *hopeful*, when the first thing that always sprang to mind was a breach of the peace order. Followed swiftly by that rising panic as reality sank in— the wedding wasn't happening and he was breaking her heart. He didn't love her.

She hadn't made it work no matter how hard she'd tried. He'd stomped on her heart and broken her faith in everlasting promises.

She didn't believe in love anymore, plain and simple.

Pretty dumb place for a wedding planner to be.

'Yoo-hoo!' The door rattled and, along with a whoosh of cool air, in walked Mum, arms full of sweet-scented baking and a basket of fabric swatches, thread and general haberdashery frippery. 'Is it me or is it unseasonably cold today? Oh, hello gorgeous little girl. Girls.' She beamed at them all in turn. Then homed in on Chloe. 'You look tired.'

'I'm fine.'

'No, you're not. Fretting over himself again?' Her native Irish accent always came out when she was anxious.

'For goodness' sake, no. And I told you, stop talking about it. I don't ever want to hear his name again. And stop looking at each other behind my back—I know what you're doing.' Chloe cleared a space on the overstuffed sofa, indicated for them all to sit, drew up the coffee table and then fetched plates and forks. As they began to eat, Chloe called the meeting to order. 'Right, let's talk Davidson and Wright. Where are we up to with the bridesmaid's dresses? When's the last fitting scheduled for?'

Back when Chloe had bought this flat with Jason, he'd worried about being so close to her mum and sister who lived on the next street across. He'd laid down strict visiting rules, which they'd all had to abide by. He didn't want them popping in uninvited, in case Chloe and he were having mind-blowing sex on the kitchen table. Not that they ever had either. The sex wasn't mind-blowing, although it had been perfectly fine. Well, maybe not so frequent towards the wedding, but she'd been busy, and they'd had a lot to discuss. You can't talk and have sex, he'd said. One or the other. As if making love to her had been something he'd had to focus on very carefully.

And definitely never on the kitchen table. *Why would we do that?* he'd said. *We have a perfectly fine bed. Do they have to be here all the time?* he'd moaned. *It's like living in a goldfish bowl.*

Now she was grateful of her family's proximity—they popped in and out whenever they wanted, sharing keys and food, and everything. They supported each other but had some space. Right now, she was very glad they were here.

They got through the business in record time. One thing Chloe was proud of was her ability to keep everyone focused and on task. Unfortunately, having so little on her books meant that there was too much time left over to discuss their favourite topic. Her love life.

It was her Mum who started it. 'I should have throttled him, really. I should have gone round to his house and cut off his—'

'Mum!' Jenna shook her head. 'Children present.'

'I was going to say, cut off his buttons. It was a lovely suit. Those buttons were gorgeous, the perfect shade of grey.'

'Yes, Mum, we know. Like polished steel,' the sisters chorused together. Jenna leant in and whispered behind her hand to Chloe, 'Wait for it… wait for it. I bet you a fiver she'll mention the Cassidy curse.'

'Such a shame. Neither one of you is settled now.' Their mother leant back and crossed her arms. 'Of course, it's the Cassidy Curse, you know.'

'We know,' they chorused back. Jenna hissed, 'You owe me.'

'No chance. It was a no-brainer.'

'Happened to your grandmother. Then me. And look at you two. Not a husband between you.' With what could only be described as relish Mum looked over to her grand-daughter, knee-deep in building bricks. 'Not that either one of you is to blame. We're just unlucky. We need to break it if Evie's ever going to have a chance at being happy.'

Chloe collected the plates up. 'That is, of course, if you believe a woman can only be happy with a man. I, for one, think you can be perfectly happy on your own.'

'And you're proving that, aren't you? Being grumpy with clients, moping around, refusing dates…' Her mum's tone had turned a little darker. After all, she'd been on her own for nearly thirty years. And they all knew she was lonely, but she'd never admit it. Hence the cruises and the ghost hunting. But she'd stepped over the line when she'd arranged a blind date with one of her friend's sons.

'Mum, I will not go out with someone you set me up with.'

'He was a good catch.'

'If you like middle-aged, dour funeral directors with more than their fair share of dandruff.'

Her mum shook her head and tutted. 'Beggars can't be choosers. You can always invest in medicated shampoo or white suits. Give him a chance. Or why don't you sign up for that Timber thing on your phone? Maggie says her daughter's using it to find men.'

Chloe shot her sister a look that begged her to change the subject, but she wasn't biting. Traitor. 'It's Tinder, and no one uses it for dating, anyway. It's just for hook-ups.'

'Isn't that the same thing?'

'No, Mum. It really isn't.' She would not go into the literal ins and outs of a dating app with her mother. In a moment of drunken weakness, she'd downloaded it and given it a very brief play. Chloe had been horrified to be rejected by men she'd liked the look of, and had tried not to take it personally. But really? How dare they left-swipe her? It was just rude. 'Now, please can we not talk about this? How about Jenna? Let's talk about her love life instead.'

Jenna looked up from stacking bricks, panic all over her face. 'Too soon. Really. Just too soon.'

'It's been over three years, honey.'

'Exactly. Way too soon.'

Mum rummaged in her sewing basket and brought out some buttons she was covering in the palest pink silk, then sat back with that telltale, self-satisfied look on her face. 'Then looks like it's all eyes on you, clever Chloe.'

Clueless, more like.

Jenna had started playing another game with Evie. 'Okay, sweetie, let me think... Oh, I know! I spy with my little eye something beginning with... red. Oh, look, oh...' Her gaze was fixed on a man walking past the window. Chloe followed her line of vision and then closed her eyes as her gut contorted in panic.

No.

Muffled against the wind, he wore a thick, dark grey scarf around his neck and an overcoat pulled up to his ears. All that was visible was a mess of dark hair, as if he'd literally just got out of bed, and an aura of something exotic. 'Isn't that... Chloe, come here. Is that Vaughn Brooks?'

At the mention of his name, Chloe went cold. The last time she'd seen him, he'd been nursing a lump on his head from when he'd hit the church tiles after her rugby tackle. Last thing she'd heard, he'd gone overseas to open one of his restaurants. He had a chain now. London, Manchester and Paris, apparently—which she'd hoped meant she'd never lay eyes on him again.

She barely afforded a glance out of the window; it was all she could manage as she slunk down on the sofa, hoping against hope he wouldn't see her. 'I wouldn't know. Or care. That guy looks like his hair needs a decent comb, so it could be, I guess. Come away from the window.'

'Pretty good looking, though, right?'

'I never noticed, to be honest.' Well, actually she had. On a good day, he might be described as dishevelled. He had dark, swarthy skin as if he'd been brought up in full Mediterranean sun. A smug glower. She hadn't noticed if he'd smiled but was pretty sure he hadn't, so she had no idea what his teeth were like.

But thinking back... maybe her sister had a point. There had been that one look he'd given Chloe as she'd left the police station that could have been construed as genuinely sorry. 'Anyway, the exotic look isn't my type.'

'So what is then?' Jenna leant in, suddenly interested.

Someone who might turn up to his own wedding would be

a good place to start. Chloe shrugged. This was the last thing she wanted to talk about. 'I haven't got one.'

'When we played with that phone app you left-swiped a lot of dark-haired men. So I guess you like blonds?'

'You reckon? Jason is blond. I hate blond.'

'You hate Jason. That's a different thing altogether.' Jenna had a strange look on her face as she tapped her biro against her lip. 'So... no blonds or brunettes. Doesn't leave us much to go on. Redheads. Baldies. Short-to-average heights are out, given you're five foot six.'

Whoa. This was all getting too personal. 'What are you doing?'

Jenna raised an eyebrow. 'Casual conversation. Come on, you used to spend hours dreaming of the ideal man.'

'When?'

'Aged ten until, what, sixteen? Then you met Jason, and you declared you'd found him. Or you were hell-bent on turning him into Mr Perfect.'

'I was not.'

Her mum looked up. 'Yes, you were.'

'Geez, great, you're all ganging up on me. Evie? Help me out here?'

'Ribbit,' she gurgled.

Great support there from the three-year-old.

Jenna's eyes were on Chloe again. 'You like a laugh, so sense of humour is very important, yes? Well turned out. Successful. Definitely own income. Kids? Would you mind taking on someone else's kids?'

'I don't know. Should I mind? What is this?' She watched her sister write something down on her notepad. 'Why are you taking notes?'

'Me? Hmm, I'm not, just something for my... shopping...

list.' She shoved her pad back into her bag but not before her cheeks pinked. 'It's getting late. I suppose I should go and give Evie her bath. Come on, sweetheart, let's get you home.'

Taking in her sister's under-eye dark circles and her mum's steady focus on the pink buttons, Chloe decided she'd do them both a favour. 'I can bath her here if you like? I love bath time with my niece. We could have a story and milk and a cuddle because I think I'm owed a few.'

Jenna smiled wearily, her shoulders sagging. 'That would be so lovely. To be honest, I'm knackered. She had me awake at four this morning wanting me to sing to her. I am so over 'The Wheels on the Bus', but she loves it. Oh, and would you mind if I borrowed your laptop while you're in there? I need to check something on my email.'

'Your phone can do that quite well. I thought I'd shown you?'

'Er… no, my phone's playing up.' Jenna's eyes darted away, and Chloe got a strange feeling in her belly.

'What are you up to?'

'Me? Nothing at all.'

'What. Are. You. Doing?'

Her little sister didn't bat an eyelid. 'See, the thing is, if you don't believe in love, you can't be happy for anyone else in love. Ergo, you can't do your job properly. And we need you to do that. *You* need to do that. You worked so hard for your wedding planner's diploma. You work so hard, full stop. So what we need to do is find you someone to love.'

The panic she'd seen earlier in her sister's face now rebounded in Chloe's chest. Why couldn't they all just leave her alone to wallow? 'Oh, no we don't. That is some strangely skewed logic. FYI, I'm never doing the relationship thing again.'

'Well, you won't if you sit here. And why do you still have

that there?' Jenna was pointing to the newspaper article on the pinboard.

'To remind me never to make the same mistake again.'

'So, I'm over this. You need an intervention. This is it. The end. New chapter.' Jenna stormed across the room, ripped the paper from the pin and tore it into tiny pieces. It floated to the floor like confetti, a strange, sad irony that Chloe didn't miss.

'No—'

'Yes. I want my lovely sister back. Well, most of her; you can keep the bridezilla bit.' Jenna looked at her, a mix of frustration and love in her eyes. 'You need to start believing in the thing you sell. You need to have a good time, get laid. Sorry, Mum. Have fun. And then you need to fall in love. Hopelessly and totally.'

The panic spread to Chloe's tummy. 'I don't want to. It isn't fun; it's terrifying. I don't want to go back out there and get on the horse or whatever else you're going to try to tell me to do. Leave me alone.'

'I did leave you alone, for three months. But now it stops. You need cheering up. You need to meet some guys—play a little. Remember what it was like to want to know someone so badly your heart hurts? When thinking about them makes you smile, randomly, for no real reason except... because. When you can't get enough of their smell. When you argue over who puts the phone down first.'

Chloe shrugged. 'Most people communicate by emojicons these days. It's hardly, 'You put the phone down first... no you... no you. I love you. I love you more.' It's more like, smiley face, love heart, thumbs up, now where are the grumpy cat memes?'

'Cynic.' Jenna wrapped her into a hug. 'They're not all bad. Ollie was a good man. A very good man. There are plenty of good men out there. You just have to find someone.'

'No, I don't.' Chloe took Evie by the hand and motioned her towards the bathroom. 'How am I going to do that if I'm not even interested in looking?'

'Oh.' Her sister gave a nonchalant raise of her shoulders and spoke so softly Chloe could barely hear her over her niece's happy giggles. 'I'm sure we'll find a way.'

CHAPTER 2

*H*ey*, loving the dark tresses, and look at those gorgeous brown
eyes. You have depths I'd like to plumb, DaydreamBeliever.
And I have the perfect tool for the job. Chat me back?*

What the hell? Chloe blinked. And again. Another random
message had dropped into her inbox. That made three today.
Five yesterday. A few on Sunday, which was when they'd started
to arrive. That spam filter needed a good clean. She deleted the
message and went back to working on the black-and-white-mov-
ies-themed wedding. She called Jane Davidson. 'Hi, good time
to talk?'

'Oh, yes! How's it going, Chloe? I went to see your mum the
other day for a fitting and the dress is so adorable. I mean, really
beautiful. The flare of the skirt is so Marilyn Monroe. Tim's going
to fall totally in love with me.'

'He already has, I hope?' One jilting was enough already.
Unless she turned her business into a jilting agency. Chloe could

see the by-line now: *Don't want to go through with I do? Call Something Borrowed for a guaranteed jilt of a lifetime; we break it off, so you don't have to.*

There were a couple of things belonging to Jason that she'd liked to have "broken off", one in particular.

'Yes, yes, yes,' Jane replied, her voice taking on that breathless, excited tone Chloe knew so well. Every bride was the same, utterly in love with the wedding as well as the groom. Sometimes, more in love with the wedding. 'I mean, he'll just die when he sees me. Do you remember we met at a fancy dress party and I was Marilyn, and he was King Kong?'

'Yes, of course I remember, and yes, you did.' Jane and Chloe had worked together years ago in the early days of her Inland Revenue career and stayed in contact with each other sharing a wider group of friends. And, in fact, Chloe had been at that fancy dress party, along with Jason.

She also remembered how much time and attention she'd put into her own dress-up outfit: Galadriel from Lord of the Rings. While Jason had gone as James Bond. He hadn't wanted to wear anything 'too out there' in case he looked like a fool, and thought the suit gave him a suave edge. It hadn't. And yet, even then she hadn't been able to see past the love she had for him. 'I remember it was love at first growl. You were clearly destined to marry.'

'And you're making it happen. Did I tell you already how brilliant you are? How are the plans coming along? Anything else to report?'

'Lots.' Vintage Hollywood was proving a lot more enjoyable to explore than frogs promised to be. Frank Sinatra songs, movie quotes and high glamour were just perfect for these two film buffs; hiring out the Movie Museum for the wedding was icing. Chloe had pulled in a lot of favours with an old friend from uni to get the date they'd wanted. 'I've sourced some great little place cards for the tables—you can have them like cinema ticket stubs, or old camera film, or even clapperboards. I'll show you when we meet next week. The photo booth's all booked too. They'll come to the reception area at three, set up and be ready for play straight after the first dance 'til ten. They always go down well—such fun.'

Fun. That word again. Why hadn't she thought about doing something like this with Jason? She'd been determined to have the whole fairy tale catastrophe, the dream she'd had since she was a little girl; the church, a solemn service, a serious place to commit their serious love for each other.

And in hindsight, she perhaps might have been a teeny weeny bit of a stickler for detail. Perfection, actually. Okay, she might have exhibited slight OCD tendencies in the minutiae, and that may have irritated him a little. Maybe if she'd dressed up like a dead movie star he might have hung around long enough to say I do. 'We need to look at the seating plan too.'

'Oh, yes... about that...' Jane suddenly sounded a little panicked. 'Er, well... look, I have to run now, Chloe. Talk soon?'

'Sure? Okay. Don't stress; we've got it all in hand. Bye.' A little strange, but then most brides panicked about the seating plan. Who to seat next to Great Aunt Madge who smelt just a little bit of wee? Or Uncle Fred, who had a bad case of wandering palms.

Another beep. Chloe glanced at her laptop screen. Another message: *DaydreamBeliever? Very cool name. How about I give you something to dream about?*

Then another: *You look familiar. Location West London? Local to Portobello, maybe? I think I've seen you in the market? I work in the Chatswood Arms, gangly bloke, glasses, receding hairline (don't judge me). Chat me back. We could have a coffee? Wine? Meaningless sex?*

Wait a minute. This wasn't spam at all. How did he know she was in Portobello? How did the other guy know she had brown eyes? What exactly were they looking at? This was—she clicked through—this was a dating site. *I'll kill her.* She couldn't get to her phone fast enough. 'Jenna!'

'Hey, perfect timing. I was just about to call you.' Her sister's voice reverberated down the line, all shiny and happy. 'I've just been talking to Stacey Taylor about the flowers and everything and she was saying she was thinking about venues, and they want their reception—'

'What in hell's name is matchyou.co.uk?'

'I don't... Oh.' Jenna dragged in an audible breath. 'Listen, this is important... about Stacey... she said they wanted to meet with you and—'

'Why is my photo on it? *I believe in positivity and kindness...?* What on earth? Since when? You'll be saying I want to dedicate myself to achieving world peace and to run a foster home for stray puppies next. Oh—you just did. Great. This isn't Miss bloody World. It's my life.'

Her sister had the decency to sound contrite. A little. 'Ah, that. Yes. Welcome to my Love Plan. I decided you need to get out more. No more Cassidy Curse. Good-bye, angry Chloe. Hello, happy clients.'

'Hello insanity, more like. Love Plan? Are you mad? Have you any idea what kind of shitstorm is happening? One of these men knows me.'

Jenna laughed. Actually laughed. 'That's good then, isn't it? And he likes your profile enough to contact you, so you're already one foot in the saddle. No awkward small talk?'

'No talk at all. Remove me from this website immediately. Pleeease.' She didn't want to be the object that someone else assessed and then found wanting. She'd had enough of that. 'I don't want to be judged, or have to be nice to someone just so they'll like me, or pretend I love rugby or motorbikes just to be accepted. It feels like I'm in a shop window and men are looking at me deciding whether or not to buy. I'm not for sale, Jenna.' After a few random clicks, Chloe found herself hammering the keyboard a little too intensely. 'Is there an easy way to log out?'

'I... um... don't know.'

'Great. Thanks. Thanks a lot, Jenna.' Chloe breathed in and out slowly, utilising the yogic breathing she'd learned at that one and only hot yoga class she'd attended. Not the most successful attempt at relaxation. She'd clamped her hand over her right nostril, inhaled through the left and then woken up in the reception area outside, being revived by a no-necked weightlifter who smelled of medicated rub. Turns out hot yoga can drop blood pressure pretty quickly.

Yeah, in hindsight it had been a rough few months.

She clicked a few more times and found a photo of herself in the centre of an animated love heart made up entirely of men's photographs. Today's love matches. Apparently. 'I'm surrounded by men, and believe me, that's not remotely as attractive as it sounds. One of them has the username of '*StiffRoger*.'' A shudder ran down Chloe's back. 'That's wrong on so many levels.'

Jenna's voice was laced with a soothing smile. 'I didn't say you'd meet The One immediately. These things take time. Let's talk later. When you've calmed down? If—?'

'I haven't time for this. I have a long to-do list today, sourcing place cards and Hollywood-themed favours. Trying to design a contest flyer for the wedding show. Confirming the band for Jenkins and Tomlinson.' She paused as she stopped at the next point on her list and her heart fell. 'Ahem... researching frogs. I'm trying to make our business work. For you and Mum and Evie.' She was trying her best, and she didn't need do-gooder distractions. She'd got a handle on it all. She had.

'Right. Yes. Of course.' There was a pause, and then her sister was back. 'Look, here's another thing... don't be angry—'

'What now?'

'Er... Stacey's insisting we go to Vaughn's to talk about potential menus and dates.'

That shudder just intensified down her spine. Perfect. Just perfect. 'Vaughn's as in Vaughn Brooks? So arrogant he named his restaurant after his favourite chef—*himself*. She wants to go there? Why there all of a sudden? We talked about somewhere in the city. I was just about to confirm Home House. She liked it there; she said it was perfect. We haven't got much time to get this organised and by some miracle they had a space on the twenty-first. But they had other couples booked in to have a look too—'

'Yes, I know...,' Jenna butted in. 'Vaughn's just picked up another award. There was a review in the Sunday paper, and Stacey saw it. By all accounts, it's a fabulous place. Whitewashed brick walls and crystal chandeliers. Intimate and beautiful. Outstanding food. Vaughn's restaurant is apparently quirky but perfect.'

'Unlike Vaughn the man. Who is arrogant and conniving. He said to that journalist that Jason and I had been a bad match from the start. I wouldn't be surprised if he'd talked Jason out of marrying me in the first place.'

In fact, next to Jilting Jason, Vaughn Brooks was on Chloe's list of men she'd like to kill. It was a list of two, and it wasn't strange at all that they were related.

So it was more than her ego was worth to go there and negotiate a deal that would advantage him in any way. And it had absolutely nothing to do with the fact that she'd accosted him with a bunch of flowers at St Catherine's Church altar and would wear that mortification forever.

She clutched at the only straw she could think of. 'He doesn't do weddings.'

'Since when?'

'Right this second.'

Jenna sighed. 'Oh, Chloe, honey, he does do weddings, actually. Stacey rang him while she was here. She was so excited; she had the review in her sticky little hand. He said they could have the service in his walled garden if she wanted. They have a canopy for rainy days. He has some time this afternoon before they open for dinner and said he could squeeze her in. I said that would be okay. It is okay, right? I mean, we have to at least allow our clients some independent thought?'

'Not if it messes with my head.' Chloe squeezed the bridge of her nose and closed her eyes. But what choice did she have? Keep the customer satisfied no matter what the personal cost. The clutched-at straw moved ever further from her grasp. 'You'll come with me? Safety in numbers?'

'Ah, no. Evie has Ballet Tots at four thirty. He wants Stacey there at five, timing's all wrong.'

'Traitor. Matchmaker. And now you want me to smile sweetly at Vaughn Brooks, too? Double traitor.'

Jenna sighed. 'Hey, he wasn't the bad guy there. At least he actually turned up at the church; give him a break. And I'm sorry about matchyou.co.uk. I was trying to help, honestly. It was so easy in the olden days when people made the match for you.'

'This is not *Pride and Prejudice*, Jenna. This is my life. Mr Darcy is not going to walk through a pond for me.'

'It was a lake, actually, and more's the pity. Because it's a truth universally acknowledged that a single woman, in possession of a teeny misfortune, must be in want of a bloody good shag. Or just a date. Some fun?' She laughed. 'Sometimes I get carried away with ideas and don't always think things through. I didn't mean to upset you, really. Truth is, I'm worried about you. I love you, and I don't want you to be so down in the dumps.'

'Oh.' There was a little clutch at Chloe's heart. Jenna had meant well. Even if the emails had given Chloe a bit of a panic. But her family needed to learn she could handle her love life on her own, or, in other words, avoid ever having one again. There was no way she was going to risk everything on a man. Bad enough that her business was breaking, but that was nothing in comparison to how her heart had felt when Vaughn Brooks had walked up the aisle with that smug yet pitying look in his eyes. Her whole life had stopped then. Everything had broken, and she was only just starting to feel she had a handle on things. Surely only a masochist would ever risk that kind of hurt again? 'Oh, it's okay. I know you were trying to do a good thing. Just unsubscribe me, please?'

'Consider it done.' Jenna's voice was upbeat again. 'So, go on, girl. Face your demons and go to Vaughn's. You just need to look him in the eye once and then it will all be forgotten.'

'Never in my whole life will I forget. But if Stacey wants to go, then who am I to say no?' *Great.* A meeting with a man who everyone thought she'd tried to disembowel with white roses, silver pine cones and a delicate but not overpowering smattering of heather.

And now she had an inbox relentlessly bleeping with guys who thought she was interested in having a life. She wasn't. Things were getting just a little too out of her control for comfort. The last time that had happened, it had ended badly.

Just ask Vaughn Brooks.

Jenna

FIVE YEARS AGO...

Sender: Jennacass567@gmail.com

Hey, Nick!

Sorry my first email arrived out of the blue. You must have had a shock! Thanks for taking the time to reply. No, it doesn't seem like five minutes since we were at St Peter's, never mind five years! I wasn't really in that 'cool' group at school for long—they ditched me as soon as they found out I bought my uniform from the second-hand shop. But you weren't to know any of that. You seemed to stay out of our way a lot. I guess we didn't have much in common back then, and that group really was a collection of little bitches.

But yeah, your mum said you'd signed up for the army graduate officer scheme and been gone two years already! As I said in my last email, I knew you were into war gaming, but I couldn't believe you'd actually joined the army. Hero!

Shame we lost touch when we left school. I remember how you and I used to have a laugh in concert band back in Year Seven. I have to be honest, though, I haven't touched the clarinet since! Anyway, when I bumped into your mum a few months ago at a friend's housewarming, it was such a funny coincidence that I thought I'd write to you. I'm glad you think it's okay if we write to each other every now and then.

It sounds pretty tough wherever you are. I appreciate you can't tell me any details, but wow, camel riding sounds great! Good to hear you can have some fun in your downtime. I can appreciate too, that it gets frustrating just sitting around and waiting for something to happen. I'd hate that. I can never sit still for long.

Your girlfriend sounds nice, although it must be tricky when you're deployed to different places—how do you ever get to see each other? I presume you must have met her while you were 'at work'? Is that allowed? (You dark horse, you!)

I went to the St Peter's five-year reunion last week, and it was full of the old faces. What can I tell you? I'll try to remember… Oh yes, Ayesha Patel got into Harvard to do a master's in physics! Can you believe it? Well, I can. She was always so much better at sciences than any of us. And Ged Foster is a reporter on the TV lunchtime news. Amazing! Every time I see him, I remember the day he got drunk on the spiked punch at the prom and vomited all over my feet. I bet the BBC wouldn't have taken him on if they'd known that! Mr Pritchard has finally retired. About time too! He must be nearly ninety.

We've all decided to meet up once a year from now on. I hope you can join us one day!

Nick, I'm so sorry to hear about your friend. It must be hard losing someone you've become close to. You said you'd trained with him, so you must have known him a long time, and I can imagine it's pretty intense living conditions out there, so you're in one another's pockets all the time. Friendships must get deep pretty quickly. I'm sending you heaps of hugs and love. You know where I am if you want to rant. Please feel free.

Are you planning on coming home soon? You sounded a bit fed up with army life. Can you leave? I don't know what the rules are, but I seem to remember someone saying you have to sign up for seven years?

And finally... Drum roll... You'll never believe the juicy gossip today.................................

I'm getting married!

Ollie proposed. OMG, it was the most romantic thing, ever. We were on a day trip to Brighton and in a really fancy restaurant. He made a toast to 'us' and then got down on one knee. In front of the whole restaurant! I was gobsmacked. I mean, really. I wasn't expecting it at all. But I love him so much. He's just perfect in every way (he's your typical tall, dark and handsome. He has a building company and says one day he's going to build me a house. Okay, I know you just did a gagging action. Sorry.)

Of course, I said yes! My sister, Chloe, is a wedding planner—I think I told you in my brief first email? She's just starting out, so I'm one of her first clients. And, of course, Mum is going to make my dress. I thought I might try my hand at doing the flowers. It's something I've always been interested in and a bit different to working as a hairdresser. Anyway, I imagine that's all too much information for a soldier on active duty and who is probably not interested in such domestic things... so, I'll go.

Every time I hear about the Middle East on the news, I get nervous. Stay safe.

Jenna x

CHAPTER 3

Vaughn's restaurant was on Portland Road, a nice brisk walk away on a blustery spring afternoon. A weak sun filtered through high, thin clouds casting the antique shops, clothing merchants and bustling cafes in a magical halo of soft light. As she walked, Chloe tried to get rid of the tightness in her chest, focusing instead on her surroundings and the peace of mind she got being in this slice of Notting Hill.

'Hey, Chloe, love! How are you?' Don, one of the antique shop owners, walked past, takeaway coffee in one hand, a horse racing newspaper in the other. He gave her a big smile. 'Cheer up, love, worse could happen.'

Could it? What could be worse than going to a meeting with the man she'd assaulted on her wedding day? 'Yes. Yes. Have a nice day, Don.'

Next, it was the lady from the Chinese restaurant, sweeping out the front of her shop. She nodded, grinning. 'Hello.'

'Hi.' Chloe smiled and waited to cross to the sunnier side of the street.

Two young skateboarders skimmed down the centre of the road, slapping their boards on the concrete as they came to a halt to let her cross. 'Age before beauty, right, miss?'

'Watch it, you two.' Despite Vaughn Brook's presence in the area, she loved this place. The friendliness of the people, the fresh edge of bars and mismatch of trendy stores, the buskers and their eclectic choice of songs—which weren't always to her taste, but added a definite buzz and a smile to her step.

She liked the eccentricity of the market, the way each day had a different feel, a distinct personality; the quiet of the week and the bustle of the weekend with tourists snapping endless photos and local shoppers hoping to find a bargain. Jason had suggested, a few times, that they move out to somewhere cheaper, to somewhere with a community. Couldn't he see that, despite being in a big bustling city, there was a real community right here?

The trees along her route were coming to life again after a long, cold winter; tender, burgeoning buds promising blossom in a month or so. Daffodils had given way to tulips brightening the regimented Edwardian buildings, creating a colourful path. Despite all this, Chloe still felt a little like Dorothy on her way to Oz, surrounded by amazing things yet with nothing in her heart but the anxiety of trying to find her way back to safety again.

Vaughn Brooks. Just her luck.

She located the restaurant in a parade of shops selling chic and not cheap knickknacks, next to an organic butcher's and a juice bar. Exquisite wrought iron railings separated the first-floor apartments from the ground floor businesses. *Vaughn's* stood proudly in the centre of the parade with pristine white canopies hanging over the shop front, the lettering of his name painted in a swirl of flamboyance on the canopy fabric and across the windows. A cluster of tables and chairs on the footpath gave it a distinctly Mediterranean feel.

Chloe stole a look at the menu on a board outside the door. Twice cooked pork belly, Chinese spiced duck… Which, in any other eating establishment, would sound wonderful, but right now gave her heartburn.

'Chloe!' Grinning widely, Stacey appeared at the restaurant door with Mark, the groom-to-be, standing next to her. They looked completely at home and, unfortunately, utterly smitten. 'Oh, it's just divine. Come and have a look. The garden is perfect. I can't believe you didn't suggest it before.'

Chloe pasted on a shiny, happy smile that her sister would be proud of and refused to show any sign of irritation. 'It's fairly new. I haven't been here myself yet. Can't wait to see it.' There had been talk, just before the wedding, of an invitation to the restaurant's grand opening with celebrities and famous TV chefs and the diverse clientele of the area. It had sounded right up her street. She presumed the invitation been lost in the post.

With Vaughn working overseas for most of his adult life, Chloe hadn't met him until The Jilting. As a cousin who'd spent long childhood summer holidays with Jason, then forging his stellar career abroad, he'd been a well-kept secret. He'd been too busy, too elusive—too damned selfish, she'd privately thought—to come back for the engagement party or Jason's father's funeral. He had a reputation of jumping from one job to the next, suddenly uprooting and going travelling on a whim. Doing exactly what suited him with no regard for anyone else. But he'd always been top-pick for best man, no hesitation. A pact, she'd heard, Jason and Vaughn had made years ago.

Then he was suddenly there, his presence bigger than ever. She hadn't even stepped over the threshold, and her heart began to hammer. Out of the shadows he came, slowly coming into focus. The smile he'd worn slipped as he realised who she was.

There was a silence as they stared at each other. His hair, as she'd remembered, was a mess of dark waves. His eyes narrowed, black as midnight and matching his collared shirt, which was haphazardly stuffed into dark jeans. The linen covered a body she'd actually touched, and suddenly, the hardness of those muscles under her fingertips rebounded into her brain. Briefly, she wondered whether he'd honed them just by lifting heavy-duty kitchenware or if he worked out. For a second, she couldn't breathe.

His jaw was fixed. 'Chloe Cassidy.' He regained whatever composure might have momentarily slipped with his smile. Whether it was subconscious or not, she didn't know, but he rubbed his forehead with his forefingers. The exact spot she'd cut as she'd inadvertently wrestled him to the ground. 'Do I need to duck or run for my life? Should I call the police right now or wait to see how things unfold?'

The smile she found was gracious and forgiving—but, she hoped, sarcastic to the point of piercing his well-inflated ego. 'Don't worry, I have no need to take you down this time. You are perfectly safe.'

'So *you* are Stacey's wedding planner?'

'Yes.' Was that so difficult to imagine? It was hard trying to speak with a throat that felt rubbed raw with sand and a mouth faux-grinning as wide as a bullfrog's. But Jenna was right. She had to be here for her client. She stuck out her hand. 'Mr Brooks. Good of you to fit us in at such short notice.'

He gave a swift glance to her hand, then to their clients. 'Chloe. And you can call me Vaughn—after all, we're not exactly strangers.'

'Okay, Vaughn it is.' His handshake was firm and warm. And

the briefest she'd ever experienced. Clearly, he was as put out about this as she was. *Good.*

But that didn't explain the shiver of something that went through her as she touched him. She reached into her bag for her planner, hoping to wipe all traces of him from her skin. Maybe that would stop the strange tingle in her fingertips. It didn't. 'Yes, so, we're looking at the twenty-first of June. I'm sure Stacey's told you all about their plans? And I'm also sure you'll be busy that day; mid-summer and all that, busiest time of the year, right? And we'd like to seat around a hundred; that's quite a lot for a small place like...' Chloe flashed a look around the room as she stepped in. Damn. It would seat a hundred comfortably.

And wow, it was startling. There was indeed whitewashed brickwork, which she'd expected to look tacky, but actually looked authentically French, Italian, or something. Like a villa she'd once stayed in high on the Tuscan hills, comfortable and welcoming, yet stylish. Crystal chandeliers reflected the natural light, and crisp white tablecloths adorned white ironwork tables with matching chairs in a long room with towering ferns and greenery, illuminated by large cathedral candles on white candlesticks. There was even a small raised section, perfect for the main wedding group to sit in full view of their guests. In essence, it was perfect.

Double damn.

At the end of the room were huge glass French doors. Chloe gestured to them. 'May I look at the garden? Obviously, being a summer wedding, it would be just perfect to be outside. Although, I doubt...' *That I'll like it. That it'll fit a hundred. That I can hold this smile much longer.*

With fingers crossed that it would be totally unsuitable, Chloe led the little troupe down the room and out into a... well, a slice of heaven. More whitewashed walls, more candelabra, and more glass reflecting even more light. Strings of tiny fairy lights cascaded down the walls. It was simple, stylish, sophisticated perfection to the point her breath stalled in her chest. This time her smile was genuine. 'Wow. Are you allergic to colour or something?'

He gave a nonchalant shrug that he'd clearly learned in the kitchens of the foreign restaurants where he'd spent a good part of his life. 'I prefer to keep things simple. Too much of anything detracts from my food. Believe me, that is what will make you say wow.'

The arrogance again. Shame she wouldn't be going anywhere near his food.

Vaughn stood by the French doors and cranked a large handle into gear. 'We use this when it rains.' With a couple of twists, he released a canopy of the lightest gossamer cloth that provided cover but preserved the light. 'It's delicate, but 100 per cent waterproof. I imported it from Naples.'

He'd thought of everything.

With a whelp, Stacey clapped her hands, her voice as high-pitched as Chloe imagined hers would be, if she were capable of more speech. 'Oh my, it's beautiful. Please say you're available on the twenty-first? Please?'

Chloe lay a warning hand on her client's arm and whispered, 'We haven't talked prices. It could be way over budget; I don't want you getting your hopes up. And what does Mark think?'

'I'll tell Mark what to think.' Stacey hissed back through a forced smile as she regarded her fiancé. 'Bugger the cost. It'll be worth every penny.'

'One question.' Chloe caught Vaughn's self-satisfied, hooded gaze and her heart did a little loop-the-loop. That was what frank annoyance did to you—palpitations. 'Why are you available at such short notice?'

He handed them each a menu. 'I've only just got my alcohol

licence. It took more time than I thought possible. Bureaucracy here is even worse than in France. If you've seen enough here, perhaps we can talk potential menus for the big day? Go in, take a seat.' He motioned for them all to go back inside. Stacey and Mark led the way, Vaughn went next, stopping at the door to wind in the canopy. There was nothing she could do but wait until he'd finished—that, or crush past him. No way.

She looked down at her shoes and wished she'd worn ruby slippers, doubting that clicking nude heels together three times would get her anywhere near home.

After a couple of twists, Vaughn turned to her. The well-rehearsed business pretence dropped, and he stared at her with stark annoyance. 'Well, hell, Chloe Cassidy. I'd heard your business had all but dried up. I didn't imagine I'd see you again. Not in my worse nightmares.'

Wait a minute. *She* was the nightmare? 'Hey, it's not my fault if you have trouble sleeping. I wasn't the one breaking up a marriage.'

He froze. 'Shoot the messenger, why don't you? And it was just a wedding, not a marriage.'

'Just a wedding? Just a wedding? It was *my* wedding. Your cousin's wedding. But it all went swimmingly well for you in the end, didn't it? Not a good match, you said. It was for the best, you said. So you got what you wanted.' She stopped glowering at him for a second and raised her hand to a concerned-looking Stacey, who was waving a menu at her. 'I'll be there in just a minute. Ironing out some minor details here. Have a chat with Mark about what dishes you want.'

Vaughn stopped winding but didn't make to go back inside. On her wedding day, she'd had plenty of other things to think about, so she hadn't realised just how tall he was, how broad shouldered. How nice he smelt—like an exotic vanilla, mixed with spice and something she couldn't quite put her finger on. Delicious. It was a shock, considering she shouldn't have been smelling him at all. She should have carried on walking through into the main room with Stacey and Mark and taken a chance on brushing past him. Or walked out. Refused to come in the first place.

And now, to add to that, she was so close she could see his dark eyes weren't like midnight at all; they were a curious mix of dark grey and silver. They were quite astonishing. Extraordinary, in fact. And holding some kind of irritated dare or that same self-righteous smugness.

Apart from the scar she'd inflicted on his forehead from the rugby tackle, his features were unblemished. His nose was perfectly straight. Lines crossed his forehead, getting deeper with every second they glared at each other. She tried not to look at his mouth because her stomach went strangely tumbly when she looked there, probably due to the fact that whenever he spoke, a veiled insult, or harmful intent, or just plain anger came out.

'Really? You think I broke up your relationship with Jason? It was my fault? Get real, Chloe. What I thought didn't come into it. I was helping out my cousin who was worried about how you'd react. And he was right, wasn't he?' But there was a hint of a smile there in his voice, and the corners of his mouth twitched. Was he laughing at her? 'I'm still getting headaches...'

'Oh? God, did I give you a concussion?' Genuine concern wriggled through her. For some reason, she had the urge to touch the place on his forehead that had the tiniest of scars. 'Brain damage? I gave you a concussion and brain damage?'

'No, don't get all panicky. It's just the memory of that day brings on head pain. You don't take disappointment well.' He shook his head, eyes glinting a little. 'But, you've got a great tackle. Watch out, England might call you up for the world cup; God knows they need all the help they can get.'

Chloe shrugged and hoped he'd erased the memory of her whacking him on the backside with her bouquet. 'I work out.'

'So I gathered. How's the anger management thing going?' If for a moment she'd thought there was a friendly tone in his voice, it was gone.

'Oh, come on. I didn't hurt you intentionally, you know that. The damage only happened because your head hit the slate tiles. It was bad timing, an accident.'

She'd lunged at him with no intention of actually touching him, but her feet had tangled in her wedding dress train, and she'd lost her balance, propelling forward with force and taking him down to the floor. Then, frustrated, annoyed and humiliated, she'd smacked him on his bottom with her wedding bouquet.

She'd explained it all to the police, and they'd let her go with a warning. In fact, they'd laughed. It wasn't assault. It wasn't GBH. It was an over exuberance of her frustration, and she had never, ever hit anyone before or since, which was making his overreaction a little hard to bear. 'Anger management classes were only a suggestion; the police didn't actually make me go.'

'Pity.' He stepped back and let her go past him into the restaurant.

But she stopped and turned to him, her back to her clients so they couldn't hear her. 'You need to know I'm going to recommend to Stacey that she doesn't have her wedding here. That's for the best, don't you think?'

Those dark eyes widened and the temper she'd imagined he'd have flared. 'Not for me it isn't. It's money. It's business, *my* business, and I'll encourage them to book. In fact, I'll bend over backwards to help them. Is this because of what happened? Because of Jason?'

'I try not to let my personal life intrude on my professional, so please don't think I have any special grudge against you or your business, but there are plenty of other wedding venues in London. I'm not 100 per cent sure this is the right place for Stacey and Mark. We have quite a few more to see. We'll be in touch if we want to take things further.'

'I think she's already made her mind up. And we both know you'll want to keep her happy. I've already put it in my diary.' He put distance between them with the cool tone of his words. 'You can't avoid everyone who was at the wedding-that-never-happened, forever, you know. I presume you're going to Jane Davidson's wedding?'

'Going to it? Of course, I'm organising it. She's been my friend for years.' She put the emphasis on *my*. When she and Jason had split their goods and chattels—via text, because she did not want to see him again ever—they'd also divided their friends up, too. She'd made a list. She liked lists; they made everything seem so much more clear-cut. It took the emotion of everything. At least, that had been the idea.

Sadly, no matter what she'd done, the emotion had got in anyway. Some of their friends had shown their loyalties either to Chloe or to Jace, so those ones hadn't been a difficult decision. Jane had stayed friends with Chloe. Actually, Jane had begged Chloe to continue planning the Hollywood wedding; they'd arranged so much together it was a shame not to continue so close to the big day. Chloe had taken that as a measure of Jane's loyalty. 'It's going to be magnificent.'

Vaughn's lips thinned. 'Has she mentioned that I'm going? Only, I thought I should warn you. I wouldn't want to put myself at risk of a second bouquet battering.'

'For goodness' sake, it was a bunch of wilting flowers, and don't think for a minute that I would waste my energy on you ever again.' Just as she'd thought her irritation was subsiding, it began to rise again, starting as a swell of heat in the knot in her stomach. 'Why would you go to Jane's wedding anyway? You hardly know her.'

'Why wouldn't I? Tim's a mate, and it's his wedding too. Although you women often seem to forget that a man is involved.'

The irritation quickly spread to her fingers, which she tapped on her notepad. Although, even worse, she was annoyed at herself for allowing him to niggle away at her. 'I am a professional wedding planner, and I am fully aware there are two people involved. Since when have you been Tim's friend? You've only been back...'

'Three months.' As if he knew the effect he was having on her, he grinned. 'A lot can happen in three months. We go mountain biking sometimes, rock climbing and play football together.'

'With Jason too? He plays with Tim on Sunday evenings. Has been for years.' Her shoulders slumped a little as she realised their lives had continued as if nothing had changed. Well, she supposed, nothing much had changed for them. They'd all been able to carry on dreaming and planning. It was only Chloe who'd been hung out to dry, living in a strange limbo for three months where sleeping had been sporadic, and worrying had become her norm. She'd been forced to find cash to buy Jason out of the mortgage and run her business against rumour and innuendo. While they all blissfully carried on, situation normal.

Damn, it was just bloody unfair.

Vaughn's chest puffed out just a little. 'We just won the league.'

'Yippee-bloody-daa. I'll call up the papers, shall I?' Something akin to a large lump of ice landed on her chest as she realised the ramifications of his previous statement. 'Whoa, hang on... does that mean Jason is going to the wedding too? That I'm organising? For *my* friend.'

'Yes. And Amy.'

Chloe let that sit with her for a moment while a riot of emotions flitted across her heart.

Of course.

That was why Jane had been so reticent to talk about the seating plan. She'd invited her wedding planner's ex, her ex-best friend and the best man from the wedding-that-never-happened.

Jane had been her friend in the beginning, but that had been a long time ago. In fact, apart from the occasional wedding planning meeting, Chloe had hibernated and snubbed any social contact, licking her wounds and wallowing in her own pity party. So why wouldn't Jane invite her and Tim's current friends to their wedding? Her cheeks started to burn. 'We... well, we haven't gone over the guest list and seating plan yet.'

Vaughn looked a little concerned. 'You didn't know about this?'

'Yes... yes, of course. It just slipped my mind, that's all.'

'Are you okay? You look a little... upset.' He took a step backwards. 'Getting out of the way of your left hook, just in case.'

And then, damn it, he smiled. If she hadn't been about to self-combust with humiliation, she might have found that smile just a little bit interesting. But here, now, she saw it as pity for her messy life and, probably, a good comeuppance for what she did to him in that church.

Chloe pressed a hand to her cheeks in an effort to cool the burning sensation down. 'I'm absolutely fine. In fact, couldn't be better.'

For a fleeting moment, she considered not going to the wedding at all, but everyone knew that weddings begot weddings. The women became teary-eyed and hopeful, and the men got drunk and thought, why not? And they all remembered how fabulous the wedding had been, and now, who was that amazing planner with such careful attention to detail? And they all knew exactly who she was because she was sure to leave all her contact details in the small print on the favour bags and place cards, on the back of the order of service, and as a contact point for the well-wisher's book. It was the prime place for a wedding planner to drum up more business, and that was what she needed more than anything.

She had to go to that wedding and face them all, no matter what.

By now Stacey and Mark had grown bored of waiting and were walking over, looking less than impressed. Vaughn smiled at their clients, then leaned in a little to Chloe's ear. 'I can talk to Jason if you want? Suggest he doesn't go?'

'Why?'

'If it's going to be awkward for you. It's hard after a breakup. Apparently.'

'Apparently?' Which was it? That he'd never had a breakup, or he'd never found one hard? *What the hell?*

There was a shrug of one shoulder. 'Yes. He hurt you.'

'I'm fine. I've totally forgotten all about Jason.' It was even worse that Vaughn was trying to be nice to her. Why was he trying to be nice to her? Was that how it was going to be at the wedding? Everyone carefully choosing their words and tiptoeing around her as if she was the sad old aunt who smelt of wee. As if she was the one who had to be avoided at all costs. God, how awful that would be.

She needed to prove to everyone that she really was okay, that she'd found the courage to move on. Suddenly, brain one step behind her mouth, she found herself blurting out, 'I'm very good, actually. Great, in fact! I'm seeing someone.'

Vaughn's eyes narrowed as he scrutinised her face. 'Oh? Who? Do I know him?'

'No.' *And, strangely enough, neither do I. Yet.* 'I doubt it. I may bring him to the wedding; I haven't decided.'

She ignored the panic that reverberated in her voice and through her body. What in hell was she doing? Inventing a man just to save face? Of all the ridiculous things she'd done, this had to be up there with the best of them. But she was damned well going to get back on that horse, or in the sack or… something. Because she couldn't turn up at that wedding without a date and let them all think she hadn't got over Jason. She had.

But more, worse than being betrayed, would be the pity. From the other guests. From Jason and Amy. From Vaughn Brooks. She would not give them the satisfaction of thinking she was beaten. She was a strong woman. She was capable. She was a consummate professional. She was brave.

Well, she was going to be.

She turned to Vaughn and smiled, feeling a sense of purpose for the first time in forever. She was… she was like the trees she'd walked past to get here; renewed, refreshed, ready. Well, maybe not quite ready, but she was going to find a date for that wedding. She was going to hold her head up high and show them all. She was going to go to the wedding and beget more weddings and more and more. She was going to have a successful life and support her sister and her niece and her mother and anyone else who came along. She could do it. She could.

It was time to reactivate Jenna's Love Plan.

Jenna

Sender: Jennacass567@gmail.com

Hi, Nick!

YES! I think you should definitely propose to her! She'd be an idiot to say no. Let me know every detail. Every single one!

Of course, I'm speaking through rose-tinted glasses. We had a wonderful day. Sorry you couldn't make it, but I didn't really expect the army to let you out just to see me get married! There are photos online if you want to take a sneaky peak. I'll put the link in at the end of the email. It was all just perfect, apart from the rain just as we were having the photos taken, but I didn't let that spoil it.

We had a honeymoon in Crete, which was gorgeous apart from Ollie getting food poisoning. The only time we left the resort, he got sick. Typical! We spent the rest of the holiday in bed... but then we'd

spent the first part in bed too (I know, too much information! Sorry!).
The weather was great; it was sunny every day, and we had a nice
balcony with a lovely view, so when he was ill, I often just sat out
and stared out into a deep blue sky and thought how lucky I was to
be there with him.

I imagine your life is so very different out there in a war zone. I
can't imagine what it must be like.

It's fine if you can't write often. Really, I understand. Special ops
sounds very exciting. Are you like James Bond? (Although, I hope,
without the tuxedo! If you're having to sleep in mud at times, you'd
ruin it!). I'd be so scared with all those mortar attacks going on
around me; I'd be just waiting for one with my name on it. I guess
you can't think like that. How do you manage? You must be on edge
the whole time.

We're just rolling into summer here too. Although a British
summer is hardly as hot as where you are somewhere out there in the
desert. We managed one decent sunny day last week, and the whole
of London suddenly got summer fever. So many white legs and fake
tan disasters! We tried to organise a barbecue for the weekend, but
as always, we ended up cooking under an umbrella. This must all
seem boring to you, but in your last email, you said you liked to hear
about everyday things. I hope you're not falling asleep reading this.

Anyway, I must go… I've got to go to the chemist and get home
before Ollie… I have… Oooh, I shouldn't tell you. No, I won't. I
can't tell you yet. I have to tell him first.

Maybe in my next email I will have some exciting news! ;-)
Stay safe, Nick, and good luck with the proposal!
Jenna x

CHAPTER 4

W hat's his name, then?' Jenna asked, her eyes all-agog with vicarious excitement as she leaned over in the manicurist's chair and nudged her sister.

'Carl. Or rather *TheBigCarlhuna*, according to his profile.' Chloe tried to hide her mortification from her sister and the two nail artistes giving them the pedi part of the mani-pedi. But she could tell, just by the way the young girls at their feet glanced at each other with unconcealed mirth in their eyes, that she was going to be the topic of conversation later. 'Believe me, he is the best of a bad bunch of today's Special Love Matches. And I'm staying well away from *StiffRoger*, who seems to pop up way too often. All puns intended.'

Buoyed by potential ex-shaming and the need to prove herself to smug Vaughn, she'd plucked up the courage, reactivated her matchyou.co.uk membership and perused the sappy love heart surrounding her profile with renewed interest. She'd picked a couple of guys who looked interesting and arranged a meeting with the only one who answered her coy message of, '*hi*'. It was hardly the most profound thing she'd ever written, but *TheBigCarlhuna* had answered with a smiley face, and thus, it had begun.

'And how do you feel about this... date?'

'It's just a coffee, seriously. How bad can it be?' *About as bad as any very bad thing ever.* But she'd arranged it now, and it was the only way she was going to get a plus-one for the wedding, unless she took up her mum's suggestion of the dandruff-ridden funeral director. *No, thank you.* Chloe looked down at her toes. 'So, what's the score with this nail varnish malarkey? Age old dilemma: do you have the same colour on your fingers as your toes?'

'You can have a different colour on each damned digit if you like.' Jenna handed her the plastic colour sample swatches with so many colours Chloe didn't know where to start. It was aeons since her last first date, and once she'd got engaged and fallen into a settled routine, her interest in such things as painting nails had been overtaken by house buying and mortgages and wedding planning. This felt like a guilty pleasure, but it was nice to get out with Jenna for some one-on-one, uninterrupted sister time, and they were using a voucher Jenna had received for her birthday, so no added expense. 'What do you know about this Carl guy? How do you know he's not an axe murderer? What does he look like? For that matter, what do axe murderers look like? When you see their profiles on TV, you always think *he looks like an axe murderer, how did nobody know?* But probably, being their neighbour or something, you wouldn't guess they had it in them. *Such a lovely man, used to feed my cat... Bit of a loner...*'

'Oh, now's really not the time to throw that at me, Jenna. I'm only at this point because of you, but I don't think matchyou.co.uk allows axe murderers to sign up. I'm sure it's part of their terms and conditions. I'll check his pockets for axes, shall I?'

'Don't go anywhere near his pockets on a first date.' Jenna laughed, then wriggled as her pedicure reached the tickle foot massage part. But, suddenly, she was dead serious. 'Just be careful, okay?'

'Of course.'

'No dark alleys or wide-open spaces where he could bury a body. Don't go anywhere with him alone.'

'Well, wow, you're quite the merchant of doom.' But Chloe's courage took a little nosedive. Maybe dating was a bad idea after all. No—she wasn't dating; she was interviewing for a plus-one role. Although, in Jenna's eyes, if Chloe wasn't just about to be done away with, she was going to find fun and fall in love with love again… Or something. It was all in the framing. 'Oh, God, I don't know what the rules are these days. The last time I went on a first date was nearly ten years ago. I'm well out of practice. And anyway, I thought with all these dating apps, people went straight to sex and cut out the middle bit?'

Jenna sighed. 'Don't ask me. I wouldn't have a clue. I'm so glad it's not me doing it.'

You should, Chloe thought, looking at her beautiful sister, all pink-faced and smiling her pretend-happy smile. Maybe dating would rub the sad part off at least just a little. But she knew Jenna wouldn't hear of it. Flatly refused.

The thing was, whilst Chloe didn't believe that love was enough to keep two people together, Jenna believed she'd had her one chance for life, and no one would ever be as good as Ollie. And Chloe didn't want to stress her sister, so she let it drop. She contemplated the swatches in her hand. 'Okay, virginal white or vampy red?'

Jenna looked thoughtful. 'Red. With some artwork? Stripes? Flowers? Have you chatted him?'

'Chatted him? Is that an actual verb now? Yes, we talked a little on the video link thing.' This was so bloody hard. 'It's like window shopping and being window-shopped. There's no romance in it, not like the golden days of seeing someone across a crowded room and taking a chance. The shy but slow burn of a fledgling love.' When only *TheBigCarlhuna* had responded to her messages, she'd had no choice but to go with the video link flow. 'To be honest, I was starting to feel like I was the coffee cream on the pick and mix stand, the one people only choose when there's nothing else left.'

Jenna frowned. 'You're not the coffee cream, lovely sister of mine. You're... you're the Valrhona of the pick and mix stand, the Cadbury creme egg—original version, naturally. You're the best damned chocolate in the universe. Just remember that when you're talking to him.'

I am Valrhona. Dark, mysterious and delicious. For the first time since this whole debacle began, Chloe laughed. 'I'm sure he'll be fine, and if not, I can make a quick getaway, right? Text me fifteen minutes in and I can use you as an excuse if I need to. Yes, I like the red, it makes me feel adventurous, but I'm not sure I'm up to art as well.'

Her sister scrutinised the handiwork. 'You're probably right. I like the plain red; it's forthright without being in your face. So, after you've been with him a few minutes, nip to the loo and text me that you're okay, just a thumbs up or down. And leave your find-a-friend app on so we can trace you if needs be... You know, if you...' She did a slashing motion with her fingers across her throat.

'Gee, thanks... I'm really feeling the trust vibes here. I'll be fine. Really. He's a musician, and he's two years older than me. He seems nice, with a kind of overly zealous smile and a soft voice. Mostly we just murmured. God, it was embarrassing. I think he was more nervous than I was. What the heck are we supposed to say? I can't remember how to flirt.' And then there might be a kiss... and maybe more? She was bonkers for doing this. 'What if he wants more? What if he doesn't? What if he hates me? Aaargh! It's so much easier staying in and binge-watching box sets.'

But that wouldn't get her a date for the wedding. And not going would mean she took a risk on drumming up more clients. So she was stuck with it.

Maybe she could get a date-by-mail order? Was that really even a thing? Tick-boxing all the right attributes: tall, dark, and handsome. Messy hair. Dark, haunted eyes...

And then that thought took her on a strange trail that ricocheted from her own wedding and back to yesterday at Vaughn's, and the strange tummy-tumbling thing started to happen all over again. And that was enough to convince her that she needed to be focused on the coffee this afternoon and not thinking about the best man shenanigans, because all that did was produce anxiety.

Jenna did that sisterly thing of patting Chloe's arm. 'Just be yourself, honey. *TheBigCarlhuna* will love you.'

'The new me with the gel nail varnish and freshly manicured lady garden? Instead of bitten to the quick fingernails and... well, let's just say it's been a while since anyone's been down there.'

'You're having a bikini wax? Today?' Her sister jerked around and then stilled as her nail artiste pulled her foot back towards the bubbling foot spa and tsked. 'And you're meeting him tonight?'

'Sure. Why not?' No big deal. It was just a tidy up.

'Your thighs are going to look like a freshly plucked chicken. What on earth were you thinking?'

'I wasn't thinking anything. I met the guy online this morning. I don't intend for him to go anywhere near there; it was more just for a confidence boost.' Chloe sighed. 'To be honest, I need more than a bikini deforestation to make me feel up to meeting a man. What if he's horrible? Worse, what if he isn't? What then? Because it's all well and good trying to find someone, but what if I really like him? What if I fall in love with him, deeply, honestly, totally, and then what if this new man, The One, the love of my life—?'

'I thought that was Jason.'

'What if the love of my life, *version two*, does a runner too?' What then for her heart? 'I can't cope with another Jilting.'

'I think you're getting way ahead of yourself, Chlo. It's just a little fun and finding a plus-one.'

'No, of course. You're right.' It was nothing at all to do with falling in love.

After the mani-pedi, Chloe confirmed the get-out-of-date-quick texting plans, kissed Jenna goodbye and made her way to the waxing salon for what she anticipated was going to be one of the probably many excruciatingly painful experiences of the day. Trying to flirt with a murmuring musician would be small fry after this.

'Hey, love, pop these on.' The beautician threw a packet onto the very bright pink therapy table in the overly pink room. 'Just going to wash my hands. I'll be back in a mo'.'

Chloe picked up the packet. This was the first time she'd visited Smooth, preferring to go somewhere new so she wouldn't have to relive her embarrassing past with Michelle, her usual beauty therapist. The last time she'd seen her was the day before the wedding.

Big mistake. Michelle never threw packets at her. She was more the *hoik yourself up on the table and let's get on with it* kind of beauty therapist. She definitely didn't have hot pink decor, leopard print wallpaper and a beehive hairstyle.

Sensing she was going to be way out of her comfort zone in more ways than one, Chloe tore the packet open and found two pieces of paper joined together by two pieces of string.

Ooookaaay. How would she 'pop' these on? They didn't look suitable for any part of her anatomy; there was a square of paper, string, then another smaller square, more string… nothing to give her any clue as to where it would fit. A hair protector for when she lay down? Did the string go over her ears? It didn't look big enough for anything else. Certainly not a thigh. Or two. Definitely not her bottom. 'Er… Shona… Sheena… Sheila?' Oh, why hadn't she paid attention when the woman had introduced herself? 'Hello?'

'Ready, love? Right.' Shona/Sheena/Sheila bustled back into the room and came to a sharp halt, making a pursing shape with her lips and staring hard; dark blue pupils popped in bloodshot white. Chloe guessed it was a botoxed attempt at a frown, and it was peering at the paper thing. 'Oh. You just want a straight Brazilian, then?'

'What? No! I just didn't know what to do with this?' Chloe held out the paper… thing. 'What's it for?'

'It's knickers, love.'

'But I have some on. Thank you, anyway. And these don't look remotely like—'

'Knickers. Love.' Sheena/Shona/Sheila regarded her for a minute, again with the deer in the headlights stare, wide and a little wild. She slowly shook her head and sighed, long and deep. Then, she spoke as Chloe often did to little Evie… carefully enunciating, 'Is this your first time? Really? Where have you been? Mongolia? Because I'm sure they have grooming there too. Never mind. We'll work around it. Now. Hop. Up.'

'No… I've just never been given… oh, never mind.' After wriggling her lovely favourite electric blue wool skirt up to her waist, Chloe lay on the bed. And no, having someone peruse her lady garden never got any easier, stranger or not. 'Short, back and sides, please,' she said, attempting a joke to cut the icy atmosphere.

'Hmm.' Sheena/Shona/Sheila looked for a few seconds at Chloe's nether regions, the dying whale muzak in the background clearly having no calming effect on her mood as she sighed irritatedly. Her head popped up. 'First date?'

'What? How did you guess?'

'It's a bit busy down here. Not been getting any action? Know what I mean, right? Ha, ha!' She tucked tissue paper into Chloe's knicker seam and pulled her left leg into an impossibly painful position, bent at the knee, toes touching her right thigh. The hot yoga had been a whole lot easier, before she'd fainted, obviously. 'Or were you growing it out for a reason?'

Chloe closed her eyes and died a little inside. Over the last three months, she'd had more on her mind than waxing. 'No, I've just been… busy.'

'Well, good news is, you have enough fluff to make a lovely shape. You want a shape? I can do hearts, a star. No? A landing strip? I've got bling if you want? You want some vajazzle?' The Sh lady gave her first genuine smile of the consultation, clearly convinced she was dealing with a halfwit. 'What's his name, love? I could do his initial.'

Good God. No. No man was worth this. Ever.

Anyway, would she do B for Big or C for Carlhuna? Too many probables. 'No, just a regular front bottom shape will do. Thanks. Just a little less hair, please.'

'If you're sure. Though, that could take a while.' The wax was just a little too hot as Madame Sheena/Shona/Sheila schlepped it onto Chloe's inner thigh. Then she rolled up her bright cerise sleeves. 'Okay, darling, take a big deep breath and let it out slowly. I'm going in.'

CHAPTER 5

*A*s it was, it took more than a while and now Chloe was running late. Not running as such, because Sheena/Shona/Sheila hadn't been as adept with the waxing silks as she could have been, and Chloe's inner thighs *schtuck* together painfully as she rushed towards Covent Garden.

Every step made her feel exactly as she imagined Velcro to feel—if it were part of the human anatomy—every rip apart was an exquisite agony. She was beginning to regret not wearing any tights, but the only possibility of relief was the gentle breeze that blew up her skirt as she half strode, half hobbled across the square, the meet cafe in sight.

Well, it certainly was busy—no opportunity for any axe wielding here, she mused with relief. Her phone vibrated in her pocket as she squeezed through the door someone was holding open for her.

Jenna: All okay?

Chloe quickly texted back: Not met him yet TXT again in 15

'Reminding yourself of what I look like?' A voice from behind had her turning round. There stood a man, maybe three inches shorter than she was and grinning nervously. His strawberry-blond hair was pulled back into a little neat man bun. He had nice eyes. Palest blue. Yes, he was the man from her laptop, no need to check. 'Chloe? Right? I thought I might have to have a sneaky look at your picture again too. Mind you, it makes little difference what with Photoshop these days. You, however, look just like you did on Chat. Reassuringly. Although, quite a lot thinner. I'm Carl, and I'm garbling. Sorry.'

'Hi, Carl. It was just a text; I wasn't checking your photo.' She waved her phone at him then didn't quite know what to do next. What was first date etiquette? As she pondered this conundrum, he tiptoed and leant towards her face, clearly about to kiss her hello. She ducked to the left at the same moment he ducked to her left too. Their foreheads grazed. Her cheeks heated. Her heart pounded. 'Oh shit. Sorry. I'm not good at this.'

'Me neither. Over here. Come sit down.' He walked her to a table that had a guitar propped against it. *Oh God, please don't let him sing.* 'Coffee?'

'Yes, please. Just black, and filter if they have it.'

'Got it. I'll be back.' Which would have been fine if he hadn't said it with an Arnold Schwarzenegger accent. But, well, clearly he liked a joke. That was a good thing. Wasn't it? A man with a sense of humour was very sexy. Usually. Sometimes? So far, so good. Height notwithstanding. But they could deal with that. She could stick to flats for the wedding— couldn't she?

She was all about compromise these days. She'd learnt her lesson the hard way. *There are two people in a wedding, Chloe.* Who'd said that? Ah yes, Vaughn Bloody Brooks; a fine time for him to jettison himself into her thought processes. Suddenly, she felt herself trembling just a little, her heart doing a strange thumpety-thump. First date nerves. Obviously.

Then *Carlhuna* was back, still smiling. 'Your coffee will be here in a minute. She said she'll bring it over. It was four pounds fifty. You don't half pick the expensive places.' He stuck his hand out, and it took her a second to realise he was asking for the money for her drink.

Fair enough. Days of equality, and all that. She rooted around in her purse for change. 'I've only got four pounds thirty.'

'You can owe me the rest, or pay me back in kind.' He winked, pocketing the coins.

God. Really? So soon? She didn't even know his surname. Was that the way things were done these days? *Hello, here's a coffee. Fancy a shag?* 'Oh. Okay. I'll give you an IOU? Twenty pence?' She made a play of looking for a piece of paper, finally settling on a napkin and writing IOU 20p, signed, Chloe.

Carl shook his hand and screwed the napkin up. 'It was another joke. A very bad one. Look, I've never done this…'

'Me neither.' Her sense of humour seemed to have fled along with her courage.

'Okay, so we're both rubbish; that's one thing in common, right? There must be other things? Let's start.' He straightened up in the chair and leaned across the table as if it were a job interview. Actually, it felt like one. 'Tell me about yourself, Chloe? Why are you single?'

'Er… I've just got out of a ten-year relationship. Well, three months ago. And I'm trying… this… out. You?' Another thing on her hit list for Jason: making her do awkward small talk with a miserly musician midget.

Carl picked up his guitar, glancing at her. 'Sorry. It helps me relax. This whole dating thing makes me nervous.' Then he started strumming. It wasn't horrible, or intrusive, or bad. It was just strange. *Please don't sing.*

It was a tune she'd heard around the place. No. No, actually, for the love of God, it was the tune she'd chosen for her and Jason's first dance. How bloody ironic. *TheBigCarlhuna* hummed a bit then, *'My heart's so full...'* He grinned. 'No, I'm not going to sing to you, don't worry. I'm just trying to decide where to start. We were married for a couple of years, together for eight all up. Didn't work out. I was doing the circuit trying to make a living, you know; gigs, bars, clubs and she wanted me home. We grew apart. No. No, we didn't. She fell in love with someone else. Bloody cow.' His eyes glistened, and his voice wobbled. 'You're my first since... Since she left.'

Please don't cry. God, she couldn't spend all her time with him wishing the poor man to *please don't... cry, sing... kiss me.* He clearly wasn't over his ex.

Chloe didn't want a man trying it on with her just to get over an adulterous wife. She didn't want to be the rebound woman. That brought a whole load of problems she didn't want to deal with. She had enough already trying to drum up business to pay her sister and put food on her niece's plate.

But maybe things between them could grow to a slow burn. She wouldn't be his rebound woman then; she'd be his real woman. A musician's muse. It could be fun. Maybe. He could pluck those guitar strings and sing through those thin lips, gaze adoringly at her through his nice eyes. *But* he had a sickly pale skin that told of endless nights in bars and sleeping during the daytime. He was a musical vampire. With no sparkle. She tried to imagine *TheBigCarlhuna* standing on a box and kissing her, his intense gaze piercing her soul.

She checked her body for any kind of reaction to that thought. No gentle flutter, no zing in her freshly plucked nether regions, no yearning of any sort. Nope. Nothing. Nada. Zero.

There was no chemistry.

These things took time.

To try to help her relax, she crossed her legs, but a searing pain ripped through her—a sort of kind of zing, but not at all the zing she was looking for.

Then she couldn't uncross them. Not without a bit of extra effort.

No. She couldn't uncross them. Full stop. And she wanted to. In fact, uncrossing her legs suddenly became the single most pressing thing on her brain. Some relief. Fresh air. Ungluing.

But it wouldn't be a simple uncrossing. It felt like it would be a giant rip of flesh.

So, she kept them crossed. And tried to focus on him instead, and not on the tight stickiness—super strength glue—at the top of her thighs. 'I see, so she left you. I'm sorry.'

'Yeah, me too.'

She tried to distract herself further away from the pain and looked more deeply into those pale blue eyes to summon some kind of proper zing. A horny zing. A sex driven zing. A craving. A fierce urge. But no. Nothing.

But she sure as hell wanted to uncross her legs.

There was no fighting it; she had to uncross them. 'Oh! Ow!'

'You okay?' He put the guitar down and covered her hand with his; it was warm and a little sweaty. 'You look a bit… overwhelmed.'

'I'm fine, thanks, honestly.'

She wasn't. Not at all.

Bad enough that she felt as if someone had set fire to her nether regions, but now what to do about the hand? Here she was skin-on-sweaty-skin, and she still felt nothing. No zing or tingle. She almost laughed; she'd even felt a tingle with Vaughn Bloody Brooks, although that had been a whole mix of anger and frustration and humiliation.

And directly on cue, as she thought about Vaughn's face, her heart began a strange upbeat again. She willed it back to slow and pushed away her odd response to him. He just made her angry over and over.

So, great, some kind of response to prove she was still alive came from her nemesis, but she couldn't summon up so much as a frisson of a tingle with Big Carl here.

Big Carl, eh? Well, he clearly didn't mean his height, so…? She took a surreptitious look at his feet. No. Average-sized feet. Which left…?

Things might have got interesting. If only there was a tingle.

And that got her thinking about Vaughn again. *Go away,* she chastised the image in her head. This time, it was of when she'd been on top of him in the church. His mouth so close and so angry. The spark in his eyes.

Probably not a good sign if she was with one man and another, albeit annoying man, kept intruding on her thoughts.

The coffee arrived at the same time as her phone beeped. She took it out of her pocket and saw the words OKAY? CHECKED FOR AXES? And smiled. Then flicked a quick horizontal thumb emoji to her sister; the jury was still out.

'Sorry,' she said to Carl, as he stopped strumming again and frowned. 'That was rude of me. I thought it might be important.'

'Your get-out plan?' His phone buzzed on the table, and he gave her a shy grin. 'Mine too. You can't be too careful about who you meet. Women can be axe murderers too, you know.'

'That thought had never crossed my mind.' And with that, all fear fled. Carl seemed okay. A little short, and a little sad, but okay. He was worried about the same things; he'd been through the same experience. Maybe she could help him not be sad?

Oh, what the hell—she might as well be honest. She sipped some coffee, which was hot and strong and fortifying for her needs right now. 'Look, cards on the table, Carl; I don't suppose you're free a week on Saturday? I have a wedding to go to, and I really need a date.'

'Not your wedding, I hope?' He tipped back his ponytailed head, showing a row of straight white teeth, and laughed. 'That would be hilarious. Groom doesn't show up and guest steps in. Only, stranger things have happened.'

Hilarious indeed, and far too close to the truth. 'No, actually, I'm a wedding planner, and I don't normally take a date, but this is a friend's wedding, and she said I could bring someone. I thought it'd be fun.'

'I'll check.' He swiped his phone a couple of times, and she noticed he had manicured fingernails, which she wasn't sure about, at all. Just a little too pointy, and a little too long. He shook his head. 'No, sorry, I've got a gig that night. I can do tomorrow night? How about a drink? We could go for a pint? Somewhere a bit cheaper than Covent Garden, though.' His hand was back on hers, oddly unnerving.

'I'll just check my diary.' Unsure about how good a liar she was, Chloe dragged her hand out from under his and grabbed her phone, deflated. If he wasn't going to be her wedding date, then should she lead him on?

She crossed her legs again, but not without a searing pain that pinged from the top of one of her thighs to the other and brought swift tears to her eyes. 'Ow!'

'Do you have…?' He grimaced. 'I don't know how to put this. Do you have Tourette's? Only you keep squealing for no apparent reason. And that's fine, you know. We all have little foibles, and I'm totally okay with it. In fact, I've got—'

'No. I don't have Tourette's.' *And please don't add anything else to my list of please don'ts…* Okay. She was going to have to sort this out. Right now. 'I'm… I'm just going to the loo. Back in a mo.'

She shuffled, in not a little pain, semi-cross-legged to the bathroom where she darted into the first empty cubicle, hauled up her clothes and took a good look.

Oh. My. God. Little bits of fluff from her blue woollen skirt had rolled itself into tiny balls and attached to the leftover pink wax bits in the creases of her thighs. Down under she looked like a hairy mammoth crossed with a smurf. Frantic, she started to try to pull the fluff off, but, *Oh Holy Mother…* Her underneath… *What?* Tiny red spots. She'd either had a reaction to the wax, or the fluff, or a lethal combination of the two? A smurf with measles.

Please don't sing, cry, kiss me or try anything else on until I a) feel tingles, b) no longer resemble a pox-ridden blue dwarf.

Her phone rang. The cavalry, thank God. 'Hey, Jenna.'

'Why are you answering?'

'Because you rang. Why are you calling?'

'We didn't have a code sign for thumbs horizontal. What does it mean?'

'That he's *okay*,' she hissed. Having de-fluffed as much as she could, Chloe pressed the phone to her ear, secured it with her shoulder, dragged down her skirt and went out to wash her hands. 'But unavailable for next weekend, unfortunately. A little short, and shy and sad. More to the point, though, any tips on gentle fluff removal from raw genital areas?'

'What the hell, girl?'

'Never mind, I'll just have a bath when I get home. He won't be seeing that tonight.'

'But? Do you like him?'

Did she? 'I don't know. I don't know what I'm doing. He seems okay. He has a guitar.'

'Is that good or bad?'

'Aaargh. I just don't know. We're planning a drink tomorrow. A real drink, with alcohol and everything.' Maybe that would help with the tingles? Chloe pushed the bathroom door open with her bottom and stepped back into the cafe. 'Got to go. I'll keep in touch. See you—Oh. Oh, great. Charming.'

'What's wrong?'

Chloe looked around the café. There was no sign of man nor instrument. 'He's gone. Taken the guitar and everything. Gone.'

She wandered back to their table and her half-filled cup of expensive coffee. There was her screwed-up IOU in a little puddle of coffee spill with scrawly spidery writing on it. Limp and sad-looking, just, she realised, how she imagined she must look. 'He's left a note on a napkin: *DaydreamBeliever, sorry to disappoint but I didn't feel any chemistry. You seem nice, but you're just not my type. Didn't want you getting your hopes up. Good luck. Carl.*'

Getting her hopes up? He wished. He'd gone, just like that, when she'd been feeling sorry for him?

Sad thing was, she found it hard to really care about *TheBigCarlhuna's* jilting. She felt precisely… nothing, about him. She supposed that proved to her it wasn't meant to be.

She didn't remember dating being so awkward, or was it that it hadn't been? She and Jason had hit it off immediately. They'd been in the same group of friends hanging around at school, and it had felt inevitable that they'd get together.

The rest of her life didn't feel inevitable at all now. It just felt kind of bare. A whole fresh canvas, Jenna would say.

Chloe screwed up the note again and threw it into the half-filled cup. *Another one bites the dust.*

One thing did niggle her, though; what was it about men that they couldn't look her in the eye and let her down gently? Why did they all take the coward's way out and run off before facing her?

In truth, the only man who'd been honest with her was Vaughn Bloody Brooks, and that had been some showdown, but he'd at least had the decency to turn up.

And why, in heaven's name, did every thought keep turning back to him today? All it did was remind her of what she needed to do to save face next week and gave her a bad case of the jitters.

Chloe sighed and made her way towards the covered market for some serious window shopping—scarves and jewellery this time, not men. At least there was a chance she might find something she actually fancied here.

Ah well, she didn't have to worry about her blue-rinsed nether regions anymore.

Back to the drawing board.

Jenna

Sender: Jennacass567@gmail.com

Nick,

Thanks for your card and emails. Obviously you heard about Ollie and thanks for your thoughts and the flowers at the funeral.

It was sad. So very sad. One minute he was there being my husband, planning a life—a good life, Nick, with a baby on the way and a wife who adores him. Sorry, adored him—that seems such a final way of saying things. And a big contract on the horizon that meant we could finally plan our first proper home. The next minute, he was gone. Run over by a lawyer who was texting while driving and who's trying to wheedle her way out of prison.

I don't think she's ever been married, and she doesn't have any kids, and I don't think she has any idea what I'm going through;

otherwise, she wouldn't make us relive it over and over by refusing to take responsibility.

So, I'm sorry I haven't written in a while and that I couldn't see you when you came back to visit your mum. I've been lost in a black hole. I mean, totally lost, Nick, and I don't know how to pull myself out. I have this beautiful baby girl who has his eyes, and every time I look at her, I see him, and it hurts so badly all over again. She's adorable, I can see that, but I only do what I have to do to get through this and to keep her safe.

I'm scared to love her. I'm scared to go through all that again, Nick. What if I lose her, too? I could because now I know that there is no safety net out there. Ollie's accident was just one of those random things that happens. Something that you see every week in the papers, and you gloss on over because it's not relevant. But it is. I grieve now for every lost soul I read about—somebody's husband, somebody's son, somebody's father—it's like having my chest ripped open again. Raw. I feel raw. And I can't ever let myself love someone so much that I feel this much pain without them.

Actually, there are days where I feel nothing at all, and that scares me even more. I need to feel something for little Evie and I... just... can't.

I know you lost your good friend—and more now too, for which I'm so very sorry. I know it feels as if there's a part of your heart that's gone forever. A part that was truly only theirs and that you'll never get back.

No. It feels as if someone has punched my heart right out of my body.

I hope you had a good Christmas and birthday, and that Santa brought you something nice even in all that heat. I'm grateful I don't know where you are because there are some terrible things happening out there, and I'd just be glued to the TV looking for you.

We had a very quiet Christmas with just family. None of us felt like celebrating, although Mum and Chloe tried hard to make it special for Evie's first Christmas. I took Evie over to Ollie's mum and dad's for Boxing Day, but we all sat around trying to smile for the baby's sake. In the end, I said she was overly excited by all the presents and brought her home. Mostly I just like it when I'm home, surrounded by my familiar things. By Ollie's.

I didn't go to the school reunion this year. I couldn't face all those pitying faces. But I did bump into Sandy Christiansen in the market, and she said she was engaged to a Canadian guy and was moving over there in the summer. I guess she's probably almost there by now. People keep on living their lives—I must try to start doing that—or at least not envy that they can live theirs when I feel as if mine is over.

I'll try to write again when I'm in a better headspace.

Jenna x

CHAPTER 6

By Tuesday, Chloe was starting to get a little desperate. None of the online men had seemed quite suitable, and she wasn't just being fussy. There simply wasn't anyone who ticked the boxes. She was running out of time to vet a date and deem him capable of conversation, nice enough to actually spend an evening with, and suitably house trained.

'Today's love matches are mostly a repeat of yesterday's, with a couple of novelty ones thrown in. Here we have *PrinceAlbert*. I really hope that doesn't mean what I think it means,' she mused to Jenna who was over with Evie for a marathon Jane Austen evening and sleepover. Evie was settled in bed in the spare room, and there was a chilled chardonnay with Chloe's name on it. She just wanted to get through today's offerings with a clear head before she consumed alcohol. 'I've messaged a couple, and I'm just waiting to hear back. It's worse than waiting for blood test results.'

Jenna pushed her sideways to make room on the sofa and peered over her shoulder. 'Just do some random click-throughs.' She grabbed the laptop. 'Come here, let me do it. How about *FantasticFreddie*?'

'The one from Essex? I tried him the other day; he didn't answer. You know, I think you're enjoying this. Looking, but not touching. Doesn't it make you just a little bit intrigued to know what you're missing out on?'

'Hell no. I'm just vetting for you, that's all.' Her sister raised her eyebrows in a warning not to pursue this line of conversation.

Chloe wasn't biting. 'You could sign up too. We could have some double dates. Get out a little.'

'I go out.' Jenna twisted on the sofa, pulling her feet under her bottom and balancing the laptop on her knees. 'I go to ballet tots, sing-a-long and story time at the library. I go to nursery and the swing park and the supermarket. Now, back to the task in hand. Let's find another one quickly, so we can open that wine.' Jenna scanned the pages. 'Ugh. *MagicMike*? They don't have great imaginations for names, do they? Oh, no. Really. No.' She clicked again. 'Oh, my God... no.'

'What is it?'

Jenna's mouth formed a very plastic smile as she clicked frantically. 'Nothing. Next page.' Whatever image had shocked her was gone and there was *FullThrottle* in full high-vis gear on a motorbike. Another swipe non-starter.

Chloe leaned over. 'What is it? Not *TheBigCarlhuna* again? I thought he'd deleted his profile? When I went in to award his dating stars, he wasn't there.'

'No. It was no one—'

'Let me see.' Something wasn't right. Chloe grabbed the laptop, backtracked and squinted at a shabby, blurred photo of a topless guy in a garden. Her stomach felt as if it had dropped like an elevator, about forty-four floors. She gripped the laptop more tightly. *'Jason?'*

Of course it was. She'd taken the damned photo at Kew Gardens years ago. He wasn't using his real name, but Chloe would have known that cheating smile anywhere. And that body. 'That's Jason. Isn't it? It's Jason. Isn't he still with Amy? Vaughn said they were both going to the wedding. What's he doing on a dating website? Wait a sec… *Searching4U*. Urgh. His profile name is Searching For You. When he'd already found me, and then found Amy, and lost me. Member since two thousand and thirteen? We were engaged by then. He was on this when we were together. He cheated on me, and he's doing it all again with Amy.' She could feel her blood pressure rising. 'I should tell her.'

'Not your problem.' Jenna took the laptop back and clicked off his annoying face. 'Seriously, honey. Do not get involved. Whatever you say will only look like sour grapes.'

'No. No, you're right, it's none of my business.' But Chloe had often wondered whether Amy had been the first philandering he'd committed. 'Why didn't I see it? Why was I so blind to him? I gave everything to that relationship, committed all my energy to it. All he did was use me as a steppingstone to the next poor victim. Men. *Bloody* men.'

'I hope you're not going to become one of those women who sits around moaning and complaining? Jason is in the past. You're supposed to be moving on. And at least, if he's being unfaithful to Amy, it means he's just a serial non-committer. It isn't your fault, sweetie.'

Chloe shuddered at the thought of how many women he might have had. 'Poor Amy.'

So, that was a first, feeling sorry for the woman who ran off with her fiancé.

Her sister nudged her. 'Look, you've got a reply from someone.

Someone who isn't half bad looking. *DrewsAmused*. He wants to meet. He likes your photo and thinks you might *connect*.'

'Please don't read my messages.'

'He's cute. Dark, wavy hair, nice smile.' Jenna jolted up, took the computer over to Chloe's desk and started to type. 'Hi. Yes, I'd love to meet for a coffee. Based near Notting Hill. You?'

'Oi, what in hell are you doing?' It was definitely wine o'clock. Without so much as a backwards glance, Chloe opened the chardonnay and poured two large glasses.

Jenna took one and grinned. 'I'm moving things along. You don't have a lot of time, right? Conveniently, he's in Shepherd's Bush, so you could meet halfway. When's that wedding?'

'Saturday.'

'Drastic measures, then. How about tomorrow? Lunch?' She typed. 'No? Coffee? Afternoon? Evening? Five o'clock? Five it is, he says. EAT on Holland Park Avenue? Great, see you there! See? Child's play.'

'It is until you want to do it for yourself.' Chloe shrugged, wondering whether she'd need to take a box for him to stand on or tissues for his tears. Or extra cash in case he complained about the severe prices in this part of town. But she never once contemplated another wax. He'd have to take her as he found her. If he was ever down in that neck of the woods. And that wouldn't be for some time. She focused back on her sister. 'Would you like me to set you up on a date, too?'

Jenna looked at her for a long moment. 'Oh, can you hear Evie? I think she's crying. I'll take her some milk, give her a cuddle. She's probably having a bad dream. Can you get *Pride and Prejudice* set up? The Keira one.'

Jenna's get-out plan was always to hide behind her daughter. But time would come when her daughter grew up, left home, and Jenna would be lonely. Lonelier than she was now. She deserved some good times, to share her life, to have someone to adore her, to love her.

I'm fine on my own, Chloe thought, *but Jenna would enjoy sharing things with someone;* she was a nurturer, she was kind, and she deserved someone to be there for her. Whereas, Chloe quite liked the freedom to do what she wanted, when she wanted. If it wasn't for that wedding, she'd be entirely happy to sit inside and watch Jane Austen forever. She flicked on the TV, grabbed her wine and put the DVD in.

Ah, those days of chivalry and manners, of men being heroic and strong and willing to face whatever challenge befell them. Men who would fight for what they believed in, who were courageous and brave and loyal. She didn't doubt that there were many men around like that today; they just hadn't signed up to matchyou.co.uk.

And suddenly, unbidden, an image of Vaughn Brooks popped into her head again. This time, it was the moment when he strode towards her down the aisle in his black morning suit. Yes, there had been embarrassment in his face, but something else in his eyes. Something intense, fresh and raw. Even though he had a reputation of being unreliable and even though he couldn't have found much in that task appealing, he had done it for his cousin, and for her. And she kept remembering it. And him. And his touch on her skin. And his smell. Everything kept coming back to him.

Chloe had a very bad feeling about this.

* * *

With finalising details for the rehearsal coming up on Friday and the wedding on Saturday, Chloe had no time to chat with Drew online, so she was reliant on recognising him from his photo. But when she got to EAT, she couldn't see anyone who looked remotely like him. However, she'd purposefully arrived five minutes late because she'd read that that was what you were supposed to do. But maybe that plan had backfired; perhaps he'd already left?

One of her favourite haunts in the area, EAT was busy as always; downstairs was a cool coffee bar that had a diverse menu and shelves and shelves of books, with comfy chairs to sit and read in. While upstairs, DRINK, catered for the evening crowd with tapas and music and a great choice of wine. She ordered a 'cheaper than Covent Garden, Mr Carlhuna, see what you're missing?' coffee and grabbed an empty table in a prime position so she could monitor the door. Presently a mature-looking guy walked in, wearing a crumpled suit—no, more than crumpled. He looked as if he were, basically, homeless or embracing an iron-free lifestyle. With wild grey hair and a moderate beer belly, and well into his forties.

He glanced over and smiled. Friendly, too. She gave him a brief smile, then looked around for Drew. Unfortunately, homeless man approached. 'DaydreamBeliever? Right? Wow—you look just like your photograph.'

'Er, oh…' *And you so do not, DrewsAmused.* Words failed her. He'd lied, big time.

He grinned sheepishly. 'Sorry I'm late. I couldn't find anyone to look after my dog.'

That would explain the fur on his jacket. And the smell. And God forgive her, call her shallow, but this was not the man she'd been expecting, or indeed, the man she'd seen on matchyou. co.uk.

Conflicted only went halfway to describe her dilemma. Because she wasn't just about appearances—even though that was really all she'd had to go on—but she just knew from the second she'd set eyes on him that he was not the guy for her. She preferred her men to be around her age and, preferably, in possession of an iron. And a lint roller. A comb needn't be mandatory but perhaps brought out on special occasions. Like a first date.

The fifteen-minute get-out-of-date-quick text couldn't come soon enough.

'I see.' She looked him up and down. 'So where is it?'

'The dog?' Drew gave her another sheepish grin and pointed to his rucksack. 'He's asleep. Don't say anything; they don't allow pets in here.'

For a reason! He was breaking a zillion health and safety rules, although he looked as if he didn't care about anything other than his dog's happiness. Kind of cute. He was, at least, a man with a heart. 'You couldn't just leave him at home?'

By this time, Drew had taken a seat opposite her, but he recoiled in horror. 'Hell no. We go everywhere together.'

'That's very… nice.' The second of what she imagined would be quite a few alarm bells during this meeting started to ring in her head. He'd used an old photograph—or someone else's—to con her into thinking he was somebody he wasn't. And he was a dog devotee, which was fine and she loved them, all waggy tails and sniffing bottoms, but she had a bad feeling dogs would not be permitted at the wedding on Saturday, and that was the name of the game for her. Plus-one hunting. Saving face. Building business.

'So…' Still lost for words, she stared at him. Why would anyone lie with a photograph? Surely he must have known she'd be expecting a younger, fitter version? And it wasn't that she was disappointed—well, okay, she was a little—but actually, he'd outright lied. Surely he was breaking the Trade Descriptions Act? She put on her best polite smile. 'Drew, see, the truth is, I'm not good at this.'

'Oh.' His shoulders sagged a little. 'First time?'

'Second, actually.' And definitely the last, because nothing would ever entice her to do this again. 'I'm a little out of my depth.' Drowning, actually.

'Well, relax. I don't bite.' The rucksack started to move, and she could have sworn she heard a growl.

'That's good. Does he?'

'No. But he is very protective of me. We've been through a lot together. He was my rescue puppy—and I was his. We met when we both needed someone. We're both victims of abuse. Him physical, me verbal.' He smiled, his eyes were kind and sad. And it was okay. He looked okay, although crumpled in a sort of mad professor way. And about fifty years older than her. But still, for some woman he'd be the perfect guy. Just not her. This was hopeless. 'He's a softie really. He likes to lick my feet.'

'Oh.' She closed her eyes for a moment as she swallowed back the bile in her throat. 'Look, I'm not sure...' God, this was hard. 'Er... I don't think...' No wonder Carl and Jason had run off instead of facing her because this was actually too bloody difficult. Even more so because it felt so trivial. *Hi, I just met you. You're not my perfect man, so I'm going.* It seemed so callous. At what point, she wondered, had Jason sat opposite her and realised he wanted out of their relationship?

At what point had he swallowed back the bile too? 'So, tell me, what's with the profile photograph? You look very different.'

Drew shook his head but laughed. 'I admit, it's a few years old. Maybe ten. Or, perhaps fifteen. I mean, look at me, d'you think I'd get many dates if I put a picture up of how I look now?'

'Actually, I think you'd get a lot more second dates if women knew who they were meeting from the get go.'

'Believe me, I've tried. No one even clicked on me. I used to be all right, eh? I've let myself go a bit. Since the divorce.

Well, before, really, if I'm honest. I think it was the medication I was on. It made me put on weight. Aww, look he's trying to see who I'm talking to.' He reached a hand into his bag and made a soothing noise as the rucksack began to move across the floor. Eventually, one furry ear popped out of the top, then another. Then a nose. And it began to whine. Sweat dripped from Drew's large forehead. 'He's getting restless. It's always the same; he smells food then he wants some, and he won't shut up until he gets it. I think we should go before we get chucked out. Do you want to come back to mine? I make a mean spaghetti bolognaise and I have some cider? It's not that far.'

She could just imagine his place, all fur-flecked furniture and interesting smells. And it probably wouldn't be very hygienic if his clothes were anything to go by. No way would she go. It wouldn't be fair to give him any false hope. And geez, now she was sounding like Carlhuna.

She hated that she thought that, and that she judged *DrewsAmused*. But wasn't that what this was all about? Judging suitability? It was just a more prolonged and painful version of swiping. It was horrible, and she just didn't have the guts for it.

The Love Plan fail, part two.

No doubt there were many happy couplings made from internet dating. Hell, some of her previous clients had been deliriously happy and married after they'd met online. It did work, but then so did regular dating, if you found the right guy. The One. For the lucky ones.

But dammit, luck had never been her friend, and she didn't have the heart or the nerve to keep doing this. Even if that meant she was single forever. Even if it meant she was humiliated at the wedding on Saturday in front of all her old friends and saw pity in every single eye. She didn't have the energy to meet someone and break up with them in ten minutes. Over and over. Ad nauseum.

What the hell had she been thinking? She definitely didn't need a man to make her look successful, for God's sake. She would go to the wedding and hand out a business card to every one there. She would tell them she had some booking slots available and to let anyone thinking of getting hitched know about her services. She would imply things were going well and that she was content with her life and her business. She didn't need a man for that. She didn't need a man at all.

Yeah. *I am woman. Hear me... er, roar... or, miaow at least.*

Her phone beeped. *Thank you, Jenna.*

'Sorry, I'll just get this?' Chloe read her text and pretended to be horrified—although, a lot of her act was real. Because how had she ended up doing this? Here? With him? She looked up at Drew and smiled weakly. 'Oh. Look, I'm sorry. There's been a... thing happening. I need to go.'

But he'd been here before, she knew, as he shook his head. 'Looks like I'm not the only one being economical with the truth here, then. Who's that? Your mum? Sister? Best friend? Checking in? Giving you an excuse to make a hasty exit? As if I'm some kind of axe murderer?'

The axe murderer thing again. It was hardly as if she'd ever seen anyone carrying an axe around the streets. Mind you, she'd never seen anyone carrying a dog in a rucksack either.

She nodded, a little shamefaced, flicked the phone onto silent and threw it into her pocket just in case it beeped again and he got even more despondent. 'My sister, actually. I... just... well, the thing is, I don't think this is going to work.' Chloe stood to leave, wondering why she didn't feel as relieved as she wanted to, then realised that guilt was getting in the way. 'I'm so sorry. I shouldn't have agreed to come. I can't do this. I have to go. Good luck, Drew.'

He picked up the rucksack and pressed it close to his chest

and her heart broke just a little bit. At least he had the dog to love. 'It's Andrew, actually. I just thought Drew was more vibrant.'

Right now, in here, squeezing a tatty old rucksack like a comfort blanket, he was the furthest thing from vibrant that she'd ever met, but that was okay, too. Everyone shone in their own way. He was probably a demon in bed, or a prolific plane watcher, or a fabulous dancer or a great cook, but she'd never know.

Some other woman would be lucky to find him. And, as for herself? She didn't feel exactly bursting with colour and energy either. In truth, dating was proving to be a lot harder than she'd thought it would be. 'Just be yourself, Andrew. That's all we ever ask for. Just be honest.'

'Yeah.' He gave her a weak smile as he shuffled through the door, his mutt now on a lead at his feet. 'You too.'

Jenna

Sender: Jennacass567@gmail.com

Hi, Nick,

Thanks for your emails. You always write so many to me and I feel guilty when I only manage the odd one back, but please know that I'm thinking of you and hoping you're safe. I saw the news the other day that some more of your platoon were killed. I know this sounds terrible, but I was so glad it was someone else and not you. I couldn't bear losing anyone else.

Evie is growing fast. I know I'm biased, but she's absolutely gorgeous. I've attached some photos. As you can see, she has my hair and nose, and her dad's eyes. She's starting to show her character a bit more now, and she's got quite a stubborn streak these days (takes after her mum on that front, too). She's also prone to having major meltdowns in supermarket aisles. It used to bother me a lot, but I have to admit I just laugh these days. Life's too short to get stressed by a crying child who just wants an ice cream. (Believe me, it took a lot of crying and working things through in my head to be able to say that!) But I'm starting to feel a little better about things, can you tell? It's as if there is a little light through the clouds. That light is Evie.

I was sorry to hear about Helen. Are affairs within a regiment quite common? I suppose it must be a result of all that claustrophobic living. I hope you feel better about it all now that she's left the army, and you won't, hopefully, need to see her again. Although, it will be tough to get over. It must have been awful thinking you were going to be a dad, then finding it was all a lie and that the baby wasn't yours. That was pretty cruel of her. I don't blame you for cutting her off.

I know I don't send emails as regularly as I should, but please don't stop writing to me. It's nice to know that there's someone out there thinking about me and wishing me good things. I'll try to be a better correspondent in future. In fact, to be honest, just writing this has made me feel a whole lot better about today. I'm taking it one day at a time.

I hope the sand's stopped rubbing in places you can't mention! (That made me smile, so thank you, a smile doesn't happen often these days). And that you got over your sunstroke. Honestly, you really should take better care of yourself (Was it because you were too distracted thinking about Helen? No, sorry, don't answer that, that was just me, being too nosy again.).

If you ever venture near Notting Hill when you're on leave again, please pop by. I'm back living with my mum. I can't afford to move into a place of my own. Ollie's money didn't go far. He hadn't got around to sorting out life insurance. He was only twenty-six! No one should die that young.

I hope the sun's shining where you are, Nick, and I hope one day we'll get to catch up over a coffee. Let's look forward to that, shall we? I think we both need something to look forward to.

To happier times! Stay safe.

Jenna x

CHAPTER 7

*N*ow, completely gasping for a coffee, Chloe crossed the main road and started to walk back towards the tube station. But she quickly realised that by the time she'd changed tube lines at Shepherd's Bush, she'd be just as quick walking all the way home. And since she'd given up her evening spin class to meet Drew, she needed the exercise. Maybe she could walk her frustration out of her system, and pick up a bottle of wine to go with dinner along the way.

She meandered for a while, checking out what she could see through the windows of the houses and apartments of the ultra rich of Holland Park and the gorgeous delicatessen and handmade shoe shops, but suddenly she heard raised voices and came to a halt.

Oh, hell.

She was almost outside Vaughn's restaurant. A closed sign hung on the front door, but Vaughn was having a loud discussion with a woman on the pavement. She was pretty, young and very angry. Unable to walk by without being seen, Chloe hung back, pretending to be window-shopping for expensive knickknacks in the shop next door as she listened.

'I told you, Vaughn, I won't tolerate you changing everything at the last minute again. It's disruptive and makes us all look like idiots. If the staff don't know what they're selling, they can't sell it. You won't make any money. I won't get paid.'

He stood completely still and frowned. In his dark suit on her wedding day, he'd seemed impenetrable, aloof and formidable. Same, last week, in his casual work clothes. But today, in chef whites he looked messy—not in a *DrewsAmused* kind of way but in a hot dishevelled TV chef kind of way. Hot and—whoa, that thought had come out of nowhere and took her aback a little.

Hot? She'd never knowingly aligned Vaughn and hot before. But, well, he was more than hot, actually. He was quite beautiful when she thought about it. With no man bun or wild mess of mad professor hair, no dog hairs and no guitar. And there was so much more she hadn't really taken in. He was tall. And broad. And toned.

His eyes were expressive—she knew that because she'd seen the gamut of emotions cross his face. Including pity, she reminded herself. That soft pitying smile. And raw hot anger as she'd lain on top of him in her wedding dress and tried to beat him senseless with her flowers. *Raw hot anger.*

Whoa. Was that a tingle somewhere low in her belly? No. It couldn't have been. It was just a little chilly out here in the spring sunshine that promised a lot but never quite delivered the heat she wanted.

His voice was controlled and deep. 'It's called market forces, Laura. Availability. Creativity. And finally, it's called my restaurant. So I can do what the hell I want.'

So, he was pretty to look at, but still bloody annoying with his *I know everything* stance and taut corded muscles. Chloe's inner warrior woman fist-pumped as Laura stuck her hands on her hips and raised her voice even more. *Go, sister.*

'Yeah, well it's now your restaurant without a manager, too. You can't run a business like this, chopping and changing from one day to the next. At least, I can't. And that's why you employed me? Right? To run things while you worked your Michelin-star magic in the kitchen? Only, to achieve perfection, you're working yourself too hard and working us even harder.'

'I would never expect my staff to work harder than me.' Frowning, he raised his hands. 'Lots of places change their menus every day.'

'The specials, yes. But not the whole damned menu.' The woman's shoulders lifted in a kind of *I'm over it* shrug as she shook some menus at him. 'But that's not it, really, Vaughn. I just can't get a handle on you anymore. If it's not the menu, it's the decor or the suppliers... you don't like this or that, you decide to change something and let us know afterwards. There's no reasoning with you. You don't listen; you just plough onwards on your own little journey, and just as we manage to catch up in your slipstream, you change tack. Some call it brilliant; I call it difficult, and I can't do it anymore. I'm out of here.'

'No. It's absolutely out of the question.' He remained completely in control as if her words and their meaning had little effect on him. 'Marco Collini is coming tonight. It's an open secret. I need you here.'

'No, Vaughn you don't. You don't need anyone; you never have and you never will. You just do exactly what you want and don't listen to anyone else. It's like you have armour plating or something. Tough luck on Marco Collini. Maybe he'll get a taste for what you're really like. A food genius, maybe, but bloody frustrating. Completely impractical, and yet exacting at the same time. I've had enough.'

'You can't just leave. Laura…'

'Watch me.'

'Laura.' His voice grew louder, but he still didn't lose his cool. Chloe wondered whether he saved that particular luxury just for her. He watched his manager storm back into the restaurant only to return a minute later with her handbag, then walk away. She was a woman of her word, clearly.

Shaking his head, Vaughn sat down on one of the wrought iron chairs and swore. Quite loudly and for quite a long time. His long fingers tapped against the table top as he contemplated his situation. Then, he stood and paced a little, hands shoved deep in his pockets. Finally, he sat again, chin in his hands as he leant on the table, staring into the distance.

Far from feeling at one with Laura, Chloe's gut began to twist. Even she'd heard of Marco Collini, London's most celebrated food reviewer. One word from him could make or break a restaurant. And yes, she imagined Vaughn could be a genuinely giant pain in the backside, but to leave him tonight, of all nights? Harsh.

'Problem?' The word was out of her mouth before she could stop it.

He looked up at her and scratched the stubble on his jaw. It was a refined jaw. Stubborn. Fixed. But it was his eyes that caught her off guard. Dark. So very dark. 'Chloe? Chloe Cassidy. Of course—perfect. Absolutely perfect. Why wouldn't you be here to add to my already shitty day?' A pause and a little sarcastic laugh. 'Everything is going swimmingly.'

For no discernible reason she could find, Chloe found herself dragging a chair to sit opposite him. 'Are you saying that because you don't want to admit you're in a pickle, or because you truly believe it's fine, or because you're worried I might offer to help?'

'All of the above.' There was a hint of a smile. 'I've had worse problems, believe me. Today no one has died. A manager quitting is inconvenient, in fact very difficult and annoying, but not insurmountable.'

'Creative differences?'

'You could say that.' He looked at her, an unreadable expression on his face. Then he looked away, up at his Vaughn's restaurant sign as if he had a puzzle to solve. And well, actually, he did.

The tummy-tumbling thing had started to happen again, but Chloe decided it was all to do with the anxiety of watching two adults fight. She'd never seen that happen at home, her dad having died when Jenna was very little. She'd never liked the way anger made her feel inside. And possibly it wasn't helped by Drew's lies and condescension. And the fact she was now well and truly date-less for Saturday. Still, there were more pressing matters. 'Do you really change the whole menu every day?'

'She was exaggerating. But I do change it a lot. My dishes are reliant on seasonal supply, so I have to create something new and fresh based on what I buy. It's part of the appeal of the place, of my style of cooking. No one knows what to expect.' He broke out in a smile. 'Not even me, sometimes. And she knew that when I hired her; I don't see the problem. It's just a bit of extra typing.'

'And a whole new menu to learn. I've worked tables before; it's embarrassing when a customer asks you for specific details, and you get caught out.'

'Hey, if I have to cook it, the least they can do is learn what's in it. It's not rocket science. Whose side are you on?'

'Theirs, obviously.'

'Of course.'

She flashed him a smile. 'I like to hold grudges; they make me feel better.'

'Good to know. But why against me?'

'Where to start? You are clearly demanding of your staff, wanting everyone to be as invested as you are, but they are employees, so why should they care as much as you do?' She knew what it was like to run a business and the dangers of letting things get out of control. That was just one reason why she did all the administration for *Something Borrowed*. She couldn't allow anyone else to take that responsibility, not after it had been her fault things had gone haywire in the first place. And also, if no one else saw the bank statements, they wouldn't know just how bad things were financially, so she could stall them and work smarter, get more clients and her sister and mother would never know how close to closing they'd been.

None of this was relevant right now, of course. She was face-to-face with Vaughn Bloody Brooks and his impending disaster. Which, given the nature of her own, felt like small fry. 'Besides, why should I make you feel better?'

'Because you feel guilty about attacking me.' He grinned and his eyes lost a little darkness.

'That bouquet and rugby tackle are never ever going to be forgotten, are they?' They were like a giant, hovering swarm of flies, pestering and flitting around them. Just when she thought she'd wafted them away, they came back, buzzing around their heads.

'Nope. Not ever.'

'It was an instinctive reaction to a broken heart. Why should I feel guilty?'

'Because you scarred me for life and I will never look at pine cones in the same way again.' He shuddered. 'So, be honest, you're taking Laura's side because you want to get your own back. Because I broke the bad news to you in the church. Because I was quoted out of context. I did ring the journalist, by the way, and tried to get her to retract the piece, especially my bit, but she refused. Said it was good copy. I know it wasn't. I know it was your life being ruined.'

Vaughn's gaze caught hers and he was so, so serious. She felt as if someone was tipping her sideways as her heart, no, her whole body jolted. It was uplifting and scary and weird all in one. There was something in his eyes; a heat, a mystery, and she was drawn to look deeper. But she had to turn away, because he was Vaughn Bloody Brooks and he was on her hit list of two, and she could not, would not, think he was anything other than her worst nightmare.

Which meant she couldn't like his eyes, all grey and dark and mysterious. Or the muscles in his forearms, or the way he held his jaw, so aloof, so... Vaughn. Or be entranced just by the deep timbre of his voice. She would not.

She didn't know if he'd felt the same physical reaction, but he looked away, swallowed and closed his eyes briefly as if shaking something off—a bad memory, a feeling. Her.

Then he waved a hand. 'Basically, you hate me, and it's all because of Jason.'

Jason? Jason who? 'No...' The power of speech seemed to be eluding her. Vaughn had nice arms, strong. His voice... 'It's... it's nothing to do with him.'

Vaughn shook his head. 'Anyway, I need to go. Because as well as prepping, I now have to sort out typing and printing off the menus.'

'What about your other staff, can't they do it?'

'Some are on their break after lunch service. Others are setting up for dinner service, and they all have enough to do. Now is the time Laura usually does the admin and all this' —he threw the obsolete menus on to the table— 'stuff.'

'Get a blackboard and write up the menu?'

'You really are a regular problem solver, aren't you? And while it's a great idea, I don't have time to go out and buy a blackboard.' He stood. 'I'll see you at the wedding on Saturday, shall I? Still going?'

'Of course. As I told you, I attend every wedding I organise.' Regardless of date-status.

'With your mysterious plus-one?'

She thought about what to say and about the online dating and the disastrous results—about the blue fluff, *TheBigCarlhuna*, the guitar and the dog in the rucksack. And that if she didn't go to the wedding on Saturday, she'd miss the chance of advertising her skills to potential clients.

If she didn't go, her mum would have to cancel her long awaited cruise, the unsatisfying job at the Inland Revenue would become a reality and, worse—so much worse—Chloe would have to sit her sad, widowed sister down and explain that yes, a job on a flower stall in the freezing cold and the sometimes driving rain would be on the horizon for her, because there was simply not enough money to support them all.

Because Chloe had failed them.

But in the end, she decided that no explanation was needed, especially not to him. 'No. No date. I'll be by myself.'

'Good.' Whatever the heck that meant. But he didn't look like he was going to elucidate any further.

'Okay. See you then.'

'Bye, Chloe.' He turned and started towards the restaurant entrance and she stood, contemplating the walk home and her empty flat. Nothing to do because she'd done all the organising down to the tiniest detail and there really wasn't anything else left except to look up more frog facts.

And she couldn't face doing that right now; she'd had her fill of tadpoles and learning the difference between frogs and toads, and the fact that frogs absorb water through their skin and, therefore, have no need to drink. But humans did; she was dying of thirst, and she still hadn't had a coffee. Perhaps Vaughn could make a real espresso?

So that must have been the reason why she suddenly found herself saying, 'I can do it for you if you like? In exchange for a decent cup of coffee?'

He stopped, hand on the door handle, frowning. Quite confronting, that frown, in such a confident body. 'Do what?'

'The menu. It's not exactly difficult; it just takes a little time. Of which, I happen to have plenty today.'

Now, he leant against the door and looked decidedly suspicious. 'Why would you do that?'

'Because I can. I have a business degree and a wedding planning diploma. I know my way around a spreadsheet and a word processing programme with my eyes closed. Just direct me to your office, scribble down the details and I'll work my magic in there. It'll take me two minutes.'

'You really want to help me?' His eyebrows shot up, and his eyes widened, and he shook his head more vehemently. 'Thank you, but no. I can manage it all perfectly well. Before I got the stars, I ran a small place in Bordeaux. You have to do everything yourself or it doesn't get done.'

She gave him a half-hearted shrug, because, after all, she'd extended that hand. If he didn't want to take it, it was his problem. 'Okay. Your funeral. Or rather, you're missing a five-star review for the sake of a bit of humility and two minutes of my company. You are allowed to get help sometimes, you know.'

Again, he held her gaze as if weighing her up. As if contemplating what kind of fresh hell he'd have to endure if he let her into his restaurant. The dark eyes narrowed a little, and she wondered what else was going on in that brain of his.

He'd been described as revolutionary with his food, an in-génue, an upstart even. He was clever, inventive. And sharp, so it seemed. Was that all, or was there more there? He certainly didn't tolerate fools, if his conversation with Laura was anything to go by, and would not allow himself to be swayed or bullied into doing something he didn't want to.

'Okay. But, you have been warned, it's not pretty. There's a reason I took Laura on—I'm not great with organisation.' So maybe letting Chloe in seemed preferable to doing it on his own. Or rather, he was fast running out of time.

He held the door open for her and she walked into the wonderland of his whitewashed world, the scent of rosemary and garlic filling her nostrils. She put her bag down on the bar and wondered why she was here instead of walking home and collecting wine as she passed Go. But he didn't give her time to think too hard.

'Through here.' He picked up Chloe's bag and walked her towards another door, one that she hadn't noticed last time she was here. 'I'd prefer it if you kept your eyes focused just on the typing and don't look around too closely. It got a little messy before I hired Laura and she was working her way through it.'

They walked into an office—at least, that's what she assumed it had originally been, only now it looked as if someone had tipped every file they'd owned for the last ten years onto the desk from a great height. Some of the papers had landed in a heap—or a group of heaps, whatever the plural for that was—and some had landed on the floor.

There were photographs in dark wood frames covering almost one whole wall, a large lumpy sofa in a deep claret colour and a huge quirky lamp in the shape of a teardrop that cast a soothing orange glow. Where the rest of the restaurant was post-modernist stark, this was clutter central.

Chloe walked towards the desk, straddling various piles of receipts and open ring binder files. 'Whoa. You have serious filing problems.'

'I know. I've been busy getting planning permission and the alcohol licence and the council consent for this, that and the other, and all about the food. And this is a lot of the paperwork from my other places too. I wanted to keep everything in one place and try to use the same suppliers as best I could, so I can keep a similar feel across the three places. But of course that's not always possible, and some of the paperwork needs to be kept in situ; things like licences and local council stuff, policy documents, health and safety. You wouldn't believe what you need to do to even set a restaurant up never mind run the damned thing. Laura was supposed to be dealing with all this. She kept telling me she was on top of it, but I didn't have time to delve any deeper. The laptop is...' Reaching across the desk, he rummaged through some important-looking papers, pulled out a state of the art laptop and opened it. '...here.'

Chloe started to stack the paper into a couple of piles so she had a clear space to work. As she did so, she automatically put invoices into one pile and flyers for everything from an organic garden festival to a small electrical repairer into another. 'Won't take long.'

'Er... What are you doing?'

She put a piece of paper down and focused on him. Not difficult. The man possessed the room; his energy bounced from him and off the walls, she was fascinated by him, by the curve of his mouth, the steady gaze, and the pushed-up sleeves that revealed forearms that moved with grace and strength. God, she'd never, ever even looked at a man's arms before, never mind been entranced by the contraction of sinew and muscle. It was... well, it made her feel a little breathless. And a little bit hot.

'I'm just sorting them like for like and then you can go through and work out which invoices have been paid and which ones are outstanding when you reconcile your bank statement. I'll label them clearly. It's not a problem. Is it?' Only she couldn't tell, because he was looking at her in a strange way, his hypnotic eyes belying a deeper thought process that she wished she could have x-ray vision into.

'Jason never told me you could be helpful.' The suspicion was laced with a small smile.

'I imagine that, by the time you actually came back to England and saw Jason face to face, he was passed thinking of me in any kind of positive light at all. You know how it is; once you've decided you don't like something, you convince yourself everything about it is wrong.'

'I was away too long.' He'd picked up a file, but stood with it crushed in his hand as he scowled at nothing in particular. If she wasn't mistaken, there was an air of sadness and pain in his face, which was strange for him. Raw energy and anger, yes. Pain, now that was new.She hadn't thought that his relationship with Jason had been so important to him. Or maybe it was something else?

'He thought so too. He missed you. He'd have liked you around more, but he knew you were too busy off doing your own thing rather than coming back to see your family.' Then she thought she might have stepped on some toes, or spoken out of turn, and she felt a strange loyalty to her ex-fiancé and the way he'd idolised his older cousin who had chosen to stay distant, which was weird. Or maybe she'd just wanted Vaughn to know some truths. 'I shouldn't have said that. Really, none of my business.'

'I had my reasons. He knew what they were.'

'Oh, you know Jason; he's all about himself. He never said

why you didn't come home, just that it would have been nice to see you more often. Hey, you'll never guess what I found on...'

Oops.

If she told Vaughn she'd been on a dating website and found Jason on there too, she'd be admitting she'd been on a dating website, period. That wasn't going to happen.

Vaughn looked up from a piece of paper that he was writing on—the menu, she presumed. 'What did you find, Chloe?'

'Oh.' Panicking slightly, she glanced over the contents of the table. 'This. It's a... bill for the chandeliers. It's a red one. Do you want me to put it somewhere particular?'

'Damn.' In what had probably amounted to a whole thirty minutes overall that she'd spent with Vaughn in her entire life, she'd noticed a little muscle in the side of his jaw that twitched when he was annoyed. It had happened a lot at the church and was happening again now. 'Laura was supposed to pay this weeks ago. Why didn't she? Do you mind if I...?'

He leant across and took the computer from her. Then he stood, close. So close. Too close. She got a waft of his vanilla-spice smell and caught a close-up of impossibly long lashes framing his dark eyes, and she felt that tingle again. It was becoming a little annoying and inappropriate.

When he began to speak, she edged away from him. 'Apart from the fact she just quit, I'm beginning to regret taking her on at all. She's the sister of a friend and wanted a leg up in the industry. I owed him, so I offered her the job. Looks like she was in a little too deep. Great maître d', but wanted extra hours so I gave her the admin to do, too. Clearly that was a mistake. *Damn.* These are good suppliers, and they gave me a hefty discount. I need to keep them sweet.' Tapping on the keyboard with intent to maim, he opened his bank account page, set up a direct credit and paid for the chandeliers. 'I doubt they'll have me back as a client again. I had no idea. And now I'm really running late.'

'Do you have an accounting software programme?'

'Yes. It's here…' He clicked again. 'But I have to go and prep. Here's the menu. The computer's wi-fied to the printer. I'll grab you something to drink?'

'Yes, please, a coffee. Espresso?'

'Okay. I'll be right back.'

And they both knew he could easily have typed the menu up and printed it off by now, but he hadn't. And neither had she.

She didn't want to think what that meant.

CHAPTER 8

The late afternoon morphed into the evening and, fuelled by the best coffee she'd had in London, Chloe printed off his menus, sorted his papers, filed bills and even made a start on entering data into the accounting software. Surprisingly, he'd only looked a little shocked when she'd asked for his password and only mentioned industrial sabotage once under his breath as he'd given her pretty much full computer access. He had stopped short at allowing her into his bank account, though, and she supposed she couldn't really blame him.

Out in the restaurant, there was a murmur of hushed voices, the clang of pans and even more delicious aromas floating across the air. An unobtrusive soundtrack played, and she felt almost serene as she put everything into neat order. There was a lot soothing about changing chaos into calm. And, to be honest, it was nice to be focused on something other than her own problems.

A few hours later, he came into the office and stopped short.

His hair had fluffed up in the steamy kitchen atmosphere; his face was pink with heat, and he had chaos in his eyes. She wondered what it would take to soothe that into calm too. Then she wondered why her gaze flicked to his mouth when kissing a man like Vaughn would instil anything but calm.

And hot on the heels of that thought was shock that kissing him had been the first thing to enter her head when she'd looked at him.

He gave her a startled smile as if he'd just woken up and found a tasty treat in his bed. 'Oh, Chloe, still here?'

'Believe me, I could go through this all night and only make a tiny dent.'

'Wait right there.' He was gone for a few minutes but returned with a grin and a tray filled with olives, fresh warm bread, some kind of bright pink whipped-cream dip, hummus and an array of Mediterranean-style vegetables dripping with a fragrant olive oil. There was also a bottle of dark red juice, a tall glass and a napkin. He placed the tray in front of her. 'Eat this. Order anything you want from the menu. In fact, order anything not on the menu too, and I'll cook it for you. Then I'll call you a cab to get you home. You've been here too long.'

'All going okay out there?'

'Great. Look, Chloe, you don't need to do this.'

'I know.'

'So why are you doing it?'

'If I'm planning to hold a wedding here, I need to make sure you keep open long enough for it to actually happen. I don't want you letting my clients down. I have enough problems without you adding to them. And, also, because you have paper that I can shuffle. I don't have much paper to shuffle. No piles of invoices to put in glorious, perfect A to Z order. A lot of bills, though...'

She nodded at the thought of them all looming over her and of having to use the electricity money this month to pay the council tax. 'Yes, a lot of bills.'

He looked at her for a moment, and she felt strangely exposed. She'd said too much. Again. 'Things not going so well after all?'

'On the contrary, how did you put it? Everything's going swimmingly. Now, let me try this food. And thank you again. It looks very... pink.' She scooped some cerise dip onto her bread and took a bite, trying to take the attention away from her business. She didn't want news to get back to her old group of friends that she was failing.

No.

She refused to believe she was failing. Things would work out. They would. She was back on her feet now. And spending time here doing mindless filing had freed up her subconscious to think about fun ways to attract new clients. She actually felt a little more positive about the way forward and had even jotted down a couple of notes she would turn into actions. So, in a round about way, she had something to thank him for. 'Oh, wow. This is delicious. I mean, *really* delicious. Smokey and tangy. What is it?'

'Beetroot, feta cheese and a little magic. A secret recipe I picked up in Turkey, and if I tell you the ingredients, I'll have to kill you. But it's nice, yes?' He grinned, and it was genuine and refreshing, and she realised he was starting to relax in her company. No more hesitant glances towards things that could be used as weapons. Which, for them, was pretty huge.

'Yes, it's lovely. Now, go back to the kitchen and work your magic there, too, chef. You can't waste all your time in here. When's Collini coming?'

His mouth turned up at the corners. 'Someone who's more of a slave driver than me. Interesting. He's here already. That's why I haven't been in to see you for a while. Entree and main down. Just dessert to go. Jacques, my sous chef, is just putting the finishing touches on.'

'And you trust him with Collini?'

'I'd trust him with my life, which is worth a lot less than Collini's praise.'

Chloe looked towards the door and wished she could take a sneaky peek outside and see what this mysterious reviewer looked like. 'Can you read anything from his body language?'

'No, he's notoriously deadpan about his eating experiences. We'll just have to wait until the review's out tomorrow. He chose the duck entree, which is always a crowd pleaser, and the lamb rack main, which is my signature dish, so finger's crossed.'

She watched as his face lit up at the thought of his food creations and remembered when she used to be so abuzz about her own job. To the point of not letting anyone else in, apparently. But it takes time and effort to build a successful business, at least Vaughn understood that. 'Be honest, you forgot I was in here, didn't you?'

'Don't be ridiculous.' He looked so taken aback that she believed him. So that didn't account for his startled reaction as he'd come into the room. What did?

'It's okay if you did forget me. I understand. It's a big deal having a reviewer here; you need to focus on that. In fact, you'd better get back in there and work that kitchen.' She glanced at her watch before she saved and closed the accounting programme. 'Wow, I didn't realise it was so late. I'll get going. I have to get a decent sleep to finalise everything for the rehearsal on Friday.'

Vaughn's face fell from its gastronomic high. 'You don't want dinner?'

'The dips and bread were enough. So no, I won't. Not this time.' Then she inwardly cringed. *This time?* Was she sounding as if there'd be a next time? Because she wasn't going to do his books for him, that gem of a job would have to go to someone else.

'How about a glass of wine, by way of thanks?'

She turned around and looked for her handbag. 'No. I really should go and get out of your hair.'

'Chloe, you're not in my hair.' As he shook his head, his hands locked on her shoulders, anchoring her in place. His restless energy emanated from him, and his heat, which seemed to shiver through her, coiled through her gut, tingling in parts of her that hadn't tingled in a very long time. He smiled as he spoke, and she wondered if he knew exactly what effect he was having on her. 'As you saw earlier, I like to pay my debts, and I won't take no for an answer. I don't like to be beholden to anyone. Red or white?'

God knew why she was even contemplating this when she'd thought about kissing him, and now she was tingling in response to his touch, but it seemed where Vaughn was concerned, her brain wasn't entirely decided. Evil or good? Hit list or kiss list?

She was too confused to think. Too scared to make a conscious choice one way or another. And it was, after all, only a glass of wine that he was offering. 'Okay. I'll just have one small glass, please. White. Anything. But, honestly, you don't have to do this while Collini is here.'

'It'll take my mind off things. It's not appropriate for me to go out and hover over him, and all the other punters are gone or served their last course. It's going to be an early finish tonight. Midweek can be tough on a new place.'

'But business is picking up?'

'Sure. That last great review certainly increased bookings. I just have to get word out. Wait here.'

There was a clear space now on the lumpy sofa, so she sat on that and looked around the room. There were framed certificates on the wall and photos of what she assumed were Vaughn's other restaurants, one that was clearly in Paris. Another was taken on a busy city street in what she assumed was Manchester. And then some photos were obviously of places he'd visited; the Taj Mahal, Machu Pichu and Morocco. A music festival somewhere. Sydney. Snow. The Great Wall of China.

No wonder he hadn't had time to come home and see his cousin; Vaughn had packed his life with living.

'Here we go.' He placed a tray on the table and handed her a glass. 'New Zealand Sauvignon Blanc. This should speak for itself.'

She took a sip. He was right. The taste of gooseberries and lime filled her mouth. It was showy at first but had complex flavours and depth. A little like Vaughn, she smiled to herself. 'I was just looking at all these photographs. Well, wow, you've been to a lot of places.'

He shrugged. 'Just going through the list, you know. The usual tourist trails.'

'And now you have what? Three restaurants, as well? You're certainly ploughing through life experiences.'

He glanced up at the photos and then back at her. His voice was softer when he spoke again. 'It is the general idea of having a life, isn't it? There's no point sitting around just waiting for death to happen.'

She nodded, a man after her own heart. 'Sometimes I feel as if that's what Jenna's doing. Jenna, my sister—'

'Aha. I remember a few women from the church. Was she the one who dragged you off me?'

Chloe's cheeks went redder than the beetroot dip. 'God, yes, that was her. Oh, the shame. Anyway, she has lovely little Evie, who she adores. But she's too afraid to get involved with a real life. It's like she's watching from the side, too scared to dive in.'

'Why's that?'

'Her husband died. Run over. Rather, he was mowed down as he waited at a bus stop to come home after work. She was pregnant at the time, and it was terrible. I mean, really terrible. Such a huge shock for everyone, but, obviously, especially Jenna. You don't imagine how a life can just stop. But hers did.' Chloe refused to allow her voice to crack as she spoke, even though the memory and the pain were still there. 'She used to be so fun-loving and outgoing; she'd grasped life by the balls. And it's as if she's been acting through the last few years with a pretend smile and refusing to talk to anyone about it. Ever since Ollie died, she's held back just enough to stop her from enjoying herself. It's as if she feels like having a laugh would be a betrayal to the fact that he's not here to laugh with her.'

Vaughn's eyebrows rose as he listened; then he nodded. 'Losing someone can do that to you. Or you can go the other way, too far over the other edge.'

'What do you mean?'

'All that life's too short stuff. Carpe diem, and all that. It's just a licence to have a good time and bugger the consequences.' He looked up at the wall of photos, and she noticed something in his eyes. A haunted darkness, which he let linger a moment, then brushed it off with a shrug. 'But you do have to get out there. It's hard to find the right way to grieve. Actually, there is no right way. You just get through it.'

'Have you…?' She wanted to ask him if he'd been there, had lost someone close to him, but didn't know whether it was the right moment. Didn't know him well enough to pry. And surely Jason would have mentioned if something so momentous had happened.

'Yes. Yes, I have.' Vaughn seemed to understand exactly what she was asking. There was a pause where he looked anywhere but at her. Mostly, he looked at the photographs, and where she'd seen darkness in his gaze, she now saw that lighten a little. 'It was a long time ago.'

'I'm sorry.'

'Yeah. Me too.' Judging by the look on his face, he must have loved her very much. 'And now I'm trying to live up to the promises I made. You say things, you know? At the time. You make promises, and you intend to keep them all. Everyone.'

God, she wanted to ask him so many questions, but it just wasn't the right time. 'Tough?'

'Sometimes.' He put his glass down on the tray and she was surprised that he looked a little embarrassed. For Vaughn Brooks, that was a very strange turn of affairs. 'I keep busy. Very busy.'

'Hence the restaurants?'

'I have to make a living somehow. I got interested in food when I was travelling around. Getting jobs in kitchens, then progressing to formal chef training became an easy way to see the world. I could indulge myself on so many levels.' He tipped his head and smiled up at the photos and his memories. 'And I did. Hedonist at heart, you see.'

'I envy you that freedom. It must be nice to just please yourself.' Although he'd obviously been through some hard times, so maybe he deserved to do what he pleased, just like Jenna did. She'd been through enough to decide exactly what she wanted to do and be. Although, Chloe knew, sometimes people also just choose the easiest path.

Vaughn was the most serious she'd ever seen him, and with it, there was a stillness in his body, as if he'd given it all a lot of thought and was totally content with his decisions. 'Being my own boss in every aspect of my life has served me very well. No disagreements. No compromises. No complications or responsibilities past myself, oh, and the staff obviously. But there's little emotion spent there. I like it that way. I chose this way of life, and it suits me.'

Bingo, Chloe thought, as he took her empty glass from her hand and put it next to his on the tray. Was being alone the easiest way for him? Staying aloof and not getting in too deep? Being a grumpy old sod?

He turned the heat on her. 'So why did you decide to be a wedding planner of all things, Chloe? Instead of a bank manager or a doctor? Or a scientist?'

'Why do you want to know?'

'You hinted that things weren't going so well. So, I'm trying to find the passion you once had for it. You can't run a business half-heartedly. Why a wedding planner?'

'I didn't start out wanting to be one. When I was younger, I was happy studying for my business degree and then getting a paying job. God, it was nice to get a pay cheque; it meant I could start to plan and save. I've always been a planner, you see. I had my career path all mapped out, and I thought I was sorted for life. But my mum had always talked so passionately about her wedding day; the dress, the bridesmaids, the church. She made it sound so wonderful, like a fairy tale. Believe me, I am so over that idea right now. But, rewind a few years, I got bored working for the tax office with little opportunity to advance, and at the back of my mind, I'd always thought how amazing it would be to make other women's dreams come true. Plus, like I say, I'm a born planner, and, okay, just a little bossy.'

'You don't say?' His eyebrows rose, and he laughed.

So did she, because there was, she realised, a certain amount of truth in the bridezilla comment, but it had stemmed from being a perfectionist and not from being a spoilt bitch. Although, it may not have come across like that at the time. 'Well, okay then, I'm a lot bossy. But I struck out and started up my own business. Jenna's was my first wedding. Then one of her friends wanted me to help her, and it snowballed. It's a great job. I can choose the hours I work. I meet generally nice people and go to wonderful venues and create a fairy tale. It's fun. I love it.'

Loved it.

'And now? It's a trial because clients are few and far between?'

Yes, let's stick with that and not the whole fallen out of love with love thing. 'I need a pep, yes. Actually, I need a fairy godmother with a magic wand. Basically, Jason cleaned me out when he left me with a full mortgage to pay and a business to run.' She stopped short at trying to explain the Jenna and their mum conundrum.

'And you just offer wedding planning? Not other events?'

'What kind of other events?'

He shrugged. 'I don't know, Chloe. You have to think out of the box. Something wedding related? Honeymoons? Proposals?'

'I think there are plenty of people who have cornered those markets already.'

'Engagements? Baby showers? Divorce parties? Okay, that last one was a joke.'

'Because it would be funny to organise weddings *and* divorces wouldn't it? Hilarious. Yep, we cover you from the fairy tale to the nightmare and beyond. Funerals too? Why not? Yes, let's add those to the list.' It probably wasn't funny, but she laughed anyway. And so did he. Their eyes met as they both swayed forward a little, and for a moment, they sat there just looking and smiling and there was a feeling… something new… in her gut. And heat.

Was there…? Was she imagining heat in his eyes too? She didn't dare to think. That was a stupid idea. He was her ex's cousin. He was committed to life alone like a martyred poet or something. He was everything she didn't like in a man. He was Vaughn Bloody Brooks, for God's sake.

She swatted any idea of his lips and his eyes and his heat away and focused on the conversation. 'But a general party planner, I guess that could work. I do need to develop, but I'd have to change the name of my company. And then there's my mum and sister to think about. They need to be doing the flowers and the dresses so they can make a living.'

His smile slipped. 'And all the responsibility for your whole family falls to you? I presume you've talked to them about the financials?'

'No. I couldn't. Really. I can't tell them. It's the way we work. I run the show and drum up business, and they do the other stuff. We do what we're good at.'

'Which puts a lot of pressure on you.'

Yes, it did. But Chloe didn't want to come across as some kind of victim or airy fairy whinger. 'I can handle it. Jenna has little Evie to worry about. And Mum... well, Mum hasn't had an easy time. When Dad died, she had to look after us on her own. She didn't have a network of family, and she barely had any friends. They hadn't been over from Ireland very long, and she couldn't afford to take us back and find a life there. She has mood swings, depression. But the sewing steadies her. I couldn't make her give it up and get another job. But you do have a point; we need to diversify. Maybe costumes for parties, bespoke ones, obviously. Perhaps party planning... yes. Proposals, engagements, venue sourcing, wedding-related things—I like the sound of that. Maybe advertise that we relish taking on special themes. That we specialise in the strange and the wonderful.' There was no way she would tell him about the frogs yet, if ever. 'I've just been so stuck in one headspace I haven't been able to see round it.'

He grinned and sat back, satisfied. 'Glad it helped. You need to work out a point of difference or run some special offers. Talk to venues and suppliers and get some dual deals organised.'

'Oh yes, what a great idea.' She sat up straight and looked him in the eye. 'Right, Mr Brooks, what kind of deal can you do for me? If I bring clients here, what discount will you offer?'

He threw his hands up. 'Whoa. I'm just starting out here, too.'

'In London, yes. But you do have two other restaurants, which means this is part of a freaking chain. You are a corporate restaurant baron, Vaughn Brooks, and I'm just a lowly wench dragging myself up. And I'm actually starting to feel a little excited about things for the first time in forever.'

To be honest, just thrashing out ideas with someone else had made her more positive about her work again. Lately, sleeping had been put on the back burner while worrying filled her nights. Sometimes she felt as if she was going to explode with all the exhausting thoughts in her head. She didn't want to worry her mother and sister with the dire state of affairs, but these thoughts, looking forward with new ideas, were actually quite exciting. How the hell she'd execute them, she didn't know.

She realised she was grinning inanely. Or even insanely. Somehow they'd ended up chatting so animatedly they were facing each other, knees almost touching. Almost too close. She looked up into his face, at those steady, dark eyes and the smile. Vaughn Brooks could smile a beautiful smile. Who knew?

A silence fell, and it felt as if the air shimmered around them in the soft orange half-light. As if something magical could happen, as if anything was possible. She was acutely aware of the rise and fall of his chest. Of the closeness of his mouth. Of the heat in his eyes. Yes, definitely heat. And a need that was thick and... *there*, shining brightly between them.

For the second time that evening, she thought about placing her mouth against his, of how he would taste. Of how much she wanted to kiss him.

And of the many, many reasons why she shouldn't. Couldn't. Wouldn't kiss Vaughn Brooks.

The thumpety-thump began to hammer in her chest, and her hands became as sweaty as TheBigCarlhuna's. If this was how she felt without even touching the man, then God help her if she ever had any kind of physical contact with him.

Not going to happen.

She stood, brushing her skirt down, willing her limbs to stop shaking. 'Righty-oh. I've been here way too long. I should go.'

There he was looking at her again, with a question in his gaze. Searching. Then he nodded assertively and the spell between them was broken. 'Absolutely. I'll take you home.'

'No!' There was no way she was going to sit with him in a car, so close. She turned away and picked up her bag. The atmosphere that had been charged and heated and expectant started to cool into awkwardness. 'No, really, a cab will be fine. You have to go out there and finish up. Give Collini a good send off.'

She followed him to the door, through the restaurant and to the street. Every step was difficult, forced, taking her away from a bubble of intimacy she'd relished. Taking her away from a risk. A chance. A danger.

Once outside, the cool air breathed around them. She didn't know what to say, so she smiled and clutched her bag to her side.

And he stood next to her, tall and graceful and steady, his breathing wasn't all over the place like hers was. He seemed completely calm. As the cab rolled up, he opened the car door. 'Thanks for tonight, Chloe. You helped me out of a fix.'

And helped her right into one. 'Make sure you go straight to a temp agency and get someone to come tomorrow to finish off all that paperwork. And then get a permanent office manager.'

He gave her a salute. 'Aye, aye, Captain.' Then he leant forward, and his lips grazed her cheek.

Heat slammed into her, but she stayed stock-still, frozen. *No complications.* It was a good motto to have and one she'd do well to adhere to. There was absolutely no point in getting carried away with the way he made her feel, because if anything intimate came of this attraction, she had no doubt that a few days or months down the line he would be making her feel very alone all over again. And a little less together.

When he pulled back, he was smiling. 'I've been meaning to say... I am very sorry about what happened in the church. You didn't deserve that. It was a cruel thing to do. I made sure I told Jason what I thought.'

He'd stuck up for her? 'Thank you, Vaughn. I doubt it made any difference to him, though. Jason can be very single-minded when he wants to be.'

'The man's a bloody idiot, what can I say?'

And before she could read anything into that, Vaughn closed the door, and the cab was pulling away.

Yes, her ex was a raving lunatic, that was a given. But his cousin? He was a completely different puzzle. And definitely not one she was about to try to solve.

CHAPTER 9

The taxi pulled up outside her apartment building, and Chloe was surprised to see a light on in the lounge and... was that a twitch of her curtains? Strange.

She paid the driver, and as she got out of the cab, she noticed a police car parked on the road, too. Not unusual, not really, in this part of London, but in conjunction with the light and the curtain twitch, it made her heart speed up.

What the hell?

Was everything okay? A break-in? Mum? Jenna?

Shit.

A million scenarios gunned through her head, none of them pleasant. Dashing up the steps, she simultaneously dug around in her bag for her key, but as she was about to thrust it into the lock, the door swung wide open.

'Chloe! Thank God, you're okay!' Jenna's arms wrapped around her and pulled her into a tight hug. 'We thought you were dead. Oh, God, thank goodness you're okay.'

'Dead? Why the hell would you think that?'

She followed her sister, who was shouting in wobbly but relieved tones to rapturous applause, 'She's fine! She's alive!' into her lounge to find two police officers—one male and one female—squished into her sofa with china teacups in their hands. Snuggled up against them was her mother. Who had lost her usual soft smile.

On various dining and comfy chairs pulled into a half circle facing the sofa, sat Mrs Singh, who was her mother's next-door neighbour, Faith from the pub, Saskia from the yoga studio and Kat, Chloe's oldest friend from school. At their feet were sagging cloth bags bulging with books. Opened bottles of wine on the coffee table vied for space with cheese and crackers and dips and a large box of chocolates.

Book Group. Was that tonight? Damn, it was. She'd clean forgotten. Not that she'd had time to read a word of the latest crime bestseller—ironically, about a woman who'd disappeared after Internet dating.

'Thank the Lord! You're safe.' Her mother stood, her mousy hair falling into her eyes, eyes that were blotchy and red-rimmed. She ran trembling hands down Chloe's arms. 'And back just in time. I thought we were going to have to talk about books. Now, we can just keep going with the gossip. Tell us now, where've you been? What the hell's been going on?'

'I'm fine, Mum. Honestly. I was just—' Chloe looked around the room at the gaping mouths, all of them hanging on her every word.

And cops? Had someone arranged a show and tell to go with the crime theme?

The female officer spoke into her collar. 'Copy that, yes, she's returned. Unharmed by the looks of it. No, she hasn't clarified who the perpetrator was.'

'Perpetrator?' Chloe squeezed past the book group personnel wall and looked at the officer. 'What's going on?'

'Your sister filed a report that you may have been abducted by a…' The officer glanced at her regulation, small, black notebook and frowned. She sounded almost disappointed now that Chloe had been found. 'Male, caucasian, going under the name of *DrewsAmused.*'

'What? No? Don't be ridiculous. That poor man. You haven't… Oh, you haven't arrested him or anything?' Sure, he was a little odd, but he was hardly abductor material.

'He's helping with enquiries, ma'am,' the male cop answered.

'Oh, no. Please leave the poor guy alone. We weren't a great match, but he wasn't too upset by it. He certainly wasn't dangerous. This is so ridiculous; it's not even funny. You can't go around thinking people are like that. He was actually quite nice. I left him hours ago. I've been at—'

Chloe stopped.

There would be questions. Lots and lots and lots of questions, she knew there would. They would read things into the situation that just didn't exist. They would make wild leaps of imagination and such a fuss. They would want every tiny detail, and they would all be entirely happy creating scenarios in their heads that hadn't happened. Even though she had to admit to having fantasised about kissing Vaughn, telling them about it just wasn't worth the hassle. She turned to Jenna. 'Why didn't you just call me instead of the police?'

'I did. A thousand times. You never miss book group. You never don't answer.'

Chloe pulled her phone out of her bag. It was switched to silent mode. And with a long line of missed calls and texts getting more and more frantic. 'I see, yes. I must have, er, left it on silent.' *While I got cosy with Vaughn Brooks in the back room of his restaurant.*

'So where were you?' It was Jenna. This time a little more intent than before. 'We were worried sick. I mean, really, really worried. I thought you were—oh, Chloe, you have no idea what was going through my head.'

Sadly, Chloe did. She remembered the day Jenna's husband hadn't come home. How her sister had sat, white-faced and numb waiting for information, as if she knew, deep down, that he wasn't coming back. Jenna had the same look on her face now. The one that said she knew bad things happened, that this had been a hard reality for her, not a little inconsequential flirtation. The look begged her not to send her world into another devastating tailspin.

Chloe felt guilt shimmy through her. The poor woman had been through enough, small wonder she panicked out of proportion. She would explain it all to her sister in private. Later.

Chloe looked at them all in turn and tried for a smile. 'Hey, can't a girl go out without being subject to an interrogation?'

Eight pairs of eyes blinked back at her as if she were completely out of her mind. 'No,' they all replied in unison.

'Maybe she was on a booty call.' Mrs Singh nudged Chloe's mum and giggled. 'Naughty girl.'

'Not our Chloe. She wouldn't do that.' Her mum patted the policeman's hand, almost spilling his tea, which Chloe was absolutely sure her mum must have made because that was what she did. *Manners maketh a man, girls.* Sadly, keeping daughter's love lives private didn't make a woman. 'She's a good girl, despite what the papers say. She's tried Timber, but it didn't work out. And so Jenna's set up this internet dating thing—I don't think anything will come of it. Not in the long run, anyway. Unlucky in love we are; we're cursed. Sorry to have been a bother. Thank you for coming so quickly.'

The officers stood in sync, shaking their heads and rolling

their eyes. The female one gave a wry smile, and now that Chloe thought about it, she seemed vaguely familiar. 'Yes, well, we make it a priority to come out for single women. Especially ones with form. Now, have a good evening. And, Chloe, do your family a favour and check in with them every now and then. It makes all of our lives a lot easier.'

The thumping in her chest got harder. 'Form? You said I had form? What does that mean?'

'Previous. You know, you're known to us, Miss Cassidy.' She leant in and winked. 'From the church? The assault on the best man? Best call out I'd had in a while, that was.'

'I see.' Chloe felt the heat in her cheeks burning like a beacon. 'I thought it wasn't on record.'

'Oh, no, it's not, not officially anyway. But we do have very good memories.' They walked to the door. 'Have a good evening.'

That was unlikely. Bad enough to be reminded about The Jilting all over again, and her humiliation, and Vaughn Brooks and the bouquet, but there would be more questions now. And the only people better at interrogation than the police were a group of bored women, two glasses of wine down and with very vivid imaginations.

'Now, to the nitty-gritty, Chloe. Jenna tells us you had a date? And it was from that internet?' Their mum had a habit of clarifying things loudly. 'Who was he? If he didn't abduct you, then how did it go?'

'He was nice. He has a dog. He just wasn't my type. He was quite a lot older than me too.'

'Sugar daddy. Yum.' Mrs Singh again. That woman was incorrigible. She fixed Mum in her sights. 'You should do this internet thing, Bridget. You're always on about the Cassidy curse, but it's just plain rubbish. You need to find a decent man and keep a tight hold of him. You all do.'

Their mum folded her arms and pursed her lips. Never a good sign. 'It's not as easy as all that.'

'Phooey. You brought that *curse* on yourself, Bridget. Graham wasn't all bad. Maybe you should have tried to work things out with him instead of kicking him out. I said so at the time… you could have talked to someone, a counsellor… a priest… marriage… guidance.' Mrs Singh came to slow halt.

And the room began to spin.

Mum's face was fuchsia pink as she fussed around with her bag. 'Well, it's been an interesting evening. I'll be going now.'

Faith, Saskia and Kat stared, open-mouthed. Because, like Jenna and Chloe, they'd all heard time and again, at countless book groups when discussing romances with lovely hopeful endings, about poor Mrs Cassidy's curse. About the wonderful husband that had died a premature death and left her with two little ones to deal with. About her broken heart. About her loneliness and her struggles.

Never, not once, had she mentioned that she'd *kicked him out*.

Chloe tried to keep her voice level, but emotion spilt around her words. 'Mum?'

'Early start tomorrow.' Flustered and turning from pink to scarlet, Mum stood, grabbed her bag and made her way through the chairs and the people and the bags of books towards the door. 'There's some work to be done on that dress before Friday.'

'Mum!' Jenna now. 'You can't. You just can't go. Not now.'

Mum turned to face them, slowly now, every inch the tired and lonely fifty-eight-year-old. She glared at Mrs Singh, who shook her head and looked away. Then she stared at each woman in turn. She looked guilt-ridden but cowed too.

She'd lied for twenty-eight years. Almost three decades of untruths, of Chloe and Jenna believing something that simply wasn't true: that their mum and dad had had a fairy-tale marriage. That he'd been The One. That no one would ever compare with Graham Cassidy. That there was a Cassidy curse that meant they would never be married or happy or both. But that true love existed. Something pure, ethereal and perfect.

It was the foundation for *Something Borrowed*.

It was all lies.

Mum straightened, and her voice was calm. 'He was having an affair. It wasn't the first, and I knew it wouldn't be the last. He didn't like being a family man. He didn't want the responsibility of two little girls. Oh, he adored you, but he didn't want to be the one who fed and clothed you, who had to be serious about your future. I put up with it for two years, and then one day I looked at you both, and I thought *what example am I showing them*? That you lie down and take it? Or that you stand up and fight? I didn't know how much you understood. And he made it clear he wasn't going to help out. I told him to choose between me and her. *You're on yer own,* he said. And he went.'

Chloe's mouth was dry, and she realised her hands were shaking. 'But why lie? Why not tell us the truth about being a strong woman and kicking him out?'

'You were so little. I didn't want to burst that lovely bubble of adoration.'

'But you said he'd died when he hadn't? Is he—?' Chloe couldn't think straight. She had a dad somewhere out there? All this time? 'Is he still alive?'

Mum shook her head. 'Two years after he'd gone, he drowned in the Thames. Drunk as a skunk.'

'In those two years, didn't he ever come back? Didn't he want to see us?' Chloe thought about how she would have felt if someone had taken her niece away. How hard she'd have fought to see her, to have regular access. Hell, she'd force them to make

Evie live with her. She wouldn't just leave her to it. Forget about her. How could anyone do that to their own flesh and blood? 'Didn't he want to work it out? Didn't he care about us? Why didn't he ever come back to see us?'

'Ah, love.' Chloe's mum dropped her bags and came back over to her daughter. She cupped Chloe's face in her hands. Hands that had worked, stitched, cooked and washed until they were red raw. That had waved good-bye to her every morning as she'd gone off to school, then to university and then to work. Hands that had wiped away her tears and had held her tight as she'd sobbed for what felt like forever after The Jilting. Yes, Chloe knew her mum's worth in her life and loved her unconditionally, but really? This was one hell of a lie.

Her mum continued. 'I think he was relieved to be gone. He was too young to be tied down. Too selfish to think of what anyone else needed. I'm sorry, love. I mean, really, really sorry. About the lies and everything. About him, if I'm honest. The lazy wastrel. I thought it'd be easier if you thought he was a saint. I didn't want you to have all that toxic stuff in your lives.'

Chloe extricated herself from her mother's hands and shifted back on the sofa, just too shocked to know what to do. 'So you internalised it instead? And held him up as some sort of idol?'

'I hoped he'd see the light and come home. I loved him, Chloe. Too much, to be honest.' She probably still did, which would explain why her mum hadn't been near another man ever since. She'd also had to come to terms with her husband leaving and then his death only two years later. Two lots of grieving for a man who didn't care about anyone but himself, allegedly, but then, he wasn't here to defend himself, although his actions hadn't exactly proved the opposite, had they?

Chloe's throat felt as if sandpaper had been rubbed up and

down it. Why had every man she'd ever cared for walked away? Why did none of them have the guts to face her and be honest? And now this, her mother's lies.

'I'm sorry, Mum, but that's not good enough. Everything I've believed in has been a bloody lie. You lied to us over and over.'

It was harsh; God, it was a horrible thing to say and Chloe wished those words hadn't come from her mouth. And maybe it wasn't just about the lies her mum had told; it was about the fantasy world Chloe had created in her head about her father, the man who would have given her horse-riding lessons and taught her how to fish and walked her up the aisle… like that had even happened anyway. But he would have supported her, challenged Jason to a duel or some modern day equivalent. Her father would have protected her against all life's difficult times, sheltering her from the hurt and the ugly. Except he hadn't. And he never would have. 'I shouldn't have said that, Mum. I'm sorry. But… what a bloody mess.'

'Yes. Yes, it is.' With that, her mum straightened again, eyes still darting to the door at irregular intervals. Clearly she'd rather have been anywhere else than here.

'We should go. I think it's at Jenna's house next month, right?' Faith had her hand on Chloe's shoulder. They'd all gathered their things up, and each of them was heading towards the door as some sort of evacuation nirvana. There was a queue and Mrs Singh was wedged in the doorframe, vying for first place out with Saskia. Faith mouthed *call me* to Chloe and made a phone shape out of her hand.

'Please. No.' *Don't go.* 'I'm sorry. Please stay.'

Faith shook her head and pulled Kat with her. 'You've got things to sort out. We don't need to hear them. Believe me, I want to, but it's better if you three stay and get it all out there.' With a final grunt and a heave, the two front-runners popped through the door, followed hastily by the rest of the non-Cassidy family members.

Then, silence.

Chloe looked at her mum, then at Jenna, and back to her mum who was standing empty-handed next to the chair looking uncertain as to whether to sit or to leave, too. Judging by the sideways glances towards the door, Chloe imagined her mum would much rather be walking home with Mrs Singh, even if only to kill her en route for letting slip a secret that would probably have been better never being unearthed.

But it had.

'And then there were three.' Jenna finally spoke. Her voice was hushed and raw, almost as if she didn't believe the reality they'd found themselves in. From a tight circle of unerring mutual support, they'd suddenly been ripped apart. She didn't appear to be reeling with anger like Chloe, but she was so pale, and her voice was so quiet it was worrying. 'Mum, seriously, how could you? Even Mrs Singh knew.'

Mum was popping pins in and out of a small pincushion on her wrist, her actions getting faster as she spoke. 'Anjini has been a good friend to me. But she can be a little loose with her words. When I find her, I will kill her.'

'She's kept her mouth closed for twenty-odd years. So, not that loose, not really,' Jenna snapped. 'Is there anything else you weren't truthful about? Any more lies we should know about?'

'Probably a whole lot, Jenna. But they were told for your own good.' Things were starting to turn bitter if Mum's tone was anything to go by, which was a very bad sign. Over the years, she'd had her fair share of nerve troubles, and Chloe hoped this wasn't going to jump start a downwards spiral. 'Now don't be bothering me anymore about it. I did what I thought was the right thing to do. I'm going home to relieve the babysitter. You can come with me, Jenna, or you can come along later, after you two have had a chance to b.i.t.c.h. about me behind my back.'

What? This was somehow going to be their fault? Chloe's grip on her temper was fast slipping out of her control. 'And now we're the bad guys?'

'Oh? Bad now is it? I'm *bad*? Is that what you're saying?' The fuchsia colour deepened, and with a flourish, Mum indignantly grabbed her bag. 'Bad for protecting you? Well, thanks for nothing. Now, I'm going to see little Evie—at least she might appreciate me.'

With a huff, she turned her back.

With a slam of the door, she was gone.

Chloe stared after her. What a night. What a day. What a bloody life. 'Aaaargh. She's so infuriating.'

'Yes.'

'Over the top?' she asked Jenna, who was slouched sullenly on the sofa, absentmindedly worrying her wedding ring. Something she did when she was tense as if she was trying to seek comfort from Ollie. Chloe hoped she found it, she really did.

'Yes. We were acting like spoilt brats, and I can imagine she's going to feel as if we ganged up on her. She had her reasons for lying, I suppose. It would have been hard for her to decide what was for the best. What would you have done in her shoes?'

'You are becoming far too reasonable, little sister. But I don't know. I just don't know.' Chloe hated this bad feeling between them all. They'd been through so much together and had built such a good life. A good business—most of the time.

Ah, yes. The truth of that wasn't exactly comfortable, and she'd chosen not to say anything because she didn't want to worry them. Which, of course, was the same thing her Mum had done when they were little kids, sugar-coated the truth. Chloe was doing the same kind of thing now, and they were all grown adults. 'I'll come with you and talk to her.'

Jenna frowned. 'Now? Oh no, I don't think so, Chlo.'

'Why not? It's better not to sleep on something like this.'

'It's late, and I know what you two can be like when you get fired up. I don't want you coming in and things getting out of hand and upsetting Evie.'

'Won't she be asleep?'

'Probably. But kids feed off all that negativity. I think she's had enough in her life, don't you? You can come over tomorrow and apologise first thing.'

Reluctantly, Chloe admitted that Jenna had a point. 'Okay. I will. Hopefully, she'll have calmed down by then, too. Tell her I'm sorry, though.'

'Of course.' With a soft smile, Jenna wrapped her sister in a hug. It was lovely. Until... 'So where were you. Tonight? Really?'

'I was honestly just helping a friend out with some admin work.' For some reason, Chloe felt she needed to keep the evening's activities to herself a little while longer. Nothing had happened; she had indeed just been helping someone out. In the end. That was all. Nothing else. Nothing. Absolutely nothing. And she would tell Jenna everything as soon as she'd got her own head around the strange way her body was reacting to him.

'You were working for someone else until ten thirty? I hope she paid you well?'

She? Chloe let that hang there, but she didn't go out of her way to correct the assumption. Had she been well paid? Vaughn had certainly fed her well, given her wine and helped her thrash out ideas. Chloe had no intention of thinking about the way he'd made her feel and certainly not talking about it, not now, after everything. She was so damned tired, and there was another long day ahead, no doubt, especially trying to get Mum back on side. 'Sort of. Yes. It was fine.'

'And the date?'

'Was terrible. A complete disaster. I will never do that again, Jenna, ever. I'd rather be single for the rest of my life than have to meet up on a string of blind dates over and over. Please don't make me.'

Her sister looked at her a long time, clearly weighing up the pros and cons of winding Chloe up. 'Okay. I won't. But next time you disappear, keep your phone on. Okay? Please don't make me worry about you like that again.'

'Okay. I'm so sorry, Jen. I didn't mean to upset you.' And there wouldn't be a next time, of that she was sure. One evening with Vaughn had been far too much already.

'Right, well, I'll be off to wave the white flag of surrender.' Jenna gave her a quick peck on the cheek. 'Oh, and before I forget, could you have Evie for me two weeks on Sunday?'

'Sure. Why?'

'I'm helping a friend move house. Actually, move back in to the area.'

'Oh? Anyone I know?'

'Just Nick Welsh. From school?'

'Nerdy Nick Welsh? The spotty geek who was into war gaming and shocked everyone when he actually joined up to fight with real weapons?'

Jenna nodded, hand covering a yawn, muffling her words a little. 'Yes, him. He's moving back to the area, and I said I'd give him a hand.'

Seemed a strange choice of pen pal to Chloe. So unlike Jenna. In fact, the whole scenario sounded a bit fishy. So many secrets. Did she really know these people at all? Did they know her? But perhaps this one was more positive. A man. A friend. Just what Jenna needed. 'You stayed in touch with him?'

'Ah, you know, we email every now and then, no biggie, just keeping him up to date with gossip from school, really. He's been gone a long time, nearly ten years, I think. He's renting a flat in Talbot Mews, and I said I'd give him a hand to get things straight. You wouldn't mind? Having Evie? I don't want her getting under our feet if we're lugging heavy furniture and unpacking things. I wouldn't ask, but it's the day Mum goes on her trip to Warwick.'

'The ghost hunting trip? What the heck is that all about? It's hard enough being in touch with some of the living, never mind about the great departed. But, anyway. Sure thing. No problem. My head's full of stuff, so remind me closer to the time.'

'I will. Sleep well, sis.'

'Thanks.' Chloe looked around the room. The chairs were still in a haphazard crescent. There were dips and crisp crumbs and a whole box of untouched chocolate mints on the coffee table. It would take some time to clear all that up. Still, it would take her mind off the bombshells of tonight.

Her mother. Her father. Her sister. Vaughn Bloody Brooks.

With all that running through her head, she doubted very much that sleeping well was going to happen anytime soon.

CHAPTER 10

'S he's having one of her attacks,' Jenna told Chloe as she poured water into the kettle at their mum's house the next morning. 'I thought she might, after last night. The usual. She won't get out of bed. Won't talk to me. She just about managed to shuffle out to say good-bye to Evie; then she went back to bed.'

The kitchen smelt of brewed coffee, fresh laundry and freesias; the familiar scents of their childhood home. Chloe would have sat down at the large pine table that was older than her, had it not been for the mess of home too; teetering piles of little stripy leggings in acid colours sat next to delicate fairy wings and soft toys. Mum's sewing basket had been plonked on top of what looked like a week's worth of newspapers, bridal magazines with lots of different coloured post-it notes stuck to relevant pages. And, in probably what had been the only space available earlier this morning, was now a Peppa Pig matching cup and plate with toast crumbs, crusts and greasy blobs of peanut butter.

And it was all very comforting, but Chloe was happy to just visit and not have to live with the chaos that was a three-year-old and a late-fifties, hormonal woman amid her mid-life crisis—ghost hunting indeed. Lies.

Actually, their mum had suffered from *attacks* on and off over the years. But regardless of the circumstances leading up to being a single mum, she'd worked hard to bring her girls up through bouts of the blues.

And now Chloe felt even worse. 'Should I go up and talk to her?'

Jenna rinsed out the coffee plunger and put two hefty scoops of grounds in. 'I'm on my third already, and it's only nine thirty. She's delicate and a little demanding. So, no. Don't you dare go up, you'll only make her worse.'

'I won't. I'll be nice.'

'Which is a lovely thought, Chloe, it really is. But I'm not sure you can pull it off.'

'Ouch.' Sometimes her sister's *honesty is the best policy* approach hurt. 'Great. Thanks.'

'You know what she's like; it's always you who gets the brunt of it.'

'Because I'm the eldest, yeah. Great.'

'I'm sorry, sis. I couldn't change that, could I?' Jenna threw her a conciliatory look. And she was right; being born first had put Chloe under a lot of strain over the years, mainly because she had this innate need to look after everyone. But it was hardly Jenna's fault. Her little sister shrugged. 'Okay, so I'll take her up this coffee and see if she'll come down and have a chat. I think she's embarrassed about it all, really. Don't worry, it'll blow over.'

'I feel really strange about it, to be honest. I was angry, and now, I have to admit, I'm a little curious about what happened. Okay, well, call me nosy, but I'm a lot curious.'

'Me too.' Jenna put a steaming cup on the counter for Chloe and cradled the other one close to her chest. 'I know this is going to sound strange, but I always felt I had this sort of… don't laugh… widow's connection with Mum. Like she was the only person who could relate to what I was going through, because she'd been through it too, that we'd shared something really tragic and yet survived. But now…' her words petered out, and she looked a little lost.

Chloe stroked her hand, like older sisters do when they can't think of anything to say. Because the whole situation was hurtful and strange and she hadn't ever been a widow and so didn't share that connection. Real or otherwise. 'Oh Jen. I'm so sorry. I hadn't even thought about that. It must feel weird.'

'Wait here.' Jen slipped her hand out from under Chloe's. 'I'll take her coffee up.'

'Will you ask her if she's finished Jane's alterations yet? The bridesmaids'? A couple of them needed some crystals sewing on if I remember? And if she responds positively to that, will you ask her if she's finished my dress for the wedding too?'

The only problem with being a planner *and* a guest was that Chloe was expected to join in with all the themes. Hollywood glamour was all well and good, but not great for running around after the photographer, chasing the venue manager about the myriad of things that could go wrong and setting out place cards, room decorations and generally making sure the whole day ran smoothly.

Jenna nodded. 'Okay. One thing at a time. I'm going to take the coffee up and see if she responds to that.'

'But I need at least two things by tomorrow.'

'And you won't get either of them unless you let her take

things at her pace.' Which was precisely why Chloe had always been so thorough in her planning and her nagging—some called it *checking in*—because Mum had a habit of taking things at her own pace. Which on good days was grand, but on bad days was like watching paint dry. 'She's never let you down before.'

'But she's been perilously close to the edge with things she doesn't think are important, or if she doesn't feel like doing them.'

'Don't be silly, Chlo. This is a wedding. *Our* business.' Jenna glowered and ducked out the door, Mum's coffee in her hand as she called out, 'She knows this is important.'

Not as much as I do.

The table was in such a mess, the whole house was, to be honest, but it was what she'd grown up with, so Chloe wasn't overly perturbed. There were plenty of other things to spend time on, rather than clearing up, but she made a start on picking up Evie's breakfast dishes and was just about to carry them to the dishwasher when something on a folded page of newspaper caught her eye.

The review of Vaughn's restaurant. She picked up the paper, a little anxiously, she had to admit to herself, even though it had nothing to do with her. If Vaughn got a great or a terrible review, it wasn't going to affect her life in any way.

'The food showed flair and creativity. Chef's special was infused with spices reminiscent of a Moroccan souk, a perfect piquant blend, and a perfect main course served with fluffed and fragrant couscous and eastern-style vegetables with just enough bite. The chocolate tower was divine and smooth and with more than a little oomph. In short, Vaughn's restaurant had a lot of promise but disappointing follow-through on service. Wait staff didn't know the menu with enough depth and had to keep checking their notes or asking other staff for guidance. And time between courses was woefully long. A weak 7/10.'

'Shit.' Chloe snapped the paper shut and shook her head. Her far-from-perfect poached egg on toast breakfast settled in a congealed lump in her tummy. 'Shit. Shit.'

That review could be make or break for Vaughn. Really terrible would have been awful, but a draw for the macabre; punters would have gone to eat there just for the novelty value. Because Collini's reviews tended to be either magnificent or humiliating, a nine or a ten would have been excellent. But a middling score was neither here nor there. It was just… *meh*. And people didn't respond to meh the same way they responded to heinous or glorious.

Should she call him?

Her hand went instinctively to her phone, and she almost tapped his name in. But, well, why should she? Why would he care what she thought? Why did it bother her so much that things hadn't gone perfectly for him?

In truth, she felt as if she'd spent the whole damned night with him anyway. He'd been there in her head walking around her dreams, hand feeding her little morsels of food by the light of an open fridge door—a huge steel fridge with a bright light—like in some kind of porn movie. A food-porn movie. God yes, food porn. At one point, she'd almost kissed him. Actually, at a few points, she'd almost kissed him too…

And there she was, getting hot and bothered at the thought of it. This just wasn't what she needed. The man had made her forget all about the book group meeting, which had led to the police and her mum's revelation. Maybe if Chloe had gone straight home after her failed date with *DrewsAmused*, things wouldn't be in such a hot mess now.

So no, she wasn't going to call him; she had other things to do. Like appease her mum. But, well, 'Shit and bollocks, anyway.'

'What on earth's the matter?' It was Jenna. Her eyes flicked to the paper then back at Chloe, scrutinising her face. 'Oh, that, yes I saw. Not great for his business. But what the hell do you care about Vaughn's restaurant? I thought you couldn't bear to be in the same room as him?'

Chloe wanted to off-load right then to Jenna and confess that she'd been at Vaughn's place last night and that she'd dreamt about kissing him and a lot of other x-rated things. But what was the point? It wasn't as if it mattered. He'd helped reignite some passion in her business, in her life, and, it appeared, in her dreams. But saying it out loud would only make her have to think about it more, explain it even. And she couldn't. Turns out he was hot. And friendly. And so off limits, he might as well be on Mars.

So instead, Chloe went for bright. 'Oh, you know, just interested in the gossip. I want to make sure there will still be a restaurant for my client on the twenty-first. Anyway, the issue in hand? What did she say? Has she done the dresses?'

'There's some hemming needed on your dress, but Jane's and the bridesmaids' are finished and hanging in the workroom.' Where other people had a dining room, Bridget Cassidy had a workroom; it was the only space in the house that was meticulously clean and tidy and where no one under the age of twelve was allowed.

Chloe's mood improved no end hearing this. 'Right, I'll take them all with me. I'll drop Jane's and the bridesmaids' off tomorrow and do the hem myself on mine.'

Her sister paused then nodded. Her mood was clearly nowhere near as improved as Chloe's. In fact, she looked quite tense. 'I'm worried about her, Chlo. She hasn't touched the other two coffees and she's very pale. Her spark's just gone again. She's flat. Completely flat, as if someone flicked a switch. You know, like in ninety-seven.' The Year of Bed. Seven months their mum had stayed there. Getting up only in the morning to see her girls off to school, then shuffling back in and staying there until the next day. Chloe had seen to the shopping, cooking, cleaning…

But God forgive her, but rather than her usual concern for her mum, her first thought was for the other dresses she needed to finish for the remaining weddings. Would they be done in time? Harsh? Probably. She was doomed to hell—or was she already there?

Then she looked closer at Jenna, at her sad sloping face and at the messy room and all the things that needed doing. The wedding ring that her sister still wore brought to mind her poor dead husband and her little girl who was so bright and light and fresh. Then came the problems they'd have if those weddings were a failure at all. *At all.*

So Chloe sparked into action. She opened the dishwasher and put the dirty plates and cups in. Then she tidied up the cereal packets, pushed the toaster back on the counter, wiped the crumbs away with a cloth, poured in some dishwashing powder and switched the machine on. Entering the workroom, she gathered the heavy dresses together and hung them on the door handle, ready to take them home. Then she hauled every ounce of positivity she had left and smiled at Jenna. 'Hey, don't worry, she'll be fine. It's just a temporary thing. We'll fix her. We will.'

'How?'

Good question. 'I don't know, love. I'll find a way. But don't you go worrying about it, seriously, leave it with me. I'll apologise. I'll beg for forgiveness. I'll ply her with gin. Buy her favourite chocolates. All of the above.'

She'd just add it to her list. Find Jenna a husband. Sort out the money. Build up the business. Fix Mum.

And stop thinking about Vaughn Bloody Brooks and his bad review and his dreamy eyes and nice mouth and the way she felt when he touched her—even just by accident.

Unfortunately, she knew, the last thing on her list was going to be the hardest thing to do.

* * *

By seven thirty-two on Saturday evening, Chloe was exhausted and ready to climb into her bed.

Unfortunately, she had five more hours of smooching and smoothing and generally making sure there were no hitches at the Hollywood hitching.

She was just starting to relax, a little. So far she'd managed to busy herself with details, keeping her distance from the guests and focusing entirely on the wedding party. Although, she had to admit that her first sighting of Vaughn in the crowd had made her heart do a funny loop-the-loop thing. Unlike seeing Jason with Amy, which had just made her rage inside.

'Excuse me? Julia? Anyone sitting here?' A deep voice said from behind her. Vaughn? Her shoulders tensed, and her silly heart did that thing again, conveniently forgetting that he was so not the man for her. And he was talking to someone called Julia, which was interesting in itself, considering he'd barely spoken to anyone all day.

He'd stayed just a little out of reach, aloof wasn't the right word—detached? Yes, detached from everything and everyone. Sure, she'd seen him share a joke with the groom and have a drink with Jason, but there was always something just a little unconnected about him, as if he tolerated company rather than enjoyed it. Almost as if he was reluctant to let anyone past an invisible shield he held in front of him. And, sure, she knew the reasons for that, losing someone you loved would make anyone wary of any deep connection again. Feigning disinterest, she didn't turn her head towards him and took another sip of wine instead.

'Julia?' The voice was definitely being directed in her ear. 'At least I'm assuming that's who you're meant to be. Aren't you wearing her dress? Chloe?'

Julia. Of course. How stupid of her. Patting her French knot up-do and making sure it was still hair-sprayed to within an inch of its life, she turned and clashed gazes with a very dapper Vaughn, resplendent in black suit, white shirt, and black tie. His normally messy hair had been slicked to one side, a la nineteen thirties leading man, which made his dark eyes stand out even more.

Without meaning to, she inhaled sharply. God almighty, he was gorgeous. Actually, the man would have been gorgeous in a paper bag on a dark night, during a lunar eclipse. She worked on keeping her voice even and cooling the heated buzz that thrummed through her veins. 'Yes, you're right. Top of the class, Mr Brooks. Julia Roberts, Academy Awards night two thousand and one, only with a much shorter train. How did you know? Men aren't usually interested in women's dresses.'

He took a seat next to her; chair turned out to face the dance floor like her. Then he leant in a little to talk over the music. He smelt clean and fresh, with a discreet hint of masculine cologne on his jaw, and he was so close her heart wouldn't stop its silly *hello Vaughn* dance. And hell, this was Vaughn Brooks—the man she'd hated. Should still hate.

But clearly she didn't hate him at all. Her body was practically begging for his touch.

'Come on, Chloe, Julia Roberts was every boy's fantasy back then. Black dress, white straps. Diamonds. Long legs. Big smile. What's not to like? And you rock the look spectacularly.'

'Thank you. Clearly, apart from the long legs, the beautiful red hair, the famous caramel-coloured eyes and the Yankee drawl, I'm the double of Julia Roberts.'

He laughed as his gaze met hers for a little longer than she was used to. 'You'll do.'

'I'll take that as a compliment, shall I? I think it's the best one I'll get today.' Probably the only one. 'You look very nice, too. Very… er… who are you meant to be, exactly?'

'Pick any man from any awards ceremony any year, last century, last decade, and this. We all get to wear the same thing. Suit, tie…' He smiled, and she remembered the review and her heart swelled a little. *Meh, indeed.* There was nothing about this man that was meh. A little brooding at times, definitely with grump potential as she knew only too well following the bouquet incident, and sometimes distracted by his own bloody genius creativity—but never, ever meh. He took a drink from his pint of beer then turned to her again. 'Things going okay? It seems as if everyone's happy. You've done well, not that I know anything about these things. But I didn't notice any problems during the ceremony, and it's a great venue.'

Yes, let's talk about work, shall we? 'So far so good. It's a perfect place and they've gone overboard helping us dress the set for a wedding.' The staff had pulled out all the stops with a glamorous nineteen thirties' style gin palace with echoes of *The Great Gatsby* as a reception venue. The waiters wore spats and black and white outfits, and the waitresses all had black bob wigs.

The actual wedding ceremony had taken place in the main gallery in front of a huge bower of beautiful white flowers reminiscent of *Twilight*. It had taken Jenna hours to make it and taken them both hours to install it in front of some props from a recent movie about a dragon prince, so there was magic and mystery and a little bit of sorcery happening too. Much like the job of a wedding planner, Chloe mused to herself. 'I saw people enjoying the cute clapperboard place cards and awards trophy chocolate favours. But I can't get complacent; we still have a few hours to go.'

'And the dress was a definite hit, so that should please your mum.'

'She's nothing if not talented with a needle. I'll give her that.' Jane's dress was indeed phenomenal. A confection of white satin, it was a copy of Marilyn Munroe's iconic halter dress from *Seven Year Itch* that billowed over a New York subway grate. It had been elevated to wedding dress status by the addition of Swarovski crystals beaded heavily across the fitted bodice, and a filmy, frothy, tulle overlay on the skirt.

As she'd walked down the makeshift aisle, the guests had sighed at the beauty of it all and Chloe had noticed the satisfied coy smile the bride wore as she'd made her vows.

'Any more business happened yet? People begging you to plan their nuptials? Your diary is brimming with events? Bar Mitzvahs, christenings, Halloweens?' He lowered his voice so she had to crane in to hear. 'D.I.V.O.R.C.Es?'

'Hush that mouth, Vaughn Brooks. Never mention that word in my presence again. At least, not at a wedding.' She pointed to the empty space around them; everyone else was joining in a conga dance. They were having a good time and that, at least, was down to her planning and DJ recommendations. She was good at this. 'Can't you see the queue of clients forming around the block?'

'It will happen, give it time.' Vaughn gave her an encouraging smile that warmed her through. With his infectious positivity, she could start to believe that things really would happen. And a little nugget of self-belief was there too, glowing timidly in the centre of her chest. Yes, she could do this.

'I hope so. I've taken every opportunity to let people know I'm available. My business cards are everywhere, and my website is printed on everything. I almost thought about having it tattooed on my forehead… too much?'

'Let me see…' He laughed and reached out to her side-swept fringe, tugging it gently up to reveal her forehead. Such an intimate gesture that it had her stomach twirling. Out of the corner of her eye, she saw Jason standing at the bar watching her with a strange look on his face. Her heart picked up its rhythm, and she focused back on Vaughn and his touch. All too soon, he dropped his hand, and she wanted to grab it, just to feel his heat under her fingertips. He was still laughing, and she liked that, even though he hadn't spent much time talking to anyone, he'd sought her out and was giving her his full attention. 'A tattoo would be just a little over the top, I think. Business cards and word of mouth will do just fine. Maybe draw up some flyers? Take some photos of this wedding if you're going to go down the weird and wonderful route.'

'Jane said she'd write me a testimonial about how smoothly everything's gone and that I can use a couple of her official wedding photos when she gets them. Although, I've already taken a few on my phone.' For something to do with her hands, she lifted out her phone and showed him. He seemed genuinely interested and talked about composition, layout and the rule of thirds in photography. Once again, she started to relax with him. It was nice having someone to talk these things through with. Jenna and her mum were invested in getting things done, but they weren't interested in spreadsheets and marketing budgets and branding.

Vaughn nodded as she scrolled through her photos of the flowers and close-ups of some exquisite detailing on the dress. 'You need more photos of the venue and the tables if you're going to sell yourself as a general party planner and not just weddings. Do close-ups of the quirky things, like the place cards because they will highlight your attention to detail. But steady as you go, it won't happen overnight.'

'Such a shame, because I could really do with overnight success, believe me. I never was very good at that patience malarkey.'

'No, I've already had the brunt of that particular personality trait.' He rubbed his head and winked. 'Have you discussed things with your family yet?'

'Do not talk to me about families.' She couldn't help but laugh, remembering picking up Jenna and the flowers this morning, and their mum not even coming downstairs to talk. Or the lack of response to Chloe knocking on the bedroom door and calling through to *get well soon, Mum. I love you.* Or the blackcurrant jam stain, from Evie, down her favourite cream Zara trousers. And the way Jenna kept looking at Chloe as if everything was her fault. Talking about the business was way down on her list. Survival was at the top.

Vaughn's eyes narrowed. 'Why not? Trouble?'

'Where to start? If my mum taking to her bed and refusing to budge for three whole days is what you might loosely describe as trouble, then yes. Trouble it is.'

He looked as if he regretted asking that first question, never mind the second. Or third. 'Is she sick?'

'No. Yes. I don't know. She's been hiding a secret for twenty odd years, and we all found out about it the other night… about my dad. Turns out, he didn't die. Well, he did, but he didn't die immediately. She kicked him out. And then he died.'

There was a deep furrow above Vaughn's eyes as he tried to keep up. 'He died because she kicked him out?'

'No.'

He held his hands up. 'So whoa, I am way out of my depth here. It sounds very complicated.'

'It is. She wanted to protect us because we were little, but the lie sort of grew and then she didn't feel like she could tell us the truth. Anyhoo, it means that we don't have a Cassidy curse after all. She was just making it all up. I think. I'm not sure about the last bit, to be honest. But it means that she wasn't really a widow after all, although I don't know if they ever got around to getting a divorce either. And now Jenna's cross with her too, which never happens. Jenna's the favourite.'

She hauled in a breath and was just about to explain about the book group night, but he jumped in. 'Chloe, is anything straightforward with you?'

She looked over at Jason, still standing at the bar, then back at Vaughn. 'No. I don't think it is.'

Vaughn nodded slowly. 'I thought not.'

'Is that good or bad?'

'Neither. I just think of it more as a warning.' He grinned. 'I'm not good at complications.'

'I know, you said before. Is that a warning too?'

He thought about it for a moment then shrugged. 'I suppose so.'

'Right, then. We're both well... er... warned. You don't do complications or commitments. Noted. And my life is just crazy.'

'Also noted.' He smiled, and it was such a warm, soft smile. Then his hand brushed against hers, and she shivered with the biggest tingle rush she'd ever had. 'Glad we got that out of the way.'

She felt way, way out of her depth. No, actually, she felt as if she wanted to throw caution to the wind and dive right into those non-committal arms and stay there. That was the trouble with warnings; they made you want to ignore them completely and test the dangerous waters for yourself.

She also wanted to deflect attention away from her and this, because she'd already spoken far too much and he was looking at her with a kind of pity that was muted by a sad smile that said he felt sorry for her. She didn't want to talk about herself anymore, but how to broach the next subject?

In the end, she channelled Jenna and went for honesty being the best policy. She moved her hand away. 'Look, Vaughn, I saw the review.'

'Ah. Yes. That.' His eyebrows rose and he gave a sort of shrug that she figured was supposed to indicate that he didn't give a toss about the review, but it was clear from the fall in his mouth and the faded light in his eyes that he did care. A lot. If she wasn't mistaken, he was also a little embarrassed as he looked down at his empty glass. 'You want another drink?'

She reached for his arm and gave it a little squeeze that she tried to turn into a gentle, friendly punch, in case she gave him the wrong idea. 'It is okay to talk about these things, you know.'

He frowned. 'Yes, I was going to. I just need something to help smooth things over first. Just to bolster my ego, you know.'

'Oh. Right. Okay. I'll just finish this; then you can get me another chardonnay.'

'No hurry. I can wait all week to talk about a very average review.' He was going to talk to her about how he felt. And he didn't seem scared about the prospect or worried. It was the most masculine thing she'd ever heard.

She glanced away and noticed that the catering guy was gesticulating at her from across the room. He was making a sawing motion with his hand, which she deduced was about the cutting of the wedding cake. *Perfect bloody timing, mate.* Although, to be fair, she already had plenty of reasons to leave Vaughn well alone.

One of them was still staring at her from the bar; Jason's face was screwed up tight and even from this distance she could see he was not happy at all. In fact, she could feel the pinpoints of daggers at her heart the more he stared. Probably, because she was talking to his cousin. Or the simple fact she was here at all, making his new Chloe-less life just that little bit more difficult.

When he saw her looking over, Jason raised his eyebrows, making sure eye contact was made.

She looked away quickly.

'Oh. Sorry, Vaughn, but… I… actually… I need to go. I think I'm needed for the cake cutting.'

Vaughn followed her gaze over to Jason, then back. He nodded and frowned. 'It seems like I'm always trying to convince you to have a drink, Chloe. Don't have one on my account. It's fine.'

She looked at the catering guy who was still gesticulating, then at Jason, who was still frowning, then at Vaughn, who was starting to walk away. No man for months then three all wanting her attention at the same time. *Typical.* 'No. No, it's not that. I will. I'd love a drink, thank you. Once I've sorted out the cake cutting.' She held her empty glass out to him. 'Chardonnay please, and line them up.'

'If you insist.'

And with that, man number one turned away. She watched him walk towards the bar, breathing a silent sigh that Jason had seemingly disappeared. Now, for the cake cutting and man number two, who was the one with the sharp knives, so she should probably have made him man number one.

She stood up, turned to head to the kitchen area out back and smacked hard into… man number three. 'Oh. Jason.'

Damn.

'Chloe. Hi.' It came out as a slur, more like *Chloeeehi.* Too much wine, knowing Jason. He was like that, guzzling the free booze as if there was a prize for whoever drank the most and he was determined to win it.

He was very close and, what? Leaning in?

No!

That thin mouth puckered tight, and pale blue eyes closed as he swayed towards her. Closer and closer he came. She could smell his aftershave, the same one he'd worn for the last ten years, and the memories rolled through her. She'd loved him and offered him her heart, and for a good few years, they'd been happy.

Then he'd run off with her friend. At their wedding.

Closer and closer still. The mole just above his upper lip was in perfect focus.

Yes, he was going to kiss her cheek. She could feel a collective intake of breath and the eyes of every single guest watching. Including Vaughn.

But she couldn't make a scene, or walk away in case he made one. She had to just stand there and find a smile and allow him to do this one act of cringe-worthy, anger-inducing faux-friendliness.

Yes, her lumbering ex was going to kiss her right here in front of everyone, and she was going to have to take it, literally, on the cheek. Shame and humiliation mingled with the rush of memories of what they'd had. And what he'd taken away.

Double damn. From somewhere deeper than she ever thought possible, she found a smile and offered her cheek, freezing at the contact, wondering how she could have loved that face so much.

'Hi, Jason, lovely to see you. You're looking great today. Very smart.' But heck, she wanted to stamp her feet and shout *What the hell were you thinking? How bloody could you?*

But she couldn't because she had a ridiculous need to be nice, which should have stemmed from a desire to prove to him and everyone else that she could rise above the humiliation and be civil. Or it should have come from a desire not to cause a scene and jeopardise the wedding and subsequently any knock-on business.

It didn't.

Mortifyingly, it came from a deep-seated need to endear herself to him. Because that was who she was. She was the girl who men ran away from. The one not worth hanging around for. The one they couldn't even look in the eye and say *I'm sorry for hurting you.*

She realised with a hard lump in her throat that she really was that girl. The one who had an entrenched need to be nice to everyone, because that way they might like her enough to stay around.

CHAPTER 11

Chlooeeee…' It was said through a smile that was at once possessive and disarming. 'What are you still doing here? Shouldn't you have gone home by now?'

Oh, and passive-aggressive, another of Jason's many stellar talents. She kept her voice steady and polite, even if he didn't deserve it, the bride and groom did. 'I have to stay to the end, you know that. Why? Is there a problem?'

'Amy's embarrassed, and she asked me to talk to you, although God knows why. I said you'd be cool with it.' His eyes darted over to the table where Amy was sitting, watching them, looking glum. She wasn't sure, but Chloe couldn't detect an ounce of real compassion in Jason's face, for either of them.

'Cool with what, exactly?' She lowered her voice and turned him away from the rest of the crowd, and the need to be nice to him started to wither in direct proportion to her rising anger. 'The two-timing? The betrayal? The Jilting? Going on our honeymoon without me? Leaving me financially ruined?'

He leant in. 'With us being here. You know… me and her, together. And you. It's not awkward, right? She thinks it is.'

It hadn't been, Chloe had managed to navigate through it quite successfully using stealth tactics the British Army would be proud of, but it certainly was difficult now. She cringed. 'Me? Feeling awkward? No! Not at all. I'm fine. This is work to me, Jason, that's all.'

'Work, work, work. That'd be right. Because that's all that matters to you, isn't it?' He was swaying again and seemed to be having trouble controlling the volume switch on his voice. Amongst the long list of other things, Chloe's commitment to her work had irritated Jason. 'Weddings and flowers and dresses. Blah, blah.'

'I need to make a living like everyone else,' she managed not to hiss, then tried to find some control for herself. God, he could be odious when he was drunk. And his profile on that website kept flashing in front of her eyes. *Searching4U*. Maybe he'd taken it down now? Maybe he'd committed to Amy 100 per cent. 'How's things? With you and Amy?'

'Depends on who you ask.' His jaw lifted, defensively. Yes, that was it—he was feeling all the awkwardness and was trying hard to be defensive and manly about it.

'What do you mean?'

He didn't meet her eyes; in fact, he stared at a spot somewhere in the far distance and for a fleeting second there was a hint of humanity in his eyes. He looked a little lost, out of his depth to the point where she almost felt a little sorry for him.

And that was the problem with Jason, he tried hard to be macho and heroic, but inside he was really just immature. He was all about the fun, and nothing about the responsibility. One day he'd grow up and be a decent citizen—he really would. He just hadn't evolved that far yet. 'Amy's pregnant.'

'Oh. Wow. Well, wow. A baby? Wow. That's a surprise.' It felt like a fierce stab to her heart. It was stupid to even think it, let alone feel it viscerally, but Chloe's gut hurt as if her own child had been ripped away from her. It was no secret that she'd planned to have babies, a family. Jason hadn't wanted one, at least not yet. *Too young,* he'd said, *to be tied down to children. We should be having fun while we're young. Wait.* So she had. And waited. And waited. Until another woman had taken her place. That poor woman who didn't know he was still searching for someone. 'That's... well, that's wonderful. Fabulous!'

'Is it?' His head snapped up to meet her eyes now. There was what she could only describe as fear in his gaze.

Chloe dropped the gushing exuberance; she didn't feel it and clearly neither did he. 'You're not happy about it?'

'*We're* ecstatic. Can't you tell? Delighted.' His eyes flicked again to Amy, who was still nibbling her fingernails and looked as far from ecstatic as anyone could be about carrying Jason's offspring. 'Over the bloody moon.'

'Well, it's great news, and it's happening whether you're ecstatic or not. Congratulations to you both.' Her voice seemed to echo a little, and it took Chloe a moment to realise that the DJ had stopped the music, and people were starting to gather near the cake, although their eyes were on Jason. And her. And she felt the creep of more humiliation steal through her veins, through her limbs. 'Look after her, Jason. Treat her well.'

'And what do you care?' Now his voice was really loud. 'I mean, really, Chloe? Why the hell does it matter to you?'

'I guess you and Amy don't matter to me. But a baby matters, a real human being that you're going to have to take care of. And obviously it matters to Amy, so it should be bloody important to you.' So he needed to grow up and stop acting like a hormone-fu-elled teenager who couldn't own up to his responsibilities. Of course, she'd only realised this in the last three months. Before that, she'd been buoyed by his youthful outlook and enchanted by his enthusiasm to have fun.

From the corner of her eye, Chloe saw Vaughn take a step towards them carrying two glasses of white wine. She shook her head minutely to stop him. This was between her and her ex, any other contributors would start making way more of it than it was. She could handle it, smooth things over and stop it being such a big deal. At least, outwardly, anyway. Inwardly, her stomach twisted tight, and there was a lump in her throat.

A baby.

She focused on Jason. 'Please give my congratulations to Amy. You need to think about her and what she needs now.'

'Ah, well… Thing is, Chlo…' He gave her a weak smile, as he seemed to take a moment to centre himself. His body softened the longer he looked at her as if he were remembering good times, good things. 'Thing is… I'm trying to think about her. I am. It's just, I can't stop thinking about you.'

'Well, tough, Jace. Tough, if you feel guilty about it. You made a decision, and you have to live with it.'

'I don't think I can.' And to her horror, he reached out and touched her face. *Oh, good God. No.*

Really? He wasn't feeling guilty about what he'd done to her; he wanted her back. Or wanted her, *as well.*

She prayed no one was watching, that they were all distracted by the amazing cake or… something. She hoped no one would see this drunken morose idiot spouting nonsense, and her standing there taking his thinly veiled passive-aggressive rubbish all over again. Not anymore.

She didn't want him to like her anymore.

Taking a step back, Chloe took a deep breath. 'Please don't touch me.'

He looked sulkily at her. 'You used to like it.'

'When we were together, yes. And now we're not. You're with Amy. And she's watching. *And pregnant.* In fact, everyone's watching. Including Jane, the bride, *my client.*' Jane was standing, cake knife gripped in her hand, her face thick with anger and frustration as if contemplating where to stick that knife next. Chloe had a few ideas... 'Jason, please go back to Amy.'

'I don't want to go. I want to stay here with you.'

She took hold of his hand and pulled it away from her face, flashing a smile to the watching crowd while simultaneously silently praying for the ground to swallow her up. 'You're drunk, Jace, and you'll regret all this tomorrow. Just go back to your girlfriend and stop making a scene. You're going to ruin this for Jane and Tim, and for me. You have no idea how bad this looks.'

He shook his head. 'That'd be right. It was always about you, wasn't it? What you wanted.'

'I'm going.' Chloe took a few steps towards the group but was stopped by Jason's hand on her arm.

'You can't go.' He was shouting now. 'Stay here. Stay here, Chloe. Do not walk away.'

'Jason! What are you doing? Why are you touching her?' Amy's wobbling voice echoed around the room as she marched towards them. There was no sign of a pregnancy, no tell-tale little bump or waddle, but she did look very angry.

Chloe's heart plummeted. This was worse than a dreadful daytime soap opera. She walked towards her ex-best friend, palms up and open in surrender and made her voice as soothing as possible, 'Amy, it's fine. Really. There's nothing happening here.'

Amy glared at her. 'You're just jealous, that's all. It doesn't suit you, you know. Poor Jason feels sorry for you, and he's a bit vulnerable right now. So just leave him alone.'

Vulnerable? There was that internet profile again running

through her head like a TV news report. But what could she say? They'd only accuse her of making things up, or stalking him or some other rubbish. This was all such a bad idea.

'Okay, both of you, that is enough. Stop it. Stop it right now. I am fine with everything—you both made your choices, and that's okay. We've all moved on, and we all have to get along. Now, there's a wedding going on here, let's enjoy it, right?'

She managed to extricate herself and did a walk of shame through the silent crowd and the clients and the gaping guests to the magnificent five-tiered wedding cake resplendent with the whitest of white icing and a deep red carpet running from bottom to top. Hollywood glamour in fondant icing. On the very top was a clapperboard with the words Mr and Mrs Wright. Wedding. Act One. It had taken her days to find the most accomplished cake maker for this. It was a flipping masterpiece and all to Chloe's own design. 'Okay, let's get this show on the road, eh? Who's for cake?'

And yes, her voice was wobbling almost as much as her legs, but she thought she just might have got away with it.

'About time, too. We've been standing here like idiots while you sort out your disastrous love life,' Jane hissed through clenched teeth as the caterer carved the bottom tier into pieces. In the far corner of the room, Chloe could see Vaughn and Jason having a heated discussion. Jason was shrugging weak shoulders as Vaughn towered over him, face black as thunder. Everywhere she turned there was an argument. Jane was still hissing. 'What the hell did you think you were doing there? How dare you try to ruin my wedding? We're supposed to be in the limelight, not you.'

'I am so, so sorry, Jane. He gets a little boisterous when he's been drinking.' So maybe things hadn't gone quite as unnoticed as Chloe had hoped. It was her job to ensure the bride and groom's day went off without a hitch, that the bride had the happiest day of her life. She was supposed to be giving her the fairy tale, not the nightmare incorporating a stand-up row in the middle of the dance floor at cake cutting time.

'I know what he did was hurtful, Chloe, but you can't take it out on him here, at my wedding.' Frosty was an understatement; Jane would have frozen a blowtorch in a heat wave.

'But, I… wasn't taking it out—' Was there any use in arguing?

'And poor Amy. She's pregnant, you know. It hasn't been easy for her. Morning sickness is horrible.'

'Poor Amy?' The one who got the man and the baby? 'I mean… yes, poor Amy. Morning sickness is terrible.'

The bride's eyes narrowed as she glared at Chloe. 'She's been a good friend to me while you've been hibernating and refusing to come out. I couldn't have done all this without her support.'

'What? I arranged the whole thing…'

'You did some phoning around, yes, but *she* was there for me when I needed to talk ideas through. She was so concerned about you being here today. She was in pieces over it, I mean real ugly tears, and I had to deal with all that. People told me to get another planner after what happened at your own wedding and the police and the newspaper article and everything, and that you can be… *emotional* about things, but I stuck by you. And now you show us up in front of everyone by arguing with him? Here? At my wedding?'

The hot sting of anger welled up from Chloe's chest. 'But… I didn't… he… I… Wait a minute… *which* people told you to get another wedding planner?'

Jane looked nervously towards her friends. Their friends. The ones who'd chosen Jason. 'Honestly, Chloe, do you think I'm going to tell you that?'

'No. It doesn't matter, really, it doesn't.' Tears stung the back of her eyes. But damn it if she was going to show them she was upset by it all. Clearly, they'd already made up their minds about who's side they were on, and it wasn't hers. She made a play of looking at her watch. 'Oh, I think the DJ's going to start up again in a minute. Eight thirty? That's right?'

'I don't know, you're the planner, aren't you? I'm just the bride, remember?'

How could I forget?

Chloe started to say more, but Jane turned away and started talking to another guest, all smiles and serenity as if Chloe and her problems didn't exist.

In fact, as Chloe did a three-sixty degree turn, she realised everyone had grouped off into little huddles. One of which was around Amy. Old friends—of Chloe's too—were stroking her back and making cooing noises. Jason was nowhere to be seen. And as for Vaughn, he'd disappeared too.

So she was on her own. Entirely on her own, and yet surrounded by hundreds of guests. Which had been her plan, after all, once the dating thing hadn't worked out. She'd been absolutely fine about being here purely for business, with no one to support her or to take her side or to help. She was still fine about it. She was a strong professional woman, after all, and she had absolutely nothing to prove to any of them.

She just hadn't realised how lonely it would feel.

'So, you didn't tell me you were going to be the main act tonight. Quite a show.' *Vaughn.* There was that little flip in her stomach. He'd appeared from nowhere again, handing her a glass of wine and wrapping an arm around her shoulder, which felt strangely wonderful and comforting, as he steered her towards an open door. 'But that's quite enough for now, Chloe. Let's get you out of the spotlight. Take this and drink.'

The museum was housed in an old wharf building over-looking the River Thames. Out front, there was a wooden deck, usually closed off to the public, but open for private functions, with views across to Tower Bridge. They stepped outside and breathed in the cool spring air. The sun was dipping behind the buildings, casting red streaks over the city. It could have been beautiful. It was, but Chloe didn't feel it. She just felt righteously annoyed, and strangely beyond glad that Vaughn was here.

He had a cool edge to him that was cross and angry, but she didn't think it was with her as he pressed the glass to her mouth and tipped. 'Now, drink some more. A big gulp. That's it, and another one. That'll make you feel better.'

The wine slipped down very easily, fresh and cooling. And hell, she needed it. 'That bad, eh?'

He grinned, his hand still resting loosely on her neck as she drank. 'No, not at all. No one really noticed World War Three starting in the middle of the dance floor between you and my feckless cousin and his sappy girlfriend.'

'Now you're just outright lying.' She couldn't help but smile. He had a way of making things feel better. No, actually, of making her feel better. 'It was hardly a world war, just a little… er… disagreement.'

'Okay, if you say so. But let's just say the wedding-that-never-was is the main topic of conversation at the wedding-that-currently-is.' His smile was gentle, but he removed his arm and leant against the railings. His smile fell as he looked at her. 'It'll blow over, Chloe. Don't worry.'

There was a cool breeze where his arm had been, and she missed his heat already. Craved it. There was something strange going on here inside her, something that longed to feel his touch on her skin. And more. There was a heat inside her, too, that only ever flickered into life when she was with him. But, right now, there were more pressing matters. 'Don't worry? My client hates me. Amy hates me. My ex hates me—'

'That's not what he was saying to me.' Vaughn looked at her and she couldn't read what he was thinking.

'Which was…? Come on? What did you say to Jason? Rather, what did he say to you? No. Don't answer that. He's your cousin; you probably have a secret Bro code or something.'

'Why do you want to know?' Vaughn took a noticeable step back. 'Do you still love him? After everything he did to you?'

'Of course not.'

'Amy said you were jealous.'

'Don't be ridiculous. Seriously? What does she know? She hasn't ever asked me how I feel. But for the record, I'm not. Jealous, that is.' Not about Jason, but maybe about the baby. Yes, about the baby. Chloe's ears went pink and her cheeks blazed—talking about this personal stuff with Vaughn was plain embarrassing. He'd been there, after all, at her most humiliating moment. And again now, at her second most humiliating moment. Maybe it was him? Maybe he was the humiliation catalyst? 'I just want to make sure that Jason has left the building.'

'I can confirm that he has.'

'Good. Good riddance.' She had to get the words out somehow because if she didn't, they would sit in her gut and rot. 'You know she's pregnant? Amy?'

Vaughn nodded, looking grim. 'I do. And I'm sorry.'

Chloe raised her chin. 'It's fine.'

'It isn't.'

Her heart squeezed; there was no point in lying to him when he could clearly read her mind. 'No, it isn't. But it will be. I'm just a bit shocked. It was supposed to me, you know. That baby—it was supposed to be ours. One day, anyway. We had plans, at least, I did. He had plans too, just not the same ones as me, obviously. I do want a baby, at some point, and now Amy's got that too.'

'Oh, Chloe. Come here.' Vaughn wrapped her into a hug and held her there for a few minutes. Just held her. No words, no soothing noises or empty phrases. Just his warmth around her. As she breathed in his scent, she felt the strength in his arms and matched her breathing to his. It felt amazing just to have someone hold her after such a long time. To feel as if someone cared.

She'd read somewhere that a hug of more than twenty seconds had actual real medically proven healing properties, so she made sure to hang on to him for a few seconds longer, just to test out the hypothesis.

And, for the record, she certainly felt a whole lot better being wrapped up in Vaughn Bloody Brooks than she had before.

She looked up at him, and noticed the little lines around his dark eyes as he smiled, the hair that was supposed to be neat and now wasn't, and the smart dark suit that did not make him look like every male movie star ever. It made him look much more unapproachable and sexier and just more beautiful.

And it all made her feel a little off balance. Because Jason was his cousin, but Vaughn had been the one defending her. And that made her feel a little sad because she didn't want to get in between two cousins. Cousins were family, and the one thing she knew more than anything else was that family should always stick together.

Then she felt a little bump in her heart at the thought of her mum in bed, feeling sick because she'd lied. And the anger still deep in Chloe's gut about the lie. And the fact she'd lied to her mum and to Jenna about money. And it was all out of love and a desire to protect family from hurt.

All in all, families were very confusing.

He's Jason's family.

'Thanks for that.' Feeling much better and a little guilty, she wriggled out of his arms and dredged up a smile. 'I'm fine. Really.'

'I know you are. You are more than fine, Chloe Cassidy.' Vaughn tapped her gently on the nose, then settled against the rail again. 'And he isn't. I told him he was an idiot to make a scene, and that he was making a fool of himself and you. Then I hailed a cab and sent them both packing. He shouldn't have even come tonight.'

'He was drunk.'

'He's got a very poor track record of making decent decisions.'

'Too right.' Exhibit A, m'lord: *Searching4U*. 'Well, he's ruined it for me tonight. No one's going to book *Something Borrowed* for a wedding after that, and I doubt Jane's going to recommend me to anyone anytime soon.'

Vaughn's eyes softened, and on such a big, masculine man, it looked… well, it looked adorable. Who'd have thought the bouquet-battered best man could look like this? 'Forget it. Screw them all, Chloe. There are other people who will book you.'

'Please explain that to the bank when they come knocking at my door.'

'It won't get to that. You have plenty of things you can fall back on. Haven't you?'

The Inland Revenue job she hated? But there it was, she had people relying on her, so she had to do what she had to do if it came to winding up the business. 'I just wish I didn't have to. Bloody Jason. Again. I should have just ignored him, or told him to piss off. Why is it only afterwards that you think of things you should have said and done?'

'Trust me on this. You can't change the past. You can only

move forward.' Vaughn tipped his drink at her in a kind of salute, nudging her gently forwards. 'Think of ways to do that and don't focus on Jason.'

'Believe me, it's not like I want to, but he was so entwined in my life for so long. Ten years, over a third of my life. And he keeps turning up and reminding me all over again.' But she had been focusing too much on her past, and Vaughn was right; it was definitely time to strategise a future rather than looking behind her all the time at the bad bits and the things that went wrong. Like her mum and dad, and the Jilting.

Then she thought about the bad Collini review and Vaughn's lost loved one and wondered how far forward he could move, too, when things kept getting sticky and too hard to push past. 'I can certainly go into damage limitation mode. But it sounds as if Jane was only tolerating me because we'd already arranged so much before my wedding and I was in too deep for her to extricate herself. I'm not sure she'll be overly keen to let me use her photos now.'

'So? You have your own. And here... I've taken a few too, so we can pool resources. There's bound to be something you can use out of this lot.' He reached for his phone and showed her some very arty-looking close-ups of the flowers and the costumes and the venue, with a filter that made them look retro and vintage and chic and exactly the kind of look she was aiming for.

'Wow, you're really good at this.'

One side of his mouth tipped up in a smile, and she got the feeling people didn't pay him compliments very often. Which was a crime! The world needed to see that smile more often. 'It's just something I picked up. My... er...' He looked out across the water. 'Someone I used to know was a photographer.'

'Well, you learnt well. And thank you.' She was intrigued by the sad smile, but he had a sort of hands-off look about him that told her this topic was clearly not up for discussion.

For a few moments, they stood in silence staring out over the river, the evening breeze fluttering around them. Tugboats sloped by, bars emptied and filled, people carried on their busy Saturday night lives. Inside the museum, the DJ had started to play some 80s tunes and the dance floor creaked with jumping bodies. Out here on the balcony, it was quiet and peaceful and for once Chloe didn't feel the need to speak to fill the silence.

Eventually, Vaughn turned to her, edging a little closer. Once again his scent washed over her, tugging at her heart and her gut and the deeper parts of her. He glanced at the door. 'You want to dance?'

She didn't want to break this precious moment of solidarity. Or to call it anything other than that, even though she suspected there were things happening inside her that were so much more than solidarity with Vaughn. 'Dance? In there? With that lot? No thanks. Is it wrong of me to want to grasp some peace out here just a little while longer?'

'No. Do exactly what you want. What do you want, Chloe?'

Lots and lots of things and so many of them seemed to in-volve him——kissing him, for example. That was at the forefront of her mind right this second. Running her tongue over his lips. Inhaling him. Tasting him. All the things she shouldn't be doing or thinking about when she was at work. All the things she'd missed these past three months; just being held, a forehead kiss, Mind-blowing sex.

Just being held.

Spending time with someone who made your heart sing, who *got* you in a way that no one else did. Who you were excited to see. All the things that would be on her list of reasons to avoid Vaughn—the man who couldn't commit because of something, or someone, that happened to him years ago, and that had taught him to steer clear of complications.

Never mind the fact that despite what she hoped in her heart of hearts, maybe there really was a Cassidy curse, because so far she'd been pretty unlucky where men were concerned.

But for once, she was going to go with her gut and decide what she wanted to do and just put it out to the universe. 'Actually, I'd like to dance out here.'

'Then that's what you'll do, madam.' And even though the music was an up tempo, bass boom-boom beat, he reached for her waist and pulled her closer.

Not close enough… there was a distance that he still maintained, not just in the outstretch of his hand that held her apart, but it was all around him, worn like an aura. It was who he was, and she was okay with that. He had no pretences or agenda. She couldn't imagine him having an affair or keeping a dating website profile when he was in a committed relationship.

But she did wonder if he ever let anyone truly in. And again her mind trailed to the Lost One and who she'd been and how much he had really lost—all of his heart or just a part of it? All of his hope? A good part of his future? Because she knew that once you'd truly loved someone, then a part of you goes when they do.

She looked up at him. 'Thank you, Vaughn. Thank you for the photos and the support and for this. It's good to know I have at least one… *friend?*'

'I may live to regret this, but yes. You do. I'd like us to be friends.' An eyebrow rose. 'God knows what I'm letting myself in for. And remind me to keep well back from the bouquet throwing and table arrangements in there. I know what you're like around flowers.'

'You're safe. For now,' although, she didn't feel very safe at all. Dancing with him was a wild step into the unknown, and she felt as if the ground was shifting and she was losing her footing. She reached a hand to his shoulder and one to his waist, steadying herself, feeling his heat through the expensive linen. Feeling the honed muscles under her fingertips, making her breath hitch a little in her chest.

Because friends didn't act like this. Did they?

They moved slowly side to side, each single step to a double beat of music. It was out of time and out of sync but seemed to perfectly match their tune. And it felt totally natural to talk to him as they moved. 'I also wanted to say that clearly Collini doesn't know anything about food.'

'Actually, he does.' Vaughn shrugged at the admission as if he were giving up something huge by saying those words. 'But he liked the food, right? To be honest, he was right about the service. And if I want to shoot myself in the foot, I have to admit that Laura was right too. Even you suggested I was being a jerk by changing things on a daily basis.'

'I never said that. Jerk wasn't a term I actually said out loud.' *Oops.* 'Was it?'

'No. You didn't have to.' His thumb smoothed over the back of her hand in mesmerising strokes, and she wondered if he even realised. The gentle rhythmic movement stoked something hot inside her, making her legs shake a little. He didn't seem to notice that either as he kept right on holding her. 'That's not to say you were right. But if three people are telling me something, I do need to sit up and take notice. I'm big enough to accept when I'm possibly, just a teeny bit... mistaken.'

She dug her fingers underneath his ribs and laughed as he squirmed away. 'Wrong, you mean? I think you'll find the word is *wrong.* Go on, say it. I bet you can't. You can't say the words, *I'm wrong.*'

He opened and closed his mouth a few times like a goldfish,

frowning and laughing at the same time. Then he shook his head. 'No. No, I can't.' He laughed again, eyes dancing before his forehead rested lightly against hers, the gap between them closing just a fraction. His voice softened to almost a whisper. 'And don't push it, Chloe Cassidy. There's a line you're about to cross.'

'A line? Why?' Her heart hammered at the shift in atmosphere. It felt as if static electricity twitched between them—urgent and bright and shocking. She lifted her head and looked up into those gunmetal eyes. She saw a lot of heat there, underwritten by something she'd never noticed before... unease? Guarding. Something that held that distance between them. 'What will you do if I cross it?'

'Don't tempt me, Chloe. I mean, really... don't...'

'Why not?' She licked her bottom lip and bit down, holding his gaze. Her breath had become strangely ragged, and she felt an overwhelming need to kiss him.

He traced his thumb across her cheek, sending shivers of need spiralling through her. His touch was gentle, yet confident. In his eyes heat blazed, eradicating the guarding. He trailed his thumb to her mouth and ran it slowly, achingly slowly, across her top lip. For a moment, she couldn't breathe as all air stripped from her lungs. Low down, deep inside, a longing unfurled.

She wanted to more than kiss him. She wanted to touch him, skin on skin. She wanted to run her hands over that magnificent body and haul him to her. In her?

Bloody hell.

Then he lowered his mouth to hers.

Bloody, bloody hell. Her heart all but stalled in her chest.

She shuddered in anticipation, closing her eyes. Her heart beat a riotous rhythm and her mouth dried, waiting for the feel of his lips on hers. Waiting for the gentle pressure and the taste of him.

When it didn't come, she opened her eyes to see him looking at her with such confusion, pain almost, and definitely frustration.

Then, almost as keenly, she not only physically felt him withdraw, but saw him consciously disconnect from her too in the closed-down face and the tone of his strained voice. 'Damn it, Chloe Cassidy. Damn it all to hell.'

He gave her one last brooding look and opened the door. A riot of noisy disco music split the peaceful London hum and shattered the happy bubble of excitement in Chloe's chest at the same time. He'd gone. No kiss. The friendship muddied.

Damn it all to hell, indeed.

Jenna

Sender: Jennacass567@gmail.com

Hi, Nick!

Not long to go now!

I'm so looking forward to seeing you next week. No, you're most definitely not imposing by asking me to help you. It will be fun, I'm sure. We have a lot to catch up on. I think you're going to like living here again. It's April, and there's a hint of warmth in the air and spring flowers are everywhere. The whole neighbourhood smells of creole cooking and freesias. There are daffodils and tulips on the stalls, and yes, I talk too much about flowers, don't I? Sorry.

I've managed to score a babysitter, so I can help the whole day if you need me to. Would you like me to bring something over for lunch?

Send me the details of where to meet.

One thing, I'm not sure you'll recognise me. Just so you know, the grief diet didn't go quite the way it does for a lot of women. I have a tendency to comfort eat, so don't be surprised when you see me. You have been warned. I will understand the subtext of 'You look well'.

In other news, Evie is starting to show major talents on the dancing front (Not! Unfortunately, she takes after her mother with two left feet and being totally un-co). Her ballet tots teacher has picked her to be the 'magical tree' for the Mayday show. It's a major role showcasing Evie's innate ability to sway right and left and jump up and down on the spot like a heifer (and all out of time to the music). She's very excited, and I've managed to convince her that the magical tree in Cinderella is a hugely important thing to be, even if there's no mention of it in any of the fairy-tale books we own.

Ah, well, if dancing isn't for her (I don't think it is!), she definitely has a future in arboreal-themed slapstick comedy. I hope you'll get to meet her one day. I'm sure you will, once things have settled down a little for you.

Are you looking forward to your new job? It must be exciting to have a change, although police work can't really be all that different to being a soldier these days, right? (I'm only partly joking—the London streets can be pretty scary these days).

So, I'll see you on Sunday, then. I'm pumping iron to make sure my biceps are strong enough for the furniture lugging. (Joke! But seriously, lifting flowers all day doesn't exactly tax the muscles!)

Excited! (About moving furniture? Clearly, I don't get out nearly as often as I should!)

Jenna x

CHAPTER 12

*F*inally, something's going right.' Chloe did a mental fist pump as the delivery man arrived with all the things for the nautical-themed wedding on Saturday. Little red and white bottle openers in the shape of lifesaver rings, cake boxes decorated with anchors, and yards and yards of blue and white striped fabric for curtain tie-backs and seat covers.

All she had to do now was make the damned things, which was going to be challenging given she wasn't bestowed with her mother's seamstress skills. Still, if ever there was a woman who would give anything a go, it was Chloe Cassidy, she mused, as she brandished scissors above the stretched out material.

And—she paused and looked at the lovely fresh uncut fabric—one false move, and that would be hundreds of pounds down the drain.

But... there was no one here to help her. Mum was still remaining... well, Mum. The silent treatment was in full flow.

There were three days until the wedding. Taylor Jenkins had particularly chosen this material after days and days of trudging around the fabric stalls and shops across London. It was perfect, and the last remaining swatch left in the city. Probably the whole country.

If only Mum was here to help. Or Jenna, to just push her into it.

Or Vaughn. He'd tell her to just get the hell on with it.

She lay the material out onto the floor, stretching it almost from one end of the room to the other. Hell, if he was here, it was unlikely she'd be snipping at fabric. His pained face had barely been out of her head for the last two weeks. The way he'd clearly wanted to follow through with the kiss, but hadn't—for whatever reason.

What if…?

What if he'd kissed her? Her heart pinged a little, and there was a low warning ache in her belly.

But he hadn't, had he? He'd left.

Story of her life.

Oh hell, just do it! She made a cut, snipping along one of the blue lines all the way across the full length of the fabric. On and on and on and on. Across the fabric, across the floor…

Success!

Then she picked up one half to move it out of the way to make a start on the next length. Some of it came with her, some of it stayed on the floor. Some if it sort of hung from her grip, a sad wiggly line of extremely badly-cut fabric.

Shit. Her stomach felt as if it was dropping. Jolting. Crashing. She'd meant to fold it in half and double cut, but the bottom half hadn't been flattened out straight. In fact, it was ridged and buckled and completely hacked. In the wrong places.

Shit and bollocks. Chloe hauled in a deep breath and surveyed the damage. She'd cut across some of the stripes and nowhere near to the size or width she'd been aiming at. This piece was maybe a third of what she'd needed for the chairs. But there wasn't enough left of the other to be able to fix it.

Maybe she could use this as curtain tie-backs? Was it wide enough to be doubled and sewn? Could she…? She held a piece up then another next to it. There would be a seam right where there shouldn't be one. Plus, she'd have to chuck all that wobbly cut stuff out and start again.

Help? Anyone? Give her a spreadsheet any day. This was impossible.

She stabbed numbers into her phone. 'Jenna?'

'What have you done now?'

'Are you telepathic?' Not just that second nature sister thing but something real and scary? Yes, she was. And now she was sounding like their Mum and all her third eye, ghosts and ghouls and curses thing. 'How do you know I've done anything? I could be phoning to see how you are. Or something.'

Jenna laughed. 'You have your guilty voice on. What's the matter?'

Chloe swallowed what was left of her pride. 'I need help. This is an emergency.'

'Why?'

'I've bolloxed the chair swatches up. I made a stupid mistake and cut the fabric in the wrong place, and now I have a… well, a mess.'

Jenna snorted. 'Sorry, I shouldn't laugh, I know. No big deal. I'm sure it'll be easy to sort.'

'For you and Mum, maybe I'm missing the homemaker gene, remember. Please. Help me?'

There was a hustle and bustle in the background. Some fussing over a grisly three-year-old. An argument over which dress a teddy should be wearing. Then, a sigh from Jenna who sounded frazzled and tired. 'I can come over later? Wait, no. I've got a counselling session tonight. Tomorrow? Wait. No. I've got to make a start on the table arrangements and the grooms' corsages.'

'Now's good?'

'I'm already on track to be late for ballet tots. And that, my dear, is certain dancing death. Or ostracism. Or both.'

Chloe hated asking, she really did, but there was nothing else she could do. 'Can't you miss it, just once?'

Another sigh, this time, it wasn't an *I'll do anything to help you out*. It was more, *you just don't understand*. 'No. Evie's got to practice for the show. It's very high pressure; miss one rehearsal between now and the big day and you're out. No excuses. Sansa Bell's already been struck out. There was a hell of a showdown between her mum and Madame Emilie, believe me. The poor kid only missed because she had foot, hand and mouth disease and the doctor said she was still infectious. Or contagious, or whatever. She was preventing the other kids from catching it—so saving the show, really. But no. No chance for Sansa to make up with extra rehearsals or anything.'

'They are three-years-old. And *Sansa*? Really?' Of course. The new vogue in kid's names—popular culture characters who have had a particularly harrowing and unpleasant life… right. Grand.

'I know. I agree with you, Chlo. But I can't jeopardise Evie's chances.'

Chloe stamped a barefoot on the damned stripy fabric, just… because, and breathed out. 'No, clearly. Being a magic tree is far more important than helping me out of a crisis.' Even as she said it, she knew how that must have sounded. 'Sorry, that came out wrong. It really did. It was bitchy, and I shouldn't have said it. I'm just getting a little desperate. I need you.'

'Chlo—' There was a warning in her sister's voice that told

Chloe not to push it, that Jenna was doing her best under the circumstances. And she was. It was unfair to ask her to drop everything just because Chloe was incapable of wielding scissors and straightening out a piece of material properly. Her mother would have had a fit if she'd seen her do it. Bridget's first rule of fabric management was: check and check and check some more.

And really, the second rule should have been: Do not think about Vaughn Brooks while laying out expensive fabric.

Do not think about Vaughn Brooks and then cut expensive fabric.

Do not think about Vaughn Brooks at all. Or the almost-kiss. Or the thumb running over her lip thing. The heat in his eyes...

Where was she? Ah. Yes. Impending disaster. And none of this had anything to do with her sister.

'Look, I totally get it, Jenna; you have to do what you have to do and if it means her being a tree, then so be it. If I had a child, I'd be exactly the same.' Would she, though? It wasn't as if she was going to find out anytime soon. And having a baby hadn't been on her radar until Amy's announcement, but now there was a hole in her chest at the thing Chloe had lost. Which was stupid, because she hadn't even had it. So how could she feel bereft? But she did.

'Put Evie first. Jenna, always put your daughter first, I mean it. I will always support you for putting Evie first. But you do understand what I have to do now, don't you? I have to...' Chloe hauled in a breath. 'I have to ask Mum for help.'

Jenna's voice had a smile in it. 'Good. Maybe that's not such a bad idea. It's a step forward. It shows her how much you value her.'

'No. It shows how desperate I am. *And* how much I value her.'

* * *

An hour later, Bridget was sitting in the lounge, tutting and eye rolling and holding pieces of fabric together like a jigsaw puzzle. Apart from a brief and curt *good afternoon*, she'd said nothing else. The atmosphere was thick with tension and the elephant sat big and uncomfortably in the corner of the room. Dad. Lies. Pain.

Tut number thirty-three came from Mum's lips. 'Chloe, girl, would you look at the mess you made? You know the first rule—'

'Yes, yes. Check and check and check some more.' Still, it was the most they'd spoken in a week. It wasn't much, but it was at least something. 'The first rule should be: get Bridget Cassidy to do it. I should have asked you in the first place. I know.'

Mum lifted her head then and looked over. Her eyes were pale. Her skin was pale. Guilt and love washed over Chloe; Bridget didn't look sick, but she did look exhausted. Sleeping nineteen hours a day did that to you. What she needed was a good walk in the fresh air, some exercise. A man, some company, at least, who wasn't just Mrs Singh and a gossip-fest.

Mum gave a weak *about time too* smile. 'Well, apology accepted, our Chloe.'

'Apology? What? Since when was *I should have asked you in the first place*, an apology?'

Another eye roll. 'A mother knows when you're sorry, even if you don't know it yourself.'

'I have nothing to be sorry for.'

'And. Neither. Do. I.' There was a harrumph and a shake of the head. 'Now do you want me to fix your messes, or not, Chloe Cassidy?'

'Yes, please. And thank you.' That kernel of love bloomed into a knobbly pain in Chloe's chest and a sting at the back of her eyes. Because she knew that whatever mess Chloe made, she'd always have her mum's support. Support that really should be a two-way thing, regardless of the past. But it was still fresh and raw, and there were too many questions, personal questions, that Chloe wanted answers to that she was sure her mum wouldn't want asked.

They would get there, she supposed, but in the meantime, they had to shuffle over the hurdles of hurt pride and betrayal, and that could be a long and bumpy road.

And so Bridget sat, back rigid and taut, mouth pursed in concentration and repressed annoyance, pins sticking out from her lips as she fixed up the fabric into a neat pile of curtain swags. The woman was a sewing genius.

And, at times, a royal pain in the arse. The difficult silence was split by the doorbell.

The cavalry? Someone? Anyone?

Grateful for a diversion, Chloe dashed to the door, expecting another delivery or something for the upstairs people who were always getting things by courier. She hauled the door open and inhaled sharply as she blinked into the late afternoon light. *Vaughn?* 'Vaughn?'

He was standing on her doorstep, hands shoved deep in leather jacket pockets, hair tousled by the cold northwesterly. He nodded, gave a brief hesitant smile and rocked back on his heels, looking far more attractive than he had any right too. 'Bad time?'

Trying to calm her auto-response drumming heart rate, she stepped back and let him in. 'Not at all. Come on in. How did you know where I live?'

'Your website has your contact details, and I would change that to a PO Box if I were you. You never know who might just turn up.'

'Hmmm. Good point. I mean, anyone could just turn up, right? Uninvited?'

He grinned. 'Exactly. I was passing, and I owe you an apology for the other week.' He followed her into the front room. As she turned, Chloe caught the slight raise of the eyebrows as he noted Mum on the couch. 'Hello.'

'Oh good, someone who actually knows when they're apologising.' Mum sat back in the chair, clutching the fabric in her hands, and waited, as if she was watching a movie and she'd just got to the best bit. 'This should be good. Don't mind me, go right ahead and say it. Your apology.'

Oh, God, really? 'Thank you, Mum, but isn't it time you were going?' Chloe tried, and failed, to give Mum a telepathic hitch up and out the room. The telepathy thing clearly only worked with Jenna.

Bridget pushed the fabric towards Chloe and rolled her eyes again.

I will never do that to my kids, Chloe promised silently. Or lie to them.

'Chloe Cassidy, do you want me to finish fixing your mess or not?' She pointed an accusatory finger at Vaughn. 'Is this another man from that Timber dating thing? Because you remember what happened last time? Ah, no… that wasn't Timber, was it? That was the online dating thing? Right you are.' She smiled at Vaughn and explained slowly as if letting him on a huge secret, which it was, or at least had been, 'We had the police round, *again*…'

Only she pronounced it *po*-lice, in a tone that was deeply unsympathetic.

Chloe's cheeks burned. It was fast becoming her normal whenever her mother or Vaughn were around. Having them both in the same room meant she was doomed to look like a beetroot forever. 'No. Mum. Please. Really, Vaughn, it's nothing like that.'

'Like what?' He grinned, clearly eager for the secret-spilling to continue. '*Timber?* Online dating? Chloe? You never mentioned this.'

Before she could answer, Bridget cut in. 'She's after a man, you know. Since The Jilting.'

'The Jilting.' He pressed his lips together as if holding in a snort. 'It has a title, like it was an official event? Like, The Diamond Jubilee? The World Cup? The Jilting.'

Let me die. Now. 'No. Who'd do anything like that? No, Mum, he has nothing to do with online anything. This is Vaughn. *Vaughn Brooks.*'

'Brooks.' Mum's eyes narrowed, and she tapped her foot, her way of trying to jog her memory. Very little of what Bridget Cassidy did made sense to anyone but her. 'Brooks. Aren't you… didn't you… weren't you…? How do I know you? You look familiar.'

'Yes, Mum, you have met him before. Very briefly. Vaughn, this is my mum, Bridget.'

He stuck out his hand. 'Vaughn Brooks, Jason's best man. Yes. Hello, again.'

Bridget stared at his hand, but she didn't take it. 'And what are you doing here?' Her eyes pigged towards Chloe. 'Chloe? Why's he here?'

'I'm helping Chloe with her…' Vaughn drew his hand back, smiled a soft secret smile, then looked at the material and the nautical things out on the desk. 'Navy wedding?'

Thank you, Lord, for a change of subject. Chloe grasped it. 'Not exactly. Taylor used to sing on a cruise ship. He likes boats and thought it was appropriate.'

A frown. 'The wife-to-be? Naval at all?'

'No, *he's* a dentist. Nathan. Gay wedding,' she explained. 'The pink pound's normally a goldmine, so I'm hopeful of getting more work from this. It's going to be spectacular.' Or would have been had she not stuffed up the chair backs. Still, they were fixed. Crisis over. Thank God for Mum.

Vaughn scratched his head and again had that look as if he was trying hard to keep up. 'Oh. A wedding, on a boat.'

'A *love boat*. Lots of people get married on boats. It's a thing… a theme. More common than you'd think, actually, and even more poignant for them because of Taylor's past on the cruise ship.' Chloe shook her head in despair. 'It doesn't have to make sense, Vaughn. It's love.'

'Oh yeah.' He scratched his head, looking bemused and incredulous. As if love was something that made his head hurt rather than his heart soar. Sore, maybe, and Chloe knew all about that.

Bridget butted in, fixing him with her evil eye. 'And you've come to help our Chloe with…?'

Please, for the love of God, leave the man alone.

Vaughn stuck his hands back in his pockets. 'Her brochures. I've also got a proposition.'

Now Bridget looked straight at Chloe. 'Say yes.'

'Mum!'

'Beggars can't be choosers, Chloe.'

'Please, Mum, you don't know what he's here for. He might be wanting to sell me into the slave trade.'

'Good luck with that. I hope they don't want you to do any sewing for them. Or cooking for that matter. She's a useless homemaker, Mr Brooks. Good with numbers, though. Know anyone who wants a slave administrator? She's your girl.'

Chloe glared and mouthed *shut up* to her mum, then turned back to Vaughn. 'Kitchen? We can talk without interruptions there.'

'No need.' Bridget gathered up the fabric into neat piles and shuffled to standing. 'Don't worry about me. I know when I'm not wanted.'

Far from being glad her mum was leaving, Chloe's gut knotted up. Things between them were a long way from back to normal. Then she looked over at Vaughn; things had never been normal there. Back to her mum. 'You don't have to go, Mum. Seriously. Stay.'

Vaughn took a step forward. 'No, please don't leave on my account, Mrs Cassidy. What I have to say to Chloe can be said in front of you, don't worry, it isn't an inappropriate proposition. I'm not going to sell her into the slave trade.'

'More's the pity. But never mind. Three's a crowd, right you are. I'll take this, Chloe, and fix your mess up good and proper. Be sure to pop round later, if you're not too busy, then. We have some talking to do.' For a second, her Mum was serious and focused. 'There's things I need to say.'

'Yes, Mum.' Chloe walked her to the door and gave her a hug, holding on just a little longer, hoping the healing properties would help her Mum. Help them both. 'I'll call round later. And thank you. Really. You're a star.'

'Yes, and don't forget it.' She was gone in a huff and a quick slam of the door.

Silence.

And then, as Jenna would say, there were two.

CHAPTER 13

There was a grin the size of Cheshire on Vaughn's smug face. He was still standing in the middle of the room, filling the space with his height and his presence. Her apartment felt shabby in comparison with his bright aura, which was still guarded, but it shone. Just shone. She tried to look at her place from his eyes, then remembered the chaos of his office.

Then she forgot about that and was just captivated by his eyes, glittering and steely grey as they were, while he laughed. 'Timber? Chloe, really? Any luck?'

'No. It was hideous. I don't want to talk about it. Why are you here?'

His shoulders seemed to tense up. 'Like I said, I owe you an apology for walking out on Saturday.'

Saturday. The almost-kiss scenario. The hours afterwards of quiet, but insistent sexual frustration. More dreams of food porn. 'You don't have to apologise, really. Honestly, it's fine.'

'It's not fine at all. So, I'm sorry.'

'Aha.' She tapped her foot, because in her language, that meant she was waiting impatiently for more.

He frowned as he looked down at her tapping boot. 'What's the matter?'

'I'm waiting.'

'For?'

Chloe sighed. *Men.* 'An explanation.'

'You want an explanation? An apology isn't enough?'

'No. I'm not entirely sure what you're sorry about. The fact that you left in a hurry, or the fact that you... I thought you might... Vaughn, why did you just up and leave like that? Explain yourself.'

'That's not fair. Usually, an apology is enough.' He shook his head and thrust his hands back into his pockets. But after a second, his mouth twisted into a thoughtful kind of pout that had a smile in it. 'But this isn't usual, is it? Okay then, I'll trade you. An explanation for an explanation.'

Her heart thrummed. 'An explanation about what?'

'What happened'—he made quote marks with his fingers as he said the next words— "*last time—more* po-*lice?*"

She couldn't help laughing at his woeful interpretation of her mother's accent. 'Not bloody likely. Not going there. At all. Some things have got to stay private.'

'Too bad.' A shrug of lovely broad shoulders. 'Then you can accept my apology without an explanation, and we're both off the hook.'

'I can see right through your games, but you've chosen the wrong person to play with.' And was it hot in here? Ever since he'd stepped foot in her apartment, the temperature had skyrocketed. And did he need to push his sleeves up on his sweater so she could see his muscular arms and the tiny dark hairs that accentuated his many trips to European sunspots?

She leant across the table-cum-desk and pulled the rickety sash window open. Strains of music from the market billowed in along with a gentle spring breeze and the smell of Thai cooking. The whole of Portobello probably knew about the *po-lice* by now. Mrs Singh wasn't just the sari shop owner; she was the human version of The London Evening Standard. Like it or not, Vaughn was a local business owner, so at some point Chloe's goings-on would filter back to him, either at a small business network meeting or generally through the loudhailer dressed in a gold and red traditional Indian dress, chatting loudly to anyone who'd listen in the middle of Portobello Road.

Chloe turned to him, her heart thrilling as her gaze settled on his face. A dark rush of heat ran through her. 'Okay, Vaughn, I'll tell you my sordid story, if you tell me yours.'

The smile grew. 'How old are you, Chloe Cassidy? Five? You go first.'

'How old are you? Six?'

But he kept his mouth firmly shut and glared, looking as if he could comfortably stand there all night and not utter a single word. And she so wanted to know about his dark, sad past that there was nothing to do except talk. 'Okaaaay. There was a date, and it went badly, but I was late home, and Mum called the police. Your turn.'

'How badly?' His fists were curled tight by his sides, and her breath hitched a little at his response. He was agitated because the date had gone badly? Maybe he was the rescuer type? Maybe that was why he'd broken Jason's news to her at the altar, and why he was so helpful at the wedding? It was just his natural default.

But then she thought about his brooding eyes, standoff looks, the way he'd argued with Laura and his admission about not wanting complications. He wasn't a rescuer. Far from it. He was a leaver. A loner. A heartbreaker, no doubt, too.

His heartbreaker eyes narrowed. 'Did he hurt you? Drug you? Chloe, you can't be too careful these days.'

'No! No, it was nothing like that. Seriously. It was just, well...' She thought about poor *DrewsAmused*—what a lot of nonsense over a harmless meeting—and laughed. 'It was all just a little surreal. Now, don't think you can get out of it that easily. It's your turn, so spill,' she urged.

Vaughn took a breath, eyes no longer glittering, now just a dull polished steel. 'I had a relationship a few years ago, and it didn't work out the way I hoped it would.'

That was it? That was all he was prepared to say? 'I gathered all that last time you refused to speak about it. But that's all the details you're prepared to give?'

'It's around about the same number of syllables as you. And as opaque. Your choice, Chloe.' The look he gave her was insistent and assertive, and she knew that for things to move forward in any way, she had to be honest with him.

She went in to the kitchen and called back, 'Drink first?'

'In the afternoon? Must be serious.' He followed her, leaning against the doorframe as she opened and closed cupboards trying to find some long-lost booze.

'If I have to spill my guts to you, then yes, I need a drink.'

'Sure. If you like.' His eyebrows rose as he watched her scoot down and search in the lower cupboards. And yes, they needed work. They were a chipped, scratched, cheap pine from another decade, and to a sophisticated kitchen person's eye, like Vaughn's, they must have seemed very twee. Or just plain bad taste. Certainly not in the food-porn league of his steel professional kitchen. Her kitchen needed work. Or rather, a bomb. Jason had been about to rip it out—no. No more Jason. His cousin grinned. 'What do you have?'

'Aha. I knew they were in there somewhere.' Wishing she

was offering him something grand, akin to his dream-inducing mouth-watering morsels, she pulled two sticky bottles out and presented them to him. Hardly food porn generating. Probably not even fit for consumption. 'Crème de menthe or Jägermeister?'

'Bleurgh.' He looked as if he was about to throw up as he scanned the bottles and the sticky ooze down the sides. 'No. But thank you, anyway.'

'If I'm honest, they're probably all well past their use by dates. I think I bought them for Jenna's twenty-first, which was... five years ago? Yeah, I'm twenty-eight, and she's two years younger. Yes, five years. Anyhoo, I'm not a regular drinker.'

His mouth contorted as if he'd swallowed a ball of acid. 'So I gather. I should have brought wine. I'll stick to tea. No? Coffee? No? Ah well, hit me with it—not the crème de menthe or the Jägermeister—the po-lice thing, or you won't get the photos or my proposition.'

'Bloody hell, you drive a hard bargain.'

'So I've been told. It's part of my charm.' He looked at the frown on her face. Eyebrows rising more as he gave a kind of *I give in* shrug. 'Or not. Talk.'

So she leant against her trusty ancient wood-effect melamine kitchen counter and told him about the Cassidy Curse and Jenna's Love Plan, about *TheBigCarlhuna* and his guitar and long, pale fingers and the coffee-stained goodbye note, and about *DrewsAmused* and the dog in the bag. Surprisingly, Vaughn managed to keep a reasonably straight face. Although she did omit to mention the blue smurf fluff escapade, because that was going just a little too deep into her personal life and he hadn't earned anything like a preview into that territory as yet. Verbally or otherwise.

When she'd finished, he leant back and smothered a grin. 'So, well. I was right—nothing is straightforward with you at all. But why would you go to all that trouble just for a wedding date?'

Her cheeks heated, because even though the humiliation was great enough when she talked about her dating failures, it was utterly complete with the explanation as to why. 'Because for some dumb reason, I told you I was bringing a plus-one. It was on the hoof, and I dug a huge hole and promptly jumped right into it. But more, it was really because I wanted to prove to them that I was still someone. To you all.'

'You are someone, Chloe Cassidy, and you're worth a million more than them.'

Something bloomed fierce in the centre of her chest. He was very, very good for her ego. And yet still she didn't tell him about Jason and his dating profile. 'Now, your turn.'

Oddly, he reached into his pocket and pulled out a USB stick with the *Vaughn's* restaurant logo. Then he wandered back through to the lounge, calling through, 'Actually before I forget, here's a stick with my photos. I was going to email them to you, but there's quite a few of them, and they're quite big files. I wasn't sure if your internet connection would be up to big downloads. I thought you might want to have them all together.'

'That's kind, thank you.' She popped the USB stick onto the coffee table and then folded her arms, waiting for him to talk about his past.

'Grab your laptop and we can make a start choosing some good ones for the brochures. I've also added some samples of my flyers and the address of my guy who will do them on the cheap for you.' He flicked his wrist out and checked the time. 'I've got dinner starting soon, so I can't stay long. How about we have a quick look?'

She pulled out her laptop and loaded the photos. On the larger screen, they were very good. He tugged the machine towards him and made a few clicks. 'See, if you crop this one, it pulls the table flowers into focus. And this one... look, the movie backdrop with the yellow brick road swerving off to the right draws your eyes. You could have your logo up there at the top where the road ends.'

Chloe dragged up a chair and sat next to him, mesmerised by his hands as he worked. They were large hands, solid and safe with a history she knew nothing about. A history she suddenly was desperate to learn. 'You're avoiding telling me the story, aren't you?'

His eyes were kind but still guarded. 'Nothing gets past you, does it? Chloe, this isn't the time. But safe to say, I'm not a great bet when it comes to relationships. So, in case... you know, the friends thing and the dancing? I don't do long term.' He patted his chest over his heart. 'Scarred for life, I'm afraid.'

Loved and lost. Her heart squeezed a little, but instead of being disappointed, her estimation of him increased tenfold. He was at least honest, as she'd imagined he would be. And that made everything a million times worse. Because the better he became, the higher her chance was of actually liking him. She did not want to like Vaughn Brooks. 'You're like Jenna.'

'Possibly.'

'She won't take any more risks either.'

He frowned again. 'It's not about taking risks. It's about...' He ran a hand through his hair and grimaced. 'It's about taking risks.'

'And you're telling me this, why?'

'Self-protection, really.' Well, geez, the man was definitely honest, which made it even more dangerous to be with him. She didn't know much about honest men; she was realising. 'And for your own good.'

'Thank you, but it's fine. Really. I'm not looking for anything either. I'm through with love. Completely. In fact, I'd go as far as to say I don't believe in it.'

'Really?' He actually looked affronted.

She tried to explain. 'Okay, hear me out on this. How can love be such a great thing if it tears you up inside? If it breaks your heart?'

'Then it wasn't love. Not a true kind of love. That's got to come from both sides. One plus one makes a whole lot more than two. It makes a whole world.'

'Well, wow.' He'd had that, she guessed, an all-consuming, giving and taking, non-selfish love. That once in a lifetime thing. 'I lucked out then. What with the curse and everything. I don't even want to try to find it.'

'So you say.' He made a few more clicks of the mouse and cropped a photo of the wedding cake and copied and pasted it onto a mock-up of a business flyer. Then he rotated it a few degrees sideways. 'Hence the online dating thing?'

'Don't make things sound more complicated than they are. I just needed a wedding date, and you know why.' The man was a marvel at Photoshop or crop or whatever it was. But it was all just hedging. She tried to sound casual and light but failed as her voice wobbled and came out high-pitched and a little intense. 'And… the Lost Love?'

His hand froze over the touchpad. 'Lost love?'

'Sorry, the relationship that didn't work out the way you hoped it would?'

His fingers tensed, and as she watched, that tension spiral through his arm, his shoulder and his jaw, and he looked so devastated, she regretted pushing him. Because whatever he was going to say, she didn't want to hear come from his mouth. 'No more questions now, Chloe, okay? But yeah… she died.'

And that bombshell was meant to stop her asking more questions? It wasn't as if she hadn't imagined that would be the case. Who would have gone to such an extent to purge themselves, as he had done? Travelling the world, immersing himself in his business and making sure there were no connections made. Oh, and the whole *scarred heart* thing.

'So, you are like Jenna then. You two have a lot in common.'

'Not something I want to have in common with anyone.' She could see he'd closed down and shut himself off emotionally. He hadn't wanted to talk about it, and she'd pushed him too far.

'No, of course not. I'm sorry. I just meant, she'd understand.'

'I don't think anyone does, Chloe, not really.'

They sat for a few minutes staring at the computer screen in silence, yet seeing nothing except maybe a little deeper into territory it was probably inadvisable to explore. And Chloe wondered what it was like to have loved someone so utterly that it meant you weren't willing to give even a part of yourself up in case the same thing happened again.

She realised now that, whilst she'd thought she'd loved Jason, it had been more a familiar love than a desperate, soul-mate kind of thing. At a young age, she'd decided he'd do, and they'd got on with it.

Part of her yearned for that kind of once in a lifetime connection, but the sensible part of her knew it was uplifting and fulfilling and ultimately, possibly, damaging—if it didn't work out well. Like Jenna. And her Mum. And Vaughn. All of whom had decided to have an unfulfilled life rather than risk it all again.

He shrugged, seemingly dispelling the cloak of poignancy that shrouded him. 'Right, let's talk about my proposition?'

'Okay. Are you sure you want to still make it, given that neither of us are keen for... anything?' God, the lies were pouring out of her now. She was keen for a kiss. Did that make her shallow? She wanted to kiss away the pain that had clouded his eyes at the mention of his woman's death, to soothe the crack in his voice.

'Yes, this is purely business, Chloe. I'm in the market for an administration person, as you know, and you need some cash flow. So, I wondered whether you'd be willing to take on the task until I can find someone permanent?'

'You're offering me a temp job?' Now she just felt ridiculous. Of course it was about work; he wasn't going to make a prop-osition about… *that*. 'You're offering me a temp job that has nothing to do with event planning?'

'It has everything to do with event planning. I have daily phone calls from people wanting to hire my restaurant. Even yesterday I had a call from a film company wanting to use it as part of a set, but I'm juggling the phones and the cooking. I haven't had time to look for someone to take over. I'm too busy. It's a classic chicken-egg scenario. I need someone to help me find more time, but I haven't the time to look for them.'

He paused and weighed up her reaction, which she was trying to hide under a smile she'd plastered onto her lips as she nodded for him to continue. He'd told her he didn't want complicated, but surely working with him would make things a zillion times more complicated, especially when being in the same room as him made her want to kiss him, to lay her head against his chest and breathe in the strength and calm he exuded.

'The way I see it, it makes sense, Chloe. I'm too busy with the restaurant, and you're having a lull. Just for a month or so? It'll give you easy cash, and you can work on your business from my office—once you tidy it—if you need to, and find me a permanent member of staff at the same time.'

'I don't know. I really don't want to work in a restaurant; that's not what I had in mind.'

His gaze met hers and held there for a few moments. When

she didn't agree or turn away, he shook his head. 'Okay, well, it was just an idea. But now I really do need to shoot because I've left Jacques in charge and I don't want to do it too often. Think about it, at least?'

'Okay, okay, I will.' Beggars can't be choosers, as her mum had said. She walked him to the door and held it open as he stepped through, taking a little of her heart with him. Because, even though the special people in her life were all about protecting their own hearts, Chloe had a bad feeling that hers had a mind of its own and was hell bent on falling for the totally wrong kind of person.

The kind that just couldn't fall for her.

CHAPTER 14

So, is that it? You're giving up on *Something Borrowed*? On us?' Jenna's voice, down the phone, sounded exasperated and tired. 'Mum said he was round last evening, all smiles and beautiful eyes.'

Chloe took a deep breath. Discussing this was only going to add more resentment. After twenty-four hours of thinking things over, she had decided to take Vaughn up on his offer. Spurred largely by the telephone call from her bank manager yesterday refusing an increase in the overdraft. She was going to work on his business because she couldn't afford to work on her own. Yeah, a classic chicken-egg thing, indeed. 'Don't be silly. I'm still 100 per cent committed to our business. I'm just helping him out. It's only temporary.'

'But you might learn to love it. You might never want to work with us again. Mum also said that when you came round to pick up the curtain tie-backs, you barely said a word. That you didn't stay for a cuppa, or want to chat.' Her sister's voice rose a little. 'Are you going off us, is that it? Because, Chloe, Mum knows things aren't right. You just have to give her a chance to explain.'

'I will, I promise. I just didn't feel like talking much last night. I was tired, and she was watching Ghost Hunters. It didn't seem like the right time to nut out something so personal as what the heck happened to Daddy.' Truth be known, Chloe was reeling from the strange feelings Vaughn instilled in her and worrying about having this conversation. 'You must know you are my priority. The business is my priority. I'm still going to be working with you and Mum. *Something Borrowed* is always going to be the most important thing to me, after you and Evie. And Mum, obviously. I just need…' *To pay the bills.* 'To fill my time and flex my administrative muscles. This is a good opportunity to keep my skills up to date.'

'But you won't be able to spend any extra time growing *our* business.'

'The one I spend every waking hour on?' And some sleeping ones. When she wasn't having food-porn dreams. 'Oh, don't worry, I will. I'll make sure of it. And Vaughn's got some great ideas and is going to help me design a flyer for the wedding fayre.'

'*Vaughn. Vaughn. Vaughn.* What's going on there, Chlo? What's with the sudden interest? I thought you were sworn off men?'

'I am, and it's not like that between us.' Just like that, another lie; they were coming thick and fast and tripped off her lips with ease these days. 'Besides which, the Love Plan was your idea in the first place. What was all that about if you didn't want me to find someone?'

'I do. But not Vaughn. He's… grumpy. And too close to Jason, who broke your heart.'

'Trust me, Jenna. There will not be another heart breaking.

Not for me and definitely not by Vaughn. He seems quite decent, actually, underneath it all. He doesn't want any involvement; he's not interested in me like that. We're friends, which is nice. And, bottom line, it's a temporary job. It's money in the bank, not a bloody marriage proposal.'

* * *

'Here I am, reporting for duty, sir.' Chloe walked through the restaurant doors, breathing in the delicious smells of garlic and cinnamon and cumin. At least, that was what she thought they were. In truth, it could have been parsley, sage, rosemary and thyme, for all she knew.

'Excellent. Er… I'll give you a proper tour this time.' Once again, in his own environment, Vaughn seemed a little distracted. He was, she mused, very dedicated to his business and creating mouth-watering gems for the public. She followed him into the sparkling, pristine, industrial kitchen, relieved to see there was an order and pride here that he clearly didn't have for bits of paper. They would make a good team because she did paper very well.

'The kitchen. As you can see, we've already started prep.' He pointed to the stacks of vegetables sitting on kitchen paper. 'Salting the aubergines before I roast them. If you get hungry or thirsty, please help yourself to things from this fridge here. This is for staff use. That one'—he pointed to a huge stainless steel industrial fridge—'is for restaurant use only. Do not touch it.'

Touch it? She could barely breathe at the sight of it. Her dreams came back to her in full sensual replay. Heat shimmied through her, scooting through her veins, melting into her gut. Her breath caught in her throat. Yep, that was pretty much the whole food-porn fridge, right there.

Frightened he might see something of it in her eyes, she

turned away. This was a huge mistake. How could she work here with him, so close, and yet be lukewarm in her reactions to him?

'Hungry?' He smiled. 'I could fix you something?'

'No. Not at all. Let's just get on with what needs to be done. I've decided to work three days a week for you. Will that be enough to tide you over?' She'd calculated the minimum she needed to bring in and would work for that. Stuck between appeasing Jenna and helping Vaughn, she was willing to compromise. 'I do need to work on my business too.'

His smile faded. 'I was hoping for something more full-time.'

'I can't. It's that or nothing, I'm afraid. I'm squeezing my time as it is.'

'Okay. Then let's make a start. If I only get you for a few hours, I need to make the most of you.' And did his eyes glitter just a little as his smile found its way back?

Two hours later, he stalked into the office, bringing with him a morning tea snack of freshly baked and still warm scones, real butter, what looked like homemade jam and a large pot of coffee. 'Break time. How's it all going?'

Chloe looked around at the organised piles she'd carved through his chaos. 'I've managed to file most things into some kind of order, and I'm making my way through the urgent invoices. Did you know you spend a phenomenal amount of money on laundry?'

'It's a necessity.'

'I appreciate that, but can't you shop around for better quotes? These seem a little over the top.'

His eyebrows furrowed. 'I could. But I don't have time. Could you?'

She nodded. 'I'll add it to my ever-growing list.'

'Excellent.' He plunged the coffee, poured and handed her a cup. 'How's your business going?'

'Hmmm. The wedding on Saturday should help. Actually, they live close to here. If you want, I could make some recommendations for you? Slip this restaurant into the conversation? Have you got some more business cards? I could add them to the gift packs on the sly? Just drop them in.'

'Er... no. We need to order some more? I use Printworks—'

'I'll add it to the list. Consider it done.'

'Excellent. Now eat.' He pushed the plate towards her.

'Wow.' She looked at her thin frame, which wasn't as thin as it had been. 'If you keep bringing me food, I'm going to be the size of a horse. Jason used to say I was getting chubby—'

'Don't talk about Jason.' It wasn't a suggestion. It was an order. *What the hell?* He stared at her, clearly surprised at his own vehemence. Then checked himself. 'By which I mean, you can talk about anything or anyone you like, Chloe. And you can damned well eat what you like too.'

'Yes. Yes, I can.' So she did. A scone with cream and jam. Then another one, and they were melt-in-the-mouth soft and sweet. The coffee was brewed to perfection, strong and earthy. He watched with a wry smile as she drained the last drop. 'That was definitely what I needed.'

'You looked as if you were enjoying it.' And there—right there in his eyes—was the heat and the need mirrored back at her. It was more erotic than the food-porn dream. Although, it was a close run thing.

Oblivious to anything else, they sat there grinning at each other for a few moments. God knew what was going on in his head, but in Chloe's, there was a running commentary. *He's so bloody gorgeous. Those eyes, dark and mysterious, yet honest and open. Those hands. God, those hands... the things they could do. The feelings they induced. And his breathing seems a bit fast. Is it? Is his breathing as fast as mine? And God...*

He drew his eyes away and picked up his coffee cup. 'Okay, I have an idea. Not a life-changing one, but food for thought. At the very least it might be inspirational.'

'Yes?'

'It's my turn to go to the market tomorrow to speak to the suppliers and put in an order for the weekend. With me taking time off for the wedding last Saturday, it's not fair to ask Jacques to cook and order all week. If he's extra lucky, I'll even suggest we keep the menu as we have it today. Such a shame Laura has gone. She'd have enjoyed seeing me with egg on my face.'

So no rampant sex in the office then? More's the pity. 'And what's this got to do with my business?'

'Just a loose idea. Maybe you need to diversify a little? Up for some fun? Smithfield market's got some great venues for weddings; it's apparently haunted too. There's a lot of history there.'

The coffee was buzzing around her system, but the heat in the room was making her laconic. It was a strange juxtaposition; feeling both wired and loose-limbed at the same time. But underneath everything was a constant thread of tension that had wormed its way into her bones. Her head was constantly working overtime and finding things to worry about. Maybe a bit of fun would release some of that pressure.

And hell, Jason's parting text to her had been particularly cutting: *The fun went out of it a long time ago, Chlo. Actually, the fun went out of you.*

'Haunted? My mum would be interested in that. She's taken to ghost hunting for some reason. And that's given me another idea. What do you think about haunted parties? Mum seems to have a few strangely-dressed friends if her Facebook page is anything to go by. Maybe I could tap into that? Ghost weddings? Haunted parties?'

He made a face that told her he wasn't convinced. 'I'm not

sure how to answer that, and definitely not qualified to, but why not?'

'Okay. Well, it might be something else to add to my portfolio. Let's do it. The market.'

'Right. Excellent. I'll pick you up at six.' He was gathering the plates and cups together onto the tray, and she stood and squeezed past him to get back to the desk. Another lung full of his scent had her shallow breathing. She straddled a pile of papers and then found herself slipping sideways as her foot lost purchase on... A football? What the hell—?

'Watch yourself, there.' He reached a hand to her waist to steady her. It was warm through the soft fabric of her cardigan. He was all too close again, with a tight hold on her. 'Whoa.' Her body went on full blush-alert and tingles pinged across her skin. She wiggled away and picked up the football. 'Really? A ball in a restaurant?'

'Why not? Sometimes we take it to Holland Park and have a quick game.'

'It's an office.'

'It's storage. It's the dumping ground.' He ticked the list off on his fingers. 'It's the staff changing room, so be warned, you may find semi-naked men in here from time to time. It's also the party room, the counselling room and the engine room, where we brainstorm menu ideas.'

'And now, it's my office.' She tried for authoritarian but laced with a tease, as she put the ball into his empty hand. The one that had come too close to her skin. 'So no more balls. Or anything else that shouldn't be in here. Okay?'

He nodded and the easy glint was back. 'Yes, ma'am. Noted. No balls.'

She couldn't stop the laugh. 'Right you are. Now, six o'clock, you said? Why don't we just go straight from here after work?'

'No. Six tomorrow morning.'

'In the morning?' Well, at least it wouldn't infringe on her working day. 'When do you sleep?'

'I don't. Much.' She wasn't sure if it was the thought of his hand pressing gently on her back or his next words that made her shiver. Either way, it made the promise of seeing him tomorrow a little more dangerous. 'Not if I can find something more interesting to be doing.'

'Like what?' The words were out before she could stop them. And, despite the warnings and his hands-off approach, the man's hands had most definitely been on. She wanted to feel them not just on her waist or her cheek, but all over her.

This was so not going to work.

He stopped short, and the earth began to tilt in a strange way as he looked at her. But his voice held another warning. 'Chloe—'

'I know. It's okay.' She swallowed, and her mouth was wet, but her throat was dry. It was so easy to say things, but feeling them was another thing altogether.

'Don't—'

'I know, Vaughn.' Her hands shook and her legs were like jelly, without thinking through the consequences, she reached out and gripped his wrist.

He put the tray and the football down on the desk and then held her hands just as tight, his forehead resting, like last time, on hers. 'No, you don't know anything, Chloe. You don't know how bloody hard this is right now.'

'I do know.' But unlike last time, she was not going to let him walk away until this business was sorted, once and for all.

His hand cupped her cheek. 'Because—'

'I know. I *know*, Vaughn.' She was pretending that she was in control when in reality, her heart pounded, her hands were clammy, and she felt dizzy with daring, adrenalin and so much need.

She reached for his waist, tugged gently at him, urging him to do what she'd wanted him to do for so long. And despite all the reasons not to, she wanted to feel him against her. To taste him. There was no way she could stop even if she wanted to.

With a daring she didn't know she possessed, she tiptoed up and pressed her mouth against his. She felt a little resistance as the shock registered. Then, with a groan, he returned the kiss. Soft and tentative at first, he nibbled on her bottom lip, snagging it in his teeth. Another groan tore from him as he finally gave in to whatever it was that he'd been fighting.

Then he kissed her full and open-mouthed as his hand tightened around the back of her head, hauling her closer.

He tasted of all things male. Divine, like his food. Like him. Like nothing she'd ever experienced before. Like everything she'd imagined and more. Heat curled around her, around them, locking them in a world of just two. This was what she'd been dreaming of.

All he needed to do now was feed her dainty morsels by the light of his industrial fridge—

'Chloe.' He pulled away a little, not enough to deter her, and his hand was still on her cheek, but there was definitely distance. 'We can't. I said… you know why.'

'I know. I know. I know.' Her voice was surprisingly throaty, and she was shocked at how wanton she sounded. 'It's complicated. I'm complicated.'

'Yes. Very.'

'I don't want to stop.' She turned her head away, but he pulled her to face him again. Time stretched for a few moments as he looked at her with so much regret and desire and growing passion.

'Neither do I, but… Goddamn.' He fisted his hands in her hair as he tried to gain control. But she saw the moment he stopped trying to be the good man; in a deep breath, a curse and a decision made. His voice was hoarse and thick with need. 'Who doesn't have a little complication in their lives every now and then?'

'Yes. That. That exactly.' It was still difficult to haul oxygen into her lungs as every cell in her body hummed with fierce desire.

'And hell, there's only so much I can resist.'

'So don't.'

'That easy?' Then his mouth slammed on hers, a decisive act that told her just how much he wanted her, just how much trouble they were in, and just how deep she was falling, even with his warnings and her own promises.

He walked her backwards and crushed her against the door, capturing her hands above her head, his tongue dancing with hers. Then he kissed a trail along her cheek, her neck, and on to that place just behind her earlobe that made her squirm with delight.

And in turn, she found a place on his throat that smelt so delicious she nuzzled against it, relishing the strength in his body, in the heart that beat rapidly against her ribcage. His hands held her tight, and yet with a tenderness she'd barely known could exist from a man so big and so strong.

Then his hand found her breast and she melted against him as he stroked first over her top then under it. And she responded by pressing herself against him. Closer. Ever closer.

She heard a moan and realised with a shock that it was her. When had Jason ever made her moan?

She banished all thoughts of Vaughn's cousin from her head. But they fought their way back.

She'd had her heart broken—more, she'd had her trust deci-
mated by a man who was a blood relative of Vaughn.

She opened her eyes and saw, over his shoulder, the wall of
photographs. The stark reminder of what Vaughn had lost and
what he held so dear, and his determination not to get involved
rang in her ears.

Scarred, he'd said. *Scared*, she thought. But who could blame
him? He'd lost the love of his life, and Chloe would be forever
competing with that. With a ghost, a memory, with someone
capable of shattering his heart.

And now he was capable of doing the same thing to hers.
Because if this wasn't getting involved, she didn't know what was.

So for the first time in her life, she knew it was her turn to
walk away. But she wouldn't be like all those men who hadn't had
the balls to face her. She'd deal with it head on.

She managed to wriggle away from him, pulling her arms
down and pushing lightly on his chest.

The moment she did it, and he stepped back frowning, she
regretted it. But it was the right thing to do, for him. For them.
'You're right, Vaughn. We shouldn't be doing this. There are too
many reasons why not.'

For a few moments, he looked at her. His eyes were kind
and sad and heated as he tugged her top straight and pressed
his mouth to the bridge of her nose. 'Yes, you're right. I'm sorry.
Sorry.'

Worse thing was, he looked it too.

She dug very, very deep and found a quiet equilibrium—on
the outside at least—and gave him a smile that she just knew
would be fake and overdone, but it was the very best she could
muster given the circumstances. 'Nothing to be sorry for. It was
an itch, and we scratched it. But I don't think I'll be coming to
the markets tomorrow if that's okay with you?'

His eyes briefly shuttered closed. 'No. Maybe not.'

'And we should probably keep the office door open in future. That is, if you still want me here?'

He was all business as he reached for the tray and the ball, and he gave her a regretful smile that didn't stretch to his eyes. Damn it, it barely reached his mouth. 'Of course I do. I think we both need you to work here, Chloe. But no kissing from now on, okay?'

'No kissing. Good idea. Good job. Right then, let's get on to it.' She gestured to the door and ushered him towards it. 'Come on, skedaddle. I've got people to phone. Things to do.' *Feelings to compartmentalise.*

He left without a single glance backwards. And, as she slumped against the wall and tried to cool down, she wondered exactly why it was that giving in to temptation was always so much easier than fighting it.

CHAPTER 15

*C*hloe, darling, this has been the best day of my life. And it's absolutely down to you. Thank you, thank you, thank you. I love this boat; it's all been perfect. I just want this night to last forever.' Taylor may well have been one drink short of a barf, but he was a very, very happy drunk. The perfect client, in fact. No sarcastic comments, no barbs about Chloe's woeful love life and best of all... there were no exes hanging around with pregnancy news. Yes, keeping business and personal life completely separate was infinitely better for her blood pressure, her mental health and her bank balance—if the large tip Taylor had added to Chloe's bill was anything to go by.

Plus, she'd been so busy having fun dancing the night away on the love boat that she hadn't thought about that kiss once.

Well, maybe once. Or twice. Okay—so when the grooms had stared into each other's eyes and then kissed so gently during their first dance, Chloe had felt a rush of heat as she'd remembered the way Vaughn's lips had met hers. The tingle through her body as he'd deepened the kiss. The heat of his hands on her skin...

'Chloe? You okay?' Taylor looked a little concerned.

Rallying herself, she hugged her client. 'I'm fine. Honestly. Just getting a little soppy. Ignore me.'

A gentle southern breeze ruffled the striped custom-made curtain tie-backs, and she remembered the hassle they'd caused her, all because her mind had been elsewhere. It was becoming too much of a habit, and one she needed to kick.

She smiled, shoving Vaughn out of her thoughts. At least, to a corner of her head where he wouldn't cause too much trouble. The man was damaged and, for the record, so was she.

'It's been an absolute pleasure to be part of your wedding, Taylor. If there is anything I can do for either of you in the future, just let me know. You have my details.' Chloe ran a finger along the anchor favour in front of her and made sure the little sticker with her contact details was still intact in case anyone else needed to contact her too.

The disco music had stopped for the night, and the captain was steering the weary partygoers safely back to shore across the thick black water. Lights from the towering buildings on either side of the river studded the endless inky sky, and their reflections shone brightly in the shadows of the river. She'd forgotten how stunning London could be when it put on a show... or maybe she just hadn't been looking. For too long, her focus had been on the past and on how bad things were instead of pushing forward. 'Mention me to your friends, will you? I've got a couple of spare dates in my diary that I'm looking to fill.'

If only it were only a couple, not a couple of hundred.

The groom slapped a sticky kiss on her cheek. 'Hey, actually, I was wanting to organise a surprise birthday get-together for Nate in July. Something sophisticated, you know. Upmarket, but intimate. I'd love it to be outside too. Although, hello rain showers in London in the summer! But that would be adorable, right? Eating under the stars, like here? I was thinking about fifty guests? Maybe sixty? Any ideas?'

Now this, she could do. 'Lots. Dinner?'

'Of course. And lashings of bubbles. Buckets of the stuff.'

'Something trendy, but not too hipster? Cool, but not cold? Outside, but with options? I have just the place in mind. And the owner will let us decorate it in any way we like and be willing to discuss any food preferences you have. Any special meals? Favourite dishes? He'll recreate them for you.' She added that bit with her fingers crossed behind her back, because who knew whether Vaughn would be open to that?

'Darling, I knew you'd be the perfect person to ask. Oh, and—' Taylor gestured over to a couple who were leaning against the boat railings and staring out across the Thames towards Greenwich. 'Samantha and Greer are thinking of tying the knot. Girls, girls... come here. I want you to meet la belle Chloe, Wedding Planner Extraordinaire.'

Chloe found them a smile; she didn't have to dig too deeply. Wrapped around each other's arms, they were clearly besotted with each other. Love did exist, she knew. It was here; she could feel it in Taylor and Nathan's tenderness and desire to please each other, in Greer and Sam's need to be connected on a physical as well as cerebral level. It was in their eyes. Something she didn't recall having seen in Jason's—at least, not for a long time.

Maybe love just happened for other people. Maybe the Cassidy curse was real after all. 'Hello, there. I'm Chloe Cassidy, wedding planner. Taylor tells me you're planning on getting married?'

'Taylor!' The statuesque woman on the right—Greer? Gently slapped the groom's arm. 'That was our secret! We haven't even told our parents yet. But yes, and soon, hopefully.' She rested her head on her girlfriend's. 'We want to start a family. We're both so broody; all we ever seem to talk about is babies these days.'

Chloe ignored the little spike in her heart. 'No problem. I'm very discreet, but how about you surprise your parents with your fabulous news, and a save the date suggestion or two at the same time? What kind of venue were you thinking of? Party size? Let's talk details; this is so exciting!'

The women seemed thrilled to be talking through some ideas, and they spent the next hour brainstorming. This was absolutely the best outcome, and Chloe began to feel a little lift in her heart. How could she not when she was surrounded by so much love?

Then it was time to leave. The grooms were just about to disembark and ride off into their future in a fabulous vintage Jaguar car, with the requisite tin cans and 'Just Married' sign on the back. She sighed at the sight. Some traditions should never disappear.

She wrapped them both in a hug. 'Thanks so much for a fabulous evening, boys. Have a wonderful honeymoon. I want to hear all about it when you get back.'

Nate gave her a gentle slap on her bottom. 'Cheeky. You want to know *all* about it?'

'No. Really. Not everything.' She winked. 'You are just the most perfect couple.'

'Yes, we are.' Taylor pecked her on the cheek. 'Now, all we have to do is find you a perfect knight in shining armour, too.'

'Oh, don't waste your time. There's no such thing, not for me.' But the memory of that kiss flitted back into her head. Again.

Taylor tutted. 'Everyone has someone out there for them, honey. You just haven't found him yet.'

'Well, in that case, I'm open to offers. But he can leave the armour at home.'

Taylor looked around at the guests—predominantly male and predominantly gay. 'Not going to get anyone from this lot, love. You haven't got the right equipment. But don't give up hope, he's out there somewhere.'

'Yeah. One day, eh? Now go. Have fun.' She waved them down the gangplank and watched them drive off into more fun and love-filled days and nights. Then she made her way to her car.

There'd be no knight in shining armour for her, she knew. That was just a fairy tale for other people. It wasn't as if she needed one; she was an independent, professional woman who could definitely stand on her own two feet. It just got a little lonely sometimes, plotting world domination. Someone to share her hopes and dreams would have been nice.

A family…

The trouble was, once upon a time she thought she might have found that knight. But she just couldn't trust her judgement anymore.

* * *

It was past one o'clock by the time Chloe was nearing home. Her bones were weary, but she didn't feel like sleeping. Ideas for Greer and Sam's wedding were coming thick and fast, so she had to keep pulling over to the roadside to scribble notes into her trusty notebook. It was going to be an amazing celebration of their love. Then there was the booking for Nate's surprise party—she added that to her planner—she mustn't forget to add that to Vaughn's calendar at work on Monday, too. And discuss menu ideas with him.

The roads were clear, and the moon was high in a black sky. She tapped her fingers in time to the upbeat music on the radio as she drove while humming along. Suddenly, she realised she was driving past *Vaughn's*, which wasn't the wrong way home, but wasn't the most direct either.

Her brain was clearly overloaded to have taken a detour this way—on autopilot.

But, even more strange, there was a light on in the restaurant. At this time in the morning? She'd discovered he didn't live above the restaurant; he had an apartment in South Kensington, and he closed before eleven on most nights so… who?

Why?

She pulled the car to the kerb and told herself she was just checking that everything was okay and that she wasn't getting out of her car and walking up the path because she wanted to share this good feeling with him.

'Vaughn?' She tapped on the door. It was open. This was a completely stupid idea, because if she'd caught burglars mid-burgle, she was going to be in deep trouble.

As she stepped through the door, she was greeted with ear-splitting, loud rock music. The seating area was in darkness; the sound was coming from the kitchen.

'Vaughn?' she called out, breathing easier knowing he wasn't being attacked, or robbed; although his hearing was possibly being murdered by the intense, thick bass.

Her heart jittered a little. She ignored it. But when she stepped into the kitchen and saw him, his back to her, sleeves rolled up and pummelling something on the steel counter, she couldn't help notice her pulse escalate.

Even from the back he was formidable. Tall, dark and intent. Long legs in chequered chef pants, a straight back, strong, broad shoulders emanating such power.

Not wanting to stop him—and secretly wanting to watch him so engrossed in his work just for a moment—she tiptoed a couple of steps to the side and stilled. He was utterly lost in his world as he punched, threw and punched again a huge silky skein of dough. He hummed along to music that seemed to light something up inside him. He was totally focused, mesmerised by the rhythmic fluid actions, and she wondered what was going on in that head of his.

While he was kind and considerate, he was also completely content in his own company. He didn't need anyone else. Clearly. The physicality of the work suited him, too. This suited him. Here was space and time to think and breathe. Not to mention that a man who was engrossed in hard physical work, that worked muscles she could see stretching and contracting, was inordinately sexy. Just watching him sent a rush of heat through her. She ached to cup her palms around his hands and trace his movements. To press and push and pull in rhythm with him.

That wasn't the only kind of trouble she'd had in mind.

But, after a while, he seemed to sense she was there, and the spell was broken as he turned sharply, his fist curled to his chest, his breathing hard and fast. 'Shit, Chloe, you made me jump.'

Only feeling slightly guilty, she stepped towards him and looked down at the counter. 'That poor dough—what has it ever done to you?'

'It snuck up on me in the middle of the night and made me jump.' With a quick flick of his hand, he turned the amped music down so they could be heard. His eyes softened as he smiled. And her heart tripped. 'What are you doing here so late? Weren't you supposed to stop working hours ago?'

He started to push against the dough again, sinking his fingers deep as he answered, 'I could ask you the same. I'm starting the dough to let it rise overnight so we can make our famous bread rolls tomorrow. You?'

'I saw the light and wondered...' What had she wondered? She hadn't really thought this through. She'd seen the light on and wanted to talk to him, to tell him her good news and ask about his day. In truth, she'd just wanted to be with him. God, that admission sucked. 'It looks more like you're paying the dough back for some evil deed it's done you.'

He grinned. 'It's therapeutic. Come and see. Oh, and it's magic.'

Uh-oh. Another goofball. Next thing, he'd be joining her mum in a ghost hunt. 'Okay, Dumbledore, why is it magic?'

'Because you take basic ingredients—flour, water, yeast and salt—each of them nothing much on their own, but when you mix them together and encourage them to bind in a whirl of chemistry... Boom! Magic happens. Add some time and heat and it turns from a thick, sticky dough to delicious, mind-blowing bread.'

'Do you always finish your days like this?' When she worked here, she always left before the staff finished clearing up. Apparently there was a whole world of things happening that she had no idea about.

He glanced at the wall clock. 'It's been a busy night and I'm still wired. Making bread calms me down, helps me sleep.'

'But why are you making it tonight? And aren't you supposed to have the day off tomorrow, anyway? I saw the roster; you haven't had a day off in weeks.'

His shoulders rose. 'Do you ever really switch off when you have your own business to run? I was mulling over some recipe ideas; keeping my hands busy frees up my head to think. Research reckons that mundane tasks allow the subconscious to play.' Oh, and he was wise too. 'I told Jacques I'd do the bread prep for him, so he won't have to get in too early tomorrow.'

'You're very good to him.'

'He's a good chef. I want him to stay here.' He gave a quick shrug. 'When I go back to Paris, I need to know I can leave him in charge.'

Chloe's heart stuttered. She hadn't really registered that he might leave. Which of course, was foolish, he'd hardly been here in the past—why would he stay now? 'You're going back to Paris?'

'Of course. I have my business to run there.'

'And'—she tried to keep her voice light and wondered if he noticed—'what about here?'

He shrugged as if the question was irrelevant. 'I'll divide my time between the three restaurants. The key is to have great staff. That's why I need you to help me find the perfect person. Then I can go.'

Great. So her job—if she did it successfully—would ease him out of her life. There was a hollow hurt in her gut as if he'd gone already. Then it hit her: she didn't want to ease him out of her life.

Whoa. That was another huge admission.

She barely knew the man. He had his own life to lead as she did, but a part of her wanted him to stay. A lot of her wanted him to stay. And it wasn't just because he was the most attractive man in the whole damned universe. He was actually genuinely nice, considering he shared the same bloodline as Jason.

And that thought should have made her turn around and leave because the warning bells were ringing in her head. Maybe what she was feeling was becoming the one thing he hated: complicated.

But she didn't leave. Instead, she watched as he pushed his fists into the thick, creamy dough and heard it sigh as he squeezed the air out, releasing puffs of yeasty scent into the air.

The way he punched and pulled and pummelled it again was rhythmic and meditative, and she could see how repeating it over and over would relax a stressed state of mind.

She edged to the counter, wanting a bit of what he was feeling because she was far from relaxed now. He was planning on leaving.

Strange how a good mood could evaporate with just one conversation. 'Show me?'

'Of course. You have to treat it firmly, but gently. Don't be scared of it. Push the heel of your hand into it... like this.' He showed her the correct action. 'Then gather it together into a ball and push again, stretching it a little each time. You have a go. Wait! Wash your hands first.'

She saluted and winked. 'Aye, aye, Captain.'

'Clearly you spent way too much time tonight on the love boat.'

'It was fun.'

He flashed a smile that lit up his face. 'Yes, so I gather. You look different. You're glowing.'

She went to the sink, did as he asked and was back in seconds. 'So, I have news.'

'Yes? A successful night too?' He stood back and watched her as she pummelled the dough, stopping her every now and then to adjust the angle of her wrist or show her how to push with a little more force.

'It was excellent. The boys loved the wedding, the venue and everything, and now one of them wants to organise a surprise party... here!' She stopped pummelling and looked up at him, gauging his reaction. Okay, partly just to look into the gunmetal of his eyes because she wanted to languish there a little in the spark and the heat. 'But it may need a little compromise on your part.'

His eyes narrowed. 'In what way?'

'I said you'd be happy to create any favourite dishes they have. You wouldn't mind, would you?'

'It depends.'

'On what?'

His mouth hitched at the corners. 'What do I get as a reward for being so amenable? You're pimping me out, Chloe. I don't know whether to be flattered or—'

She flicked flour at him. 'I'm selling your skills, crazy man. And pimping your *restaurant*. You'll get a hefty pay cheque, a great review, happy customers and word of mouth. That is, after all, the name of the game.'

'But only if I cook what they want? What if I don't think it'll work? What if they have heinous suggestions, and I won't be able to add my signature flourish?' At her frown, his eyebrows rose. He slowly nodded. 'Okay, I'll think about it.'

'What you mean is, *Yes, Chloe, of course I'll do it.* I'll do anything. Don't hire me to help you out and then turn down my suggestions. I was right about the review, wasn't I?'

'No one likes a smart arse.' He grinned, and his eyes crinkled. 'I'll compromise, I'll compromise, don't worry. But good work, Chloe. Thank you.'

'Great!' She almost jumped up and kissed him on the cheek, but that would be a step over the line. *No kissing.* 'I knew you would. I'll book it in, yes? Plus, I have another wedding booking. Two adorable women, who want a festival-themed wedding with tents, hay bales, a live gypsy band and picnic hampers. Gourmet, of course. Do you fancy branching out into catering too? All the best chefs do.'

He started to run a knife over some of the dough, chopping it into smaller pieces, moulding it into small balls and then placing them on huge floured trays. 'Perhaps. But I do have three restaurants to run.'

Yes, and two of them weren't anywhere near here. 'You could do it as a sideline. Think about it. You could even be in supermarkets; in fact, why not do a stall at one of those hipster festivals too? You'll get your name out to a whole new market. Hot damn, I'm good at thinking up things for you. I wish I could do the same for my own business.'

'You had a successful day today—take the wins, Chloe.'

'I know, I know, I just want the world right now. Too much to ask?' She flicked her hands in the air and flour p'ffed out across the steel surfaces. 'Oops. Sorry.' Her hair was also slipping across her face so she briefly pushed it back with her wrist as she tried to keep pushing and pulling the dough he'd allowed her to play... er, work with. 'This is hard work.'

'You have to do each batch for at least ten minutes; then we leave it to rise. Wait... there's flour on your...' He pushed her hair back once more and tucked it behind her ear. Then he ran his thumb over her forehead and rubbed a little. The air stilled around them and their eyes locked. She saw a furnace blazing there, molten steel, desire that he was struggling to hide. He let his hand fall. 'Sorry... I know... Cheesy.'

'Not cheesy at all.' At just that tiny contact, she could barely breathe. His gaze burnt into hers and suddenly the air was thick with sexual need. Two people. One touch. One scorching look. A lot of desire. Boom! Magic. Without thinking, she put a hand to his chest, feeling the thud of his heart—erratic and fast, but strong. 'Vaughn—'

'Chloe—' He tore his gaze away and huffed out a groan. 'Right. Er... Are you hungry?'

'Why are you always trying to feed me?'

'Because you look too thin, and it's the best thing I do. I'll have you know, people pay a fortune to be fed by me.'

Her eyes flicked toward the huge stainless steel fridge. Her food-porn dream. Words got stuck in a dry mouth. She swallowed as she thought about sex by the light of the open fridge door. About hand-feeding each other food. Then she reminded herself that this scenario was very different from her dreams. For one, they'd agreed that neither of them was prepared to actually go there and do that. 'Yes. Er... Okay. What have you got?'

'Whatever you want. Come here.' He took her hand and tugged her to the fridge. Opening it up, he lifted out containers of cooked meat. 'See, there is everything you could possibly want to eat. Olives? Cheese? Finest prosciutto, from Friuli in northeast Italy. Try some.' He ripped a piece off and held it out to her.

He wanted to give her food because it was a distraction from the need that simmered in his eyes, she knew damned well. Because he wanted her as much as she wanted him, but he was hell-bent on fighting it. And that was his choice. But it didn't mean he wanted her any less.

He was Mr Non-Committal; he was going to leave as soon as she found a decent manager for him. There was no future for them. Whatever they did next would not only be a mark on her heart but on her soul too. She was playing a dangerous game.

But, despite everything, she still wanted to play.

Because not playing this game with Vaughn Brooks would mean a lifetime of regret, of wondering what if? Of wishing she'd had the guts to take something she wanted. So for once in her life, she was going to put herself first.

She leant forward and took the prosciutto from his out-stretched fingers—with her teeth. She didn't know who was more shocked, her or him. So, rather thank thinking about where they were heading, she concentrated on eating the delicious meat. 'Oh, God, that is amazing. You want some?'

'Aha.' There was a subtle shift in his voice, one that told her he wanted more than food. And that stoked the fire in her gut, made her bolder, braver.

She took a piece of the ham and held it to his lips. Without taking his eyes from hers, he leant forward a fraction and took it into his mouth. Then he gave her a smile that was half sexy, half tease and all sin.

'Anything else?' She tore her gaze from his and looked in the fridge. 'Ah... strawberries. Did I ever tell you how much I adore strawberries?'

'Chloe—' *No kissing.* He didn't say it, but he didn't have to. It was there in the silence.

But this was eating. Right? Just strawberries, and they weren't exactly sinful. Unless...

'I mean, I really, really, adore them. Just irresistible. They remind me of summer... and sunshine... and...' She ran her tongue over her top lip, then caught her bottom one in her teeth and gazed up at him. His eyes flickered red-hot need and he reached for the container of scarlet fruit.

Flicking off the lid, he lifted a strawberry out and held it to her open mouth, running it over her top lip, then on to the bottom one. Slowly, he placed the fruit between her teeth. She sucked it in, bit down and tasted the intensely sweet juice.

'Delicious. You try one.' She did the same to him, watching his throat work as he swallowed. 'I'd like another, please.'

'Yes, m'lady.' Breathing fast, he took another out and ran it again over her lips, then put it in his own mouth. 'You taste like heaven.'

'How would you know?'

'Because I'm pretty damned sure that Heaven would taste of strawberries and wine and sunshine. Like you probably do.'

'Want to check? Just to be sure?' Then, unable to resist any longer, she tiptoed and cupped his face in her palms. With no hesitation, she licked a trail across his lips. 'You taste pretty damned good yourself.' Then she licked a trail down his throat.

Still no kissing. Not technically.

'Do that again and I won't be able to hold back any longer,' he groaned against her forehead, but still he didn't kiss her.

So, achingly slowly, just to prove her intent, she licked again, first his bottom lip, then the top.

He edged away a fraction, holding her shoulders as he growled, 'I mean it, Chloe.'

'So do I.'

His eyes flickered closed. 'We should stop.'

'Why, when I know you want it as much as I do?'

His voice was gravel and stone. 'Because this isn't a game, Chloe, and I just can't give you what you want.'

CHAPTER 16

*Y*ou don't even know what I want. You've never asked me.'
Chloe ran her hands over his chef's whites, feeling the
hard muscle underneath, the solid wall of chest. Her
heart was beating rapidly, but she was flush with business success
and felt bold and brave. For the first time in a long time, she felt
she could actually grasp something she wanted. And if she didn't
do this, she would definitely regret it. 'Right now, I'm thinking
hot sex would be a perfect end to a great day.'

'And then what?'

Good question. 'And then the sun will rise tomorrow, and we
will carry on with our lives.'

'Simple as that?' His eyes narrowed.

'Simple as that.'

'But nothing's ever simple with you.'

'Let's just say I'm a work in progress.' Because she didn't want
to examine too deeply what on earth was happening here, she

nuzzled her head into that perfect dip between his neck and his shoulder and let her fingers stray over the top of his trousers, playful and light. Didn't matter what words he was using, if ever there was a show and tell as to what he wanted, it was this hard length against her palm.

He grasped her hand, brought it to his chest and kissed the knuckles, a gesture so tender it made her heart squeeze.

Oh. Maybe he'd meant no mouth kissing? She lowered her head to their hands and kissed his knuckles in return, relishing his sharp intake of breath as she licked across them. Curling open his fingers, she licked across his palm, over and around his wrist. With every lick, his eyes fluttered closed. Then opened again in anticipation of the next touch of her tongue on his skin. Desire emanated from him, as did a struggle to fight this deepening need. His eyelids were hooded, his breathing fast.

And God, she ached to feel his mouth on hers.

She reached for another strawberry and put it half in her mouth. Turning towards him, she leant close, offering him the other half. *Take it from me*, she told him with her eyes.

He immediately knew what she was doing. At first, he shook his head, but she kept on looking at him and nodding. She saw the moment his resolve was totally blown; heat seared his eyes, and a guttural groan escaped him.

He tipped his head down and took the other end of the fruit into his teeth and bit hard. An explosion of flavour erupted into her mouth, and as he bit, their lips grazed, and another molten rush of heat suffused her face, spreading fast across her body, lower and lower. It was as close as no kissing could ever get to kissing.

Excruciatingly sensual, her skin felt alight with desire, craving his touch. He was so close. His mouth so close, she could see the exquisite lines in his lips, the day's stubble on his jaw, fine pores, and a delicate dimple in his cheek.

This was torture—tantalising, sexy, torture—to be so near to his mouth, to be able to taste him, but not to kiss him.

She reached up to his jaw, stroking across it, increasing pressure as she smeared her fingers across his mouth. When he caught her fingers in his teeth, she gasped. When he sucked them into the heat and wet of his mouth, she closed her eyes, unable to control her breathing, her composure.

Then she felt the whisper of his breath on her face, and she dragged her damp fingers away just before he slammed his mouth over hers in a hard, greedy kiss that had her melting into him.

She opened her mouth in response, and he stroked his tongue across hers, the sweep of sensation after sensation rippling through every inch of her body. His spicy scent enveloped her. His arms reached around her neck as he hauled her against him, gripping to her as if she were a lifeline in a stormy sea. And with each moment in his arms, she felt more of her defences smashed against the rocks.

She knew why kissing was so damned dangerous. It was so intimate, so raw and so real. It opened up parts of her heart that she'd slammed shut. It made her crave him more and more and more.

His initial reluctance only proved he was trying to protect her. His tenderness showed her his heart. His steady grip gave her hope to cling to, and above all of those things, the ceaseless pulsing ache for him to be inside her, rocking with her, filling her, was a need she'd never experienced before. She curled her hands to his neck and kissed him hard, noticing the exact moment when they had stepped over that line, and that sleeping with him was not only inevitable but necessary.

'You do realise we're breaking a zillion rules,' he groaned, as he lifted her to sit on the gleaming steel counter, sending trays of rising dough skittering onto the floor with a series of crashes.

'Whatever.' She imagined he was talking about kitchen hygiene and health and safety, but what the hell. This was her dream, her rules. 'Rules are made for breaking.'

'Some are for your own good.'

'For example?'

His thumb smudged across her lips as he pushed her legs apart with his hips and stepped into the space, leaning closer, ever closer. 'No kissing.'

'How can that rule be for anyone's good?'

His hands fisted in her hair now, tugging her closer, his mouth hovering a fraction above hers. 'Because it leads on to so much more.'

'Good.' He was saying this to make sure she was okay, she understood, to smooth the way, to stop embarrassment, and to prove that he was the gentleman she knew he was. But somehow he'd relieved her of her dress; she could barely remember how, but there it was in a puddle on the floury floor. She laughed as he slicked a hot trail of kisses along her breast and sucked her nipple into his mouth. The giggle turned to a moan as he pressed against her, his erection pushing against the super-sensitive part of her thigh. She was half naked, in just bra and panties and stilettoes, yet he was still all cheffed-up and with far too many clothes on.

'Take this off.' Dragging at the hem of his top, she inched it over his head and threw it, wishing there'd been a way to do that without him taking his mouth from her skin.

But *oh, God...* she swallowed deeply, drinking him in. That French sun had been very bloody good to him. Tanned shoulders gave way to solid, thick biceps, toned pecs and a tight, ridged stomach. Her eyes widened as she focused from one exquisite part of him to another. He was a dream come true. She ran fingers across his chest. 'Wow, Vaughn. You are amazing. Bloody amazing.'

'And you are the most beautiful thing I have ever seen.' He cupped her breasts in his hands and leant to kiss them again. She wriggled her bottom to the edge of the counter and squirmed against him. At the touch of her heat, he groaned, and all talking stopped.

Kissing her again, he stripped her of her underwear then circled her thigh, nudging her legs further apart, slowly sinking fingers into her core. Intense pleasure ripped through her as he stroked and explored. She could feel pressure inside her lighting up, growing more intense as he pulsed his fingers inside her. She was on the edge. Hanging on, holding on with a tiny sliver of self-control. She wanted him inside her—only then would she allow her release.

This time, when she reached for him and felt his hardness under her hand, he didn't stop her. With shaking fingers, she undid his waistband button, and he kicked the rest of his clothes away. Then he was naked in front of her. Magnificent. Assured. Turned on.

God, how he was turned on.

She took him in her palm, relishing the strength, the heat, guiding him to her. 'Condom?'

'Sure.' He turned briefly, rummaged in a pocket in his trousers on the floor, and when he turned back, his eyes glittered with desire and a tenderness she'd never seen in him before. 'Chloe, we don't have to—'

'Yes, we bloody well do.'

'Yes. Yes, we do.' Those eyes bore into her and there was so much he wouldn't say, so much she could see in those dark irises that he refused to give a name to, and she knew then, knew with all her heart, that she was fooling herself if she thought this was going to be simple.

But it would be beautiful. It would be like her dream. It

would be hers. It would be theirs. And whatever came after she would deal with.

But for now… just for now…

His mouth covered hers, and shivers of need ran through her and over her. The kisses were hard and desperate and hot. She wanted him inside her so badly, so damned badly, and nothing else would ever be enough. Nothing… and no one. This was a man who wanted her, who connected with something in her that no one else had ever reached.

She wound her legs around his hips and wiggled to the very edge of the counter, showing him what she wanted, what she needed. And then he was pushing inside her, gently at first as she moaned his name, his mouth on hers, his eyes locked with hers. Over and over she whispered his name, and over and over he answered her, pushing harder and deeper until she was lost in the rhythm and the sensation and his scent and those dark, serious eyes that told her he was captured by this connection too.

Then there was a change in the air, a shift in his breathing and in his rhythm that sent a charge through her, rising and rising until she couldn't think anymore until every cell in her body exploded into a pulsing crescendo that had her bucking with him. Her mouth craved more kisses, and her hands ached to feel his skin under her touch—it would never ever be enough. She pressed herself closer and closer to him, moulding her body with his, sharing this release, giving him everything, losing herself in *us*, losing herself in *this*, until he lost himself too, further and deeper, and further and deeper.

And always, always, *always*, those dark grey eyes glittered with the truth; there was nothing simple about this at all.

* * *

He held her close to his chest, head on her shoulder, his lips pressed gently against the dip of her collarbone. It was the kiss of a man who wanted more, but who was satisfied for now. And he was not letting go.

It was a long time before either of them spoke. But there were still moments of tender kissing, touching his face, looking, caressing. Of wonder at what had just happened between them.

Eventually, he pulled away and looked around at the fallout. There was dough rising in small puffs on the floor. Tin trays tipped over, resting against the counter legs, discarded across the tiles.

He smiled and brushed a stray lock of her hair away from her face. Then he passed her her bra and pants with a glint in his eye. 'What do you want to do now, Chloe?'

'You know what? I want to go to sleep wrapped up in you and wake up with you in the morning. That's all. I don't want to think past these moments. I don't want to spoil this. I want it to last... at least until tomorrow.' She had a feeling she wanted so much else, but saying those words would muddy everything. 'Come home with me?'

'Of course.' And so he tidied up the kitchen and went home with her. All she'd had to do was ask. And it was pretty damned scary that he was here in her bed. Two parts scary, and two parts miracle.

It was still night-time as they lay again, exhausted and satisfied, still drunk on the magic of what had happened over the last few hours. Vaughn laughed as he wrapped his arms around her. 'I didn't have much time to look before, but this is a nice place you've got here.'

She curled her fingers into his and stared up at the huge, intricate ceiling rose in her bedroom and remembered the week she'd taken off work with Jason to decorate the room. Back before the good old days had turned bad. 'It's old and has its issues, but I do love it here. I feel like I have a haven of peace in the centre of everything. We had such a lot of plans for it.'

His words were against her neck. 'Ah, yes. Plans. The road map for life until reality gets in the way. Shit happens.'

'Life has a way of not working out how you expect, that's for sure.' Like this. Like him. But then she realised maybe he wasn't talking about now, or about Jason, maybe he was talking about his past. Chloe's heart began to beat fast. 'Are you talking about...?'

There was a long silence. She lay with it, not wanting to force him to speak, but wishing he would. In the darkness, she reached for his hand and held it tight against her heart.

Eventually, he stirred. Not asleep, then. Just thinking.

'Bella. Her name was Isabella.'

'The name of your restaurant in Paris. I always thought it just meant beautiful or was referring to the setting or the food.' It had never occurred to her to question the reason behind its name. She'd always thought he was just a little too arrogant, just a little too sure of himself. She knew different now as he lay beside her. Knew he was giving and thoughtful. 'Tell me about her.'

'Not a chance.' He shifted a little, making space between them, but his voice was still soft.

She turned over to face him, her face close to his, her body against the length of his. 'Why not?'

He smiled, but it was a reluctant one. 'Chloe, this is so not the right place.'

'Why?'

'Because I don't want you to talk about your relationship with Jason. I don't want to think about you with him, so I imagine you don't really want to know about Bella. Why would you?'

Chloe didn't know why she wanted to hear about his Lost

Love; she only knew that she did. 'It might explain a few things. It's part of you—it's good to know why you're the person you've become. If I asked about your childhood, you'd talk about that, right?'

One shoulder rose and fell. 'I guess.'

'And about your restaurants, and your parents? Family? Pets?'

'Of course.'

'So why not talk about Bella? Unless... unless it's still too painful.'

He frowned. 'If it was, I wouldn't be here.'

Good. Because she so did not want to be the rebound shag. Even if that was what he was. Was he? Actually, there was nothing about the end of her relationship with Jason that had spurred her to sleep with Vaughn. If anything, her experiences with Jason had had her running from any man. She hadn't needed sex to obliterate him from her head. Far from it, she'd wanted Vaughn to fill her mind with all those wondrous scents and tastes and memories and... yes, emotions too. She wanted to feel attractive, to be more than a sister, daughter, businesswoman. She didn't know whether that was the same kind of thing for Vaughn. 'I did wonder.'

'It was so long ago, Chloe. Such a long time ago.' He seemed to understand then that she needed to know he'd compartmentalised his feelings for Bella and done the same with any feelings he may have for Chloe. That they were separate and in no way linked. That he'd managed to lock his past back where it should be. Because she knew, despite how hard you tried, past experiences made you act in a certain way, made it harder for you to trust or to give your heart. She knew because she was struggling herself with this. She liked Vaughn—she liked him a lot—but she'd liked Jason too, and that hadn't ended well.

She wanted this to end well. Or not end at all.

He sat up and stacked the pillows against the wall before leaning against them. But that didn't seem to give him any comfort, so he turned and faced her, a sheet covering the most exquisite part of him. 'We met at uni. We were friends first—'

'I didn't realise you went to university. But then I only ever got snippets of your life from Jason… and he probably only got snippets from your mum? Right?'

'Like I've said before, Jason and I are cousins, and we made that best man pact years ago. Neither of us felt we could break it. But we're not close. I hardly wrote to him every week with details of my life.' He held her hand as he spoke, intertwining his fingers into hers and resting them on his thigh. 'I completed the first year and a term of the second. Then Bella got ill; lots of non-specific things that she shrugged off because it didn't suit her to go see a doctor. Basically, we were too busy having fun. But then she got really sick, and we couldn't ignore the obvious fact that something was seriously wrong. I took her to the hospital where she was diagnosed with cancer, and when she was forced to leave her studies to get urgent treatment, I followed. It was too much for her to go to those sessions on her own, have her appointments, and no one there to be with her.'

'That would have been hard for you to go through. What about her parents and other friends?'

Again with a shrug of one shoulder. 'She wanted me to be there, so I was. Her mum was devastated and dramatic, and that didn't help Bella at all. I ended up being a buffer between them.'

'I imagine that she reacted like that purely just out of love for her daughter?' Chloe imagined how she would react to Evie getting seriously ill. Then she struck that thought from her head. She wasn't going there.

'It was. It came from a good place, but Bella couldn't cope with all the tears and the *cloud of doom*, she called it. Bella was one of those once-in-a-lifetime people you meet.' His eyes lit up at the thought of her. Light and darkness. 'She was so upbeat, a little whacky, and full of plans and ideas and dreams. We planned that when she finished her treatment, we'd go travelling and see everything she wanted to see.'

'Sounds lovely.' Chloe sensed there was a 'but' coming.

'But she didn't finish her treatment. The chemo made her feel terrible. There were days when she couldn't lift her head from the pillow, she had no energy, she was being violently sick and in the end, she decided that this wasn't any way to live and that the chemo was only prolonging her life, not curing the cancer. That she'd rather spend the days she had left seeing wonderful things and living well.'

'With you.'

'With me.'

There was a lump in her throat, now, at the life that was interrupted at such a young age. And guilt too, that because Bella died, Chloe could be here with him at all. He'd done nothing except give everything he had to this woman. How could Bella not have loved him? 'What kind of cancer was it?'

'Liver. It had spread. There wasn't any hope. There would never be any respite or all-clear... we were kidding ourselves. They were just words I used to make each day more bearable.'

'Did you get far in your travels?'

He smiled at some memory. 'We got as far as Paris, and then she became too ill to do anything else. The cancer spread rapidly, and I had to bring her home. She didn't want to come back. She begged me not to bring her home because she knew then she was going to die. But I had to; we had no way of getting treatment in France. I didn't speak the language back then. I couldn't let her die there.' The smile was gone now along with the light as he shook his head. 'It felt like I'd failed her.'

Chloe squeezed his hand. 'But you did all that. You put your life on hold for her. You didn't fail her. You loved her.'

'Yes. Yes, I did.'

They sat for a few moments in silence as this all sunk in. She let him live through his memories, saying nothing. What could she say? What could she do? He'd been through something life-defining, something devastating, and it felt, to Chloe, as if some of her own joy had been stolen too. All the while Vaughn had been going through this, his cousin had been planning weddings, living his life, two-timing his girlfriend and never mentioned a thing. 'I still can't believe Jason wouldn't have known some of this.'

'I didn't broadcast it. Jason and I weren't in touch much then. My family tried to understand why I'd dropped out of university. They didn't particularly like Bella—she was too fiery for them, and they thought she'd ruined my life chances. Mum kept it quiet.'

He sat looking hollowed out, eyes rimmed with black and edged with a terrible emptiness. Chloe felt that asking more would be intruding on something too intimate and painful. But she didn't really know what to do or say next. She knew enough from what Jenna went through that there was nothing that could heal such intense loss. That living each day, no matter how hard, was the only way to survive. He'd been so young. So in love.

And he'd trusted her enough to share his most painful moments with her.

She also knew that sometimes there were just not enough words to offer or to comfort, so she sat with him in the half-light, her hand over his, feeling vulnerable and naked and... intrusive. 'I'm so sorry, Vaughn. That must have been terrible to live through.'

'Actually, she was very upbeat. She grasped at life and chased it hard. She was never going to let the cancer beat her spirit, even if it beat her physically. She was a lot of fun; you'd have liked her.'

'I'm sure I would.'

'She was a lot like you. But different, you know.'

Chloe didn't know how that was supposed to make her feel. But there was a chasm in her chest, and it was filling with panic and loss. She was here because some other woman had died. She was the second choice, second best. And yet, she still felt honoured that he'd chosen her.

As if suddenly waking from a dream, he shook his head and raked a hand over his face. 'God, I'm sorry. That wasn't supposed to happen. Passion killer, or what?'

'I did ask.'

'I shouldn't have gone on.'

'It's okay. It's not as if any of us come baggage-free, is it? We all have pasts; we've all been through something and survived. It's good to talk about it.'

'No, it isn't, and not here. I'm sorry.' He glanced around her bedroom as if realising for the first time that he'd committed the sin of talking about his first true love after sex with someone he wasn't committed to. He wrapped an arm around her waist and pulled her down the bed. 'Let me make it up to you.'

'No, really. It's fine. I like that we're being honest. I like that. Whatever happens between us, let's always be honest.'

'Yes. Okay. Yes. Let's always be honest.' A slow, small smile grew on his lips, and he was transformed back to the vibrant man she knew. 'Fancy something to eat?'

'Is that all you think about?'

'No, I think about other things too, but yes, food and sex, mainly. A great combination, yes?' After everything he'd just said, it didn't feel appropriate to think about a rerun of the earlier fridge-food-sex journey they'd been on. She wanted to hold him, to feel that vibrant heart beating against hers. What he'd just shared had been huge and marked a deepening of whatever it was that was happening here. 'No. I think I'm going to go to sleep. It's been a long night.'

'Chloe.'

'Yes?'

'Thanks. You know, for listening. It was an intense couple of years.' He traced a finger down her cheek. 'But now you know why I can't do any more than this.'

Her gut contracted into a tight ball. 'Because you won't be able to find anyone else to replace her? Or like Jenna, because you just don't believe you can love anyone else like that?'

'No. Because I promised her I wouldn't. She made me promise to do everything on her list, and I did. And more. I visited all those places, climbed higher, swam deeper, took weird medicine in Peru that made me sick for weeks. Bungee-jumped in New Zealand. Visited Uluru. She made me promise to work hard and be successful, and I eventually settled down enough to do that, and to name my first restaurant after her. That was a joke and a dare, but I honoured it. Finally, she made me promise never to love anyone else the way I loved her.' He shrugged, but it wasn't nonchalant, it was more determined. 'And I haven't.'

Whoa. That was a big promise to make at such a young age. Surely he could see that? But maybe he couldn't. 'And you're okay with that? Wouldn't she want you to fall in love with someone and have a family and live a life she couldn't?'

He blew out a long sigh. 'I don't know. I've never met anyone to make me question it. It'd have to be a pretty special person to have me rethink the promises I've lived by for over a decade, right?'

'Yes, yes it would.' Chloe dug deep for a reassuring smile,

trying to cover up the dismay spiralling through her. 'Hey, after my disastrous year, I'm hardly looking for anything intense, either.'

And she wasn't. Truly. Having any kind of relationship would be the kiss of death to her sanity. Maybe sometime in the future, when things had settled more for her. Ever since she'd found out about Amy's pregnancy, Chloe had been troubled by a sense of being misplaced and off balance. And she couldn't help thinking it was because there was something deep inside her that wanted the things that Amy had. Sometime. But there was so much she had to do first.

'Great. We're on the same page, as they say. Yuk… I know, it's a horrible saying.' Vaughn kissed her on her nose and brought her close to him. 'Right. Let's go into the lounge.'

'Why?'

'Because the mood's gone too dark in here. We need a change of scenery. Come on.'

After dragging on some boxers, he took her hand and pulled her from the bed, waited until she'd fastened a dressing gown around her waist, then led her through to the lounge. He pulled up the blind and peered outside. The sky was a livid orange as the sun started to spread long fingers of pale light across the horizon. Thin white clouds streaked the mauve sky. 'It's a new day, Chloe. Look at that. It's amazing.'

She wasn't sure what she was supposed to say and found it hard enough to speak with the rock in her throat. 'Yes. It's very beautiful.'

He turned to her, pressed his mouth to the nape of her neck and hugged her close. 'So are you. Come here.'

She should have told him then that there were strange things happening in her chest, that his story had made her like him more, and that far from being okay with his assertion that they couldn't get involved, she thought she might already be falling too hard for him.

She should have been honest, as they'd agreed.

But she said nothing because she truly hoped that this ache in her body was because of the amazing sex, her food-porn dream fulfilment, and his sad story, all on top of a wonderful orgasm or three. And that when he went, so would the clutch in her chest and so would the hope zinging around her body at his touch.

So she went willingly into his arms, but there was a sad hollow in her heart and a voice in her head that asked over and over and over, *'So what does this all mean?'*

And the only answer she could find was that she honestly didn't know.

CHAPTER 17

C hloe woke with a jolt. Something heavy pressed across her stomach—the weight of his arm as he cradled her to him. The divine scent of Vaughn lingered in the air.

A child laughing. Footsteps past her window, out on the street.

There was bright light outside now, but it felt like it was still the middle of the night. Having been distracted into doing more amazing things, wonderful things into the early hours, she had so not had enough sleep. Everything was out of kilter.

And he was still here. It had never ever been so perfect with anyone else. Well, Jason was the only other anyone else, and being with Vaughn had not been anything like being with Jason. Another level, another league.

Another thing to worry about.

She sat up straight, then looked over at his bare solid chest, the soft dark curls of his hair and the insanely-long-and-should-be-illegal eyelashes. God, he was divine.

Things had changed between them. How were they meant to move forward after this? After everything he'd told her about Bella, could he even have space in his heart for anyone else? Would he even want to or was Chloe just a stepping stone to healing?

And what the hell was that noise? Feet stamping. A herd of wildebeest in her lounge?

'Coo-ee! Wake up, Aunty Chlo! We're here for you to play. Remember? For the day? Where are you?' The bedroom door swung open. 'Oh! Shoot. Sorry—' Jenna's voice lowered to a stage whisper, 'Evie, no, don't go in, Aunty Chloe's still... asleep. Come with Mama into the lounge. Let's wait for her in there.'

Chloe's gut knotted tight. Play for the day? When had they—? Then a fragment of memory popped into her head. Jenna's friend. The moving day. Evie. Oh, and the fact she'd told her sister that there was nothing between her and Vaughn. That she'd believed it herself.

Things were definitely infinitely more complicated now.

'Shit. Shit, and double shit. Vaughn, I just need to get up. I'm sorry.' Wrapping the top sheet around her, she struggled out from under his arm and stood up.

'What's wrong? Come back here...' *It was an I want to eat you up,* kind of growl. And she had to admit that, with the stubble and the ruffled hair, he did look a little like a dangerous big bad wolf.

'I'm supposed to be looking after my niece today.'

'Oh. You want me to leave?' As reality finally seeped into his brain, he sat up and rubbed a hand over his face. He had sleep lines, mussed up hair and looked less than perfect, which made him, consequently, more than perfect. Because he was human after all, not some kind of god.

He was human, and here, and probably had enough faults

to put her off him. Although she hadn't found them yet, despite how hard she kept looking. He'd nursed his sick girlfriend for God's sake, taken her to Paris for her last days. Lived to Bella's rules for ten years. Named a restaurant after her.

He was a bloody hero.

'Not sure how making a grand entrance would look or what kind of impression you would make wandering through the lounge and out the door. Or what lesson little Evie will learn.' She looked down at him, still half asleep, still gorgeous, still… a little out of reach. Because even though they'd shared so much last night, it was clear there was still a part of him that he held back. A part that she doubted he'd ever give to anyone else. It was the part that would mean the difference between absolute and half-hearted. And, unfortunately, it was the bit of him she thought she might want, the sharing of himself, that deeper part of him. The soul-mate thing that people talked about. The thing he'd had with Bella. 'Maybe you should stay in here for a little while longer, lay low. I need to go talk to Jenna on my own. She's not going to be too impressed.'

His voice warmed her through. 'Chloe, it's not a crime you know. We did something very natural and normal.'

'I know. I just don't know how to deal with it. I preferred it when I hated you, to be honest. Now I don't know what to feel or think apart from embarrassed. My sister's here, so I don't have time for this.'

'Then don't think. Come here.' He flung the duvet off and strode to her, butt naked and so completely and utterly at ease with himself. He wrapped strong warm arms around her and planted a chaste kiss on her head. 'Whatever you want, Chloe. I'll stay here until you think it's a good time for me to come out, or I'll jump out the window now and run home.'

'Naked?'

'If that would make you happy and stop you fretting.'

She pushed a little on his chest, because if she stood here too long, she'd be tempted to never leave this room again. 'Don't keep doing that.'

'What?'

'Being so nice to me. I don't know how to think when you do that.'

'Okay, go. Talk to your sister. But you probably should put some clothes on…' His fingers ran teasingly along the top of the sheet, which she tightly clutched across her chest. She fought the urge to let him tear the sheet from her and take her there on the bedroom floor. Again. She fought the urge to kiss him quiet, to straddle him on the bed, to lay in his arms again and sleep forever. He grinned as if reading her mind. 'Unless you want your niece to think it's Halloween and you're playing ghost dress-ups.'

'Oh. God. *Evie.*' Chloe grabbed a T-shirt and old pair of jeans from her wardrobe and literally threw them on. With one last look over her shoulder, she reluctantly left him there along with her questions and worries.

* * *

'What the hell are you doing? *Vaughn Brooks?* Really? What is it with you and him?' Jenna hissed through clenched teeth. She was standing, arms folded, watching over her daughter who was jumping on and off the sofa with a wand in one hand and a light sabre in the other.

Jenna didn't seem cross, more disappointed, which made Chloe feel worse. 'It's just—'

'No, spare me the details. I know exactly what it is, and I don't want Evie to see it or hear it or know about it. You promised you'd do this one thing for me, Chloe, and look at you. Dishevelled, tired.' Jenna shook her head. 'You look thoroughly and totally exhausted. I'm guessing there wasn't much sleep last night? Do you need to go back for a lie down? Evie needs someone with a bit of energy today, so I can ask Mrs Singh to have her if you're too tired.'

At the sound of her name, Evie looked up and laughed. 'Aunty Chloe, I'm a buzzy bee. Look.' Then she jumped off the sofa screaming, 'Buzz! Buzz! Buzzy bee!'

Even though her head started to pound and her nerves began to jangle, Chloe smiled. Because, Evie. 'I'm perfectly fine. Don't you think I'm capable of taking care of my niece?'

'Of course I know you can.' Jenna busied herself by emptying Evie's backpack of containers of food, plastic toys, colouring books and pens and stacking them all on the desk next to the USB stick, which made Chloe think all over again about the man in the room next door. Stifling the smile, she zoned back into her sister's voice. 'It's about taking care of yourself, of your heart, Chlo. It's you I'm worried about. You've just spent three months in a foul mood and in some kind of depressive funk, and now you leap into bed with the first man that asks, who just happens to be Jason's relative. His *best man*. You need to draw a line under all that and start fresh. Are you trying to get back at him, is that it? Trying to make Jason jealous? What are you thinking?'

Don't think.

Good advice, because her head was filled with too many questions and scenarios to do with last night. She was leaping too far ahead, and she needed to focus on Evie. 'You weren't worried when you came up with the Love Plan, were you? None of this is about Jason, it's about me, and having some fun. Just leave it, Jenna. Okay? When will you be back?'

'I don't know. It depends on how much we get done. I'll try not to be too late.'

'Don't worry. Stay out as long as you want.'

Jenna glanced at Chloe's hurriedly thrown on clothes and shook her head, again. 'Do you want me to stay while you at least shower?'

'No. No, I'm great.'

'You need a shower, girlfriend. and a hairbrush. ' Jenna gave a reluctant, small smile as she ran a hand down Chloe's matted bed hair. 'But you do look great, to be honest. Glowing for the first time in a long time. Sex suits you. You look happy.'

'Yeah, it was good.' Which was weird, because although she had a whole lot of doubts about the wisdom of sleeping with Vaughn, she did certainly feel a kernel of something blooming hot, raw and fierce in her chest, which was probably better to be ignored and not encouraged. He'd only ever been honest with her, and that had gone as far as warning her not to get attached or involved with him. And she had a bad feeling she was at risk of being both. 'Go. Go and meet up with your friend and enjoy yourself. Go and be Jenna the woman, not Jenna the mum, or the daughter, sister or florist, or anything else. Go enjoy.'

Jenna gave a weary shrug that was at once filled with sadness and something Chloe could only describe as trepidation. Tears glistened in Jenna's eyes, and she looked somehow smaller than she was as if she was curling into herself. 'Thing is, Chloe, I'm not sure I know how to be anything other than Jenna, the struggling widow.'

'Oh, sweetie.' Even going out to meet an old friend was a huge step for her sister who had thrown all her life and breath into surviving her husband's death, fighting the sometimes morbid desire to follow him into the grave, and struggling to live for her daughter. Distracted by work and the business and now by Vaughn, Chloe hadn't paid enough attention to her sister's needs recently. She still needed her, no matter how much she pretended she was coping at single motherhood. Instead of being supportive and open to listening, Chloe had been defensive and secretive and argumentative with her mother, which had made the usually tight-knit three Cassidy women disparate and disconnected. That was exactly the kind of thing Jenna didn't need in her life.

Guilt wriggled into the mix of confusion and tiredness as she wrapped her sister in a hug and squeezed. Hard. 'You'll get there, gorgeous girl. A wise person recently taught me that sometimes it's good not to think at all. Go and just have fun. Relax, be yourself. Go and play house. I love you.'

'I love you too. Okay, I'll be off.' Jenna tugged her fleece jacket closer around her shoulders, but her hands were shaking, and her voice was just a little weaker than normal. 'Now, be good.'

Chloe glanced over to Evie, who was tearing paper into tiny little pieces and throwing them in the air screeching, 'It's snowing! It's snowing!'

And her heart melted. 'She will be.'

Jenna fixed Chloe with a stern look. 'I was talking to you.'

Thirty minutes later, Chloe was drawing very amateur superheroes for Evie to colour-in when Vaughn's head appeared at the door. 'Safe to come out?'

'Who's dat?' Evie's head shot up at the sound of a male voice. 'Man? Who's that man?'

'Hello. I'm Vaughn.' Now fully dressed, showered and back to his more-than-perfect appearance, he walked across the room, took Evie's hand and shook it gently, giving her the kind of smile that Chloe knew melted most women's hearts. Any minute now and Evie, hooked, lined and sinkered by him, would be lying down and getting him to rub her tummy. 'I'm Evie.'

'Yes, I've heard a lot about you. Evie, do you like pancakes?'

Eyes huge, she nodded as she beamed up at him.

'Good, because I'm going to make some. Berries, honey and chocolate. Breakfast of champions.' He threw a questioning look at Chloe, who was trying hard not to be affected by his charm and kindness. 'Okay with you, Chloe? I'm starving. Haven't eaten anything in a while.'

And she knew he was referring to last night, and the glint in his eye told her he was definitely hungry for more.

But she wasn't sure how to react to him with a small child in their company, and her focus had to be on her niece today and not worrying about the man she'd just slept with. Maybe it would just be better if he left them to it. 'Not sure I have the right ingredients for pancakes.'

'Judging by the contents of your cupboards, I'd already factored in a trip to the corner shop.'

'Me come?' Evie jumped up and fitted her tiny hand into his large one, and Chloe saw the softening in his eyes. She felt an equal softening in her chest, which she was determined to fight.

'No, Evie. You stay here with me, love. Vaughn can go on his own.'

'Aww. Want go shops.' The little girl spun around twice with her hand in his, tangled her Wellington-boot clad feet and bumped onto the floor. She rubbed her bottom. 'Ouchy.'

'Ouchy, indeed. She's fine to come with me. If you'll let her.' Vaughn picked her up before kissing Chloe gently on her head. 'Have a shower. Take some time out. We won't be long.'

'If you're sure?' How would Jenna feel if she knew Chloe had let a man they hardly knew take her daughter to the shops? 'Actually, you know what? I think I'll come with you. I'll shower when we get back. I fancy some fresh air.'

'Whatever you want.' He whipped Evie into the air, sat her

on his shoulders and with a cry of 'Duck your head down!' as he went through the doorway, they were off.

'Are you sure you're okay with her like that?' Chloe stared up at Evie, so high, laughing and giggling as she gripped Vaughn's hair. 'She might fall and hurt herself.'

'Chloe, she's a child not porcelain. She's fine. I have hold of her feet, look.' He picked up the two booted feet and showed his tight grip on them. 'I have lots of friends with kids, okay? I have kids in my restaurants; sometimes I even like them.'

Which was surprising. Jason had found Evie too much of a bind and Jenna's grief too much of an emotional drain. *When will she be back to normal?* He'd moaned.

And yet, he was the one having the baby.

Chloe's good mood threatened to spiral downwards. 'So, what do we need for pancakes?'

Biting his lip, he grinned. 'You really don't know how to cook, do you?'

'I have other talents.'

'Indeed, you do.' His eyes sparkled.

She shook her head in warning and glanced up at Evie, who was waving at everyone they passed, totally oblivious to this conversation. 'I was talking about spreadsheets.'

'I was talking about sheets too.' He pushed the corner shop door open with his foot. 'Duck, Evie!'

'Quack! Quack!' The little one giggled as she dipped her head.

'Now we need flour, baking powder, sugar, milk and eggs. And whatever delicious fillings you want. Chocolate chips, *straw-berries*,'—another wicked smile—'ham and cheese?'

Chloe unlinked her arm from his. This felt too nice, too homely, too close to a dream she'd held for too long and then had battered and dashed—by chilling, life-altering, devastating words that had come from that very mouth. 'Anything. Whatever. You're the award-winning chef, make something up.'

So he did, and it was a very special concoction that he agreed with Evie, consisting of bananas, chocolate spread and peanut butter. And, surprisingly, it worked. Seemed that magic happened whenever Vaughn was in the kitchen.

Completely full of Vaughn's cooking again, Chloe finished wiping the last of the dishes and then turned to find Evie standing at her heels holding a ball. 'Do you want to go out and play, Evie?'

'Park please.' Her curls bobbed around her face as she smiled, and there was no way Chloe could ever say no to her. 'Okay, sweetie, I'll just get your coat. We'll say thank you for the pancakes to Vaughn and bye-bye.' Then she could finally get some space to think about what her next steps were going to be. 'Come on, boots back on.'

Evie ran back to Vaughn, who was sitting on the old sofa admiring the bright pink nail varnish Evie had painted—very badly—on his fingernails. On any other guy, *Feelin' Hot-Hot-Hot!* might have looked unmanly, but he rocked it. Those large, strong hands and that muscular body, all tinged with a Sunday happy brightness, made Chloe's heart ache. He wasn't afraid to be silly, or to simply allow a little girl some pleasure. He knew life wasn't all about him, and he clearly wanted to make Evie happy.

The little mite tapped his knee. 'Thank you for pancakes, Van. And for varnish. Come to the park? Play ball?'

Chloe watched and laughed. 'Van? Van the man? No. Van has lots of things he needs to do today. Don't you?'

Thankfully, he nodded as he stood, gauging Chloe's reaction and meeting her eyes. 'Yes. I do.'

Evie tugged on his trouser leg and offered him her ball. 'Play ball?'

'No, honey, I need to go.' He went to get his jacket. 'How do I put my coat on and not smudge my nails? Geez, I have all the important questions today.'

'Normally we wait for it to dry.' Chloe laughed. 'You'll have to take it off before work tomorrow anyway. Get some nail varnish remover from the chemist on Kensington High Street. Aren't there rules about nail varnish and cooking, and health and safety?'

'More broken rules.' He cupped Chloe's chin in his pink fingernails. 'Chloe Cassidy, you'll be the ruin of me.'

A tiny foot lifted and stamped. Then the other one. A lip trembled. 'Van come too.'

'No. He's just told you, he has to go.' Chloe knew her eyes were registering a strict no, *do not give in.* But her heart was tapping away at the thought of him leaving. This close, he was in kissing distance again, and all she could think of was tasting him. Feeling his arms around her, drawing her to him as he nuzzled her throat.

Vaughn looked from Chloe to Evie and back again. There was a mirrored heat in his eyes, and yet an understanding that this was not his time. 'Hey, look, I can walk to the park with you if you like. It's on the way to my house.'

Chloe breathed. 'Okay, that's sorted then. Evie, Vaughn will come and play a little while, but then he has to go. Okay? No tears when he says good-bye.'

'Hmm. 'Kay.' The little girl gave him a huge smile and slipped her hand into his. No little fist in Auntie Chloe's. Yep, there was one more female who was totally smitten with him.

Holland Park was busy with tourists and locals alike, out in force in the May sunshine. The park borders were filled with an intense array of citrus-coloured flowers. Insects buzzed from bloom to bloom as cyclists, joggers and parents pushing pushchairs busied past. Somewhere someone was strumming a guitar—and... oh no... She double-checked it wasn't *TheBigCarlhuna*. No. Thank goodness. Although what a pretty picture the three of them would make, strolling through the park, doing normal Sunday things; that would show him.

Chloe breathed deeply again, acknowledging that just maybe she needed to let go of her animosity towards men who couldn't face her and break bad news.

Summer was only a fingertip stretch away, and the air was warm. There was a hopeful feel to the place, and she let it warm her, a thaw to the chill that had wafted around inside her, wondering whether to settle or just annoy the hell out of her for a little while.

The second they opened the playground gate, Evie ran towards the climbing frame, and for the first time that morning, there was no buffer between Chloe and Vaughn. For a few seconds, she wondered what to say or do but, making sure Evie couldn't see, Vaughn drew her into a hug and pecked a hurried kiss on Chloe's cheek, his words a whisper. 'God, I keep thinking back to last night... and this morning. I can't get the sight of you naked on my kitchen counter out of my head.'

Heat curled inside her, unbidden and unwanted, really. She didn't want to react to him the way she did, so instinctive, so raw. But she couldn't switch it off, and she couldn't control it. She couldn't hide her smile either, as memories tripped through her head of how much they'd shared yesterday. Being with him, laughing and joking with him seemed the most natural thing in the world. 'All those rules broken, though, Vaughn. Working at your place will never be the same again.'

'I don't suppose you'd fancy changing to working at night? We'd get way more privacy then.'

'And no work done.' Chloe edged away as Evie came

charging towards them. 'Do you want me to push you on the swings?'

'Don't you think I'm too big for that?' He grinned. 'I don't think I'll fit.'

'Ha ha. Evie, love, you don't want the swings? Back on the climbing frame? Okay, off you go.' Evie dealt with, Chloe turned back to Vaughn. 'Is everything a joke to you?'

'You know it isn't. I told you more about my life yesterday than I've ever told anyone.' His jaw clenched a little, and she was wondered whether he regretted letting her know more about his past. 'But you can't dwell on the bad things. Life's for the living, right?'

But not for loving. Not for loving anyone but Bella.

He'd trusted Chloe enough to share those things with her. He was giving her more and more of himself, but she only had questions. Taking a leaf out of his book and lightening up would be a good idea. 'Yes. Sorry. What with babysitting and everything, this isn't exactly how I thought today would turn out.'

'Hey, we all have commitments, family, work, things we have to do. This is fun. It's just a different part of life. Besides, today started well. Very, very well indeed.' His eyes brightened as he wound an arm around her waist, pulling her to him. He smelt of her mango-mandarin shower gel and something musky that was quintessentially him, with the chemical hint of nail varnish. 'It can end well too. Come over to mine later?'

'Do you have strawberries?'

His eyes glinted greedily. 'I can get some. I had fun last night, and I want you in my bed, Chloe. Or in yours. Whatever. Geography isn't important.'

'I don't know where you live. And I have a few things I need to do.'

Taking her by the shoulders, he looked at her, frowning. 'Are you okay? I keep getting these vibes that you're not. If you don't want me around, just let me know, okay? I don't want to play guessing games. I think we're better than that.'

She chose her words carefully, hiding the affection she felt for him. 'I'm just a little surprised that we're even having this kind of conversation, Vaughn. I wasn't expecting last night to pan out the way it did. Honestly. And I'm tired. Very tired.'

'I know. And it's all my fault. But all for a good cause.' He whispered into her hair, 'You just need to get more sleep.'

'I need a man who'll let me.' Maybe it was the lack of sleep, but her defences were down, and it was too hard to keep him at arm's length, so this time she did reach for him, because how could she not?

The memories of their lovemaking were still so fresh and clear and made her heart feel as if it was swelling out of her chest. She reached to his mouth, running her thumb over it. Smiling. Smiling at the way he made her feel. And in his eyes, she could see the same tug, the same heat, and she wanted a rerun of last night over and over and over.

Making sure Evie wasn't watching, Chloe pressed her mouth against his, snatching a tender quick kiss, ignoring the voices in her head warning, warning.

When he pulled away, Vaughn glanced at his watch. 'Shit, is that the time? Actually, I do need to get home. I've got a million things to do and kick off is at six-thirty.'

'Oh, yes.' Reality chipped away at her mood. 'Sunday football. With Jason.'

'Sure. It's a good way to keep fit.'

'I know. I used to go every week and watch.'

His face darkened. 'I didn't expect this to happen, Chloe. I won't go if that makes it any better.'

'Because of last night? Oh no, you should go. I wouldn't ever want to come between you and your cousin.'

Vaughn led her to an empty bench, and they sat watching the kids playing. 'He really hurt you, didn't he?'

It felt easy to talk to him about this, especially after the way he'd opened up to her. 'Yes, he did. You never imagine what betrayal can do to your confidence or your trust. It just eats away at you, and you're forever asking yourself if it's something you did or didn't do that made them stray. Was it me? Or is it just the way he is? Could he be faithful to someone else?' She thought then about mentioning the dating website but decided not to. It wasn't her problem anymore. 'But what is it about me that bored him? Because that's what he said it was. He was bored with us, with our life. With me, basically.'

Vaughn put his hand on her lap. 'Really? How could anyone ever get bored with you? I never know from one minute to the next if I'm going to get battered with flowers or a strange sense of calm wizardry in my office or making out like a goddess on my kitchen surfaces. You keep me on my toes. That is a rare talent you have.' He took hold of her hand. 'Did you really never suspect he was playing around?'

Chloe kept an eye on Evie, who was sitting in the sandpit, happily playing diggers alongside a boy who looked about four years old. It was all so simple at that age. 'No. I didn't. I'm far too trusting, clearly. He always said he loved me. I had no reason to think otherwise. But looking back, there were signs, obviously. I just didn't want to see them. He started to pick at me... little jeers here and there. Digs, you know... *You're no fun anymore. You always put work first. Why is your family always here?* And I guess I should have tried harder, but I was trying to keep my business afloat. My sister's husband had just died, and she had a baby. There was a lot going on, and I probably neglected him.'

'That is no excuse to treat you so badly.'

She couldn't imagine Vaughn doing anything like that. He was a man of honour. Unfortunately, to her detriment. 'Anyway, I don't want to talk about him. He's sure to bring my mood down. He's such a prat, honestly. I could kill him sometimes. And, oh God, I'm so sorry, he is your cousin.'

Clearly not remotely offended, Vaughn shrugged. 'He can be a jerk sometimes. To be honest, we all can, it's not just Jason's prerogative.'

'Well, I haven't seen any jerk symptoms appearing in you.'

'Give it time.'

'I just can't imagine it.' She looked up into his eyes and felt the connection that had been growing between them tighten even further. 'Of course, you must go and play football with him. You've known each other all your lives. And I really wouldn't want to get in the way of that. Just don't mention me, okay?'

He squeezed her hand. 'Are you embarrassed about what happened last night?'

'Of course not.'

'Do you regret it? Or—?'

'I just want to keep it private. I'm not sure I want to broadcast that we're… just having some fun.' She'd cut him off, afraid he'd ask her if she was getting in too deep, or if he was going to warn her about getting hurt when they decided to call it quits. All this misty-eyed nonsense would dissipate the minute she went back to her apartment and faced the reality of her spreadsheets. He was a good distraction, and if she wanted more, it was probably only because she was feeling tired, which always made her long for sofa cuddles and shared baths and lazy days. Like today. 'It was a good end to a great day. And yes, it would be very nice to do it again sometime.'

Looking a little relieved, he glanced around at the parents

with their little ones and then lowered his voice. 'So, Chloe Cassidy, are you saying you want to use me for sex?'

'Would it be bad of me if I said yes?' She couldn't help laughing, but deep down she knew she should have put an end to it all. But what harm were they doing? They knew what they were getting into, and getting back on the horse was a good thing. It gave her something else to think about other than all the things she had to do for the business and for her family. It gave her just a little secret something for herself. And there was nothing wrong with that.

He took both her hands in his, suddenly serious—or as serious as a man could get with hot pink nails. 'It's good to know we want the same things. Tell me if that ever changes.'

Heart pumping hard, she looked away to check on Evie and to stop herself from looking into those dark grey eyes and telling him the truth. 'It won't.'

CHAPTER 18

'Nother story… please, Auntie Coee.' A very sleepy Evie handed Chloe a fourth bedtime story book and lay back down against Chloe's chest, her chubby little thumb stuck firmly in her mouth. She'd been played out, fed to bursting by an award-winning chef and bathed in strawberry bath bubbles. Now she was snuggled up under her Peppa Pig duvet using Chloe as a pillow. Her wide eyes were starting to glaze, and she was becoming a dead weight on Chloe's chest. It was well past her niece's bedtime, but Chloe couldn't resist this extra time; there was something so very special and trusting about a small child falling asleep in your arms. It was a huge responsibility and yet a promise to hold their hearts safe.

She wondered briefly whether her father had ever felt like that. Then she tried not to think about him at all, or the loss of that trust that had dogged her life lately. She wanted to love openheartedly; she wanted to feel the intense, fierce affection for a man that she wasn't afraid to feel for her niece or her sister or mother.

Before she'd opened the book, Jenna appeared at the door. Her cheeks were unusually pink, and her blue eyes were a brighter aquamarine than usual. She tiptoed in and whispered, 'Hey, how's my little girl?'

'Just going... going... gone.' Chloe pressed a kiss to Evie's sweaty forehead as she watched the little girl's lips slacken, the thumb slipping forwards as her body finally relaxed in to the sleep she'd been fighting for the last hour. Wriggling slowly and carefully, Chloe managed to extricate herself without waking up the sleeping babe, and waited in the corridor while her sister finished tucking her daughter in. 'Fancy a quick wine before I head off? I want to hear all about your day.'

'Hell, yes.' Jenna led the way back downstairs to the lounge. 'God knows, I need one.'

Chloe poured two glasses of chardonnay while Jenna began to tidy up the debris of the last two hours' playtime; building bricks, dolls, drawing paper, Play-Doh. 'Geez, one small child sure makes a lot of mess. Right, Jenna. Stop clearing up, and sit down. I can finish this. You look knackered.'

'I am. Thanks, honey. I owe you a big one for doing this.'

'She's my gorgeous niece; I love looking after her. Now, put your feet up and spill. How was your day?'

Jenna slumped onto the sofa, stretched out her legs and took a huge gulp of wine. 'I'm exhausted, to be honest, but it was totally fine. Lovely, actually. You were right. It was nice to be out doing something different.'

'And how was this mysterious Nick?'

Jenna's eyes sort of misted and Chloe's stomach jumped a little. It had been a long time since she'd seen her sister looking so animated about anything, let alone a man. Maybe she'd finally let her precious husband go? Probably not, but maybe she was starting to move on. 'He's okay, actually. Not at all like I remember. He's got this confidence about him, kind of assured, you know. I guess that comes from giving orders to people. Although I wouldn't let him give any to me. I told him straight up—I'm here to help, but I don't do salutes, and I won't jump when you say jump.' Jenna gripped the stem of her wine glass and seemed a little distracted at the memory; her cheeks were still pink even though the room was cool. 'I hope I wasn't snappy. I tried to turn it into a joke.'

Chloe laughed. 'You? Snappy? Never.'

'He did look a bit scared at one point. Do you remember he was all lanky, spindly arms and legs at school, wasn't he? Very geeky? But he's not like that now. He's...' She took a deep breath, and Chloe could have sworn her sister actually sighed at the thought of Nick. Jenna's mouth twitched at the corners as if she was tasting something delicious. 'Well, he's pretty gorgeous actually.'

Chloe felt her eyes widening. 'Jenna? Is this really you talking?'

The pink cheeks turned a brighter shade of red, and she smiled. 'My libido might be non-existent, but I can still appreciate quality when I see it. I am a red-blooded woman after all. Yes, he's very nice. You remember that advert for the washing powder where the guy took all of his clothes off in a laundrette, except for his boxers? We were all mesmerised by his body and recorded it and kept putting it on repeat? God, he was gorgeous.'

'Who? Advert guy or Nick?'

Jenna looked away, blinking slowly. 'The advert guy, of course. But Nick, he has a couple of scars from shrapnel—oh, you know he was nearly killed in Afghanistan?—but that makes him more rugged in a way. He's kind of like advert man, but real, and better somehow, you know.'

'No, I don't know. I haven't a clue. Are you telling me he took his clothes off?'

Jenna looked simultaneously shocked and yet thrilled at the thought. 'Don't be ridiculous! It was the first time I've seen him for years, and there were removal people coming in and out, and his parents... Good God, Chloe, one night of sex and you've got it on the brain. It wasn't that kind of afternoon.'

'Thank the Lord for that.' Chloe thought back to the cosy afternoon she'd had with Evie and Vaughn, which had been a far cry from the night of sex, but nonetheless enjoyable. 'So... and... well...?'

'Well, nothing. He's just a nice guy.'

Once again, Chloe sensed a but coming. 'But?'

'But now he's moved in, and I imagine he'll be too busy with work and things.'

'Too busy to what?'

'Oh, nothing.' Jenna flushed. 'I'm just being silly. Honestly. I am. Tell me about your day. How was my girl? Was she good? Did she eat anything? I'm worried she's getting a bit fussy with her food. Apparently that can happen when they hit three.'

'That's right, change the subject. I'll humour you because you're clearly tired, but I won't let you off so easily next time. Evie ate three huge pancakes with chocolate spread, peanut butter and bananas. A pear for afternoon tea and I gave her some spaghetti on toast when we got home from the park 'cos I know it's her favourite, and I didn't have the energy for arguing.'

'She doesn't like bananas. Or peanut butter.'

'She does now.'

Jenna sat forward, eyes narrowing. 'And you don't know how to make pancakes.'

'Vaughn made them, and he had her help him.' She shouldn't have felt guilty about that, but for some reason she did, just a little. She'd shared Evie's time with him, but they'd all enjoyed it.

The way Jenna looked at her was half scrutiny, half admiration. 'So he stayed a while?'

'It's good for Evie to have positive male role models, right? He cooked breakfast, came to the park and then went to play football. With Jason.' And that felt strange and weird as if she was living some part of her old life, but from the outside looking in.

'Are you okay with that?'

'It's really none of my business.' Vaughn was his own man; she couldn't tell him what to do, and she wouldn't dream of doing so. 'But he did ask if I was okay with it. That was refreshing. New.'

Pouring another large glass, Jenna peered at her in that questioning way that sisters have. They want the truth, the whole truth and nothing but... 'So things are getting heavy with le chef?'

This time, Chloe hugged the absolute truth close to her chest. 'I'm determined to keep everything simple. He's just a bit of fun.'

'Sweetie, nothing's just a bit of fun. Trust me on this.'

'Says the woman who invented the Love Plan.'

'You needed a date. I wanted you to play a little, not invest so much in a man that you go work for him, spend your weekends with him and forget everything else for him.'

This was starting to get uncomfortable, mainly because she'd actually pinpointed Chloe's dilemma. 'So, plans to see Nick again?'

'He did ask me to have a drink next week. But I don't think I will. Is there anything on the TV?' Sluggishly, Jenna leant forward, grabbed the remote control and crossed her arms. To everyone else, this would mean she wasn't talking anymore.

To Chloe, it was an invitation to dig deeper and find out what was eating her little sister. It wasn't that she was trying to be nosy; it was because sometimes Jenna needed protecting from herself. She was determined not to have a good time. Ever again. 'Why not go out with him? I'll babysit.'

'Because I haven't got time to be doing things like that.'

'Like what? Enjoying yourself?'

There was a Cassidy roll of the eyes as if Chloe should try keeping up with Jenna's life. 'How can I enjoy myself with another man when Ollie's watching down on me? I can't. Chloe, I can't.'

'He wouldn't want you to be sad for the rest of your life. He'd want you to find someone else.'

'There is no one else. No one could ever be as perfect for me as he was. And besides, look at me, Chloe.' She pointed to her body. A perfectly good size twelve. It was a strong body; it had weathered terrible things. And sure, like everyone, there were wobbly bits, but they were glorious, well fought for curves as far as Chloe was concerned.

'You're beautiful.'

'I'm fat. That's what I am. I've got so many stretch marks on my belly and my thighs I look like an ordnance survey map. And I have saggy boobs, and most of my clothes are stained by Evie's food. I probably smell like a three-year-old's poop, and if I'm lucky, I might just have nits too.' Jenna's hand went instinctively to her head and scratched a little. 'Did you notice whether she was scratching her head?'

'No. I didn't notice. I don't think so, though. And your stretch marks are just little silver lines, sweetie.' Chloe had no idea that Jenna had such a hang up about the way she looked. 'Look at what you've been through; you gave birth, for God's sake. That's a whole new person right there that you created. You've been through an awful lot, Jenna. You've earned those damned lines.

And there're no saggy bits in the world that can compete with decent shapewear and a damned good bra. And anyway, what the heck has any of that got to do with Nick?'

'Exactly. It has nothing to do with him. He wouldn't be interested.'

Shock registered in Chloe's chest. *Jenna. Was. Interested. In. Nick.* 'Of course he would. What's wrong with a real woman?'

Jenna grimaced and downed another half a glass of wine. 'A real woman? He's been holed up in Afghanistan with a squadron of beautiful, athletic, skinny women who kick-ass and shoot guns. They're all very real. Just not my kind of ordinary-real.'

'It's the army, love, not *Survivor*. I doubt they'll walk around in bikinis with AK47s slung over their bare shoulders. And even if they do, why should that matter? You can kick-arse when you want to.'

'Because how would he ever look at me when he could have one of them?'

Chloe looked at the nearly empty bottle of wine. All of this was so not how Jenna usually acted. Where was her happy, shiny smile? 'Maybe you're exactly what he wants?'

'Well, I'm not going to find out.'

'He asked you out for a drink, but even though you fancy him you're not going?'

'No. And I don't fancy him. Stop that. I can't go out with him. I just can't.'

Well, we're going to see about that. 'It's your life, I guess. But I just don't see what the problem would be to have one teeny drink. Not like now, obviously, given you're three-quarters through a bottle. But one drink wouldn't hurt.'

'No. And that's my final answer.'

The wine was going down well, but Chloe needed to get home and put together a proposal and an estimate for the festival wedding. 'Hey, was that Evie I heard? I think she's crying. Do you want me to go up?'

'No, no. You've done enough. I'll go; I've missed her. Going out without her is a bit like having an arm missing. I kept holding my hand out to Nick to walk across the road—so embarrassing!'

'Did he take it?'

'Don't be stupid. He just looked at me as if I was a lemon. And grinned.'

'So, there's a man with a sense of humour. Big tick for that. There are worse things you could do.' Like having sex on a kitchen counter. She couldn't quite believe how she'd found the temerity to just walk up to the restaurant and ask Vaughn for sex.

If it hadn't been for Jenna setting her up on those dates, and the walk back from the cafe after *DrewsAmused*, she'd never have been in this situation. Funny how life had a way of springing things on you, pushing you in directions you couldn't ever imagine going.

An idea bloomed fresh in Chloe's head.

Maybe that's what Jenna needed—a little push in the right direction. It was nothing more than what Jenna had already done for Chloe. 'Okay, hon. I'll get going now. I have to write a proposal for a new client. Oh yes, I forgot to tell you, we have another wedding to organise. Two amazing women I met at Taylor's wedding yesterday.' Had it only been yesterday? It seemed like an age ago, so much had happened in between time. 'A festival theme with haystacks and long-stemmed bouquets, daisies in the hair and floaty dresses. Just up your street.' There was another little murmur from upstairs. 'Oh, oh, there she goes again. Give her a kiss from me. Let's talk tomorrow.'

As her sister left the room, Chloe dug deep into the bag Jenna had left on the floor by the sofa. Taking out her phone, she wrote down a number. *It's for her own good*, she convinced herself. It would be so great for Jenna to have a little excitement in her life, to have random sex in random places, to feel something again.

No harm done: a little matchmaking for the matchmaker.

* * *

The numbers were starting to make Chloe's eyes blur. Not enough sleep meant she was struggling to make the maths work, but Sam and Greer had texted to say they wanted an estimate soon so they could start the wedding ball rolling. Plus, the wine was starting to make her head feel a little woozy. Even so, there was no way she'd take a risk on losing this contract; it had to be sent tonight.

But her thoughts kept swinging her back to this morning when Vaughn had been here in this room and next door, in her bed. His scent still lingered everywhere, but the taste of him was just a memory. Down low in her gut, her body tightened at the thought of him inside her, how good he had felt.

Concentrate.

She started to do the sums again but was interrupted when the doorbell rang.

So late? Chloe glanced at the clock on her computer. Nine forty-three. Not so late in reality, but it just felt like it, given the number of hours she'd spent in bed but not sleeping, and the sheer amount of energy Evie had taken up.

God knew how Jenna managed, every single day.

She peered through the blinds.

Vaughn?

Vaughn.

Damn. Typical that he'd just turn up when she was in her PJs and with wet straggly hair. She briefly thought about changing, or not answering the door, but decided, to hell with it; he'd have to take her as she was. This was her life; this was who she was. If he didn't like it, he could walk away.

'Hey.' She opened the door, trying to control the thrumming of her heartbeat as she took in his messy hair and kind eyes. 'How was the football?'

Those eyes were like bright stars shining with pride. 'We won. Three-two.'

'Well done. And you're not out celebrating with the lads?'

'There are better ways to celebrate. I brought you a present.' Smiling, he held out a punnet of strawberries. There was no trace of pink varnish on his fingers, she noticed.

'Wow, thank you. This is… unexpected. I can't wait to… ahem… eat them.' And lovely for him to turn up unannounced, asking for more of her. 'You got rid of the varnish.'

He grinned and glanced at his fingers. 'It was either that or risk a whole lot of questions you don't want me to answer.'

'Oh, yes. Of course. Well, thank you for thinking of me.'

Now he ran the varnish-less fingers through his hair. 'Is it insane of me to say I can't stop thinking about you?'

'Hell, no. I'm very flattered.' It was so damned hard not to jump on him right now, every part of her was screaming to let him in, but she had to stick to her priorities.

He watched her reaction to him, reading her body language so well. 'Is this a bad time? I should have texted, but thought I'd surprise you. Bad idea?'

'Normally, no. Normally, a fantabulous idea. Normally the best bloody idea ever. But I'm working; I have to get a quote off tonight.'

If he thought it strange she was working late on a Sunday evening, he didn't say so. He just nodded, the smile still there, confident that she wasn't fobbing him off. 'Okay. No problem. Another time, then?'

'You can come in and wait until I'm done if you like?'

'I don't want to disturb you. You're already short on time because you're working for me. You didn't get to do this earlier today because you were caring for your sister's needs. You need time for you. I'll head off and leave you to it.' Which was so unlike Jason's usual response she was taken aback. Her ex would have spent the evening disturbing her simply because her work was diverting her attention away from him. She used to think it was endearing that he needed to be entertained by her. In hindsight, she could see it was just his insecurities toying with her innate ability to feel guilty about things she should never feel guilty about.

And hell, the thought of another night with Vaughn perked her up a surprising amount. Her body began to tingle in anticipation of his touch on her skin. She wrapped her hand around the fruit punnet, then breathed in quickly as he kissed her softly on the lips.

When he stopped, she felt the smile spreading through her body, waking up parts of her that she'd assumed would be resting tonight. 'No. Come in. If you're happy to sit and read or listen to music until I'm done?'

'I'm sure I can entertain myself.' For the first time ever, he looked a little sheepish. 'I just couldn't get you out of my head.'

'You too?' His honesty made her heart flutter, and she pulled him to her, kissing him some more, her hands finding those hard muscles of his arms and stroking the nape of his neck. It felt like there would never be enough kisses.

But he stopped her, slowing things down with his hand on hers. 'Noooo. Work first. Then you get your reward.'

She shrugged his hand away and placed hers on the waistband of his jeans. 'This first.'

He gave her a wry half smile that was so sexy it almost undid her then and there. 'Work. And then you'll need sustenance. The strawberries will do for starters. I have plenty planned for the main course.'

'Greedy. And a very, very attractive proposition.' Her eyes met his and she saw the need for her shimmering there. Vibrant, like him. He was surprising, this man. He hid what he felt, and he fought what he wanted because of a promise he'd made, but it shone there in his face, in his body. He wanted her.

He kissed the dip in her throat. Then her nose. Her eyelids. Her mouth. 'Greedy for you, yes. Bloody ravenous.'

'I'll never concentrate with you here and this'—she palmed his erection—'in the room.'

'God, Chloe,' he groaned against her mouth. It was such a sexy sound; she felt the thrill of it through her body.

She started to unzip his jeans. 'Clearly someone doesn't need a lot of encouragement.'

'No, me neither.' He laughed, his hands on her waist as he walked her into the lounge, backed her up to the sofa and lay her down.

'I can't work and want this at the same time. I can't work until we've got this out of our system, full stop.'

Soft kisses became more charged, more intense. The strawberries were discarded somewhere on the floor. Along with her pyjama top. His jacket. T-shirt. Jeans. Her pyjama bottoms.

Then he was inside her again, slow this time. Tender. Each stroke deeper and more intense than the one before. Each breath in sync. Each heartbeat in harmony. She felt as if every cell in her body was alight. Her head was blurred with the pleasure of him filling her. His taste. His strength. His care for her, and his need.

As he moved inside her, he held her there captured in his gaze. The way he looked at her filled her chest with a bright light, a flame shimmering, burning down the defences she'd built.

Erasing her reticence, it built pathways of warmth to her heart. This man. *This.*

The bright light seemed to engulf her, a powerful emotion that filled her heart, singed her skin, branded him onto her—his name, his touch, his kisses. He thrust deep and hard, and she responded by bucking against him, urging him on, wanting to savour every inch of him. Wrapping her close to him, he breathed in her ear, 'This is amazing, Chloe. You are blowing my mind.'

'Is it real?' she asked him, because it was too perfect, too right, too damned beautiful for her ever to have contemplated that sex could be like this. This went deeper than fun. This meant something. No matter how hard she tried, she couldn't stop liking him, wanting him. No matter how hard she tried, he was kissing a trail straight to her heart.

'I bloody well hope so. I want you, Chloe. I want you so damned much.' His gaze caught hers again, and she snapped her eyes closed, afraid he'd see the emotion swimming there. But it didn't help. Her kisses, her body melting into his, his name on her lips, all betrayed her. She couldn't not feel something for him. She couldn't hide this desire. And she couldn't stop.

So she kissed him some more, urgently. Greedily. Rising with him to his climax. Edging nearer and nearer to the edge. And that connection, the tiny threads strengthening, tugged them dangerously closer and closer and closer.

'Feel better?' Vaughn dragged a throw over them both and held her tight against his chest. He was laughing, which was becoming more and more common with him. He'd hidden that part of himself at first, but he'd let her in, just a little, and every day it was a little more. But at some point he'd stop, she knew, and she wouldn't hear that delightful rumble that came from deep in his chest. 'Think you can concentrate on work now?'

Never. Never while he was within the nearest hundred miles or so. 'I suppose so. If I have to.'

He tapped her bottom. 'You have to. The plan was that we celebrated after you got your work done.'

She tapped him back. *God,* he had a great backside. 'Slave driver.'

'Someone has to be. Otherwise, we'd spend all day doing this and be bankrupt by the end of the week.'

We. One word that was so tiny and yet so significant.

Her heart stretched, but she didn't want to pursue that line of thought. He'd warned her of how little he could give, and she wasn't sure how close he was to shutting her out. 'Okay, give me time to catch my breath, and I'll get to it in a minute. And you can make some tea while I'm slaving over a hot laptop. I'm parched.'

He sat up, pulling her with him, seemingly unwilling to let her go quite yet as he absentmindedly stroked the inside of her thighs. 'Are you saying you actually own tea bags now? That is a step up. Next thing, you'll have all those luxury extras like bread. Milk?'

'Whoa... baby steps. Like I said, I'm a work in progress.' She kissed him again, slipping her fingers into his. 'You ever thought about how weird this is? I mean, when I saw you striding up the aisle all grumpy and serious in your morning coat, I never imagined that this could happen. It wasn't even on my radar.'

'I would hope not, seeing as you were waiting to marry another bloke.'

She remembered his taut expression as he'd walked towards her. The tight shoulders, the fixed jaw. Every step he took closer, she knew. She just knew what he was going to say, so when he reached her, she was already at boiling point. 'I hated you. I mean, really, really hated you for ruining my day. My whole life, actually. And Jason too... I hated him more than anything.'

'I know. I'm sorry I had to do it. If it helps, I hated Jason at that moment too, to be letting you down and not having the guts to say it himself. You were the most beautiful thing I'd ever seen. The second I set eyes on you in that frothy dress and long veil, I knew you were something. I also knew my cousin was an idiot. But there you go. His loss and all that...' He laughed again. 'Of course, that was until you beat me up with the flowers; then I realised you're just plain crazy. Beautiful, but completely mad.'

'Hey! It takes one to know one.'

His legs wrapped around hers, cuddling her in. 'I'm just grateful you weren't wooed by guitar guy. Or dog-in-a-bag man. Then we might not be doing this at all.'

The Love Plan seemed such a long time ago, when she'd been trying hard to be someone she wasn't. 'Believe me, I was torn. Unfortunately, neither of them appeared to think I was remotely the girl for them. Actually, I've been thinking that *DrewsAmused* might be the kind of man my mum would fall for. If he managed the dog hair a bit better and bought a comb.'

Vaughn grunted. 'Matchmaking? Really? I don't know your mum or your sister very well, but are you sure that's such a good idea?'

'It does make me feel just a little bit weird thinking about my mum and a man.' She squirmed. 'Ugh. But we all need somebody.'

'Do we, though? I thought you were done with love.' His smile was still there, but his body language had changed. His shoulders had hitched, and there was a little twitch in his cheek.

'For stress relief. And fun.' She kissed him, trying to diffuse the emotion in her chest and trying hard to convince both of them that there were no emotions there at all. 'And strawberries, of course. Who are we to deny that to anyone? I've already texted Jenna's friend, Nick, and asked him to meet me and Jenna for a drink next week.'

He frowned. 'Are you sure it's a good thing to get involved in something like that?'

Chloe thought about how spooked Jenna was yesterday about even thinking of Nick in any way other than a friendship—and because of some misplaced loyalty, she wasn't going to let a good man into her life, friend or otherwise. That would be a shame, for herself as well as Evie. Her daughter needed good men in her life. 'I don't know if it's the right thing at all, to be honest. But she gave me a push to jump back into the dating pool and look what happened. Fun, yes?'

'We're dating?' He froze, then tried to hide it behind a grin. She was also aware of a momentary panic in his eyes that left as she brushed off any suggestion of connection between them.

'Don't be daft. I think dating involves going out, you know, for dinner, or to the cinema, dressing up nicely. I don't think a walk to the play park with a toddler or random sex in a variety of locations counts.'

He sat up a little more, putting some distance between them. 'Do you want to go out?'

Dredging up a smile, she made her voice lighter than she felt. 'When would I have the time for a date? Seriously? I work two jobs and spend the rest of my time babysitting.' Judging by the relaxation of his shoulders, he seemed suitably reassured, although she wasn't. Because the thought of dating Vaughn made her undeniably happier. Which made her feel worse. Which made her switch the conversation to something else. 'I think I need to repay Jenna after getting me back on your horse—excuse the terminology.'

'Excused.' He actually looked quite proud at that. 'Glad to oblige.'

'Although, I'm not going to suggest she does the whole beautifying thing I did. It's way too much hassle.' She saw his eyebrows raise and regretted mentioning it immediately. 'Not that you need to know anything about my bikini waxing fails.'

'Oh? I think I do.' He prodded a finger into her ribcage, again and again, making her wriggle and squirm. 'I'm not going to stop this until you tell.'

'Never!'

'Now. Biking wax fails, or I tickle you forever.'

'Stop! Stop.'

His finger prodded, but then his hand palmed her breast. 'You like this? You like this. God, I like this. But no more until you tell me.'

'Okay! I surrender! But you have to promise not to judge me or to laugh. No laughing, okay?'

'Okay.' But his mouth was tipped up in a grin, and his shoulders were already shaking.

So she told him about the blue Smurf fluff and her Velcro-ed legs and Sheila/Shona/Sheena, and his eyes grew huge, and he guffawed, pulling up the throw and diving underneath. 'Show me. Show me.'

She ducked under too, pushing his hands away playfully. 'You've already explored enough, thank you very much.'

'You are absolute gold, Chloe.' This was a side of him she didn't see very often. The man who could be silly and serious and sexy all at the same time. He cupped her face and grinned. 'You are truly one of a kind. I wish I'd seen it.'

'No, you really don't.'

He snuggled against her, his hand reaching down between her thighs. 'Hey, come to Papa Smurf.'

'Not bloody likely with that chat-up line.' But she kissed him anyway, and somehow one thing led to another, and his *magic* hands made her come *with* Papa Smurf all over again.

It took Chloe a few minutes to anchor herself back to planet Earth. The room was dark save for the glow of her laptop and the orange sheen from the street lamps filtering through the blinds.

'We are so, so good at that.' She stretched out her legs one at a time, her eyes closed, breathing in Vaughn's scent. Her limbs were languid and limp, her heart as full as it had ever been as she grabbed the throw and pulled it back over them. It had suddenly turned cold in the room. 'Well, wow. I'm definitely not stressed anymore.'

'Well, fuck it, I bloody well am.'

Chloe's stomach lurched. That was not Vaughn's voice, and it wasn't in her ear or whispering softly over her neck; it ricocheted across the room, bouncing off the walls.

Vaughn jumped up, leaving a cold space between them and a chill in her heart as it thumped loud and hard.

Her eyes snapped open. 'Jason?'

Jenna

Sender: Jennacass567@gmail.com

~~Dear Nick…~~
~~Hi Nick!~~
Nick,

Thanks for today. I love your apartment. Very nice! I like the cool blue paint you've chosen for the walls ~~and the slatted blinds~~. (Lame, Jenna!!!!!)

Here's the website I told you about for the custom shelves: www.shelfsolutions.co.uk

They're great and quick and not too expensive.

Er… You know we talked about going out for dinner? Well, the thing is… you see, ~~you're too nice, and I'm in a kind of whirl about seeing you~~ I have trouble getting a babysitter.

~~I'm scared that you're so hot, and I'm too fat and that I'm reading things into our conversations. Did I imagine that long pause and the way there was an electrical surge when our hands touched?~~

Shit. Shit and shit. This is rubbish. I can't even say the things I want to say. I'm so bloody scared about just being even a friend. What kind of person does that make me? Half of one? Because I don't really feel whole. I haven't felt whole for a long time.

It's too hard being brave all the time and sometimes I just want someone to share the difficult times with. I'm so lonely. I know I have Mum and Chloe... but they've been such a help for so long I don't want to keep going on and on. I should feel better by now. I should. But part of me doesn't want to.

Okay...
Nick, I had a lovely time today, too lovely. And it felt so nice to be with someone with no pressure to be anyone but myself. You seemed to accept me exactly for who I am. You were considerate and kind and asked about Evie, and you wanted to see the photos. And when we sat on the packing boxes, and you asked me about Ollie you looked so devastated when I told you. You held my hand and just sat in silence, and I wanted to lean against you and cry and cry and cry. I wanted to lean into your strength and your compassion and I couldn't because I just can't let go. Ever. I can't ever be that person I was, and I mourn for that innocence and the joy I know I'll never have again.

So please don't be nice to me again like that. I can't bear it. My life is all about nits and nurseries and mind-numbing things that a three-year-old wants to hear, and being a mummy and living for my daughter. And your life is just starting again—you're so positive about your move here and about your future. And I'm so glad you think you'll be happy back in London.

But for the first time in a very long time, I found myself thinking about a future too, and that spooked me so badly I wanted to cling to you and to run at the same time. That doesn't make sense. Well, it does to me. So, until I feel brave enough to step out of my comfort zone and be a new person all over again (and let's face it, I've already pushed myself into a dark corner being this person, and I've dug in hard and deep. So deep I've kind of got used to it. I don't like it, but there it is. It's where I am.) I don't think I can see you again.

Best of luck

Jenna x

CHAPTER 19

'What the hell?' Chloe sat up, blindly reaching for her clothes, which were scattered across the lounge room floor. It felt like a dress-of-shame as she wiggled to the edge of the sofa and grasped her pyjama bottoms with a hand snaking out from beneath the throw.

'I could say the same.' Jason glared at them both as he stormed into the room, mocking her words and her voice. 'What the hell, Chloe? What the hell, *VAUGHN*?'

'You gave me back your key. So how come…?' Had she forgotten to lock it? No. It was a Chubb. It locked automatically. 'I knew I should have changed the bloody locks.'

But there hadn't been any money for that, for keeping her safe. She'd trusted him to keep away and get on with living his new life. He seemed pretty happy doing that, blithely and selfishly doing what he pleased.

Not anymore, clearly.

He looked very guilty. But not as guilty as he was angry. He shrugged sullenly but remained tight-lipped.

'Did you have a spare or something?' Her gut tightened. 'Oh, my God, did you have a copy made?'

Another shrug. 'I had one made, yes. In case I needed to see you or come back home. You know, to *our* house.'

Fury started to build in her chest despite the fact she was trying to drag on inside-out pyjamas. If this was on the TV, it would have been funny. It wasn't. It bloody well wasn't. 'This is *my* home, Jason. You have nothing to do with it; you made sure of that when you demanded a payout.'

But Jason had tuned out; he was too busy staring down his cousin. 'What the fuck are you doing here?'

'Isn't that obvious?' Vaughn looked indignant, and if he hadn't been such an honourable man, she had no doubt he'd have smashed his cousin to the floor. He didn't. Staying covered by the throw, he pulled on his jeans and his T-shirt. Then he stood up and pointed to the door, simultaneously handing Chloe her pyjama top. He snarled at Jason, 'Outside.' It wasn't an invitation; it was an order. 'Can't you see Chloe needs some privacy?'

'I wondered where you'd gone after football. We always have a drink after.' Jason looked his cousin up and down and tried his hand at sneering; it came out more like a playground whine. 'If anyone's going to leave, it's you.'

Vaughn reared up. He was at least six inches taller than Jason and broader. But his inner strength came to the fore, calming his voice, keeping him steady. 'I said, come outside, Jason, just for a few minutes. We can all talk once Chloe's got some clothes on.'

Jason shook his head. 'It is true, then? You and her?'

Chloe turned to Vaughn, unable to believe he hadn't done as she'd asked. Her voice was a whisper as she asked him, 'Did you... did you tell him when I asked you not to?'

He turned to her, registering surprise. 'Of course I didn't. What do you think I am?'

'Tell me what?' Jason's hard, black eyes bore first into Vaughn, then into her as he assessed the situation. For once, he joined the dots correctly. 'It's not hard to work it out. You were dancing at that wedding, and his car's parked outside. You're doing it... in my house. On my sofa.' He clearly couldn't bring himself to say the words out loud. It had been fine when he was *doing it* with someone else in Chloe's bed.

She wouldn't lower herself to his level and have that argument. Finally dressed and feeling more confident and infinitely angrier, Chloe raised her head. 'Why are you here? Are you drunk again?'

'No. I'm very clearheaded right now, actually.' Jason took a step forward, but Vaughn didn't let him past, shielding her. 'I want to talk to you, Chloe. But only when he's gone.'

Vaughn shook his head. 'I'm not going anywhere, so whatever it is you want to say, say it.'

There were a few long moments of silence as the men weighed each other up, like alpha lions assessing other males. Chloe looked from one to the other, wishing someone would say something, do something. The tension wrapped around them and tightened.

Eventually, Jason nodded. 'So be it. I'll say it anyway and then see what happens.'

'Say what?' She had a really bad feeling about this.

Really bad.

Vaughn's eyebrows rose, but he nodded, indicating to Jason to speak.

Her ex stepped forward, took her hand and made her sit on the sofa. She felt vulnerable there, with these two men standing above her, so tall. So much testosterone, so much at stake—family ties were at risk here. A lifetime of connection compared to a month she'd shared with Vaughn. Too many years with Jace. It felt as if the room were closing in on her. 'Okay, boys, I'm going to stand up, too. Or you can both sit. Either which, I don't care. But somebody move.'

Vaughn didn't move one muscle.

Chloe stood.

Jason was still holding her hand, so he had to stand too. And they were all three of them cramped into her tiny lounge as if in some bad Victorian melodrama. One suitor grasping her hand, the other watching and grimacing. Only, of course, Vaughn was no suitor, he was... what was he? *A bit of fun.*

Ah, yes.

But the truth was, he was so much more than that, and right now watching her messy life unfold, instead of being impressed by her witty repartee about Smurf genitals and her not-committed hot, sexy kisses.

Her throat felt as if it was closing over.

Jason smiled, gently, tentatively. He pushed a lock of her hair back behind her ear with a hand that was, surprisingly, trembling. In his eyes, she could see he was scared, truly scared, and possibly being honest for the first time in his life. She didn't want to hear what he was going to say, but it was like watching a car crash unfold... she couldn't not hear it either.

'Thing is, Chloe, I made a mistake. A big bloody mistake, and I'm not afraid to say so. I know what I did was unforgivable, so I'm not expecting you to forgive me. But I want you to know that I love you.'

Vaughn coughed. Chloe glanced up at him, but he still didn't move. His eyes were burning into Jason's back with such animosity that it made her heart almost split in two. These men were cousins. This was her fault.

And yet, despite everything he'd done, there was still a scant affection there for Jason. She'd been with him for a very long time. She hadn't fallen out of love easily; she'd fought it for a while, fought it hard.

They'd shared a lot—a long past and dreams of a future together. She remembered the day he proposed, down on one knee at the top of the London Eye. The way he'd waited, breathless for her answer, like an anxious schoolboy. The day when Ollie died, and he'd cradled her in his arms and whispered sweet things to her all night. The way they used to go out dancing to Vixen nightclub, which was a dive, but was their dive where they met up with their group of weird and wonderful friends and laughed and danced into the early hours.

They'd had some good times. Some very good times. But it wasn't enough. Nowhere near. He'd been gutless and unfaithful. 'I'm sorry, Jason. I don't want you to love me.'

'But we could start again. I miss you, babe. I want to come home.' He scrubbed a hand across his face, and for a moment, she thought he was crying.

Yes, there were tears in his eyes.

None in hers. 'What about Amy?'

Jason looked back at his cousin, shook his head, then turned to Chloe. 'I've left her.'

Vaughn cursed loudly.

'Oh. Oh, I see. With a baby on the way, too?' She didn't know what to make of this. How to feel. Because once upon a time, she'd wanted him to come home and beg for her forgiveness, to admit his faults and want to work harder on their relationship. She'd wanted him to declare his love for her in front of witnesses in a church. Although, in private would have done. She'd just wanted him to love her as much as she'd loved him.

She didn't love him now, though. What she'd felt for him was nothing compared to the way Vaughn made her feel.

Which meant…

Did it?

Vaughn's voice split the room. 'You were complaining to everyone at football that Amy kicked you out.'

'Ah.' That certainly went some way to explaining things. Chloe was the fallback, the default. That indignancy she'd seen on Vaughn's face now welded to her chest. 'Did she find your dating profile. Searching4You? Is that why? The fact you've been trying—probably succeeding, although God knows how—to cheat while she's pregnant. The fact you've had a dating profile for *five years?*'

Jason let her hand drop. 'How do you know? Have you been checking up on me?'

'Don't flatter yourself. Now, I think you need to go.'

But he stayed exactly where he was. What was it with these men? No one seemed capable of budging at all. 'Give me one more chance, Chloe. I'll get it right. I'll be the perfect husband. We can start again, something new. It'll be better. We can be so much more. I'll overlook this... Vaughn issue.'

She actually laughed. Was he serious? 'Oh, that's very generous of you. But I don't want you back. I wouldn't have you back even if you did actually turn up at a church and swear everlasting love to me in front of the bloody Queen.'

'That's not what you said when you begged me to come home. When you phoned me in the middle of the night—how many times?' Jason's tone started to turn nasty, his eyes narrowing to dark slits. 'It started to frighten Amy. And all those texts, Chloe—'

'Stop it. Shut up. I was hurting. You hurt me.' Her cheeks were burning. She'd buried deep just how hard she'd tried to get Jason to see sense and come back to her. Then, how she'd just wanted an explanation. How low she'd actually been. Forgotten or pushed it aside as an embarrassing part of her life she *wanted* to forget. Now her humiliation was complete as Vaughn looked at her.

Pity. That's what she saw in his eyes. Pity and other emotions fighting there too—things she couldn't read, things she'd never ever seen before in him. Probably a huge dose of regret of ever having met her at all, and a desire to get the hell out of here as quickly as possible.

He walked over to Jason, towering above him. 'You heard her, Jason. She doesn't want anything from you. I think you'd better go.'

But Jason wasn't listening; he'd written a script in his head and was repeating words he'd rehearsed. She was supposed to say yes, she assumed and run into his arms. And only a month ago, she might just have thought about agreeing to start again—before she'd discovered the dating profile, obviously—with ground rules and a lot of talking. Talking like she did with Vaughn. About things that mattered and about stuff that didn't. About everything and nothing.

But Jason was still going on. 'We can start again. I'll help you run *Something Borrowed*. This time, we'll make it work. And I will marry you. We could have a quiet wedding, do all the things you wanted to do. Travel. Have babies. Lots of them. Settle down—chase all those dreams you had.'

Vaughn's voice got louder. 'She said no, Jason.'

Jason swivelled round. 'Was this your plan, mate? When you sat me down and convinced me not to marry her? When you told me I'd be an idiot to say I do to Chloe Cassidy? You just wanted some action with my bride?'

'Vaughn? What the hell?' It felt as if someone had struck her in the chest. 'You *convinced* him to jilt me at the altar?'

Very slowly, Vaughn turned to her. His eyes closed briefly, then opened again as he nodded, but he didn't scrabble around for lies. He lowered his voice, steady. 'He said he wasn't sure if you were the right person for him, but was going to marry you anyway. It was a hell of a lot more than second thoughts as far as I could see; it was a recipe for disaster. I didn't think it was the right thing to do.'

'So he didn't want to end it?' She wanted to hear that it was because Jason was too much of a coward to face her in the church with all those people, that he'd planned to talk to her privately but was so wracked with grief he couldn't find words. That he'd loved her too much, that he'd had things he needed to sort out before he could commit to her, but that he would and with all his heart. Not this—not that Vaughn had made him stand her up.

Vaughn continued, still in that steady voice. 'I told him you couldn't live a lie and that either he called it off, or I would.'

'So he didn't want to end it?' Incredulous, she looked from Vaughn to Jason, back to Vaughn. 'But, hang on, he was sleeping with my bridesmaid.'

'He was torn between the two of you; he said that it was possible to love two people at once. I thought that was a cop-out. Actually, it was the biggest pile of crap I ever heard.'

'And so you told him to jilt me at the altar instead? It was your idea to make a huge fool of me in front of the guests. To get me arrested, to be in the bloody paper? A laughingstock.'

Vaughn took a few steps forward until he was standing in front of her, reaching out to her, but still clearly satisfied that he'd behaved correctly. 'Chloe, if there could have been another way, believe me, I would have done it. It was too late to do anything else.'

She pushed him away, all the emotions from that day swimming in her heart. Loss. Disbelief. Anger. And the shocking thought that she just may love him. The one thing she really shouldn't do. Couldn't do. Especially now. 'Thank you for the most humiliating day of my life.'

Vaughn tipped her chin and looked into her eyes. 'I'm sorry it had to be me. But I'm not sorry I did it. I know it broke your heart, but you couldn't have married him and lived a lie.'

'But why you?'

'Because you needed to hear the truth and I couldn't trust anyone—particularly him—to tell that to you.'

Yes, she knew how much Vaughn believed in honesty. She could imagine him back then trying to talk sense into his cousin and then, having failed to do so, deciding that someone had to do the honourable thing.

Suddenly, it was all too much for her to think about. A cold, thick weight settled in her chest. Everything was, indeed, too complicated even by her standards. She needed some time to get her head around everything. 'I think you both need to go.'

'Me too?' Vaughn stared at her, confused.

'Yes. You, too. Just for a little while. I need some space.' She looked right back at him, her heart breaking at the way his eyes were soft, but questioning. He was unsure—she could tell—about what the next step should be. He had no clue how to deal with this, and neither did she. She gave him a weak smile. 'Yeah, I know. Complicated.'

'You have to believe me, Chloe.'

'I do believe you. I do. I know you wouldn't have wanted to hurt me.' She smiled a little, wishing she could feel it in her heart. Unlike Jason, Vaughn was good man. That was the problem.

'But if it wasn't for him, we could have got married.'

She looked up to see Jason watching from the doorway. 'Geez, are you still here? Get over yourself, Jason. You were the bloody groom; you did have a choice who you slept with, actually, and how you ended it with me. You could have been kinder; you could have looked after my feelings better. You could have been bloody faithful. But you know what? I'm so tired. So tired of everything. Of fighting and trying to win, trying to get one step ahead. Trying to grasp just a little bit of happiness. Trying to work out what the hell's going on, because my life is like quicksand at the moment. I think I get a foothold and then the next thing I know, I'm drowning. I can't live like this. I just can't.'

She'd just got over Jason and had started to piece her life back together. She'd devoted herself to her family and was letting them all down every single day by pretending things were okay when they really weren't. Her mother was barely speaking to her.

But she was going to keep on working and keep on fighting because family meant everything to her. She had to keep on believing things would get better, because Evie needed to see that life was what you grabbed and held on to and fought for, and that along the way, there was such a lot of fun to be had.

And that made Chloe's heart ache even more.

Because now it was Vaughn who was causing her heart so much trouble. So much deliciously nice trouble. He made her happy. He made her body tremble. He made everything seem just that little bit better when he was around. He made life exciting and comfortable and… yes, happy.

But.

But she couldn't keep hoping he'd fall for her because he wouldn't; he'd made a pact. A loyal and good, well-meaning pact with a woman he'd loved with every ounce of his being. And Chloe wanted that, wanted him to feel the same way about her.

So there it was. She couldn't keep hanging on and eventually making another gargantuan fool of herself. She couldn't pretend this was all just for fun when really, she was utterly and seriously affected by him. She needed to walk away intact, or as intact as she could possibly be with a shattered heart.

She knew what she had to do. And that she had to do it because she had to take some control and not be like the men who had let her down in the past. She had to face him with the truth.

She walked towards her ex, feeling much calmer with clearer vision.

'Jason, my answer is absolutely, categorically no. I will not ever love you. Wild horses couldn't drag me up an altar to marry you. Go back to Amy and be good to her, or I'll tell her about the dating profile. I mean it. I've already written two texts and an email and then deleted them, promising myself not to get involved. But one of these days, I might just press send. She's got my dream, yes, and she was instrumental in breaking my heart, but she deserves you to be good to her. I'll be watching. I mean it. One hint that you're straying and you'll be facing the biggest alimony fight you've ever heard of. Oh, and maybe you could try loving just one person at a time? If you're even capable of loving anyone at all.'

Jason stared at his feet and huffed out a long breath. When he eventually lifted his head and looked at her, he seemed calmer, diminished a little. Resigned. 'I fucked up, Chlo. I'm sorry. I get the message. I won't be back.'

'Okay. Good.' That was one thing dealt with, a life-door closed and feelings compartmentalised.

Vaughn stepped towards the door. 'I'll give you that space, Chloe.'

Jason nodded. 'Lots of space.'

She almost laughed; got to admit the man was a trier.

Vaughn didn't even look at his cousin or acknowledge he was in the room.

Chloe looked at Vaughn, and her heart broke because there was no compartmentalising her feelings for him. He was kind, generous, and forgiving. He'd danced with her exactly when she'd needed him to. He'd given her a job because she needed the cash. He fed her at every available opportunity—and who wouldn't love a man like that? He gave her more pleasure than anything. She could fall deeply in love him very easily. Too easily.

A little more time with that smile and that deep laugh, a little more lovemaking, and she was at serious of risk of breaking their rules. Had already, really. Because he made her feel confident about what she could do. He helped formulate her dreams. He encouraged her. He accepted her. There were no complaints, no whining, no insistence that she give him all her attention.

And then there was the dream fulfilment... food-porn dreams, kitchen-counter sex.

Tender kisses.

Everything, *everything* he did made her happy.

Her heart started to beat too fast as reality bit hard; she did love him.

She loved Vaughn Bloody Brooks.

Loved him with every piece of herself. She'd known it could happen and hadn't been able to stop. And that was the problem.

Swallowing hard, she centred herself to say possibly the most important, most ridiculous, and possibly most stupid thing ever. Because when he heard this, he'd be gone. If she kept quiet and kidded herself and lied to him, he might stay, but it would be under false pretences, and she wasn't going to be someone she wasn't; he'd taught her that much.

Be true to yourself. 'Okay, before you go, hear me out. I like you, Vaughn, probably a lot more than I should. More than you want me to, and I don't know what to do about that.'

There was a deep furrow on his forehead. 'But you said—'

'I know what I said. I know I was all bravado and just up

for the fun of it. But I think I'm dangerously falling for you. I think… I *know* that you're the kindest, most beautiful, sincere, funniest, sexiest man I've ever met. I think I might already be a bit in love with you, and I'm certainly at risk of that just getting deeper and deeper. I mean a real love. The once-in-a-lifetime thing. The thing that everyone wants and few find.' She hauled in air. 'And it surprisingly hurts more than I ever thought it would. I didn't plan it. It just sort of crept up on me. You just sort of grew on me. And I don't think I should go on pretending it's all fun when my heart is exploding every time I see you; it's not fair on either of us. And I know you can't love me back. I know you can't ever love anyone like Bella—'

He blinked at the Lost Love's name.

Chloe couldn't stop now, though. 'And you know, the worse thing about that? That's why I like you. You're good on your word. You're capable of falling so deeply in love that you'd do anything to preserve it and to honour it. You had a beautiful, amazing woman and you lost her, but she was so lucky because she had you. I can't ever be Bella. I don't want to be. I want you to love me for being Chloe, and I understand you can't do that. I don't like it. I don't want it. But I do understand. I'm sorry.'

He was so pale she thought he was going to be sick. His eyes had hollowed; dark shadows gave way to sunken cheeks. Her proclaiming everlasting love was clearly the worse thing that could ever happen to him.

And her.

She waited for a reaction. For him to say or do something. Anything. But he didn't. He looked like a deer caught in head-lights. He looked terrified. He didn't walk to her and clutch her to his chest and profess undying love for her. He didn't kneel at her feet and ask for her heart. He just kept standing there. And the longer he stood and did nothing, the more it was like a hammer into her heart, each second bringing home the message that he did not want her the way she wanted him.

The weight in her chest intensified, forcing her to fight for air. She breathed in stuttered breaths that sounded like sobs.

It wasn't until she felt the tears on her cheeks that she realised they *were* sobs, that her chest was heaving. That she was losing him. That complicated didn't come close to how things were in her head, and in her heart. That by being honest about her feelings, she was pushing him away.

'I'm so sorry, Vaughn.'

He nodded, staring at her, still mute. Still pale. Then he turned around and closed the door as he left. Taking all hope, and much of her heart, with him.

'Bloody, stupid cow. Stupid. Stupid. Stupid.' She'd watched him walk away and done nothing. Said nothing. But what could she have done to make it better?

Since he'd left, she'd been staring at the walls for hours, trying to make sense of the very bizarre scenario that had just played out. She'd lost the two men she'd ever loved. Three if she counted her dad.

Was it her? Was it something in her that made men not want to love her?

Of course it wasn't. And it wasn't the curse, either. It was just a stupid coincidence that none of the women in her family had been successful in their love lives. But that didn't mean they wouldn't be, that they couldn't be happy on their own.

Yes. That's what she was going to be—on her own. And try to be happy, if and when her heart healed. That much she was determined to believe. Chloe hauled herself from the sofa, threw the damp cushion to the floor and decided it was time for bed.

She had a busy day tomorrow, although how the hell she'd face Vaughn at work she didn't know.

Maybe she'd phone in sick. Or suggest a different working day. Whatever. She'd deal with that in the morning. Her feet felt like lead as she shuffled towards her bedroom, turning back once to switch the lounge light out.

On the table, under the window, her laptop light blinked, the lid still open.

What had she been doing before Vaughn appeared?

The quote.

Damn and blast.

Damn and bloody blast. She ran her fingers over the keypad, bringing the computer back to life. She found her document, and through the blur of her tears, she pressed Send.

Life would go on. Less vivid as it had been. Just less.

But at least she had her business. And she'd sent the quote before the hurried deadline. At least that was one good thing she achieved today.

Now she was going to climb into bed and hibernate. Possibly forever.

CHAPTER 20

Sender: Samsam1984@ymail.com

Hi Chloe,

Thanks for the estimate for your services. We were so excited having spoken to you, that we've already told our parents about our plans and want to press on and get married as soon as possible.

We've heard such great things from Nate and Taylor, and we were so excited when your email came. Obviously, however, we've had to be sensible and have reached out for three quotes. We were really hoping yours would come in at a reasonable cost, and would have stretched ourselves just to have you organise our wedding. But unfortunately, your prices were so much more than the others. We've accepted a quote from Say I Do.

We're really sorry, but we needed something within our price range.

Best wishes,
Sam and Greer

'What? No. What the hell?' Something inside her shook loose as Chloe opened her documents and checked. Double checked. 'Damn and bollocks and blast. Just effing brilliant.' She'd sent them a quote with an added zero.

She never messed up. Ever. The only thing she had control over was her business, and now... another chance ruined. It was the icing on the cake to a perfect twenty-four hours of hell.

No wonder they'd thought she was too expensive. She should have checked instead of blindly sending, but there had been too much running through her head. Blinking back tears, she rewrote the proposal, sent it with a huge apology for her oversight and asked—*begged*—them to reconsider.

Of course, they wouldn't. By sending the wrong estimate in the first place, she gave them the impression of unprofessionalism. If she couldn't do basic maths, how could they rely on her to get other things right?

Bloody men.

Vaughn Bloody Brooks. At the thought of him, her heart felt as if a red-hot poker was piercing it.

How was she going to tell Jenna about this? And how could she confess to her about the date she'd set up for her with Nick?

Would things ever be right between her and her mum?

How was she going to face Vaughn this morning?

What about her heart?

Climbing back into bed with a mug of tea and a slice of hot buttered toast, she contemplated pulling the duvet over her head and hiding from the world. Suddenly her life had got too complicated even for her.

* * *

'You lost us a contract because you were HAVING SEX WITH THAT MAN?' The bar was unusually crowded, so Jenna was shouting rather more loudly than Chloe felt comfortable. Especially as her private life was in the frame.

She cringed. 'The man, who is now out of my life. It wasn't because I was having sex; it was because I'd decided *not* to have sex with him again. And do you think you could keep your voice down?' Having told her sister all the details from last night, Chloe did feel a little better; a problem shared and all that. But the rawness of her heart was still there, and she felt on the edge of tears.

Jenna put her hand over Chloe's and squeezed. 'You did the right thing by telling him, honey. I just wish you could have told me too.'

'You had other things to think about.'

'You're my sister. I want to help you. How was he this morning at work?'

Chloe was just about to answer, but the drinks arrived, complete with umbrellas and olives. They'd gone all out on the cheesy vibes of nineteen-seventies cliché. Cocktails, at happy hour, in a seedy bar just off Portobello Road. It was all they could afford; the music was too loud, and the people were less than desirable; therefore, it was a perfect place to get drunk and forget. Or get drunk, at least.

And set up a date for a sister who didn't want to date.

Where were they? Oh, yes. Chloe's broken heart. 'Vaughn's in Paris. He flew out early this morning. Apparently, he has urgent work there, so Jacques, his sous chef, tells me. Although, seeing as I do a lot of the admin and take most of the calls, the problem wasn't something I was aware of. Very convenient, don't you think, just to up and leave? He's probably just running away from crazy Chloe, the woman who had successfully managed to

do what she'd vowed not to do and then told him all about it.'
But she was glad she had. Living a lie wasn't working for her.

'He's probably doing you both a favour by letting the dust
settle a little. Maybe you should email him?'

'He texted me, actually, this afternoon. Said we needed to
talk. I told him I didn't think he had anything more to add, and
that I needed time to rethink.'

'Finally, you do the right thing.' Jenna sipped her drink and
gave her a soft smile. 'Yummy cocktails, eh?'

'I guess.' A little sour, some salt and enough alcohol to chase
the tears away. For now. 'I am so embarrassed. I'd hand my notice
in, but I can't afford to give up working for him; that money
comes in very handy. We'll just have to hope that next weekend's
wedding fayre brings in some decent clients. And, trust me on
this, no man is going to distract me from my business. Ever again.
I phoned Sam and Greer and explained about the added zero, and
they said they'd rethink about working with me. They've signed
a contract, though, so chances are they'll stick with *Say I Do*.'

'Well, it's their loss. We'll work it out. I'll help.' Stirring her
drink with a bright pink glass stirrer, Jenna looked pensive. 'You
know, I've been thinking a lot recently. I need to start to build
my life again. I can't go on just existing like this.'

'Oh? You're doing fine.'

Jenna shook her head, determinedly. 'No, I'm not. I get that.
I've been hiding, and I feel… *less* than I was. I had my confidence
knocked, and I just couldn't shake the grief for so long. I'd think
I was doing okay, and then it would hit me out of the blue, in
waves, knocking the breath out of me, hollowing me out. But
those waves are less intense, and I'm not scared of them any more.
I know they'll always come, and I'll never forget Ollie, ever, but
I think I'm ready. You know, to start living again. My brain's
finally started to listen to all those affirmations I've been learning

at counselling.' She inhaled deeply and slowly let the breath out. 'I'm ready to move on.'

This was a huge deal for her sister. 'Oh, Jenna, that's amazing. I'll help, anything.'

'I know you will.'

'So, what do you have in mind?' Chloe breathed out heavily. This was what she'd been hoping for, for so long, but she knew there was no deadline for grief.

Jenna's eyes brightened, and she became animated, her hands moving as she spoke. 'I'm going to open a florist's shop. You know I told you about the empty place next to the pub? Well, when I was talking to Nick, he encouraged me to think about what I wanted to do with my life going forward. *You need to keep taking steps*, he said. And he's so right. I need to do something for me and Evie. I need to show her what we can achieve. I don't want her growing up with a mum who's always on the verge of taking to her bed, like we had. We don't need to perpetuate that, do we?'

'A shop is a brave move, Jenna. It's a lot to take on.'

'I know. But it's the right thing to do. I can do the wedding flowers and so much more, but this will be my business. Something for me to focus on. And it's my turn to give something back to the family, Chloe. You've put your own life on hold for me. Now I need to stand on my own two feet and help you too.'

'You are allowed to grieve, you know.'

'And I still will, but not so much anymore. It's time, I think. And thank you for everything. I couldn't have got through it without you. You've been a rock. My rock.'

Chloe gave her sister a hug. 'We'll get there, you'll see. We'll be unstoppable. *Something Borrowed* will rise from the ashes.' There was a solid lump in Chloe's chest. For so long she'd felt the pressure to fix everything, to make sure everyone was safe and cared for and not worried. Some of that pressure was being taken from her, and it was such a release. Jenna seemed to have it all worked out. She looked hopeful for the first time in years.

'In the meantime, you can work for Vaughn, and I can rent out that shop space, see how things go, but I might even try to find a place just for me and Evie to live in, too. Give mum some room.'

There were baby steps and then there was a giant leap into financial problems. 'One thing at a time, honey. Apartments are expensive, you know.'

'I know, but we could stretch a bit, don't you think?'

Eurgh, tough love was hard. 'No. We couldn't, not right now. Things aren't going well financially enough to support three homes. It'll pick up, but we need to be stringent for a while.'

'That bad?'

'That bad. But it won't be forever. Besides, she loves having you there.'

'I used to think that, but I'm not so sure now. It's not great for any of us. Evie and I share a room, and you know how tiny that is. We're all cramped. I get the message, though. I'll talk to her and see if she can pick up some more work from the dress shop, too. It's not fair to you being the one with all the money worries.'

'No. Don't. I can sort it.' Although the relief at just having said those words was palpable. Chloe felt as if she could breathe properly for the first time in ages.

'*We* can sort it. We're a team, right?' Now there was a glint in Jenna's eyes. 'She needs to move on now that we've got this Dad thing out in the open. She has to let it all go. If she was ever thinking of dating someone, she can hardly do it with me and a three-year-old under her feet.'

Chloe almost choked on her margarita. 'What? Mum? Dating?'

'It's not beyond the realms of possibility. She's still in her fifties. She still has a pulse and, I imagine, a libido, so why shouldn't she?'

'Urgh. I do not want to think about my mother's libido, thank you.' There was another round of drinks ordered and delivered in record time, which made Chloe feel an awful lot better. 'You know, Mum actually needs some more friends. Those people she sees at the ghost hunting conventions are all well and good, but none of them live nearby. Maybe a man friend would be nice company.'

Jenna smiled. 'She admitted the other day that she got into the ghost hunting because she wanted to connect with Dad. It started as Ouija boards and developed from there. Now it's more about scaring herself stupid and some strange fascination with haunted houses. But it all goes back to Dad in the end.'

There were still so many questions Chloe had for her mum, but they needed to heal a little first. 'After everything he did, why did she want to contact him?'

'Closure, apparently. To tell him how we were doing, to talk to him about his two little girls.' There was a look in Jenna's eyes that made Chloe think that she sometimes spoke to Ollie, too. 'She loves him even now, I reckon. Even after everything. But she really believes the Cassidy Curse means she'll never find another husband.'

Irritation rattled through Chloe. 'What a load of bollocks. There is no such thing as the Cassidy Curse. Look at Ollie, he was a wonderful man. And Vaughn is too. We've both loved good men; that's not a curse, it's a blessing. We'll do okay even if we never find a husband. It is the twenty-first century—women can do anything. Although sex is a bit difficult on our own, I admit, but not impossible. Just not as much fun…' She raised her glass, her mind racing once again to those strawberries. 'But we have so got to shake off our past. And I for one want to say goodbye to the stupid idea of the Cassidy Curse.'

'Good-bye and good riddance.' Jenna raised her glass, and they chinked. Then they sat in sisterly silence for a little while. Time was ticking along. Nearly seven thirty, which meant—'You look deep in thought, Chlo. Penny for them?'

Chloe shrugged and swirled the liquid around in her glass, playing for time. Because she had another secret that she wasn't about to share with Jenna anytime soon but was about to appear through the pub door any minute now. 'I was just thinking I wish we had a crystal ball to see how our lives are going to be in five years' time.'

There was a horrified look on Jenna's face. 'God, no. I'll probably be ten stone heavier.'

'And so what? There'll just be more of you to love.'

'There's enough of me already. But that's okay; I'm just a work in progress.'

The same words Chloe had used with Vaughn. Once again, there was that familiar surge of pain. She missed him. Missed his kisses. Missed the way he made her laugh. Missed the sex, even though it had only happened a few times. Even though she hadn't really known him for long, it had felt so right, as if he were her once in a lifetime. Obviously not.

'Everything will be okay, sis. I promise.' Chloe noticed the shadow at the door. Tall, broad. 'Er... talking of which.'

'Of what?'

Matchmaking. 'Of things being okay.' Chloe cringed. It had seemed like a fabulous idea in the throes of post-sexual satisfaction. Now, not so much. It didn't feel like matchmaking, more like interfering. 'Er, I think Nick just walked in. Is that him? He's coming over, that's him, right?'

The horrified look morphed into a deep blush and abject terror. 'Oh, Chloe, please tell me you didn't?'

'I might have.' Chloe hoped her sister would forgive her. She gave a little apologetic grimace. 'Just a little text inviting him for a drink. Just as friends.'

'Why the hell would you do that?' Jenna stared across the room and raised a half-hearted wave to the pretty gorgeous man walking towards them. Her face was glowing, and no wonder. Nick walked with an easy confidence. He was tall, although not quite as tall as Vaughn. *Will that man ever get the hell out of my head?* Clearly Nick was very, very fit if the muscles straining his T-shirt were anything to go by, and his hair was cropped army-short, which accentuated warm dark brown eyes that glittered as he gave Jenna a huge smile. But he stopped short of a hug. 'Hey. Hi, Jenna. How are you?'

'G-g-great. Thanks. Um….' Was it Chloe's imagination, or was her sister stuttering? Make that speechless? That was new.

He grinned. 'I'll just grab a drink. Do you want anything? Hey, you must be Chloe. I'm Nick.' He held out his hand.

Chloe took it and shook. It was nice and solid and safe. She was placing her sister into safe hands. Excellent. 'Nice to meet you, Nick. And no drinks for me, thanks. I'm going home in two seconds. But Jenna's on margaritas.' She turned to her sister as he headed to the bar, giving them a good view of a well-toned backside. 'Holy moly. Look at that fine specimen of a man.'

Jenna was looking. Boy, was she looking. Not quite tongue lolling out of her mouth looking, but near as dammit. She hissed at Chloe, 'I hate you.'

'No, you don't. You love me. Maybe not so much right now, but you'll thank me later and you know it came from a good place.'

'Why is he here? *How* is he here?'

Chloe did feel a teensy guilty but was buoyed on by the alcohol. 'One of us needs a chance at love, and I'm out of action for the time being. I texted him to say we were having a casual drink, and it would be a lovely surprise for you if he happened to be passing. I thought you need a nudge.'

'I'm so not ready for this.'

'You said you wanted to start living. Here's your chance. *He's* your chance.' She ran her hand over her sister's and squeezed it to stop it trembling. 'Breathe, girl. Breathe. It'll be fine. He is fine.'

'He is mighty fine. But I'm not.' Jenna's jaw set tight. 'No men, Chloe. I just want a business. A new life for me and my daughter. No. Men.'

'Awww. Come on, I just want you to have some fun.'

'Oh yeah. Like you?'

Chloe thought back to the steel kitchen counter and the strawberries. To the pancakes, the dancing, hiding under a throw and making love for hours. It had been beautiful and lots of fun, even if it wasn't now. Even if her heart had been smashed to smithereens, her eyes still sore from the tears and her throat still full and raw. It might have sounded crazy, but she was totally glad because Hurricane Vaughn had happened. 'Yes, honey, just like me.'

* * *

It was late afternoon the next day by the time Chloe dared to catch up with Jenna. She texted her, playing light and pushing the guilt down to a minimum. *It had been for her own good.*

Chloe: How did it go last night with Nick?

Jenna: Okay I think, but I will never forgive you

Chloe: Yes, you will. And...????

Jenna: We talked a lot. He's very lovely and kind, but only

as a friend. He didn't make a move, which was refreshing. (Or maybe it's my layers of lard that put him off)

Chloe: FFS Woman. Leave yourself alone. You're gorgeous! But I'm glad it went well.

Jenna: I told him I wasn't looking for a boyfriend... not in an intense way, I just said it in passing... and he seemed totally fine with that

Chloe: Good—he should be

Jenna: Looks like I have myself a friend, then. You know what? He's totally into Game of Thrones too. So we had a long chat about that and theories about Jon Snow *swoon*. He's got quite a sense of humour too. And... And, anyway, LEAVE ME ALONE! I have to get ready for book group. No, actually—come round now, you coward, and give me a hand. You OWE ME, BIG TIME

* * *

'So how's your man drought, Chloe? Getting any action?' Mrs Singh peered over the book she was supposed to have read, but couldn't remember anything about, so was relaying the story from the back cover. Clearly the book hadn't held her interest, unlike Chloe's sorry love life.

But before Chloe opened her mouth, her mum butted in. 'No action for either of my girls, I'm afraid. Our Chloe was after seeing a relative of Jason. He's dumped her. And Jenna's not got a hope of finding a man as she spends her life here, with me and her wee baby. More's the pity because neither of them are getting any younger.'

The strawberries that Vaughn had brought over—and that they hadn't eaten or... anything—were sitting in the middle of the table. Jenna had dipped them in chocolate. Chloe reached out for one but decided she hadn't the appetite for them anymore. Too many memories. 'For the record, ladies, *I* dumped Vaughn before things got too serious. Actually, we were very grown up about it. And, Mum, do we need to broadcast our lives to everyone?'

'These are your friends, love. They all just want to help. Don't you, girls? A problem shared is a problem halved and all that.' Mum sat back, her knitting needles clicking, in some sort of righteous assumption that she was in the right.

Faith, Kat and Saskia all nodded, eyes bright with an interest none of them had shown in the books either.

Chloe looked at them all sitting there expectantly and tried for a diversion. 'Okay. Well, in good news, Jenna is looking to secure a contract for a florist's shop next to The Duke. So you have to make sure you all buy fresh flowers every week, at the very least. If everything goes to plan, it'll be opening in a month or so.' She winked at her sister, whose cheeks were pink and flush.

Jenna took up the story, her voice light and excited. Talking about this new venture made her the most animated she'd been in years, apart from last night when she'd first set eyes on Nick. 'Yes, it's going to be called *Something Fragrant.* I wanted to keep the poem idea going: Something old, Something new, Something borrowed, Something blue. Something... *Something Fragrant* works, I think. *Something Fresh?* Unless anyone can think of anything better?'

'*Something* Better? Something Sexy? Something Sweet?' Mrs Singh laughed and tucked into the strawberries. 'I'm good at this. I'm wasted in a hardware shop.'

'You most certainly are. You have many talents, Mrs Singh. Actually, you should become a Private Investigator. You know more about everyone's lives before they know themselves.' Chloe gave her a smile. 'There are a few details we need to iron out, first. Jenna went round to have a look at the place this morning.

There's a small room out back which I can use as an office, and I can even advertise right there on the main thoroughfare. Plus, I can work in the shop when Jenna needs to drop off or pick up Evie.' It was all worked out, and Chloe had started to look forward to this next phase.

She reached into her bag and dug out some printed papers she'd been working on all afternoon, trying to keep Vaughn from hopping into her head and making her regret the words she'd said to him.

Why couldn't she have just strung him along? At least that way she'd have had more fun and more time with him. 'Here's some proofs I've done for some new flyers. I'm moving into event planning too, so anything you need a hand with, let me know. Bar Mitzvahs, birthdays, funerals, whatever. I'm your girl. Diversification is the key, right? We have to be Jills of all trades these days.'

After they'd all passed the flyers around and made comments and suggestions, there was a satisfied silence. For a short minute. Then Mum sat forward. 'Right you are. I've been mulling things over, and I've decided there're some things I need to say to my girls.'

Faith frowned softly with concern and stood up. 'Should we leave you to it?'

Bridget raised her hand and forced Faith back down in her seat. 'Oh no, you stay right there. I'm going to say it here because you all were there when the news broke.'

Even though her Mum was deadly serious, Chloe couldn't help smiling. Mum thought she was an international news item. *Breaking news… parents split up twenty-odd years ago.*

It happened. Chloe had come to realise, once the shock had worn off, that bending the truth a little just to make someone feel better wasn't the worst sin someone could commit. Shit happens, as Vaughn said. And you dust yourself off and get up and face another day. Over and over on repeat until you find a slice of sunshine that makes everything seem just a little bit better; a smile from a toddler, a group of women having wine and talking nonsense, sisters, flowers, summer.

And having her mum here, instead of taking to her bed, and trying to make her peace. That meant so much. Another bit of sunshine right there—forgiveness and reconciliation.

Bridget was saying, 'I wish I could say he tried to get in contact with you, but he didn't. I wish I had letters for you from him, but I don't. I couldn't understand how someone could do that, girls; just walk away from their own children and never want to be part of their lives. But he did.' She cleared her throat again; there was a husk to it infused with sadness and regret and embarrassment. 'It hurt me so much to see you and think of what you were missing out on. It was hard not to talk about what he'd done, to tell you the truth, but I didn't want to see that in your eyes. You were the most beautiful things in my life, you still are, and I didn't want to see your faith in love broken because of him. So I told you he was dead. I know I shouldn't have, but once I'd said it, I couldn't ever go back, could I? And then he did die… so it didn't become a problem. I'm sorry, loves. I really am.'

There was a rock in Chloe's throat, and she stumbled over and gave her a hug, tight. 'It's okay, Mum. I get it. It's amazing the things you can do when you love someone, right?' *Like walking away. And being happy that you'd held him just for a little while.*

'I love you both. To bits. Although sometimes you drive me mad with frustration.' Jenna squeezed their hands. 'Right, now, who's for wine? And Chloe's made something. I'm not sure what it is, but it's very… pink.'

Chloe leant over and gave the goo a swirl with a carrot stick and took a bite. 'It's beetroot and feta dip. It's just missing something. I never did get the proper recipe.' And then her heart started hurting a little again at the thought of Vaughn and the kiss in his office. But it was okay. Jenna had told her the hurt came in waves, but it got easier. Chloe knew that herself, though, too. She would survive. Especially with these women around her.

There was a muddle of hands with carrot sticks and pink dip and someone mumbled, 'Well, it's the first time she's ever bought food to book club, so that's a start.'

'Now…' It was Kat, the book group leader, who never led. Or read a book. 'About the books…?'

'Not a chance. I want to hear about Jenna's date.' Mrs Singh licked her lips and grinned.

Mum's eyes widened. 'Jenna had a date? Now how did I not know about that?'

'Mrs Singh, how do you know about that?' The woman was a walking miracle.

There was a glint in her eyes. 'I have my sources.'

But Jenna's mouth was all pouty, and her ears were red. 'It wasn't a date. It was just a friend. You know, Mum, the one I told you about, the soldier.'

Mrs Singh, again. 'I'm told he couldn't keep his eyes off you.'

'Probably struggling to see around me.'

'Will you ever stop talking about your weight? Hey, have you heard about the latest superfood? It's got a weird name, but don't they all. Apparently it's from the Amazon and the women there have been eating it for centuries…'

Chloe leant back in her chair and let the rush of musical chatter wash over her. Yes, it was noisy and chaotic, and they never ever talked about books, but she loved these women. There was a camaraderie here, a sisterhood that supported each other, that lifted each other up when they needed it, that made her laugh, and cry at times.

Things were going to get better. Jenna had a dream that was becoming a reality. Things were settling down between Chloe and her mum. There was a future for them, a good future if they all stuck together.

But there was still that little tug, the empty bed that was calling her, the scent of him still on her sheets and the twinge of pain in her heart.

The strawberries on the table mocked her: *We could have been something.*

Something better, something sexy, and something very special indeed.

CHAPTER 21

I think it's coffee time. Anjini, I need a hand. Come with me. I spotted a kiosk somewhere over by the entrance.' Bridget was bristling and bubbly and bruising for a fight, judging by the tight way she pulled her cardigan around her shoulders. Chloe hoped there was sufficient security here at the wedding fayre to deal with two middle-aged women who could raise merry hell when they wanted.

'That means you're going to bite my head off about spilling the peas on that curse. Again.' Mrs Singh folded her arms across her chest and steadfastly refused to move. 'No, thank you. I've had it twice now, and I don't want to hear another word. I've apologised over and over, and that should be enough. I'm staying here. Chloe needs me, don't you?'

Mum being feisty, Mrs Singh being petulant. Chloe grinned. So good to see things almost back to normal. 'Whoa, ladies, don't drag me into this. And it's *beans*. Spilling the beans, Mrs

Singh. Jenna and I can manage quite well here, thanks. I'd like a black coffee, please. Jen usually has a cappuccino, and get a hot chocolate for Evie if you can carry it. Go and sort yourselves out, ladies. Talk. Fight. Shout. Then come back as friends again. Please? I like it better when we're all friends.'

Her mum gave her a weary smile and patted Chloe's hand. 'We are friends, Chloe. Don't worry. You are allowed to have fights with friends and family without everything turning into a complete disaster forever. It's what makes things stronger.'

'Yes, she's right.' There was humour in Mrs Singh's eyes. 'She'll make a fuss. I'll make a good pretence of listening. Then we'll be done. Right, Bridget?'

'Right you are.' Mum grinned at her oldest friend. 'You're nothing but trouble, you know that?'

'Indeed, I do. And proud of it.'

Chloe watched them walk away, arm in arm, Mum's mouth working ten to the dozen. Anjini nodding and laughing and, no doubt, taking no crap whatsoever. Things were healing. Although, she expected it would take more than that to make her own heart a little less sore.

Two weeks, and still no word from Vaughn, apart from short emails about the business, and nothing… *nothing*… about what they'd shared. He was still in Paris, with a trip up to Manchester planned for next week. No diversion via London. She knew because she'd organised the damned flights.

She closed her eyes briefly and let the hurt wash through her. Acknowledging it, and then letting it go. Getting over Vaughn would be a long path, she realised, but one she could definitely walk. And she didn't miss the irony of being at a wedding fayre with a broken heart.

'Excuse me, do I know you from somewhere?' A young woman, standing in front of Chloe, was breathless and excited. Her eyes were as bright as the lighting in the large exhibition room. 'You look very familiar.'

'I just gave a presentation on the expectations of the wedding planner and the couple, in the western hall. Maybe you were there?' Chloe smiled. So far, so good. The fayre had brought in hundreds of happy couples looking for their own unique wedding experience, and there was a steady footfall of people stopping to chat with her.

Groups of bridesmaids giggled hysterically over the free vodka at a hen party company booth further down the aisle. The huge exhibition hall hummed with chatter and laughter and the giddiness of expectation and celebration. There was a cluster of people around the *Something Borrowed* stall, people interested in the photographs on the wall, the one of the yellow road and the close ups of the Marilyn Monroe dress that still made Chloe's heart ache. Because he'd taken the shots. Because he'd been there with her, trying to make her feel better.

God, she wished he was here now to make her feel better all over again. Every bit of her ached to hold him again. Every cell in her body missed him and craved his touch.

Focus.

And she did. No man was ever going to distract her from her work again.

The woman was still looking at her, clearly trying to remember where she knew her from. Chloe smiled. 'Is there anything in particular I can help you with? Are you planning a wedding? We have lots of experience and great ideas to make your day extra special. Anything. We specialise in the extraordinary.' She'd decided not to use the word quirky as that may put people off.

'Hmmm.' The woman gave her a friendly smile back. There was nothing in her that Chloe recognised. 'Not sure... really.

Something Borrowed. Something Borrowed... the name's very familiar.'

'It's probably because of the poem. Maybe? Look, I know it's totally overwhelming in here with so much on offer. Had much luck so far? Found anything that appeals to you?' Chloe glanced over to Jenna, who was grinning as she wiggled Evie on her knee, simultaneously handing out flyers and chatting to potential customers. Evie was a great draw card with her cute button nose and gorgeous floor-length ivory silk flower-girl dress.

They'd used the exhibition opportunity to showcase examples of Mum's handiwork, which were displayed on mannequins. The booth was decorated with pretty summer flowers to highlight Jenna's floristry business. The rental contract had been signed, and things were happening. Next week she'd be in her new shop.

After thinking about what Vaughn had said about her not shouldering everything, Chloe had told them about the cash flow problems, and they'd taken out a joint bank loan to cover everything. They'd also decided they'd have equal shares in the business and equal responsibility. Both her mum and her sister had stepped up to the challenge. With every passing day, she'd felt the weight of responsibility fall just a little away from her shoulders.

Chloe handed the woman a leaflet and a pen. 'There's a sign-up form here. Would you like to leave your name? One of the team can get back to you later in the week. That way you'll have had time to digest all the information and have a better idea of what you want. I'd love to hear what you're planning.'

Jenna gave her a discreet thumbs-up and a wink. *Good. Positivity. Fun.* And the strange thing was, Chloe actually felt a little of it too. Some of the shiny, happy people thing. She wasn't destined for love ever after, but others were. She was okay with that and determined to give them the best wedding experience she could.

'No, thanks. I remember now. Yes. *Something Borrowed.* That's right.' The woman's eyes narrowed as she nodded, and Chloe's gut started in free fall. 'Weren't you the wedding planner who was stood up at the altar?'

'Er... yes. That was me.' What was the point in denying it? 'Good memory.'

'That's right. I edit the Portobello Local newspaper. I'm covering the show,' The bride-to-be who clearly wasn't a bride-to-be explained, with glee. 'Great story, by the way. Especially beating up the best man. With the flowers! We had a few laughs about that in the office.'

'Oh. Good. Glad someone did.' Not even a client, just another nosy reporter wanting to cash in.

The woman put her hand to her mouth. 'Oh, God, you didn't get back together with the groom, did you?'

'No. I didn't. He's still with the bridesmaid. But it's all in the past. Life goes on, right?' Chloe glanced nervously around at the crowd who was straining to listen. The murmur of chatter went silent, and tens of pairs of eyes were all looking at her. Was this how it was going to be? Would she never be allowed to forget? She raised her voice and infused it with as much shiny shimmer as she could. Laughing. Yes, laughing to make light of it. 'It wasn't the crowning moment of my career, I'll give you that. But we have to make lemonade when life hands us lemons, right? I have safeguards in place now, and always recommend taking out insurance for the big day. But rest assured, you'll get hitched without a hitch with us.' She cringed inside. Had she really just said that? She sounded like a bad advert on the Shopping Channel.

There was a snort from Jenna. And Chloe glared at her.

'So.' The woman went on. God, she was nosy. Or thorough. Or something. 'How are things for you now?'

'Great. Couldn't be better, actually. Business is thriving. We're soooo busy.' Chloe had crossed her fingers as she said that. What of it? 'But, of course, we'll always make room for any new clients.'

'Could have gone either way, I guess. At the office, we had bets you'd be closed down within a month.' The woman rummaged through her purse and handed a card to Chloe. 'Marnie Fitzpatrick. I do love a happy ending, especially for our local businesses. Call me, and we can arrange a follow-up feel-good story. It'll be good advertising for you.'

'Thanks. I will.' When things actually got better. Although, there had been interest and most of the flyers had been taken. Hopefully, they were going to be very busy indeed. No time to wallow in self-pity over Vaughn Bloody Brooks and wishful thinking.

Marnie looked very pleased with herself. 'Oh, and I always wondered, what happened to the best man afterwards?'

We had sex. I fell in love. He broke my heart. He left. 'He—'

'He's right here.'

'Vaughn?'

The voice was dark and smooth and washed through her, warming bits that had been ice since he'd gone. Her heart jumped and jittered as she looked for him across the heads of the little crowd.

And there he was. Head and shoulders above them all, pushing his way through the wide-eyed, open-mouthed audience until he was standing in front of her.

'Vaughn.' It was the only word she could say. The rest were stuck in her throat, wedged in with the tight lump that seemed to be making breathing quite difficult.

'Hey, Chloe.' He looked around at all the eyes that had moved from her to him, even wider now and glittering with even more excitement. 'Hello, everybody.'

There was a collective intake of breath. A few 'hi's' and 'hellos.' Then silence.

'Chloe, love, here's your coffee.' Her mum was nudging her way through with a lot less panache than Vaughn had. Seeing him, she stopped short and glowered. Her hand still outstretched with coffee that, Chloe thought for a moment, might have been flung over his very nice Parisian dark blue jacket. 'Oh. Well, look at that. It's your man.'

Earth, eat me up, now. Chloe took the coffee for safekeeping. 'Yes, Mum. It's Vaughn. And he's not *my* man. Very definitely not mine. That's right, isn't it, Vaughn?'

'About that…' Vaughn reached to her arm and tugged her a little closer. 'Can we talk? Without an audience?'

'Oh, no, you don't.' Mum put her hand on his shoulder. 'Anything you've got to say, you can say in front of us. We're her family. Hurt her again and you'll have us to deal with.'

He twisted round and peered at everyone's hands. 'No bouquets? Good.'

'Not yet. But there's some in grabbing distance.' Bridget reached out for a bunch of pink and purple freesias in a pot. 'So, we're waiting… get it out, lad.'

The redness on Chloe's cheeks intensified. 'Mum!' she hissed. 'Leave the poor man alone.' Then she turned to Vaughn and drank in the sweet sexiness in his face, the dark steel eyes, the kissable mouth. *Please don't break my heart all over again.* 'What are you doing here?'

'You really want me to say it in front of everyone?'

'Yes, she does.' It was Marnie. She had her camera poised.

'For the love of—' Chloe shook her head. She did not need

witnesses to yet another humiliating heartbreak. 'No. Actually, let's go outside.'

But there was a fashion show between them and the front door. Crowds had accumulated to watch the new season's dresses. Tinny music began to play. Luckily, all heads turned towards the models.

'Over here, Chloe.' Vaughn's hand was in hers and, for a moment, she let it stay there, so warm and safe and firm. And she let the sparkle of hope in her chest fire into life. Because underneath it all, she did believe in love. Even if it was one-sided.

But if that was the case, then… why was he here?

He pulled her behind the booth and looked almost as if he was going to kiss her. She dropped his hand and pushed space between them. 'Whoa, hang on, Vaughn. What's going on? Why are you here? You're supposed to be in the air right now on the way to Manchester.'

'I had to come and see you. I couldn't breathe properly. I can't sleep. I can't do anything without having you in my head. It's driving me insane.' He put both hands on her shoulders and drew her closer. 'I shouldn't have just gone off to Paris like I did. I'm sorry. I treated you badly, and you didn't deserve that.'

'No, I didn't. You walked away from me after I'd laid my soul open to you. You hurt me. You didn't even say a word. You did what every single man has ever done to me, Vaughn. You just walked away.'

'I know. God, I am so sorry. I didn't know what to say. I didn't want to tell you how confused I was because that wasn't fair. But it was blowing my mind. Everything seemed to happen so quickly… the dance, then the kiss, then the sex, and I felt completely blindsided by it. By you. By what was developing between us. And then Jason came along and professed his undying love for you, and I had so many emotions rolling around inside me. I couldn't handle the way I was feeling.' He stroked a finger down her cheek. 'And I really didn't like the way I felt at the thought of you being with someone else. That spooked me.'

So he was just here to reconfirm what she already knew. She fought her wobbling lip and dredged a smile. 'Look, it's really busy here and I really, really need the business. So, if you're done? I accept your apology. It's okay. I understand you can't love me. Not like you loved Bella. You had a once-in-a-lifetime thing. I'm glad you did. But I think I might have, too. And… well, that hurts me more than I expected it would. Look, I really do have to go.'

She blinked away the tears that were springing up in her eyes. She would not cry over him again. She had more self-respect than that. She turned, trying to shrug off his hands.

'Chloe, wait.' He hadn't let go of her, but she'd twisted away from him. 'You're right. I can't love you like I loved Bella—'

'Yes. Okay? I understand. Now, please, let me go.' She shook her head, unwilling to let him see the traitorous single tear spill down her cheek.

'No, you don't understand, not at all. Listen to me.' He was laughing now. *Laughing.* It was a gentle rumble, delightful, playful and teasing. And sincere. Utterly, devastatingly, adorably sincere ricocheting through her heart like tiny sprinkles of stars. And it was killing her. 'I don't want to love you like I loved Bella. I want to love you the way I love *you*, Chloe.'

'I have to go—I can't be here. Wait.' Had she heard right? 'What did you say?'

He bit down on his lip. 'I said that I love you. It's been a bit of a shock; I'll admit, but I do.'

'You love me?' Out of the corner of her eye, Chloe saw a huddle of smiling faces; her mum, Jenna, Evie, Anjini and the reporter. They looked like maidens from a historical romance film, clutching each other and swooning over the happy ever after. But this was Chloe's life, and she was well aware of the scarcity of happy ever afters happening there.

But... what if? What if everything he was saying was true?

'Yes. I bloody well do love you. And I'll keep on saying it until you hear me properly. I love you, Chloe Cassidy, and I... well, I wondered'—his eyes widened as he grinned—'if you still wanted to be with me, after everything?'

'Want to be with you?' Was he joking? A thrill of heat swam through her and her heart tugged towards him.

'Yes.'

'But you walked away from me, Vaughn.'

'And I will never leave your side ever again, Chloe. In fact, would you...?' He started to get down on one knee, but she pulled him up, her heart now pounding a zillion times faster.

'Oh, no. No. No way. Don't ever propose, don't ever ask me to marry you. Don't ever do that to me. I'm happy to arrange anyone else's wedding, but I'm definitely not organising one for us. I know how that stuff ends, and it's not pretty.'

'So, I'll just have to prove that I'm true to my word then, won't I? I won't leave you again, Chloe, ever. And I won't propose if it really bothers you. But you're happy with kissing?' His mouth was close to hers now, and she felt the pull to him that she couldn't resist. She craved the taste of him, the way he smelt, the heat of his arms.

God, she loved this man. 'Aha. Kissing's good.'

'And strawberries?'

'Oh, yes. Definitely strawberries.'

As he lowered his mouth to hers, he murmured, 'Then we'll have to stick with that, then.' He winked at her, slow and sexy and full of promise for the future together. 'For now.'

EPILOGUE

Wedding Fayre Joy For Portobello Wedding Planner

There wasn't a dry eye in the house at Saturday's Wedding Fayre, held at the Westgate Centre, Shepherd's Bush, when Chloe Cassidy, head of Something Borrowed *wedding planning services had a fairy tale ending fit for any blushing bride.*

Four months ago, Cassidy was jilted at her own wedding; the news of her finance's philandering brought to her by heroic best man, Vaughn Brooks. The day ended with more than tears when, bridezilla-style, Chloe tackled Brooks to the ground, resulting in a visit to the police station for her and to the hospital for treatment for him.

Fast forward four months and love has blossomed between the star-crossed pair, culminating in an almost-proposal that had every woman in the room melting and every groom wishing he'd thought of something as clever and meaningful. A proposal to a wedding planner at a wedding fayre. What could be more perfect?

But Cassidy, once bitten and now very shy of planning her own wedding, interrupted the proposal with a kiss and a polite refusal. 'Of course, I love him and wouldn't be without him. Ever again. I'm just too busy planning a perfect day for each one of my clients,' she gushed after the almost-proposal.

Brooks just shrugged. 'Whatever she wants, she can have. I love her with, or without, the ring to prove it.'

But there was a suspicious glint in her mother's eye, and her sister was overheard saying, 'No wedding? We'll see about that. Leave it to me, Vaughn. I have a very good idea.'

So, watch this space! We'll bring more news when we hear it. Were you there? Did you witness the almost-proposal? Have photos? Have insider information? If so, contact the news desk on info@portobellolocal.co.uk

From Louisa...

Thank you for picking up **Something Borrowed**, I hope you enjoyed your visit to the Cassidy's crazy world. If you enjoyed Chloe and Vaughn's story make sure you look out for more of my weddings books and the next of my new **Something Borrowed** series coming early 2017. I also write books for Tule publishing and Harlequin Mills and Boon Medical line.

To keep up with all my release and book news, please visit me at *www.louisageorge.com* and subscribe to my newsletter. I do giveaways and cover reveals and fun stuff for my VIP subscribers. I love hearing from readers, so drop me a line, come and say hi! And *please* consider leaving a comment or review for **Something Borrowed** at your favourite online retailer or review site!

Thanks again for taking a chance on me and my books.

Happy reading!
Louisa x

Sneak Peek!

Love Christmas? Love weddings? How about Christmas weddings in paradise?

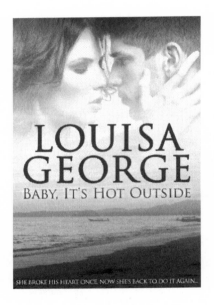

Here's an excerpt from my Christmas
novella, ***Baby, It's Hot Outside***

*D*aniel caught the scent of jasmine and honeysuckle and something else—something so familiar it had him swivelling round. He sucked in air.

Emma.

He wasn't prepared for the jolt of heat that ricocheted through him at seeing her again after these last few empty years. She'd come to an abrupt halt, eyes guarded. Cool liquid blue pupils fixed on him. A taut jaw, a tight purse of those kissable lips. Her long auburn hair had been shoved on top of her head in a high messy ponytail, but tendrils drifted round her cheeks as she whipped her head from Daniel to Bas and back again. She was wearing a soft yellow dress with thin straps that showcased her body. Curves that had fitted into his hands perfectly. Long legs that he'd loved wrapped round him.

And immediately he was flung back to that first endless summer when everything had seemed possible. Even a hastily arranged wedding. Turned out being possible and being permanent were two different things.

He figured a hug was out of the question.

"Welcome back to Waiheke, Emma. Oh, and merry Christmas." He tilted Bas's empty bottle towards her in greeting, going for casual and knowing his face was anything but. So much for all that training at cop school.

Hers went from porcelain to beetroot in a nano-second. Clearly he still had an effect on her. He wasn't sure how he felt about that. "Danny. Hello."

Danny. The only person in the world who called him that. Danny was someone else, someone in the murky past. "How was England?"

"Great. Thanks. But it's good to be back home. Er…How's things?"

Home? Since when was it home for Emma? She'd always had itchy feet. She was never going to stay on Waiheke, she'd made that clear the day she'd met him and he'd promised to chase that dream with her. But life had thrown other plans at him. "Ah, you know. I'm the same as ever."

She looked at the beer bottle in his hand. "So I see. Some things never change, eh?"

"I guess not."

But he had. And how. That was a battle he'd fought hard and won—no point locking horns with her over it. He was of the mind to let it all go. This was Bas's pre-wedding party, after all, he didn't want to spoil it.

Out of the corner of his eye he saw his friend disappear outside. *Traitor.* Daniel dragged his eyes from Emma and started towards the back door. "I should probably go and help Bas with the preparations."

"Running out on me already? Really? You can't even bear to

be in the same room as me for one whole minute?" Her eyebrows rose. She bit her bottom lip. Wary. Tense. "There was me thinking I'd left the frostbite behind."

"Still waiting for the thaw, Em." And yet there was heat mixed with the ice he'd constructed around his chest. It had been his fault she'd left without him in the first place. He wasn't angry with her, just angry with himself. With the fact that they hadn't been strong enough to deal with the crap thrown in their path. And now they were stuck in a place neither wanted to be in; married and separated and living at the opposite ends of the world. "I'm needed out there, apparently. I have a job to do...and, to be honest, I just don't know what the hell to say to you."

He should probably start with *I'm sorry*. But he'd never been good at verbalising.

"You and me both." Holding on to the back of a chair Emma took a deep breath and closed her eyes. When she opened them the wariness had diminished a little. She even attempted a smile. Small, but there it was. "Look, I know we have a lot of stuff to go through but tonight we're here for Bas and Megan—can we at least try to be civil?"

"Sure. I can do that."

"Good. Thank you. It means a lot. She is my best friend—and he's yours—and it's a special time for them. I don't want to ruin things."

"Noted. I can do civil no problem. I'll keep out of your way—that seems to work." A whole weekend of celebrations to get through where he'd be regularly rubbing shoulders with his runaway wife. Great.

Then his eyes settled on hers and held for a moment. He remembered a time when he would stare into her gaze and feel as if he could see right down to her soul. Now all he could see was awkwardness. There was so much they needed to say, so much that needed working through, but he didn't know where to start.

Worse, that tug was still there. That irresistible pull towards her. For a few years they'd circled each other, created a life of love and fun and laughter, everything had started and ended with them, with their dreams, their cozy world, their precious unbreakable bond. Now they didn't even know how to begin.

He stayed exactly where he was. "So, in the interests of being civil, tell me where you're staying? At your mum's, I presume?"

Emma sighed, her gaze dipping to the floor and then anywhere but back at him. "I should have emailed and let you know…but…well… I didn't think it would be a good idea to come back to our house, Danny. Given that we, well… given that we're in this situation." Her gaze settled on her hands and she rubbed her left ring finger. No wedding band, not even a thin white line. She'd ditched the ring a long time ago, then. There was that tug on his heart again. Damn it. She looked back at him. "I will come round. Maybe tomorrow? There are a few things of mine I need to get. If that's okay with you? When would be a good time?"

For her to close that door on their relationship forever? Never. But things had irrevocably changed, he knew. "Any time—you still have your key? Just let yourself in. It's your place too, you have a right to come and go as you please. I'm on an early shift, so won't be home until after four."

"Okay. Thanks."

"How long are you staying for?"

This time when she wrapped her arms round her chest, he wasn't sure if it was an unconscious barrier or a comfort hug. Either way she was telling him to keep his distance. "Two weeks. I have a job starting in the New Year in Brisbane."

"This hemisphere? Getting closer."

"Yeah, you take the jobs you can get these days. There's nothing in Auckland, little out of the city. Nothing here on this tiny island. But Brisbane sounds great. Mum's already booking flights, she's stoked to have me only a couple of hours away. She said you'd been to see her a few times, did the lawns." Emma's shoulders relaxed a little and there was a small smile. "That was kind, Danny. And surprising."

He took a step away. "You're surprised that I can be kind?"

"No. No, don't be silly. I didn't mean that. Of course not, I know you can be kind." Wearily she shook her head. "You were just so wrapped up in all that other stuff when I left, I wasn't sure...how you'd be."

"Two years is a long time, Emma. I'm fine."

"Yes. Yes you are." Her eyes grazed over his face, then down his chest. He wasn't sure where else because he turned away, burning under her scrutiny. Damn it, when she looked at him like that all the familiar emotions washed through him. Heat. Longing. A need to hold her. Actually, a shocking need to touch her. But guilt was there too, fraying the edges, taking off the shine. Her voice brought him back, "I was wondering whether you'd moved on...? Are you seeing anyone, Danny?"

"It's none of your business, seeing as we've barely communicated in two years. But for the record, no."

"Oh. Okay." Her eyebrows rose and her eyes darted to his left hand. And yes, he was still wearing his wedding ring. What of it?

He wanted to ask her about any significant others too, but wouldn't. It wasn't his place. He'd lost the right to know about her private life a long time ago.

Damn, this was worse than miserable. This was worse than he'd ever imagined, because in some dark part of his head he'd envisaged a huge blow-out argument, an opportunity to get all their issues out once and for all. A swift get-it-over-with end. But this? This was like a long slow painful death. And God forgive him, but all he could think was that Emma's skin had missed the New Zealand sun, that her hair was longer and glossier than it used to be, that her eyes were tired. Beautiful, but tired.

He'd missed her at first. Damn, and how. But he'd learnt to live without her. Eventually.

"Okay, so I'm going out back to give Bas a hand. Good to see you again, Emma."

"You too, Danny. And...er, merry Christmas right back."

Yeah, right. With Emma here, under the same summer sun and clearly still deep under his skin, Daniel doubted there'd be anything merry about it at all.

Baby, It's Hot Outside, Out Now!

About the Author

Award-winning author Louisa George has been an avid reader her whole life. In between chapters she managed to fit in a BA degree in Communication Studies, trained as a nurse, married her doctor hero and had two sons. Now, she spends her days writing chapters of her own in the medical romance, contemporary romance and women's fiction genres.

Louisa's books have variously been nominated for the coveted RITA® Award and the NZ Koru Award for the Short Sexy Category (which she won in 2014 and 2016) and translated into twelve languages. She lives in Auckland, New Zealand and, when not writing or reading, likes to travel, drink mojitos and do Zumba®- preferably all at the same time.

47858181R00191

Made in the USA
Middletown, DE
10 June 2019